MY TWO ALPHAS

JESSICA HALL

My Two Alphas
Copyright © 2022 by Jessica Hall

All rights reserved. This book or any portion thereof may not be reproduced or used in any manner whatsoever without the express written permission of the publisher except for the use of brief quotations in a book review.

MY TWO ALPHAS

TYSON AND ACE, TWIN hybrid brothers and direct descendants of the Moon Goddess, thought life couldn't get any more complicated than being raised by their older brother, the Alpha King. But when Ryker found his second chance mate, they learn she has a missing daughter. The twins help find her and bring her home. Only when they do, they can't help but feel drawn to the young girl.

On their seventeenth birthday, they find out she is their mate. The girl they helped raise as their own brother's step-daughter was to be theirs. Though Lucy was only twelve, they knew she would be a handful when she found out in the future. Lucy is no ordinary hybrid but a mutated version, like her mother, and there is just one problem. She has no wolf. The scientists who experimented on her as a child killed her wolf counterpart, leaving her more vampire than wolf. Now, not only do the twin brothers have to wait for her to grow up, but they also have to hope she recognizes them when she does.

Lucy has always been different. Being a mutation of her hybrid mother, raised by her stepfather, the Alpha King and his two younger twin brothers, her life was never easy. She spent the majority of her life in captivity before her mother and her mate rescued her from the facility and brought her home. Little does she know that the two young men who have always been by her side since childhood and helped raise her, are hiding a secret. She is their mate. What will happen when Lucy finds out that the twins are her mates and that they have known about it all along? Can she look at them as anything more than family? Though not blood-related, they did help raise her. Now, she understood why she had always been drawn to them. Drawn to the twin brothers, both Alphas of their packs. Will she trust fate, or will she reject them?

Chapter 1

Tyson

These bloody meetings were boring, but Ryker insisted we sit through the Alpha meet every year. We still had a year before we took over Black Moon Pack, so I thought it rather pointless when we didn't actually get a say in anything yet.

They weren't so bad, though. My entire family was here, seeing as we all came from Alpha bloodlines. My aunty Lily was here with her husband Damian, from the Crescent Pack. My older sister Lana and her two mates, Tate and Drake, from the Forest Pack were also here. And of course, my other older sister Arial and her mate Chase, from the Red River Pack were here sitting next to my mother. Black Creek Packs Alpha, Jamie, and his Luna were also here with two other packs, whom I couldn't remember for the life of me. Kind of pointless when my family ran the majority of the packs. Not like the other three packs could argue; no one wanted to piss off hybrid wolf packs. And they sure as hell didn't want to piss off my brother Ryker, the Alpha King, a title handed down from my mother, the former Alpha Queen.

Ace nudged me with his foot under the table, trying to get my attention. Looking over at him, he nodded toward the Luna of the Black Creek Pack.

"Check out the tits on her," he mind-linked, and I rolled my eyes at him.

"Close your mouth. You just drooled on the table," I shot back at him, and he smirked.

"What I would do to those puppies," he said, wiggling his eyebrows at me.

"Fucking nasty! She is old enough to be your mother!"

"Got a nice rack, though," he said, and I sighed. "Think they're fake?"

"I don't know. Why don't you ask her mate?" I told him, turning my attention back to Ryker, who was looking at maps laid on top of the round wooden conference table.

"Not possible," he said, looking at the Black Creek Alpha. He was in his fifties and thought his shit didn't stink. Couldn't stand the old fart.

"Why? What could they possibly need all that land for? They aren't even running the pack." Alpha Jamie said before glaring at me. *Shit! What did I miss?*

Ryker looked at Ace and me before nodding to us. I got up, walking over to him.

The Black Moon Pack, the pack that would be handed to my brother and me next year, ran alongside Black Creek Pack. Only a river stood between the two packs, dividing their territory.

He pointed to the map, indicating the open fields running along the river on our side.

"What about it?" I asked, kicking myself for not paying attention.

"I'll buy it off you."

"Not interested," I told him. That was a large empty space we planned on turning into training grounds.

"What could you possibly want with it?" Alpha Jamie asked.

"None of you bloody business. What do you want with it? You want more land? Go pester him for it. I'm not giving you even an inch of fucking space!" I told him, not liking the prick's tone. *Who the fuck does he think he is?*

"He has enough. He is just being greedy," Damien said, sitting back in his chair and folding his arms across his chest. Alpha Jamie was not liked by many. He was arrogant and stuck in the Stone Age with the way he ran his pack.

Alpha Jamie growled at Damian but soon quietened down with one look from my brother.

"Enough! He said no, and that's it. It is their land, their pack. Moving on," Ryker tells him.

"They are fucking seventeen, for fuck's sake! And know nothing about running a pack! What could they possibly need it for? This is bullshit! And no longer fair to the rest of the packs surrounding the area, when your family runs over half the packs around here," he said.

His Luna grabbed his arm, trying to calm him, and if looks could kill, she would be dead ten times over. She was a timid woman, she had her red hair tied in a bun and a stern face. Yet the fear of her husband was evident in her eyes as she cowered from his glare. I felt sorry for her, having a husband like him. It was clear she feared him. He tugged his arm away from her and stood up, placing his hands on the desk. His dirty-blond hair fell forward over his eyes before he swept it away with his hand.

"Fine! You want it so bad? I'll challenge you for it," Ace told him, also getting up from his seat. I folded my arms across my chest, sitting back with a silly smirk on my face. The old man had better sit down, Ace would eat him alive. The difference in size alone made Alpha Jamie look like a boy compared to my brother's large frame.

"Well, don't you think you're something!" the Alpha spat back at him.

"You want it, old man? Take it," Ace said.

Ryker sat down with a stupid grin on his face. "Offer is there, Jamie. You want the land? Challenge him for it."

"Sit down, love," His Luna told him, touching his arm. She looked petrified, and he would be an idiot to challenge Ace. Not only would he lose, but we would take his pack. Realizing that, he sat back down.

Ace also went to sit down, but the dickhead just couldn't help but run his mouth.

"Fucking hybrid mutts!" he muttered under his breath. Ace growled, about to attack him, when Reika suddenly stood. Reaching over the table, grabbing his head, and slamming it onto the table. I heard the crunch of his nose before blood splattered across it. My mother snickered in the corner of the room. Mom had a different way of dealing with Alphas when she was Queen, she could usually talk them down with reason. Reika, the new Queen, didn't share those views. Personally, I think my brother has rubbed off on her, she was more the brute-force sort of Queen.

Alpha Jamie sprang to his feet, a growl escaping his lips. His Luna shrieked as blood splattered on her.

"You fucking…"

"I dare you to finish that sentence, Jamie. See where it gets you," Ryker warned him, pulling Reika onto his lap before she let Amanda have him. Jamie, however, refused to sit back down. Reika leaned forward, and I could see Ryker's grip on her tighten as she gripped the table.

"Sit down, bitch! Or I will make you!" Reika told him, her claws slipping from her fingers and piercing through the desk.

Alpha Jamie finally sat back down, backing away from the argument. Reika looked a little upset, like she wanted him to remain standing just so she could tear him apart. Ryker whispered something to her, and she leaned back, and he kissed her shoulder.

"So. Can we wrap this shitshow up? Or do you other fools want to start some more unnecessary shit?" I asked.

They shook their heads, and I hopped up, glad to be out of this meeting. My mother came over from her place in the corner, following Ace and me out of the room.

"You boys excited for your seventeenth birthday tomorrow? You can finally find your mates. I thought you would have last year, but better late than never," she said.

"More excited about spending time with my family. It's been a while since everyone has been in one place," Ace said, wrapping his arm across her shoulders.

"Feels like yesterday that you were babies. Now look at you. All grown up and towering over me just like your brother," she said just as Lucy came bounding down the stairs. She had grown so much, her green and amber eyes lighting up when she saw us. She was twelve now.

"Grandma!" she squealed, rushing over and hugging her.

"Hey, princess. Where were you headed?"

"Looking for dad. I want to go to the creek with Melena and Josey."

"Dad's busy, sweetie. You will have to tell them not today. Maybe tomorrow, after the birthday celebrations," Mom told her, and she nodded before heading back upstairs.

"I'll take you. Go put on your swimmers," I told her, and she rushed upstairs. My mother gave me a look.

"What?"

"Reika wants her home. You two always give in to her."

"We will have her back before dark," I told my mother, and she sighed.

"Fine. But, if Reika rips your head off, I ain't helping you," she said, wandering off.

"Huh? Yeah, right! Reika will just be glad she isn't up to mischief," Ace said, heading upstairs to grab our swimmers. Ryker usually went swimming with her, because the girl was bottom-heavy. No matter how many times we tried teaching her to swim, she would just sink to the bottom like a stone.

I followed him up to our room, pushing the door open and grabbing a bag to stuff some clothes in. Lucy didn't have a wolf. Her biological father made sure of that when he forced her to shift, when she was eight, killing her wolf and awakening her vampire side. She too, died from the shift before coming back as a hybrid without a wolf.

"Here, chuck these in," Ace said, tossing me his board shorts. I chucked them in the bag. Just in time for Lucy to bound in with her towel and swimmers.

"Who are you going with? Ace or me?" I asked her.

"Ace. Your wolf is too fast," she said, and I nodded.

"Hold this. I need to pee first," I told her, and she grabbed the backpack, and I wandered down the hall to pee. Flicking the toilet seat up and unzipping. *Argh*, I thought as I let loose, only, I didn't hear it hit the water. Opening my eyes, piss was going everywhere. Like a fountain as I tried to stop midway. *That bloody brat! She cling-wrapped it again!*

"Lucy!" I screamed before hearing her giggle on the other side of the door. I grabbed a towel, mopping up the mess I'd just made before washing my hands.

Opening the door, she shrieked before rushing off.

"Get back here, you little brat!" I yelled, chasing after her. She rushed down the stairs, and Ace grabbed her before darting off with her, laughing.

"Were you in on it?" I asked him through the link while I was trying to find them.

"No. But, it was pretty funny. We are out back," he said, and I followed her scent toward the back patio. Stepping out, Lucy was giggling, hiding behind Ace and using him as a shield.

I growled at her, and she growled back, baring her teeth at me.

"Eyes closed, Luce. Gotta shift," Ace told her, and she turned around, covering her eyes with her hands while he stripped off before dumping his clothes in the bag.

He shifted quickly into his black wolf, which seemed to be a family trait among the men in the family. All our wolves were black. It would be interesting to see if Rayans would be black when he was older or if he would be snow-white like his mother.

I grabbed the bag. "You can open your eyes now," I told her, and she turned around. Ace's wolf Atticus nudged her with his nose, telling her to climb on him. And she did, pulling on his fur to climb on his back.

"Hang on tight. I will catch up," I told her, and she nodded, gripping his fur. I watched as they darted off into the trees. I stripped off before feeling a hand slap my ass, making me jump.

"Need some sun on that bum, bro," Damian said, coming out the back door and leaning on the railing, watching his daughter Amelia who was on the swings talking to a pack wolf. She is fifteen now. I shifted. Suddenly, Damian growled, making me snap my head to Amelia, who was walking off toward the forest with the boy she was talking to.

"Over my dead fucking body! Is she going off with that twerp!" Damian snapped before storming down the steps after his daughter. I chuckled before running off across the yard, heading for the trees.

◦◦◦

Chapter 2

Ace
THE NEXT DAY

I WAS SO FUCKING HUNGOVER! My head was pounding as I rolled on my side. Today was our seventeenth birthday, and Arial had decided to get us shitfaced a day early. Man, was I paying for it this morning.

I groaned, forcing myself up before running my hands over my face. Tyson also got up in the bed across from me.

"My mouth tastes like a fucking ashtray," he grumbled.

I got up, heading for the bathroom, making sure Lucy didn't cling-wrap the toilet bowl last night. No cling wrap. I quickly peed before heading back to the room.

"Want one?" Tyson asked, cracking the window open and sitting on the windowsill. I took the packet, lighting one before climbing out the window and sitting on the roof and leaning against the wall under the window.

"Fuck! My head is pounding!" I told him.

"I don't feel too bad. Surprisingly."

I could smell the BBQ going and looked at Tyson.

"What time is it?" I asked him, and he popped his head in the window, grabbing his phone from beside his bed.

"One o'clock."

"Fuck! I was supposed to meet up with Melana this morning."

"What if she isn't your mate?" he asked, and I shrugged.

"It doesn't matter. She will do till I find her," I told him. "You still seeing that blonde bitch, Tara?"

"Nah, too much of a cling-on. Fucking asked me to mark her as my chosen mate! Like I would give up a fated mate for a chosen one," he said, shaking his head.

I finished my smoke before flicking it, only to hear someone cuss. Lana walked out into the driveway.

"Fucking ass. You just flicked that on my head!" she said, looking up at me on the roof.

"My bad. Hard to see a midget from up here," I called back.

"That's it! I am done with the short jokes! I will show you fucking short!" she shrieked before stomping inside.

"I would run if I were you."

"Nah. I'm good," I said when the bedroom door burst open. Tyson snorted, and I got a whiff of Drake's scent.

"Fuck! That's fucking cheating, Lana!" I screamed when Drake climbed out the window.

"Sorry, bro. Gotta dish out some ass-kicking," he growled, and I jumped off the roof, Drake hot on my heels, as I tried to run away from him.

"Better run, Ace!" Lana called out laughing, just as I got tackled. We wrestled before Tate came running over, also helping Drake pin me down. I saw Tyson jump off the roof, laughing, before seeing a pissed-off Lana stalking toward me in her midget fury. Tate and Drake were still trying to pin me down.

"Ha! Not so cocky now?" she said.

"You fucking cheated! Had to get your mates to get me because you're too piss weak," I spat at her before tossing Drake off. She jumped on my back like a spider monkey before biting my shoulder blade. I growled at her, trying to toss her off.

"You fucking bit me!"

"Bloody pin him!" Lana screamed at her mates as they laughed at her clinging to me. I reached over my head, grabbing her shirt before pulling her over my shoulder and throwing her to the ground. She growled at me, getting up.

"Instead of laughing, how about you help?" I yelled at Tyson, who was just watching me getting attacked by the three of them. Hearing a war cry, I turned to look at all my nieces and nephews charging out of the house. *Oh, fuck!*

"Get him, kids!" Lana told them, and I ran off.

"Oh, shit!" Tyson said when he saw them running at him as well.

We both took off for the trees, knowing they couldn't enter without their parents.

"No fair," I heard Rayan call out when we went to their out-of-bounds area.

"Come on. We can go around back," Tyson said, and we trudged through the forest, heading to the back of the property.

I could just make out the swings and back area of the house as we stepped out of the trees, when I got a whiff of something that perked my wolf up.

"Fuck! Something smells good," I told Tyson, and he sniffed the air.

"Mhm. What is that?" he asked, and I shrugged. My mouth was watering at the scent. I could see my mother putting up party decorations, before Lucy skipped down the steps with some fairy lights in her hands and some lanterns.

"Mate!" both Tyson and I said at the same time, making me look at him. He growled at me, and I growled back.

"No! Mine!" he snapped at me.

"Like fuck! I saw her first!" I told him, shoving him. He shoved me back.

"Oi! What's going on?" my mother yelled at us as I punched him. Distracting me enough that Tyson's fist connected with my face. I tackled him, and my mother shrieked.

"Hey! Buttfaces," Lucy called out to us, and both of us looked over at her. Lucy had been raised alongside us, she was our brother's step-daughter and was twelve. I couldn't believe our luck. Not only were we paired with the same girl, we now had to wait years before she would recognize us. Supposing she even could, her being a hybrid mutation without a wolf.

"Can you help me hang these lights?" she asked, completely oblivious that she was our mate or would be one day.

"I'll help!" I told her, shoving Tyson back on the ground.

"No! I fucking will!" Tyson said, shoving me back and knocking me over.

"What's going on? Stop! You will scare the kids!" Ryker said, storming down the steps toward us as I swung at Tyson.

"What has gotten into you? Why are you fighting?" he asked.

"We were mucking around," Tyson said, wiping his bleeding lip.

"Doesn't look like it!" he snapped at us. I dropped my arm on Tyson's shoulder, jerking him toward me before slapping his chest.

"We are good. Right, bro?"

He slapped mine harder. "Never better," he said.

"Good! I need one of you to help me get the lights up there," Lucy said, pointing to the railing along the awning.

Tyson walked over to her, grabbing her and placing her on his shoulders. I growled at him, and Ryker looked at me, giving me a look of *what-the-fuck-is-going-on*. I shook my head, walked over, and passed the lights up to Lucy as she clipped them onto the awning.

"What's wrong with you two morons?" she asked.

Chapter 3

Lucy

As I was getting out of the car, I knew my mother was going to kill me. After nearly five years and only coming home on holiday breaks, I had finally pushed too many buttons, and they kicked me out of school.

My father had sent Jacob to get me from Avalon City. A lot of us mutations had trouble fitting in with pack wolves. So Avery and Aamon, who was alright for demons, opened a boarding school for us, as most of us were more comfortable around our own kind. Yet, I couldn't even see it out. Another thing I failed at. I only had three more months, and I would be eighteen and finished with school. She would kill me. Especially, after all the begging and pleading it took for her to let me go, only for me to fail.

"Best get it over with, Lucy. The longer you hold out, the worse it will get," Jacob told me, shutting my door and pushing me toward the front door. I looked up at the packhouse, which was also my home, yet the thought of facing her had me wanting to run. I saw the front door open and chickened out.

"Nope. Catch you later, Jacob!" I shrieked before taking off.

"You gotta come home sometime, Lucy! You can't run from me forever!" I heard my mother yell as I darted off.

"Just let her go, Jacob. I will deal with her when she gets home," I heard my mother call Jacob as he tried to catch me.

Yep! I am not coming home! I thought to myself. Breaking through the treeline, I headed to my safe place, my home away from home. Tyson and Ace, they had always been on my side, and I might just play on that a little. It took me twenty minutes before I hit the border of their pack as I raced through the forest.

Crossing over it, three wolves jump out, blocking me. They were always watching the borders. I was yet to successfully sneak onto their territory. Ace and Tyson had the place locked down like Fort Knox.

One of the wolves shifted back, the gray one with a white ear, and I looked up and recognized him instantly. It was one of their Betas. Tyson and Ace had two, being there were two Alphas in this pack.

"Lucy? You're back!" Chris said, a little shocked. Obviously, my father hadn't told anyone about my return, probably in case mom would have murdered me. *Good thinking, dad!* Chris was taller than me, but then again, most of them were. *Thanks to mom for the short genes! While mom got hit with the short stick, the fates must have thought it funny to whack me with the whole damn tree*, I thought to myself. Chris covered himself with his hand, and I raised an eyebrow at him. His long dark hair fell loosely down his back.

"Nothing I haven't seen before. Where are Tyson and Ace?" I asked him.

"Packhouse." I tried to step around them when Chris stepped in my way, blocking me. I looked up at the huge burly man and folded my arms across my chest, and he smirked. "Always up to mischief. It'll get you in trouble one day."

"Ha! Me? I'm no trouble. But if you don't move, Chris, trouble might just find you," I teased.

"Maybe a phone call would have been good first Lucy. They didn't realize you would be back," he said, crossing his arms across his chest while my eyes darted down. He quickly realized his mistake and dropped his hands to cover himself again. I chuckled at him as his face heated. He was around Tyson and Ace's age, but I could tell I was making him uncomfortable.

"Since when do I need to call ahead? Move Chris," I told him, and he sighed, motioning to the other two to get out of my way. They followed me to the packhouse.

"I know where they live. You don't need to follow me, Chris."

"I know. Just making sure you don't go off anywhere else. We've been having issues with Alpha Jamie," he said, and I turned around to face him.

"Alpha Jamie? Since when is that anything new?" He shrugged, and I looked back up at the packhouse before turning to tell him to go, only to find him and the other two wolves already gone. I walked up the porch steps before hearing a moan.

Looking out at the driveway, I saw Melana's red Suzuki Swift and rolled my eyes. I knew it shouldn't have irked me, but it did. Melana had been on and off with Ace for years now. I used to be friends with her, but I couldn't stand the woman now.

She was Josey's sister, who was my friend still, but Melana was also five years older than me and the same age as Ace and Tyson. Jumping off the porch, I walked around the side of the house, stopping at Ace's window. His curtain was wide open, and I could see the bitch jumping up and down on him like he was a pogo stick. I ducked down when she looked toward the window.

Covering my mouth as I snickered. Walking out back, I went to the shed, looking around, my eyes lighting up when I saw brake fluid on the shelf.

Grabbing it, I also found some white paint and grabbed that too. *Fine! She won't leave? I will make her!* I thought to myself as I walked back to the front yard. I tipped the brake fluid on her car, squirting it on her paint, knowing it would destroy it and eat the paint away. I tossed the bottle before grabbing the tin of white paint and walked up the porch steps while undoing the lid with my claws. The front door suddenly opened, and I hid the tin behind my back. Tyson stopped in his tracks when he saw me. A look of confusion crossed his gorgeous face.

"Lucy?" He seemed shocked but damn, did he smell good. They had always smelt nice, but his scent was mouth-watering good and so much stronger than I remembered. I hadn't seen them since last Christmas, so it had been a good eight months, but damn! He looked better than ever.

Chapter 4

"You're back?" he said before I heard Melana moan loudly, and the sound really got on my nerves, making me growl. Tyson looked over his shoulder at the door before turning back to me.

"Lucy, are you going to answer me?" Tyson asked before reaching for me. I stepped back, and his eyes darted to my arm behind my back.

"Hand it over. What have you got?" he scolded.

"Nothing," I lied when he jerked me toward him with my shirt.

"Lucy! Why do you have paint?"

"Decorating," I snorted, trying to hide my laughter when he looked over my shoulder.

"What have you done?"

"Nothing. Yet," I told him. *Damn! He smells good!* I stepped closer, inhaling his scent, and he stiffened, his entire body going tense. *What was up with him?*

"You smell different," I told him when suddenly Melana moaned out again. The sound sounded more like a war cry as if she was about to go into battle. Yet, for some reason, I wanted to claw the bitch's eyes from her skull and feed them to her. I shoved past him and into the house, with Tyson hot on my heels. He grabbed my arm just as I reached Ace's bedroom door, sparks rushing over my skin. Tyson jerked his hand away, and I gasped. He looked at me oddly, and I saw his eyes flicker to those of Tyrant, his wolf.

I was about to ask if he was alright when Melana just had to cry out, again. I tossed the door open, getting a good grip on the tin and chucking the paint over her, also covering Ace in the process. She shrieked.

"What the fuck!" Ace boomed, and I darted off, shoving the paint tin in Tyson's hands, laughing as I took off. *Bloody bitch!* I thought to myself as I darted out of the packhouse.

I heard Ace snap at Tyson. "What the fuck, bro!" Tyson didn't answer, and I rushed out the back to the shed.

Sitting in the shed, I hid behind one of the cars and snickered when I heard Melana cussing Ace and Tyson out before she got in her car, dust and dirt spraying everywhere as she tore out of the driveway.

"Lucy, come here now!" I heard Ace yell out to me, and I pressed myself against his car, refusing to come out when I heard footsteps approaching the shed. I heard them walk around the car and quickly crawled to the other side, only to see bare feet stop next to my face. I jumped back, scrambling backward on my hands when I looked up and saw Ace's muscled chest and abs covered in white paint. He was wearing a pair of shorts, his V-line slipping beneath the waistband. I shook my head, realizing I was checking him out, before I shrank under his pissed-off glare and started moving backward. My hands hit something, and I felt shoes under my hands, making me look up and see Tyson now behind me.

"Explain yourself!" Ace said, drawing my attention back to him. He folded his arms across his chest, making him even more imposing. Though I knew they would never hurt me, I suddenly felt guilty before slapping that feeling away. *Fuck Melana!*

"She was all over you!" I spat at him, and he raised an eyebrow at me, his eyes darting to Tyson behind me.

"And that bothers you, why?" he asked. I thought about what he said, yet couldn't explain why it ticked me off, but I suddenly didn't want her near him.

"I don't know," I answered lamely, and he crouched down in front of me.

"You don't know? So you just tossed paint on her because you don't know?"

"I also put brake fluid on her car," I announced, and he growled before looking up at Tyson.

Ace sighed, running a hand through his hair. "Why are you home? You don't finish for a few more months."

"No reason. Just stopping by," I lied.

"What did you do, Lucy?" Tyson asked, making me look up at him where I was practically sitting on his feet.

"I may or may not have blown up the science lab."

"You may or may not have? Exactly how does that work?"

"Innocent till proven guilty," I told him.

"So, you will be found guilty, I take it?" Ace asked, and I looked back at him.

"You always assume the worst of me."

"So, you didn't do it then?" he asked, and I pressed my lips in a line to hide my smile.

"Well, I didn't say that," I told him, and he shook his head, laughing softly.

"Of course, you did it," he muttered.

"What can I say? I was taught by the best!" I told him, and he smirked.

"Not even we blew up a science class. Come on, we should take you home," Ace said, standing up. I shook my head. Nope not going, mom was out for blood, mine in particular. The bill was huge.

"Lucy, up. Now!" Tyson said, nudging me with his foot. I rolled my eyes, getting to my feet before trying to run and escape. Ace's arms wrapped around my waist, jerking me back as I shoved past him.

"Not so fast, trouble. You are going home," Ace said, his breath fanning my face, and I leaned into him. Gosh, he smelled just as good as Tyson. Did they start wearing different cologne? It was mouth-watering. Sparks rushed across my abdomen where his arms lay, and I shivered at the sensation.

"Does your mother know you are here?" Ace asked, walking us out of the shed while I tried to escape his arms.

"Probably. I have nowhere else to go," I told him before dropping my weight and going limp, sliding out of his grip. I crawled off, trying to get to my feet. Only to be yanked upright and tossed over his shoulder.

"Lucy, you need to go home, and we need to speak to my brother and your mother. We weren't expecting you back this early," Ace said.

"Wait, you're telling on me. I confessed under the confidence you wouldn't tell her I was guilty," I told him, smacking his back before sinking my teeth into his side.

"Argh, fuck! Lucy, you cannibal!" he shrieked before his hand slammed down on my ass. I squirmed, rubbing my butt.

"That fucking hurt!" I shrieked, my ass felt like it was branded.

"So did you biting me," he growled, and I heard Tyson laugh, making me look up and see him following behind us.

"We aren't telling on you, but it is about time we spoke to her about something. Believe me, what we have to say to her will make her forget about anything you did at school," Ace said.

"Doubt it. Mom already got the damage bill," I told him, and Tyson sighed.

"Lucy! How much was it?" he asked.

"A little over twenty thousand," I told him, and he pinched the bridge of his nose before letting out a breath.

"Fine. I will take care of it. But you need to behave when you go back."

"Can't. They expelled me." Ace growled, his arm across my thighs tightening.

"Wait. What do you need to speak to mom about?" I asked curiously.

"Nothing you need to worry about right now. You'll figure it out, I am sure," Tyson said.

Ace walked up the steps of the porch before walking inside and dumping me on the lounge.

"Stay. And try not to break anything or blow it up," Ace said, wandering off and into the bathroom.

"I will get you a shirt now that yours is covered in paint," Tyson said, also walking down the hall. I got up, wandering around, looking at the photos on the wall. Most were family photos when I stopped noticing a wall that was just of me growing up with them. We had always been close, but now things felt different, they felt different.

"Here," Tyson said, coming back into the room and handing me one of his shirts. I pulled mine off, tossing it at him before pulling his shirt on. I sniffed it, it smelled like him.

"Geez! Lucy, you don't just strip off," Tyson growled, looking away.

"What? It's no different than seeing me in a bikini," I told him, not understanding his issue. He shook his head.

"Did you guys change cologne?" I asked him, sniffing his shirt, and he looked at me.

"Do we smell different to you?" he asked, and I nodded.

"Yeah, your scent is heaps stronger. You also zapped me earlier," I told him, remembering the weird sensation that rushed over my skin when he touched me. He said nothing but appeared to be thinking about something.

Ace came out fully dressed a few minutes later after showering.

"Come on. You need to face her sooner or later. Better with us with you," Ace said, gripping my elbow and pulling me toward the door.

Chapter 5

I did not want to go home. My mother would still spank me even though I was nearly eighteen. That woman was crazy and damn, did she have a good hand. I could still remember the last ass-kicking she gave me, never thinking I would walk the same again. She branded my ass real good that day.

Only this time, I really messed up. I burned the entire science lab down. I still believe it wasn't completely my fault. Yes, I burned the classroom down, but I only intended to destroy the table, not blow the entire place up. Not my fault someone left the gas on, the teacher was supposed to turn it off before locking it up.

Ace opened the back door of the car, pushing me toward it.

"How about you both go, and I wait here?" I suggested. Tyson looked over at me from the other side of the car.

"Get in the car, Lucy," he said, and I pursed my lips. *Nope! I am not going.* I turned around only to find Ace smiling down at me. *Was he really finding my potential murder amusing?*

"Get in the car, Lucy," he said as well, folding his arms across his broad chest, but this big buffoon didn't intimidate me. How could they when I grew up with them?

I raised an eyebrow at his words and was about to tell him to go suck on a big one when he leaned down, proving how short I really was.

"I can always make you," he said, and I scoffed at his words.

"Make me then," I taunted, and he went to grab me, but I saw his hands twitch a second before and did the most logical thing any girl would do. I kicked him, and the reaction was instantaneous. I almost felt my own imaginary nuts ache at the contact as he grunted, clutching his balls like his hands were the only thing leaving them attached to him, like it could somehow stop his pain.

"Ha! That will teach you for being balls deep in Melana," I told him as I darted off, heading for the forest at the back of the packhouse.

"Fuck's sake! Seriously? You couldn't just toss her in?" I heard Tyson tell him before chasing after me.

My legs moved at lightning speed as I tried to remember which way went where. I had not been to this side of the woods in years, but I knew there was a river somewhere. I just had to find it. I could follow it, knowing it led to Mitchell's place, he would help me hide from my mother and these two. He was probably the only person whom I actually liked in our pack. And who didn't look at me funny for my weird eyes.

Hearing water, I diverted, heading for it, when I heard a growl from behind me, making adrenaline course through my body as I picked up my pace. I could smell the water. I was so close that I could hear the river running downstream. I was nearly in the clear. I just had to jump over to the other side, and I knew I was free. Though that put me on our neighboring pack's territory, I would only be quick and doubted they would detect me.

I giggled when my foot left the bank before Tyson yelled through the mindlink at me, his voice booming through my head, startling me. I lost my footing, tumbling forward, the fall knocking the air from my lungs.

"Lucy, no!" he screamed just as I hit the ground on the other side. I turned to look at him when I heard growls coming from the trees near me. At first, I didn't understand when the five wolves stepped out of the trees like they were waiting for someone to cross. I was more confused because they were members of a pack in alliance with ours, but their feral growls said otherwise.

They dropped their heads, teeth bared, and I scrambled backward, not understanding, when I heard a vicious growl resonate from the trees before feeling fur brush against my arm and Tyson's scent wafting to me. I was shocked he cleared the river without falling into its depths. I was more vampire than werewolf, so for me, jumping was easy, but he was in wolf form. He growled, forcing his body over mine, and the five wolves growled back at him but backed down. His aura radiating out of him made even me tremble, though it wasn't directed at me. I saw Ace's wolf come up on my other side before stepping toward them, stalking them and daring them to step closer. Both their wolves were identical though Atticus, Ace's wolf, was slightly wider while Tyrant, Tyson's wolf, was taller. Both were equally menacing, and their paws were bigger than my hands as they towered over me, shielding me from Alpha Jamie's pack warriors.

"Get back to the other side, Lucy! Now!" Ace snapped at me through the mindlink, his eyes not leaving the five wolves. They looked too scared to move, and I would be too if I had both their deadly gazes on me at this moment.

Tyrant, Tyson's wolf, nipped my hand when I froze in place, his teeth puncturing my hand, making me hiss and jolting me out of my own head.

"Now!" Tyrant's deep gravelly voice made me whimper before I forced myself to my feet. I turned before running toward the edge and jumping across. Tyson followed in his wolf form, leaving Ace on the other side with the five wolves when he turned his back on them, yet not one of them dared move as he ran toward the river and jumped it, clearing rather easily. Atticus stalked toward me, and he grabbed my ankle, jerking me to the ground and ripping my legs out from under me. I cried out as his teeth punctured through the flesh on my ankle. They never hurt me, no matter what I did, they never carried on like this, especially their wolves, but I could feel their auras smashing against me.

"You don't ever cross the border!" Atticus snapped at me, making me flinch away from him. I didn't understand what was going on. They were an alliance pack. Ace suddenly shifted back, taking back control from his wolf, leaving him in a crouched position in front of me. His glare made my blood run cold. He stood, and I averted my gaze from his nudity.

"Get up!" he said before stepping around me and walking into the trees, heading toward the packhouse. Tyrant came over, nudging me before pulling on my shirt.

"Now, Lucy," Tyson's voice flitted through my head. I turned, getting to my feet when I felt his tongue run across my ankle. The wounds were already nearly healed, his saliva forcing them to heal instantly, and the tingling sensation returned.

"Now. Start walking," Tyson said, falling in line with me. Ace was walking ahead, and I could feel his aura even twenty meters away from him.

Chapter 6

When we got close to the packhouse, Ace stopped looking back at us, and Tyrant licked my fingers, making them tingle.

"You don't run from us under any circumstances, Lucy. And you definitely don't cross into another territory!" Ace scolded me. The look he was giving me made me feel like a naughty child. I hated it when he looked at me like that.

"Now, get in the fucking car while I go grab some clothes!" he said, storming off. Tyson followed in after him in his wolf form.

I walk toward Tyson's black Mustang before opening the door and climbing in. I couldn't understand why Alpha Jamie's pack would try to attack me. Something must have happened while I was away. Tyson came out first, climbing in the driver's seat. He didn't say a word to me, and I could feel how angry he was about me taking off. Ace climbed in the front, looking over at me.

"Seatbelt, Lucy," he said, and I huffed before clipping it in and folding my arms across my chest. Tyson reversed out of the driveway, and I tried not to think about the ass-whooping my mother would give me.

"Where were you going anyway?" Tyson asked, breaking the silence in the car.

"Mitchell's," I told him, looking out the window.

"You still talk to that fool?"

"He isn't a fool. He is my friend. At least he wouldn't hand me over to my mother like you pair are doing," I told him.

"Like he had a choice. Your mother is Queen. No one can go against her and my brother," Ace said.

"You can resist her."

"Yes, but we are Lycan descendants like my mother. But even still, your mother is Queen, and she can still command us. She just chooses not to since we are her brothers-in-law," Tyson said, looking in the rearview mirror at me. I looked away. She was going to kill me. I wondered how dad would take it. Knowing my stepfather, he would probably think it funny, half the time when my parents fought, it was over me and my misadventures.

"Stop worrying, Lucy. Your mother will completely forget about what you have done, believe me. She will be more preoccupied with killing Ace and me," Tyson said.

"Why? What did you two do?" I asked curiously. Ace, I could probably picture getting in trouble and doing something. Tyson, however, was always so serious these days. He was never like that growing up. I think when he didn't find his mate, it changed him. He used to tell me all about mates when I was growing up, and I knew he was excited to find his. He was even saving himself for his mate, which made me wonder if he was still a virgin. I knew Ace wasn't, but Tyson wasn't like Ace. I never saw him with another girl growing up. Maybe he was gay.

Leaning forward in my seat, I asked him, "Are you gay?"

Ace laughed at my words, and Tyson growled.

"What makes you think I'm gay?"

"Because you are twenty-three, and I just realized I have never seen you with a girl since I was like eleven or twelve. I know Ace isn't, obviously." The thought of him with Melana irritated me, and I wanted to claw her eyes out.

"Ace is just selfish by not waiting, and I'm not gay, Lucy. I am just saving myself for my mate," he said, looking over his shoulder at me.

"So, you're still a virgin?" I asked him.

"Yes, Lucy, he is still a virgin. I hear him wanking all the time," Ace told me, and Tyson elbowed him before growling at him.

"Why the sudden interest in our sex lives, Lucy?" Tyson asked me.

"I was just wondering, is all."

"Fine, what about yours then? Have you been saving yourself for your mate?" Ace asked, turning in his seat and looking back at me.

"I don't have a mate. You both know that. I have no wolf, so even if I did, I would never recognize him," I told them. The thought saddened me. I loved the idea of mates but knew I would never find mine unless he found me and told me. But no one wanted a mutation for a mate.

"Your mate is probably closer than you think, Lucy. You will find him," Tyson said.

"Or them!" Ace growled at him, making me furrow my brows at his sudden hostility.

"You still didn't answer my question. You better not have fooled around with that Mitchell. Can't stand his arrogant ass," Ace growled at me. I rolled my eyes at him and his overprotectiveness. They were like big brothers to me growing up, but now things felt different, and I suddenly found answering embarrassing.

"No, of course not. He is a friend," I told him, looking out the window. Their scents were overwhelming in the car. I wondered what cologne they'd changed to, it smelled divine.

I put the window down to get some fresh air. We were not far from home now, and dread was starting to fill me.

"She isn't very good at listening?" Ace mumbled, making me look at him.

"Huh?"

"You still didn't answer."

"Why do I have to?" I asked him.

"Well, you asked about Tyson's," Ace said, and I saw Tyson's eyes dart to mine in the mirror. My face heated under his intense gaze, forcing me to pull my eyes from his.

"Yes. I am saving myself for the mate I don't have, if you must know," I told Ace, and he nodded.

"Good," he said, looking back at the road. I shook my head at his words. *Did my mother tell them to ask me about my non-existent sex life?* Their curiosity confused me. Though I was curious about Tyson's, I suppose it was my own fault for bringing it up.

"So, will you tell me what you need to tell my mother? I want to know what you did that will make what I did, look like nothing," I asked them, and they looked at each other.

"Nothing yet, but she will be pissed off," Tyson said.

"She will be pissed off at you. She may kill me," Ace said, and I thought I saw regret flash across his eyes as he looked at his brother, making me wonder what it was he regretted doing.

Chapter 7

Pulling up, I groaned when I saw my mother standing out the front. If looks could kill, I would turn to ash the moment I stepped out of the car. My mother came storming over to me in all her blazing hot anger. I could practically see the steam coming off her as she boiled like a kettle about to scream at me.

"Don't you run from me!" she growled as she reached me, and Tyson stepped in front of her, her hand connecting with his chest instead of my face. I knew I deserved it, but I sure as hell didn't want to get in trouble. If she would only hear me out, I never meant to blow up the science lab. Yes, I intended to start the fire, but I never intended to destroy the building. And I still had my reasons for doing it if she would just let me explain.

"Reika!" my stepfather snapped at her as he walked out. Tyson rubbed his chest where she hit him as I cowered like the chicken I was behind him, hoping he could save me from her wrath.

"Inside now, Lucy!" my father said, glaring at my mother for trying to strike me. She dropped her head and sighed.

"Well, what do you expect? She is out of control, and I am fucking sick of it! You deal with her then!" my mother screeched at him as I ran inside and up the steps to my room. *Great! Now, I am trapped in here. Good few days, hopefully she will calm down, and I can sneak out of my room again. Or maybe she will let me explain without killing me first.* I locked it just to make sure. Flopping on my bed, I wrapped my purple comforter around me.

What a way to come home. Yet, nowhere felt like home anymore. Being away from here for years, only returning for holidays, had left me and my mother estranged slightly. She spent more time yelling at me than letting me explain. Hearing the door bang downstairs, I jumped before hearing a soft knock on the door.

"Lucy, let me in," I heard my little brother, Rayan, call through the door. I smiled, I hadn't seen him for eight months. Getting up, I walked over, unlocking the door before reaching out and jerking him inside and locking the door again. I grabbed him, squishing him against me as I picked him up and cuddled him, inhaling his scent. Gosh, I missed him. Since I last saw him, he had a growth spurt and was now up to my shoulder.

"Can't breathe," he gasped, and I let him go. Rayan was ten and the picture-perfect son in mom's eyes. He was next in line for my stepfather's title as the Alpha King. I didn't remember my father, but from what I'd heard, I was better off without him. He was the one responsible for killing my wolf and ruining my chances of ever finding my mate or leaving this pack.

I stared down at my brother. He looked like his father with his silver and gold eyes and dark curls, though the eyes he got from mom. Mom was also a mutation, born and raised in captivity like me. We were separated when I was a baby, and until she met her mate, the Alpha King, I was kept in a facility with hundreds of others like me. Experimented on and used by the hunters. With the help of his family and the other packs, my stepfather took them down and freed us. But none of us felt truly free, we all still lived with what happened. With the nightmares that plagued us.

"I missed you," he said, flopping on my bed and making himself comfortable with his bag of chips. I sat next to him, and he offered me some. I dug my hand into the bag, grabbing some before leaning back against the headboard.

"On a scale of one to ten, how much does mom want to murder me?" I asked him.

"A twelve, but don't worry. I heard Uncle Tyson say he would pay for the damage as I walked up here. Figured I would get one last glimpse of you before your death. What sort of flowers should I put on your grave?" he asked with a shrug. I nudged him with my elbow.

He laughed. "Lucy, why did you do it?"

"He pissed me off, and the piece of shit deserved it. To be fair though, I didn't know it was flammable."

"Since when is petrol not flammable?" Rayan asked with a chuckle.

"Since it was in a normal plastic bottle," I told him. He could always see straight through me. I might as well have been made of glass when it came to my little brother.

"Did you happen to bring the plastic bottle with the petrol?"

"No! Of course not!" I told him, acting appalled at his outrageously true fact.

"You did it deliberately, didn't you?"

I sighed, running my fingers through my hair. He always saw straight through me. I nodded, knowing it was no use lying to him. *Shit! It was no use lying to any of them.* They all knew I was guilty. Though, he truly deserved it. I should have burned the bastard alive! Instead, I burned his classroom down.

"Why?" he asked, and I looked at him. He was the only person who ever asked why, most just accused me and told me it had to do with being a mutated freak. To be fair, I have done my fair share of stupid shit, but I actually had a reason for once.

"Doesn't matter, Rayan," I told him before I heard screaming downstairs and things being thrown around and smashed. Rayan and I looked at each other before getting up, and I cracked the door open.

"Reika, calm down! You think we asked for this to happen?" I heard Tyson yell at her as Rayan and I rushed out, peering over the balcony to the floor below. Tyson ducked as she threw something at him, and it hit the wall behind him, leaving a dent.

"Love, enough," I heard Ryker, my stepfather, tell her.

"What? Are you fucking okay with this? It is fucking wrong!" she screamed, and curiosity got the better of Rayan and me. I crept down the steps. Rayan, also curious, followed me. One of the steps creaked under his weight, and he smiled, his teeth clenched and his eyes squinting. My mother looked up at me, her face twisting in anger at the sight of me.

"And you! You wait till I get my hands on you!" she growled, about to storm up the steps. *Thanks, Rayan. Now we don't know what they were arguing over*, I thought to myself when I saw my mother's thong flying toward me. I ducked before snorting that she just threw her shoe at me. I watched Rayan dart off, escaping her fury.

"Get here now! Do you have any idea what you have done?" she snapped at me before I felt the command wash over me. My feet moved on their own accord and marched me directly to her. I thought it was bullshit that I had no wolf and yet was still affected by her aura or any Alpha's aura, it didn't seem fair. I stopped in front of her, and I had never seen her so angry.

"You humiliated our family. Do you have any idea how hard it was getting you back into that school the first time they kicked you out?" she screamed at me. I knew it was the hormones from her being pregnant, but saying I was petrified of her was an understatement. She never hit me growing up, but I did get in trouble with her or her wolf Amanda the last four times I had been home. Before I could even answer, I felt her hand connect with the side of my face, her handprint bleeding into my skin as my head whipped to the side from the force. I felt my lip split open before blood trickled down my chin. I heard my stepfather growl furiously as she raised her hand again.

Chapter 8

Only this time, her hand didn't connect. Instead, I saw Ace grab her wrist just before she struck me again.

"Pregnant or not, I will break your fucking arm if you strike her again!" He growled at her, and I rubbed my lip with my thumb to find it bleeding.

Ryker growled, and I felt his aura rush out at the threat against his mate, my mother. Ace and Tyson could resist it slightly, being family. As for me, it dropped me on my ass, and my teeth clenched so tight I thought they would break as I screamed at the sudden agony before the command dropped and my father gripped my arms.

"Shit!, Lucy, I am sorry. It wasn't directed at you," he said, gripping my arms, hauling me upright while I tried to catch my breath.

My mother glared at me but said nothing.

"Everyone needs to cool off. Lucy, go with Tyson and Ace till your mother calms down," said Ryker.

"Are you fucking insane? She can't go with them after what they just told us!" my mother screamed at him, and he glared at her. My father had never denied her anything, nor did he ever go against her. He could usually persuade her but never directly told her what to do. But today, I could see she really got under his skin.

"Lucy is going with Tyson and Ace, and that is final. You had no right to lay a finger on her. I don't care what she did. She is our fucking daughter!" he yelled at her while pointing at me.

I flinched away from his sudden anger, which I was not used to. He was always calm and loving growing up, this was another side of him I was not used to. Though I had heard stories of the Alpha King and how cruel he was. Still, to me, he was dad.

"Fine, she can go!" she said, looking at him before turning to me. My stepfather sighed and looked relieved until the next words left her lips, shocking all of us.

"Don't come back. I am sick of digging you out every time you bury yourself. I won't have Rayan around your destructive behavior. You should be ashamed of yourself. I know I am," she said, and I felt my stomach twist painfully. I could see she was upset at what she'd said. I looked at my father, and he mindlinked me.

"I will speak with her. Just let her calm down," he said before touching my mother's shoulder.

My mother hung her head, her long blonde hair falling forward, and he pulled her to him, tucking her under his chin. I could see dad was upset for yelling at his mate, but she was being a little over the top. I never expected her to kick me out, though, and never thought she would be embarrassed by me. I knew it caused conflict with Aamon and Avery, seeing as they were mom and dad's best friends, but to say she was ashamed of me stung. I had enough shame, and she was the last person I wanted to be ashamed of me.

"Go, Lucy," he said softly, nodding toward the door. I swallowed the lump in my throat and looked to the stairs to see Rayan standing on the top step. I walked toward him when I saw tears slip down his face at me being kicked out. I felt bad I had let him down. I was only home for five minutes, and I was already being kicked out.

"Get out," my mother said, not even looking at me, and I stopped looking at my brother. I pressed my lips in a line, fighting back the tears before turning on my heels and walking away from him. I walked outside, and Tyson grabbed my arm, and I ripped my arm from his grip.

"Don't touch me. This is exactly why I didn't want to come home. She never lets me explain," I told him before walking toward the forest.

"Explain what? What did you expect Lucy, when you burned a classroom down?" Tyson said, throwing his arms in the air. I didn't bother answering, there was no point. Instead, I started running toward Mitchell's.

Mitchell's was the only place I knew I could go. I couldn't face Tyson and Ace, they seemed just as disappointed as my mother. Everyone always saw the worst in me. Maybe I was bad, maybe I asked for it? There was nothing lonelier than having no one on your side, no one you could relate to. I was basically a vampire living among wolves, the illegitimate child of the Alpha King. Though dad never treated me like I didn't belong, that didn't mean I knew I didn't. That was why I asked to go to the boarding school in the first place.

Melana and Josie thrived under the attention of being mutations. Melana enjoyed the attention she received in school, however, to me, it was just a constant reminder that I didn't belong. I was the only mutation without a wolf. The rest survived the shift. My biological father, a human, made me weaker than them, and my wolf never survived. I never survived. If I didn't have vampire genes from my mother being a hybrid mutation, I would be dead. Dying awoke the vampire gene within me, and now I was basically a bloodthirsty monster among a pack of wolves.

When Aamon and Avery opened the boarding school, I begged my mother to let me go, and it was Tyson and Ace who convinced her for me. They knew how much I struggled in school and saw how much I struggled with my own identity. Turns out I didn't belong there either. Boarding school was just another place of torment but for different reasons. The first four years were great, the last year had been a living nightmare. I put my trust in the wrong person, and that trust was abused.

"Lucy, where are you going?" came Ace's voice through the mindlink.

"I am going to Mitchell's," I told him as I tried to focus on where I was going without running into a tree. The mindlinks could become distracting, and it wouldn't be the first time I had run into something.

"Make sure you are home before dark," he said before cutting the mindlink. I could tell he was angry I ran from them, yet I didn't understand his issue with Mitchell.

Home. I wasn't going home. Tyson and Ace might have let me stay with them, but I didn't belong there. I didn't belong anywhere. Every time I came back, every holiday that I returned, it became more startlingly clear how much I didn't belong. I had no home. Mom had built a new life, and I was on the outside of it now. Not even she wanted me. I would watch her with Rayan. I was so excited when he was born, I even helped deliver him. He was so perfect, so small, and I loved him instantly, but mom was so focused on him, which was understandable, he was a baby, but I got pushed out, bit by bit.

If it wasn't for me, they would be the picture-perfect family. I felt like the dirty secret everyone knew about. I had no doubt my parents loved me, but sometimes that wasn't enough when everyone else looked at you like you didn't belong.

I stopped at the river that ran almost a full circle around the city and the borders. I walked a little further before I stopped at the green wooden house nestled among the trees. Hidden from the road on the other side of the forest, the driveway is barely visible.

Mitchell's dad was a pack warrior of my father's pack. All the packs were linked together, branching off one another now since the majority of his family now ran them. Stopping out the front, I walked up the veranda stairs. Before I could even knock, his mother had opened the door. Her curly red hair framed her heart-shaped face. Her green eyes lit up when she saw me.

"You're back!" she said, opening her arms to me. I'd always liked Meredith. She was always so happy to see me, despite me being a pain in the ass sometimes and getting her son in trouble. I wrapped my arms around her slim waist, hugging her tightly.

"You hungry? I am just about to put dinner on if you want to stay for tea?" she asked, and I nodded before thanking her.

"Mitchell, Lucy is here!" she sang out to him before walking toward the kitchen off the side of the stairs. I heard footsteps on the floor above. This house was a pole home, and it was homely, not like the packhouse that was always crisp and clean. This place had character with its exposed rounded beams, fireplaces, and family photos hanging on every wall.

"Lucy?" Mitchell said, stopping at the top of the steps. A grin gracing his face, showing his perfectly straight teeth. He swept his blond fringe out of his eyes before rushing down the steps toward me. His arms wrapped around me as he lifted me off the ground in a hug, my feet dangling in the air, and I hugged him back.

I first met Mitchell when I was playing at the river when I was ten. His family had just been accepted into the pack, and I was playing by myself when he came across me. After that, we quickly became friends and were pretty much inseparable through primary school. Once I left for boarding school, our only contact had been via phone and video chat. We still spoke every day, but it wasn't the same. I missed my friend, missed him something fierce.

He had shot right up since I last saw him eight months ago. He was well over six feet tall and had packed on quite a bit of muscle but was still lean and nowhere near the size of Ace and Tyson. He was built like a warrior, like his father, and I knew he would be a great one when he finished school.

"You came back for good?" he asked, letting me go and placing me back on my feet.

Chapter 9

Tyson

What a disaster that was. I knew Reika would be pissed off because she was our mate. Exactly why we had avoided telling her, but I wasn't expecting her to lose her shit so badly. Ryker just gave us a knowing look. Like he'd already known all along, which wouldn't surprise me, after all, he was very observant.

Ryker was more disappointed that Ace had been fooling around with Melana, knowing he had a mate. Reika didn't care about that. She was furious that we were her mates, she wanted to kill us. We couldn't help who our mate was, that wasn't up to us to decide. She knew this, and it wasn't like Lucy was actually related to us. She was in no way a blood relation to us. It didn't seem weird to me, I could understand her freaking out if she were our niece, but she wasn't. Thankfully, we didn't share the same blood because that would be disgusting, and I would have to reject her. But I wasn't going to reject her just because her mother was uncomfortable with the situation.

"Great, now what?" Ace said, leaning on the car, watching after Lucy, who'd just taken off. I felt terrible for her. She couldn't even get a word in, and it ticked me off that Reika was so angry she would hit her. I felt partially to blame, I didn't think she would have struck her if she wasn't also angry with Ace and me. Hearing the door open, I looked to the packhouse to see my brother come out.

"Reika will calm down. I know you guys didn't ask for this, but you have to realize, to her, it is a little weird," he explained, and I nodded, running a hand through my hair.

"I know she is your step-daughter, but I am not rejecting her, Ryker," I told him.

"I don't expect you to. I had my suspicions," he admitted, and Ace looked at him.

"You knew?" Ace asked, and Ryker shrugged.

"Little obvious with how you were always first to jump in when something went wrong with her. How you were constantly drawn to her the moment we got her back," he said before looking in the car. "Where is she?"

I saw Ace mindlink her, his eyes glazing over before he focused back on us. He growled. "She is going to Mitchell's," he said, and I felt a pang of hurt, knowing she had run to him and away from us.

"Does she know?" Ryker asked, and I shook my head.

"Are you going to tell her?"

"We will see if she figures it out first. Besides, Ace kind of ruined us telling her today," I told him, glaring at my twin. Ace looked away, and I could tell he wished he had now waited. He never wanted Lucy to catch him like that, especially with Melana.

"What do you mean?" Ryker growled, looking at him. Ace didn't answer.

"Lucy walked in on him with Melana," I told Ryker. Ryker growled and glared at him. I had told Ace to wait, but he was too much of a ladies' man. Bloody fool. Lucy wouldn't be happy when she found out. He should have been thinking about the effects it would have on her instead of thinking with his dick.

"Going to enjoy watching you dig yourself out that hole, Ace. She rejects you, you have no one to blame but yourself. Melana used to be her friend. How could you?" Ryker growled at him.

"I know I fucked up. Melana knows she will never be my Luna. She knows that. I made sure that was clear. She won't be an issue. I will break it off with her tonight, okay?"

"No, it's not okay! You should never have been involved with her in the first place!" Ryker yelled at him. Ace hung his head, but hey, I wouldn't be upset if she rejected him. I could have her to myself. The idea of sharing her with my brother grossed me out.

"Once Reika calms down, she can come back home. But until then, keep an eye on her," Ryker said before walking inside. I looked at Ace.

"I told her to be home by dark," he said, and I nodded before opening my car door and climbing in.

Ace climbed in beside me, shutting his door, and I started the car heading home. "Drop me at Melana's on the way."

"I swear to god, Ace, if you being with Melana fucks everything up, I will fucking kill you," I told him.

"If anything, it will stuff me over. You didn't do anything. Besides, I never wanted Melana. She was just a distraction," he said, and I rolled my eyes. I doubted Melana saw it that way.

I dropped Ace at Melana's apartment in the city, and he told me he would run home when he was done dealing with her. Driving home, I pulled up out the front and leaned my head against the headrest. Tyrant was pissed off that we had just let her run off. *But what does he want me to do?* I couldn't control her and tell her what to do. She wasn't even aware we were her mates, and the last thing I wanted her to think was that she was unwelcome here or force her here and have her hate me for it. Opening the mindlink, I felt for her teether. All our packs now branched off each other. Under the Alpha King's rule, we now had a link to any of us in an alliance well, except for Alpha Jamie's pack. He liked to make things increasingly difficult, and I knew I would have to deal with him sooner or later. I knew his pack warriors would have alerted him to Lucy's presence when she stepped across the border.

"What, Tyson?" Lucy asked when her side of the link opened up.

"Just checking on you. Make sure you come back here before dark. I don't want you roaming the streets," I told her.

"Yeah, whatever you say, Alpha," she said, and I could hear the aggravation in her voice. Sometimes, I think she hated being the only one out of my entire family who didn't have an Alpha aura or the ability to stand up for herself. Especially against her mother now that she was mated to my brother.

"You don't need to call me that, Lucy. You know that," I told her. She didn't answer, but I could feel the link open still and knew she was listening.

"What are you and Mitchell doing?" I asked her, trying to keep the jealousy from my voice. I hated how close they were even while she was away. I knew she never went a day without talking to him, even if it was just text messages.

"Nothing, but Meredith invited me to stay for dinner, so I will head back after that."

"I will come to pick you up. I don't want you walking in the dark."

"No, I am good. Mitchell can run me back," she said, and I sighed.

"Fine, but not late, Lucy. If you aren't going to school, you can start training with me in the morning."

"What? Yelling at me wasn't enough? Now you want to beat the living daylights out of me?"

"No, we can discuss it when you get here. Not late, Lucy. I mean it, or I will come and find you," I warned her, and she cut the link off. I had no problems grabbing her while she was kicking and screaming. I was used to her defiance and the major chip on her shoulder. Though it had gotten worse the last year or so. She very rarely talked to us anymore, or if she did, she shoved us out when we became a little too nosey when we would mindlink her.

Ace and I have discussed that something was off with her, but then we saw her and she was her normal loud bubbly self. She was hard to take seriously, and it didn't help that she was constantly in trouble with some authority figure. Still, something was off. I could feel it. Tyrant could feel it too. She changed. Something within her changed, or maybe she was just becoming more aware of the bond and didn't know what to make of it without having a wolf.

Chapter 10

Lucy

MITCHELL'S MOM MADE BEEF stroganoff for dinner. It felt weird sitting at a table eating with a family. Usually, I was in a dining hall full of others like me, the chatter was endless, and you could blend in easily and remain invisible. Mitchell's father was on pack patrol, so he didn't join us. It was just Meredith and Mitchell. His mom asked a never-ending amount of questions.

"Have you found your mate yet?" Meredith asked, and I saw Mitchell give his mother a look.

"What?" his mother asked, shocked by his glare.

"You know she hasn't got a wolf," Mitchell told her.

"Neither did Queen Aria when she ruled. She still found her mate," Meredith told me. Aria was my stepfather's mother. Even though I wasn't technically related, she always treated me as if I were her grandchild. I loved my family dearly, but they didn't seem to understand what it was like being an outsider and a constant disappointment. I knew what they would think, I was not stupid or blind. They thought of me as troubled. A mess they wished could clean itself up. We ate dinner in a comfortable silence after that, and then I helped Meredith do the dishes.

Mitchell walked into the kitchen before grabbing his keys. I told him about being expelled but didn't give him a reason. I just let him make it out how he wanted, I didn't care to explain myself. No one would believe me anyway.

"Want me to run you home?" Mitchell asked, grabbing his car keys. I also hadn't told him I was kicked out. Sometimes I wished I were human. They didn't realize how free they were without having to worry about pack issues, mates, or no mates. None of them had to be the illegitimate child of the Alpha Queen.

"No, it's not far. I want to go for a run anyhow," I told him, grabbing my jumper and pulling it on. Mitchell gave me a hug and walked me to the door.

"I can run you back?" he offered, but I shook my head. I wasn't even sure where I was going myself.

"Nope, I am good. It's still early. I will see you tomorrow."

"I have school. Stop by after," he called, and I nodded, heading for the treeline. I darted into the trees, heading home. Hoping my mother was calm enough to let me come back since it had been a few hours. Maybe she would at least let me stay, she didn't seem keen on me going to Ace and Tyson's place, so hopefully, she'd changed her mind. I felt the mindlink open up on the run home, Ace's voice flitting through my head.

"I told you to be home before dark. Where are you, Lucy?"

"Heading home now. I am nearly at the packhouse."

"Which side? I will meet you," he said, and I could hear Atticus mumbling about me being out in the woods. I shook my head at his wolf as he slipped through the link.

"No, I am heading home, home. Back to mom's," I told him, and he went quiet.

"So, she let you back? That's good then. I will be home tomorrow if you want to come over while everyone is at school and work," he told me, and I nodded before realizing he couldn't see me. I nearly ran into a tree, only just managing to stop before I hit a low-hanging branch.

"Yes, she has calmed down now," I lied, ducking under the branch. I was also hopeful she had, and it was just the pregnancy hormones.

"Okay. Well, come see Tyson and me tomorrow. Please," he said, and I agreed before cutting off the mindlink. Walking through the trees in the backyard, I could see my stepfather busily helping my mother in the kitchen. She had never been a good cook. The woman could burn water, but she always tried. I watched as Rayan sat up at the table with his plate, and my mother and stepfather joined him, and they looked like a picturesque family. They looked happy.

Pulling on the mindlink, I watched my brother shiver, still not used to it like I was.

"Bet you must be glad to spend time with Tyson and Ace. Mom burned dinner again. At least they can cook," he said, feeling the link open. My heart sank at his words, my mother was obviously still pissed at me.

"Ah yeah, it's great. How is mom?" I asked him, and I could see my stepfather watching him, realizing he was mindlinking someone. He no doubt knew it was me because, besides my mom and dad, he hardly used the link.

"She is still mad. You best just steer clear for a few days. Mom and dad had a huge fight after you left," he told me. I sighed. *Great, didn't leave me many options then.*

"Come see me at school tomorrow. I want to see you. You only just got here, and I can't see you anymore," he told me sadly. I suddenly felt guilty. I knew he was lonely in that house by himself, always followed around by Jacob. It was hard for him to make friends. Rayan didn't trust easily, and he hated fake people, and a lot were. Some would do anything to be friends with the next Alpha King, and Rayan didn't like that, didn't like the attention.

"Meet me at the park across the road from the school. What time does Jacob pick you up?" I asked him.

"Three, but I can get out early."

"How?"

"By ordering my teacher to let me out." He laughed, and I rolled my eyes. Of course, he could. He had an Alpha aura even though he still hadn't got his wolf yet.

"Okay, meet me at the park at twenty to three, and can you bring me some spare clothes?" I told him.

"Okay... and sis? I love you."

"I love you too. Make sure you eat your dinner so you can have your dessert," I told him before cutting off the link. *Now what?* I thought to myself. I couldn't go to Tyson and Ace's. I already told them I was at home. And I didn't really feel like listening to Melana with Ace all night. Just thinking of that ground my gears. Walking back among the trees, I headed for the only place I could think of, the river. For the most part, it was safe there. The border patrol hardly manned it because there was a mountain on the other side. There was not much activity by the packhouse, whereas near Tyson and Ace's territory across the river was Alpha Jamie's pack, but I would be safe there.

It took me twenty minutes to walk to the river, gathering wood as I went. *Just like camping*, I thought to myself. Ace and Tyson used to take me camping as a kid, and I loved it. We would stay out in the woods for days, and that was the first time I ever ate rabbit. Tyson's wolf caught it, and I was repulsed at the thought of eating the furry critter, but it didn't actually taste bad. It tasted like any other meat just off a cute furry creature. But that just reminded me of another issue I would face while out here. I needed blood. I could go a day or two, but it would become uncomfortable if I went without it for too long. I couldn't ask Rayan to grab any from the freezer. It would go yuck sitting in his bag all day.

I made a fire before flopping on the ground next to it and pulling my arms inside my jumper to keep warm. I stared at the stars littering the night sky. I used to play dot to dot with stars when I was a kid, trying to imagine joining them to make pictures. One thing about being out here was that it was peaceful. No one to judge me or look down on me. It was quiet, leaving me to my own thoughts, not that they were any less depressing.

Sometimes I actually missed the facility, at least, it was routine and predictable. No one expected anything of you there, they just let you rot in the cells. But I never had to worry about anything because we were all the same, all equally nothing. Here people expect you to be a certain way, act a certain way, and when you don't meet those expectations, you are faced with nothing but disappointment and the judgment of others.

Chapter 11

THE NEXT DAY, I spent most of my time by the river. Looking at my phone, which was nearly dead, I saw it was nearly 2 PM, and I headed into the city to meet my little brother. I sat on the swings at the park. Staring over at the packed school. It was smaller than the boarding school I'd attended. Tall gates wrapped around the entire brick building. It had small buildings branching off it and a huge brick archway that led to the front gate. Flowers ran along the footpath out the front, and a small pedestrian crossing led to the park I was sitting in next to the school car park.

My eyes lit up when I saw my brother walking toward the exit. His blue backpack was tossed over one shoulder. I watched as he looked in both directions before crossing the road. He waved as he stepped onto the footpath on this side of the road.

"Hey, sis," he called to me, and I hopped up. He rushed over and wrapped his arm around my waist. I inhaled his scent. I loved how he smelled of the forest. I let him go, sitting back on the swing, and he sat on the other before opening his bag and digging through it. He pulled out a plastic bag, handing it to me.

"I got you jeans and a turtleneck. There is also a jumper in there, a throw-over blanket and some underwear," he said, scrunching his face up at having to touch my knickers. I looked at him, laughing. He was a good brother.

"I know you're staying at the river. Your voice sounded close last night, but if I put a sleeping bag in there, mom would have noticed," he murmured. I nodded when he pulled out his lunchbox.

He unwrapped his sandwich and handed it to me. "Thanks," I told him, taking it from him and biting into it. It had peanut butter in it.

"Mom is still pissed off?" I asked him, and he sighed before nodding.

"I think you really pushed her too far this time, Luce. Mom has banned me from seeing you and says she doesn't want me to become corrupt like you." His words stung, but I knew it wasn't his intention.

"Maybe go stay with Tyson and Ace till things calm down," he said.

"No, the river won't be so bad. She will forgive me eventually. That's what mothers do," I said, though my mother wasn't like normal mothers. "Besides, Ace has Melana there all the time. I can't stand her."

"What are you going to do about blood? You can have some of mine, but I know it won't taste too good."

I shook my head. "It's fine. I will just catch something," I told him though that didn't sound all that appealing.

He nodded before digging through his bag again. "Here," he said, handing me some money. I shook my head, trying to pass it back to him.

"No, keep it. I will be fine. I don't want your pocket money, Rayan. I just wanted to see you."

"Just take it, Luce. Not like I will spend it anyway," he said, dropping it in the bag when I refused to take it from him.

"If I can get away from Jacob, I will try to sneak out and bring you a blood bag and a few things," he told me.

"Just don't get in trouble, okay? I don't want you in trouble because of me."

He nodded, and cars started pulling into the parking lot, parents waiting for their children. Rayan got up, and so did I.

"You better go before Jacob gets here. He will tell mom he saw you," he said, hugging me and giving me a tight squeeze. I squeezed him back before grabbing the plastic bag off the ground.

"I love you," I told him.

"I love you more," he said, walking back toward the school. I watched him cross the road and wait at the gate before I turned, rushing off through the street and heading back toward the river behind the packhouse. By the time I got back, the sun was blocked by the trees as it slowly went down. I found a log and jammed the bag in it before searching for firewood again.

"You didn't come over," Ace's voice said, flitting through my head.

"Was busy," I lied.

"Come over now then. I want to see you," he told me when suddenly Tyson joined the mindlink. I could feel it stretching before his voice appeared in my head along with Ace's.

"Come have dinner with us," Tyson told me.

"No, I am good, and I don't want to cause more drama. I will come see you soon, though," I told them, cutting off the mindlink before they could say anything else. I continued gathering firewood and set it inside the rocks I had placed on the dirt. I got the fire going with a lighter I'd found inside the bag. I smiled, knowing Rayan had stolen it from dad.

When I was sure it wasn't going to burn out, I stripped my clothes off, putting the new ones on. I walked over to the river washing the clothes I had on before hanging them over a low branch to dry.

Once I was done, I went in search of blood. I was already ravenous and knew going too long would become not only uncomfortable but dangerous for anyone that happened to stumble into the woods. These woods were mainly free of humans. Not many came this far out, but I had to be prepared for them on the off chance they did. Picking up their scent would end badly if I went without for too long.

I tried to remain close to my little camp. The last thing I needed was to burn the entire forest down. *Yeah, mom may actually kill me for that. Maybe even my father.*

I picked up the aromatic scent of a deer. Following the scent, I found it was only a baby and couldn't bring myself to kill it as I watched it strip a patch of grass. I looked around before deciding to leave, knowing its mother might be around. Maybe killing something would be harder than I thought as I slid over a fallen tree. The fire I'd made, I could make out just through the trees when movement caught my eye. Rabbits. Two of them next to the trunk of an old tree, I slowly crept up on them, their little ears twitching, listening for any movement when I pounced, grabbing one by its ears, the other darting off into a nearby log. I could hear its heart pounding, its little legs kicking wildly as its fearful eyes peered back at me.

I grabbed the back of its neck, holding it while it continued to kick. I felt bile rise in my throat at the thought of killing it. *Damn. I was a shit vampire.* Getting emotional over killing a rabbit. I tried to will myself to kill it, giving myself a mental pep talk as I closed my eyes.

Come on, Lucy. It's just a rabbit. Just a cute fluffy terrified little rabbit. The mental pep talk did fuck all. If anything, it made me feel worse. I opened one eye, peering at it, its little heart thumping in its chest frantically as I looked at it. I let out a breath before grabbing its kicking back legs and the back of its head. I felt my fangs slip from my gums, my saliva pooling in my mouth, and I tried to give over to my senses, let them take control, but tears slipped down my face as I sank my fangs into the furry little creature.

It squealed, the sound breaking my heart as I drained the life from it, its kicking slowing before stopping altogether. I laid the rabbit back on the ground, its blood running down my chin, and I looked to the log the other ran into, only to see it peering out. Its heart thumped loudly inside the log. I looked away from it. *Did it know what I had just done?* There was not enough blood in its tiny body, yet I couldn't bring myself to kill the other one. Instead, I wiped my tears and headed back to the campfire. I could have cooked it, but the idea of skinning it grossed me out and would ruin my clothes. Surely, mom would open the mindlink soon, instead of keeping me blocked out, and let me come home.

Chapter 12

Tyson
ONE WEEK LATER

*I*T HAD BEEN OVER a week since we saw her. I mindlinked Rayan yesterday, who kept giving me vague answers as to what she was doing. His reply was she was around, which I didn't particularly like. I tried mindlinking Reika, but she shoved me out each time, and Ryker was nearly impossible to get a hold of even via the mindlink. We kept getting interrupted before I could even ask how she was, leaving Rayan my only link to her.

Lucy always had some excuse not to come to visit us, or for some reason, she couldn't talk long, making me wonder if Reika told her we were her mates. *Was this her way of rejecting us?*

"Hurry up! He finishes school soon, and I already told Jacob we were picking him up today," Ace called to me as I finished getting dressed.

I slipped my jacket on before grabbing my car keys and walking down the long hallway toward the front of the packhouse. Ace was waiting in the living room. He had become extremely impatient, waiting for Lucy to come around. Every day he sat at home, hoping she would show up, and Atticus had been hounding him to mark her before she could reject us. Tyrant was the same, wanting to mark her, but Atticus was even more demanding of Ace because of his relationship with Melana. Atticus knew Ace stuffed up when it came to her, because Lucy wouldn't be too happy when she learned he was her mate.

I didn't understand how Ace could even go against his wolf. Tyrant wouldn't even let me entertain the idea of anyone but Lucy. So I was surprised Ace had been able to maintain any form of relationship he had with Melana. Tyrant made that impossible for me, but I wasn't interested in anyone else anyway. I feared Atticus would force Ace to mark her against her will if he couldn't see her soon. So today, we were picking up Rayan and dropping him to his father at work since Reika had appointments. This would give us time to figure out what was going on with Lucy, and I could ask Ryker what Reika had told her.

"I'm driving. You drive too slow," Ace said, holding his hand out for my keys. I rolled my eyes at him before chucking my keys at him, which he caught before grabbing his jacket.

I locked the door before climbing into the passenger seat. Ace tore out of the driveway before I could even shut my door. "Slow down, dick. You wreck my car, you're buying me another," I told him as he sprayed rocks everywhere along the gravel driveway.

We headed through the city before taking the highway out of town and heading for the pack school, which was just outside the city. The drive took thirty minutes from the packhouse to the school before we pulled into the parking lot. I got out, sat on the hood, and lit a smoke. Checking my phone, I still had five minutes before the school bell rang. Rayan had no idea we were picking him up, so I would like to see him try to avoid us. I knew Rayan and Lucy were close, so if he didn't know what was going on, I knew my last resort would be having to hunt down Mitchell, which I didn't particularly feel like doing.

When the bell rang, kids came rushing out, running in different directions. I waited to spot him, and he was the second last kid out as he dawdled. I watched as he looked around for Jacob, his bag slung over one shoulder before I whistled, his head snapping in my direction. The look on his face was almost comical. I heard him curse under his breath before dropping his head.

"Where is Jacob?" Rayan called out as he crossed the road before stomping through the garden beds that surrounded the park. He crushed the neat gardens, stomping on the flowers. Ace climbed out of the car.

"What, no hello?" Ace asked him.

"Why are you here? If it is about Lucy, ask her yourself," Rayan said, and Ace growled before taking his bag from him and opening the back door. Ace chucked his bag in the back of the car before grabbing his shirt above his shoulder, steering him to the back seat.

"Where are you taking me?" Rayan demanded, and Ace raised an eyebrow at his little Alpha voice coming through.

"To your father at work. Now, get in before I spank your ass for being a disrespectful little shit," Ace told him. Rayan huffed before sliding into the backseat and folding his arms across his chest. I climbed in the passenger seat, and Ace climbed in the driver's seat before reversing out of the car park. Once the car was moving, I turned in my seat so I could face Rayan.

"How is Lucy?"

"She is your mate. How about you tell me?" Rayan said.

"You know?" Ace asked him, looking in the rearview mirror at him as he turned at the cross-section.

"Yeah, I heard mom and dad talking about it," he said, putting his arm on the window and resting his head on his hand.

"Does Lucy know?" I asked him, and he shook his head.

"No. Mom told me not to tell her," Rayan said, exhaling loudly.

"Well, that's good, I guess, for now," Ace muttered under his breath.

"You hurt my sister, I will," Rayan said, and I smiled when Ace cut him off.

"You'll what, pipsqueak?" Ace asked, and Rayan growled at him.

"I will kick your ass, Ace! I won't be a kid for long, and then you will be answering to me," Rayan snapped at him. He was definitely his father's son. Ace smirked but said nothing else. He had a point. Rayan was next in line to become Alpha King.

"So, how is she?" I asked him, and Rayan shrugged.

"You live with her. You have to tell us something," I told him. Rayan held his hand out, rubbing his fingers together, and I rolled my eyes.

"Information costs," Rayan said with a devious smile on his face, his silver and gold eyes sparkling back at us.

I reached over into Ace's pocket. "Why do I gotta pay him? You pay him!" Ace snapped at me.

"I don't carry cash," I told him, snatching his wallet out of his pocket, Ace having to shift so I could pull it out.

I grabbed a fifty dollar note out, and Rayan raised an eyebrow at me before I grabbed all the cash out of his wallet. Rayan leaned forward, plucking the cash from my fingertips.

"You better have good information, kid. What do you need $300 for?" Ace demanded.

"I don't. I just wanted to see if you would give it to me. Thanks for that, I will add it to my stash," Rayan said, making me chuckle while Ace growled at him.

"So spill," I told him, and he rubbed his chin.

"What should I disclose? Her favorite color is purple. Oh! She has a birthmark on her hip that reminds me of a starfish. She also had this vibrating thing in her knicker drawer. Oh, and she had a drawing of your wolves in her sketchbook," Rayan said. I shook my head at him.

"No real information, like what she is doing?" I asked him.

"Why would you go through your sister's undies, you little creeper?" Ace said before shivering in disgust.

"I had to grab some stuff for her. Nothing wrong with grabbing clothes for her. Bloody thing sounded like a rocket ship about to take off. I tried to google what it was, but it kept taking me to these half-naked lady sites," he said, scrunching his face up. I snorted at this boy's innocence, he would be horrified when he got older and realized what it was.

"Why did you have to take her clothes?" Ace asked him as we pulled into the underground parking lot.

"Um…" He seemed to think for a second, and I could see worry cross his features like he thought he had said something he shouldn't have.

"Oh, we are here! I guess I will catch you two later. Thanks for the lift," he said, gripping the door handle, about to do a runner when Ace locked the door.

"Speak, Rayan! You are ticking me off," Ace told him, and I smacked his chest. I saw Ryker coming out of the elevator toward the car.

"Fine, I will ask your father then," I told him, and Ace unlocked the door, and I hopped out.

"Wait!" Rayan called out, and I stopped closing the door and looked over at him.

"Mom and Dad think she is at your house. Please, don't get her in any more trouble," Rayan said, looking out at his father walking across the parking lot toward us.

"What do you mean? Hasn't she been staying at home?" Ace said, but Rayan shook his head.

"Mom won't let her come home," Rayan said with a sigh. "Lucy didn't want to stay with you because Melana is always with Ace, so she has been sleeping at the river behind the packhouse. I got clothes for her the other day, and she met me at school. You can't tell dad! Please!" Rayan said, and I looked at Ace.

"We won't say anything. How long has she been out there for?" He didn't get a chance to answer as Ryker opened up the back door.

"Hey, kiddo," Ryker said, reaching over him and grabbing his bag off the seat beside him.

Rayan looked at us in panic, but Ace had a tight grip on the steering wheel, looking out the window.

"Everything okay?" Ryker asked as Rayan climbed out of the car.

"Yeah, something has come up. I will come to see you tomorrow," I told Ryker.

"Ace?" Ryker asked, looking at his tense body, his knuckles white as he clutched the steering wheel.

"Everything is fine, just need to deal with something," Ace gritted out, and Ryker seemed taken aback but said nothing, closing the door.

Ace reversed out of the parking lot. Fur was sprouting on his arms as he fought to control his emotions and those of Atticus.

"Calm down, Ace. We will go get her," I told him, worried he would shift.

"She wouldn't come home because of me, Tyson! Don't tell me to calm down!" Ace snapped.

Chapter 13

Lucy

I HAD AROUND TWO HOURS before the sun went down as I gathered firewood. I hadn't seen Rayan in days. After killing the rabbit, my bloodlust had gotten out of control, and I was desperate for blood but also too scared to leave the river, for fear of attacking someone. Ravenous wasn't even a strong enough word for how I felt. I was on edge, like a drug addict going through withdrawal. I was also becoming increasingly weaker, and after having blood daily, it was unbearable to suddenly go cold turkey. I grew weak quickly, just looking for firewood was taking a toll on me, and I grew tired quickly. I never realized what an impact going without blood would have.

Giving up, I sat against a tree, leaning heavily against it. I closed my eyes, trying to catch my breath when I picked up a scent. The scent was filling my nostrils, and a growl tore from my lips, the noise startling me as I looked around for what had created the scent. I noticed movement out of the corner of my eyes before seeing something dart between two trees, my eyes picking up the movement as I watched the rabbit scurry away. I felt my fangs protrude, slipping from my gums slowly and painfully. My mouth was completely dry, and I crawled to my hands and knees.

I suddenly got a burst of adrenaline, fueled by my hunger, and darted after it, moving quicker than I had in days as I snagged it in my grip. I sank my fangs into it, not even paying attention to where I bit, as it shrieked and thrashed before I realized I had sunk my teeth into its side. My canines were ripping it to pieces as I kept trying to drain it, my senses took over, telling me to feed. Yet, I couldn't bite successfully into any artery, instead, I was just bleeding it out as I tore it apart. I licked my fingers, a moan escaping my lips, when I heard a twig snap. I spun around, a growl tearing from my lips. It was animalistic and guttural as I saw two black wolves step into my path.

One of them whined, but all I could think about was the intoxicating aroma coming from them. I heard the blood pulsing through their veins, and I lunged at one. I needed blood. That was all I could think about as hunger enveloped me. I heard snapping while lunging at the one closest to me, the wolf stepping out of my way and off to the side, when I felt something grab me. I thrashed before the scent became so strong, and I turned, biting into soft flesh. A moan escaped my lips as its blood flooded into my mouth when I felt myself ripped away from them. A pair of hands grabbed my arms, yanking me away, and I growled before coming face to face with Ace. Seeing him stunned me, and I realized why the scent was familiar and intoxicating. Looking over my shoulder, I realized I had bitten Tyson, blood running down his arm from his bicep. I attacked him.

"Lucy," Ace said before I looked back at him. Yet the hunger didn't leave, it only got worse knowing I was drinking their blood.

"Lucy, wait!" Ace said, his grip getting tighter. Moisture touched my lips as Tyson's scent wafted to my nose. I grabbed his wrist that was pressed to my lips and sank my fangs into him. But he didn't pull away, pulling me against him instead, and Ace let me go before I found myself sitting in his lap as he leaned against a tree.

"Drink, love," Tyson said, yet I didn't think I could stop even if I wanted to. I could feel his blood getting weaker as he did when Ace suddenly bit his wrist before kneeling in front of me. I let Tyson go, grabbing his, and he pushed me forward into Ace, who grabbed me and pulled me closer. My hunger finally calmed down as I leaned on Ace, his body warm, and I felt myself relax against him. My fangs pulled out of his wrist, and I saw Tyson leaning against the tree across from us, watching me, breathing hard.

"How long did you go without blood?" Ace asked.

"I just had a rabbit," I told him.

"No, I mean a blood bag, Lucy."

"Since the boarding school," I told them before I felt him brush the hair out of my face as I tilted my face toward his.

He pressed his forehead against mine. "Why didn't you come home? We would have taken care of you. Instead, we found out from Rayan that you have been staying out here," Ace said, looking around as a growl escaped him.

Panic coursed through me. *Does that mean mom knows?* "Does mom know? Did you tell her?" I asked, worried she would become angrier. Tyson shook his head.

"No, but you are coming home with us, Lucy. You can't stay here," Tyson said, standing up when I realized he was naked. My eyes trailed down his muscular body before I tore my eyes away from him, my face heating when I realized I was sitting on Ace, who was also naked. I jumped up, moving off him.

"Please, shift," I told them, realizing what an awkward scenario this was. But also realizing I was checking them out. I shouldn't be thinking this way about them, let alone checking them out. They helped raise me.

"You're coming home with us, Lucy," Ace told me before gripping my elbow.

"Okay, but shift, please," I told him, and he sighed, but I heard his bones snapping before feeling fur brush my hand. I looked beside me to see Atticus standing there. I brushed his fur, and he purred, rubbing his body against me. Tyson also shifted. The sun had nearly set, and it would be dark in about half an hour. Atticus nudged me, and I shook my head.

"I'm not a little girl anymore," I told him as he tried to get me to climb on him. He jumped up, putting his paws on my shoulders before licking my face. "Down," I told him, and he growled but got down. Tyrant was brushing against the back of my legs.

"I don't need you to carry me. I can keep up," I told them, and Tyrant whined before darting off. Atticus nudged me, wanting me to follow Tyson's wolf. I rolled my eyes before chasing after him. Atticus fell in line with me and remained with me until we hit a dirt road that joined onto the driveway leading home. I saw Tyson's Mustang come into my vision before seeing him pull some shorts on while standing next to his car. I slowed down, eventually coming to a stop next to him.

"Come on. We should get back," Tyson told me, opening the back door.

Ace came over as I climbed in the back, grabbing the door as I went to close it.

"When we get home, we have something to tell you," he said before reaching down and cupping my cheek in his hand. I closed my eyes, sparks rushing over my face, and I leaned into his touch, his hand warm as he brushed his thumb over my cheek.

Chapter 14

Getting to their packhouse, I growled when I saw Melana's car parked in the driveway. This was exactly why I didn't want to come here. I was not listening to the two of them go at it all night. The thought alone made my blood boil.

"What is she doing here?" Ace said with a sigh.

"You best get rid of her, Ace. I don't want her around the packhouse," Tyson told him, pulling in next to her car, the paint flaking off where I'd squirted the brake fluid.

Great, now I get to listen to her bitching and moaning.

Ace jumped out as soon as the car stopped, marching around to the front of the packhouse. I remained in the car, and Tyson looked over the backseat at me.

"Come on, Lucy," he said, opening his car door. I remained in my seat, not wanting to go inside if Melana was staying. I'd much rather go to the river than listen to her all night.

Tyson opened my car door before looking at me. "Are you coming, Lucy?" he asked, and I shook my head, glaring at her car.

"Not if she is staying," I told him, and he sighed before looking toward the front of the house.

"Ace will make her leave. You don't need to worry about her," he said, yet by the sound of her screeching at Ace, that might take a while.

"Come inside," Tyson said, and I huffed, annoyed, but got out anyway. Looking down the driveway toward the front of the house, I could hear Ace and Melana arguing. She was angry about something.

Walking down the driveway, they were arguing on the front lawn. Melana's face turned red as she screamed at him.

"What do you mean, Ace? What? I am suddenly not good enough for you? I have been for the past five years!" she screamed at him.

"You knew this, Melana. This was only fooling around. I made that crystal clear. You have a mate out there somewhere. We agreed this was nothing more than sex. Now leave, please," Ace argued with her.

"Come," Tyson said, tugging on my arm when Melana's eyes snapped to me.

"You! This is all your fault! If you had just stayed at school, this would never have happened!" she said, turning to me.

"What are you talking about?" I asked her, stopping on the bottom step of the porch.

"Melana, time to go. Now!" Ace said, becoming angry. His body started to tremble, and Tyson tried to pull me inside.

"No! Fuck you, Ace! Everything is always about her! I am fucking over it. Five years and you toss me away like fucking garbage!"

"I told you so many times already, Melana. This was nothing serious. Now, time to go. Don't make me command you," Ace told her, walking toward the house. Melana grabbed his arm, and he tried to push her away when her hand suddenly connected with his face. His cheek turned red from her slap, the noise loud as her palm connected with his cheek. The sight of her touching him was one thing, but seeing her hit him made my blood boil. I didn't understand my actions, yet I still couldn't control the burning hatred that swept over me before I attacked her.

We both hit the ground in a heap as I landed on top of her before punching her in the face. She growled as her head whipped to the side before punching me in the boob. I grunted before she kicked me off, and I fell to my side. *Low blow*, I thought to myself before getting to my feet just as she shifted. Her patchy brown wolf lunged at me, and I stumbled back out of her way. Ace and Tyson rushed toward us, trying to break it up, when she lunged again. I was faster, being more vampire than wolf, and I kicked her in the ribs. Her body hurtled into Ace's car parked on the grass, an outline of her body crinkling the door. Melana shook out her fur before turning toward me, about to attack when Atticus jumped in her path. His teeth bared as he snapped her, and she whimpered, baring her neck to him and lying on her stomach.

Tyson gripped my arm, ripping me toward the house and up the steps when I saw Atticus walk over to her, sniffing her, making me growl at him. I couldn't understand my sudden surge of jealousy at him being so close to her. Atticus growled at her, and she darted off up the side of the house just as Tyson pulled me through the front door.

"Lucy, enough! Let Ace deal with her."

"I don't want him fucking near the whore!" I yelled at him, struggling against his grip.

"Enough, Lucy. We have had enough drama today," Tyson said, pushing me onto the couch in the living room.

I heard car tires screeching outside before hearing the sound of metal on metal, making me jump.

I could hear Ace had shifted back and was yelling at Melana. Tyson walked off quickly to the front door before I heard him use his Alpha voice. The screen door banged as he threw it open.

"Enough, Melana! Leave, or I will banish you!" Tyson snapped at her. I shivered, feeling his aura even inside. The revving of her car stopped before I heard her leave.

"Was that fucking necessary, Tyson?" I heard Ace yell at Tyson.

"Well, you weren't going to do it," Tyson told him, walking back inside.

"I said I would handle her. You had no right meddling in my relationships!" Ace snapped at him.

"She isn't yours. But, hey, you want her? Go right ahead Ace, and mark her," Tyson told him. My chest lurched at the thought of Ace making her, nausea filling my stomach at Tyson's words. I didn't understand why it bothered me so much.

"I wanted things to end on good terms, Tyson. Not cause more conflict."

"I warned you about this, Ace. Now get inside so we can speak to Lucy," Tyson told him. I heard Ace growl before hearing footsteps of him leaving.

"What about Lucy?" I heard Tyson call after him.

"We can deal with it tomorrow. I need to fix this shit because you just made things fucking worse!" Ace snapped at him.

"Fuck her, Ace. She doesn't mean shit. Get inside. Melana can drop off the face of the earth for all I care," Tyson told him. I got up, not wanting to hear anymore, and knowing Ace was leaving to see Melana ticked me off.

MY TWO ALPHAS | 73

Chapter 15

Walking down the hallway, I heard Tyson walk back inside but I quickly rushed to the bathroom. I locked the door before turning on the shower. Getting undressed, I heard Tyson knock on the bathroom door.

"Lucy, are you okay?"

"Fine, just showering." I was actually excited to use hot water, the river was freezing, and you wanted to jump out as soon as you got in.

"I will grab you some clothes," Tyson said, and I heard him walk off, his feet loud on the floorboards. I stepped in, enjoying the hot water as it cascaded down my back before grabbing the soap. The tension in my body was loosening. *I will never take hot water for granted again*! I thought to myself as the room steamed up, the scent of chamomile soap wafting through the air.

I washed myself before quickly washing my hair. I really needed to trim it, it was getting ridiculously long. I was brushing my fingers through it, trying to untangle it, when the door opened, Tyson's mouth-watering scent hitting my nose. I looked over my shoulder to see him sit on the sink basin.

"What are you doing? And how did you get in?" I asked him.

"With a butter knife, and I brought you clothes."

"Okay, you can leave now. Little wrong, don't you think?"

"Why is it wrong?"

"You are my uncle," I told him, a little weirded out.

"Don't say that, Lucy. You make me sound like a creep. We are not family and in no way related," he said. His words hurt. *How am I not family to him when he practically helped raise me? Do I mean nothing to him?*

"Get out!" I told him, my words a little harsher than I'd intended.

"No! I didn't mean it like that, Lucy," Tyson quickly said as I glared at him.

"Then how else am I supposed to take it, Tyson?"

"I'm just saying we aren't related. You mean more to me than family, Lucy. Or are you too blind to notice?" he said, making me look back at him.

"Huh?" I asked him, confused by his words.

"Doesn't matter. It can wait till Ace comes back," he said, rubbing a hand down his face.

"Well, if you aren't going to hop out, can you at least help find me a toothbrush? Mine is still at the river."

He looked under the sink basin before pulling out a few boxes. He unwrapped one from the packaging before opening the shower screen and handing it to me while I continued to keep my back to him. I started brushing my teeth, and Tyson walked out, closing the door. I let out a breath of relief. His scent was overwhelming in the steamed-up room. When I was done, I dried myself before slipping on the shirt Tyson had brought in, but there were no bottoms. The shirt fell to my mid thighs, but I felt weird not wearing anything underneath it, especially in a house with two men. I shrugged. Nudity wasn't a big thing, and I'd spent most of my childhood naked in those stupid cells. Rarely did they give us clothes, and when they did, it was only for transporting us.

I wrapped my hair in the towel before walking out. I could hear Tyson rummaging around in the kitchen and went to see what he was making.

"Ace still not back?" I asked him, leaning on the countertop.

"Nope. But he'll want to hurry up. A huge storm cell is coming over the city," he said, looking out the window, and I did too.

The wind had picked up massively, the trees swaying in the wind and the palm trees out back bending under pressure. I shivered, glad I wasn't staying at the river tonight. I was good with storms, but thunder? Nope, I hated it, the noise was so much louder being a mutation, and I always freaked out, thinking the world was ending by the deafening noise.

"Hopefully, no thunder," I told him, staring out the window.

"You're still scared of storms?" he chuckled.

"No. Just the thunder," I told him, and he smiled.

"Homemade pizza?" he asked.

I nodded. "Want some help?" I asked, moving around the other side of the counter. He nodded, grabbing another chopping board before handing me a capsicum and knife.

We cooked dinner and ate it, but by 9 PM, Ace still wasn't home when I felt the mindlink open up. Ace's voice was flitting through mine and Tyson's heads as I felt him merge both links.

"I am staying at Jacob's tonight. I am not running home in this," he said.

"The other issue?" Tyson asked him, and I glanced at him sitting on the lounge beside me.

"Dealt with. It won't be an issue anymore," Ace told him.

"Good," Tyson said, cutting off the link and shoving his brother out of our heads.

"How did you do that?" I asked him, feeling him shove Ace out of mine too.

"Alpha genes," he answered, and I turned back to watching the TV show. Halfway through the night, I must have drifted off, waking to the sound of thunder. The house was completely dark, and Tyson had chucked a blanket over me. The wind outside was howling as it whistled through the trees, lightning striking the sky and lighting up the inside of the house. I flicked the TV back on, trying to drown out the noise, so I could go back to sleep. This was the worst storm I had seen in ages.

Avalon City hardly had storms, especially with so many elemental witches in the city who could control the weather. It was completely different here, and I didn't have my meds to knock me out either, which was what I usually did when we did get the occasional storm. I'd left my meds in Jacob's car in my suitcase and hadn't seen the doctor since returning.

Getting up, I walked into the kitchen to get a drink. Goosebumps rose on my arms because of the storm as I fought the urge to shiver when thunder cracked loudly. Walking back to the living room, I stopped in the hall, looking up the dark hallway. Tyson's bedroom door was open, and I argued with myself whether it would be weird if I slept in his room with him. He was an adult now and might be creeped out if I tried hopping in his bed like I used to do when I was a kid. He had no problems walking in on me in the shower, so instead, I decided to walk down the hallway. The thunder made me jump, and I darted off into his room, my heart pounding in my chest.

Walking over to the side of his bed, I tapped on his shoulder, thinking it best to ask than have him freak out and find me next to him. I shook his shoulder, and he rolled over sleepily, staring up at me. He then moved over before tossing the blanket back.

"Hurry up then, scaredy-cat," he said, and I climbed in beside him. He moved over a little before tugging the blanket around me and draping his arm across my waist. I relaxed against him, his scent soothing as I snuggled against him. I could feel his breath against my neck as he fell back to sleep, his breathing evening out. My skin tingled where his skin was touching mine, making me wonder if he felt the weird sensation or if it was just me. It felt foreign, and I never got that tingling sensation from anyone else except Ace. I wasn't sure if I liked the sensation, but eventually, I fell asleep, feeling safe with Tyson's warm skin pressed against mine.

Chapter 16

Ace's

Melana wasn't having it. Nothing I said to her was making her see reason. I'd told her plenty of times this was just fooling around, yet the hurt look she continued to give me as I stood in her kitchen showed me how much I'd truly fucked up. She clearly didn't see this as fooling around and thought we had something more than what I would ever give her, making me wish I had listened to Tyson.

Melana's tear-stricken face made me feel like a piece of shit. "Is this because Lucy came back? I don't get it, Ace. Everything was fine until she returned," Melana cried. I looked away from her. Her wolf was shining through, and I could tell even she was hurt, but Melana was not my mate. Lucy was.

"Are you going to answer? If it is, let me speak to her. I know we haven't always gotten along, but maybe things won't feel awkward if I talk to her. I know she is meant to be staying with you for a while."

"It's not that, Melana. This was never going to work. I told you this so many times. You were never going to be my Luna," I told her, and she started crying even more. *Great, now I feel like a dick. Ah god, why won't she stop crying? I don't do tears.* I just wanted to bail now.

"I can be friends with Lucy. I know she is family, Ace," Melana said. *How has she not figured it out yet?* It had nothing to do with Lucy staying at our house. Melana just wasn't my mate.

"Just stop, Melana. It has nothing to do with Lucy being your friend or not or you not getting along with her," I told her.

"Then what? Because you were fine till she showed up!" Melana yelled at me.

"Is it because of Tyson not liking me?" she asked, stepping closer, but I stepped away from her. I could see the hurt in her eyes at my actions.

"Lucy is my mate, Melana," I told her, getting it over with. She was going to find out sooner or later. It was better if it came from me than just waking up to find Lucy had suddenly become my Luna. Melana stopped in her tracks.

"What? Since when?" she said, outraged. It was clear she didn't expect that answer.

"Since I turned seventeen. I have known for years, Melana. Why do you think I kept telling you this would never become anything more?"

"Wait! So I was just around to kill the fucking time while you waited for her to what? Grow up? You fucking prick!" She had a point, and there was no easy way to say it, but she was correct.

"Well, yeah," I admitted, looking away from her.

"You knew all this fucking time?" she screamed so loudly I had to fight the urge to cover my ears, her voice making them ring.

"I should have told you earlier. I was planning to, but I didn't think she would come back early from school," I told her. Melana started laughing, shaking her head.

"Now I know why you would suddenly disappear every time she came back from school, and I couldn't get a hold of you unless I showed up. You are a real piece of shit, Ace. I hope she fucking rejects you."

"You have a mate out there, Melana. Don't act so surprised I would pick mine over you."

She snorted, shaking her head, laughing. "This is just fucking great, you son of a bitch. I fucking rejected mine for you, you fucking asshole!" she said before shoving me.

"You did what?" I asked, a little shocked by her words.

"I found mine last year, you prick. I rejected him for you! What a waste of fucking time that was!" she screamed at me.

I didn't know what to say to that, there was no way in hell I would reject a fated mate for anyone. Yet Melana did it for me.

"I never asked you to do that, Melana. Why would you do that?" I asked, baffled. *How could she?* The thought disgusted me. If I had known, I would have told her to go be with him.

"Because I love you, that's why. He was a stranger. I barely knew him. I clearly read that fucking wrong," she told me. I swallowed, now feeling ten times worse.

"I need to go," I told her. Nothing was going to fix this, so I just needed to get out.

"Sure, fine, Ace. Run back to your fucking slut of a mate!" She growled at me, and I stopped. Atticus clawed at me and pressed forward, enraged she would call Lucy that.

"What did you say?"

"You heard me. You want to run along after someone that's been screwing her teacher, go ahead! Good luck with that."

"Lucy is a virgin, Melana. Don't be calling her names just because you can't handle the thought of her being my Luna," I told her, forcing Atticus down. He wanted to rip her apart and kill her for saying something so vile about Lucy.

Melana laughed. "Sure, believe what you want. Josey told me what she saw. Believe what you want about innocent little Lucy. She was the one fucking her science teacher. Clearly, she couldn't handle it when he broke it off with her, so she burned the classroom down. You're pathetic. Go on, run back to your mate."

"Josey is wrong. Lucy would never do that," I told her, walking toward her apartment door.

"My sister isn't a liar, Ace. She caught Lucy leaving his class half-naked. A week later, his classroom was burned down because he'd found his mate. Think what you want, if it makes you sleep better at night. But it doesn't change the fact that she is fucking whore!" Melana said.

Atticus growled, and I forced myself out of the apartment before he killed her. I'd hurt her enough already, I didn't need Atticus doing more damage over some lies Josey had told her.

Walking out of the apartment complex, though, I couldn't get her words out of my head. Was that why she burned the classroom down because he'd found his mate? I just couldn't picture Lucy sleeping with her teacher, yet Melana's words had me questioning how much I really knew Lucy. She had changed over the last year, maybe this relationship with her teacher was the reason why. Stepping outside, I found it belting down with rain. The wind was so bad it was making the trees bend as I stepped onto the city's main drag. *Fuck! I can't run home in this.* Looking around, I tried to find a cab before remembering Jacob lived nearby.

I opened the mindlink before feeling him become alert. "What's up?"

"You home, bro?"

"Yep, I am not going anywhere in this storm," he replied.

"Good, because I am staying with you tonight. I am stuck in the city," I told him, walking down the street in the direction of his apartment.

"Okay, I will buzz you in. See you soon," he said, cutting off the link.

I then mindlinked Tyson and Lucy to let them know. In a way, I was glad I was staying at Jacob's. The thought of seeing her after what Melana had just told me had Atticus hackled up and on the verge of exploding. I needed him to be calm before asking her anything about her teacher. I also needed to find out who the fuck her teacher was. He shouldn't be allowed to teach if he was taking advantage of his students. Avery and Aamon would want to know of any misconduct, but the longer I walked to Jacob's, the more it made sense. She had to have been screwing him, maybe that was why she was so upset that she would burn down his classroom. Just like with Melana, jealousy tended to do some pretty horrid things to people.

Chapter 17

Lucy

Waking up, the storm had cleared, and the sun was beaming in through Tyson's bedroom window, lighting up the back of my eyelids, making me squint as I put up my hand to shield my eyes from the blinding light.

Sitting up, I found Tyson was still asleep, but we had both shifted in our sleep and I was lying half on him, my head on his chest and arm across his waist, my skin tingling wherever his skin was connected with mine. I pulled my leg off his waist, embarrassed at the position I awoke in, only for him to grab my leg and bring it back across his waist.

"Stay," Tyson mumbled, pulling me back to him by my shoulders with the arm I was lying on. He patted his chest, and I lay back down. He turned his face, his nose going into my hair as he inhaled my scent.

"Right where you belong," Tyson said, kissing my forehead.

"Where do I belong?" I asked at his half-asleep ramblings. He chuckles softly.

"Yes, Lucy, you belong with…"

"I'm back! Where are you both at?" Ace suddenly yelled out from the front of the house, making Tyson stop whatever he was going to say before I heard Ace walking down the hallway. Tyson growled, making me look up at him.

"Lucy, Tyson, where are you both?" Ace called out.

"In here," Tyson called back to him before sighing. Ace leaned on the door frame before folding his arms across his chest and glaring at Tyson.

"Why is she in here?" I sat up at his words, realizing how indecent it was for me to be in there.

"Lucy?" Tyson said as I pulled away from him, adjusting his shirt that had risen up, and I tossed the blanket back before realizing I still didn't have panties on. I tried to pull his shirt down to cover my nakedness underneath the shirt.

"Why do you gotta be a dick?" Tyson asked Ace as I got out of his bed, suddenly feeling ashamed for being in here. *What woman is scared of storms?* I mentally scolded myself. It wasn't the storms themselves, it was the noise they created, deafening and always bringing back terrible memories of the facility in which I was kept. There was nothing worse than being locked in a glass cell during a storm. The vibrations alone would send you mad, then the rain seeping through the cracks in the concrete floor above always made me feel like a goldfish in its tank, only I couldn't breathe underwater.

"Lucy, you don't have to leave," Tyson said, sitting up and tossing the blanket back as he too got to his feet. I was on my way to the door when Ace stepped in my path, making me look up at him. He looked incredibly irritated with me for some unknown reason, making me nervous about how he glared at me.

"Morning," I told him awkwardly. I didn't understand why he was glaring at me or the disgusted look he gave me. We were only sleeping, nothing indecent was going on.

"You lied to us. Josey told Melana what you did," Ace said, making me furrow my brows in confusion. *Josey? What did Josey say that would upset him this much?* I wondered.

"What do you mean? Josey is still at school."

"She told me why you burned the classroom down. You lied to us." I felt my stomach drop. I hadn't told anyone, and I knew I never told Josey. She became distant and hardly had anything to do with me the last couple of weeks of school, always making excuses about being too busy with her studies to hang out, making that boarding school even more lonely for me. We used to be joined at the hip.

"Because anything Melana said can be taken as truth," Tyson growled at him.

"Well, it didn't take her long to climb in bed with you now, did it? Shows what sort of person she is. I honestly expected better of you, Lucy," Ace growled.

"What the fuck is that supposed to mean?" Tyson snapped at him. Yet I was growing more confused, wondering what Melana had said. I barely had a chance to speak to Josey before they turned me out, so what could she have said to her sister about me? She knew Melana and I didn't get along, and Josey wasn't one to gossip.

"Just that she had no problems fucking her teacher, and now she is in bed with you. How could you?" Ace said, turning to look at me, and I took a step away from him.

"She said I did what?!" I asked, unable to believe what just came out of his mouth.

"Are you going to tell him, or am I?"

"Tell him what? I never slept with anybody! I told you I was a virgin! How could you say such a thing?" I yelled at him. Hot tears burned my eyes at his words.

"Josey saw you leaving his classroom half-naked, Lucy. Deny it all you want, but I know what happened. Now I know why you didn't want to admit guilt for what you did. Then you burned his classroom because he found his mate and tossed you aside," Ace said, pointing his finger at me.

While I was mortified that Josey could say that. It was far from the truth. *Why would she say such a thing? Why wouldn't she ask me?* No one ever wanted to hear my side.

"Lucy, is what he is saying true?" Tyson asked, making me look back at him.

"So, because that's what Josey said, it means it's true?" I asked him.

"Why would she lie? She is your best friend, is she not?" Ace said.

I can't believe this shit! He was the one who attacked me, yet I am being blamed!

"You know what? Fuck you!" I told Ace. This was exactly why I never told anyone. *Why should I have to prove anything to anyone?* This right here was exactly why girls didn't come forward, and no one believed them. The victims were the ones having to defend themselves against the perpetrators. *Never in my life have I been made to feel more disgusting than right now.* I could deal with what he tried to do. What I couldn't live with however, was being blamed for it.

Ace still didn't move and even pushed me back when I tried to walk around him.

"Is it true, Lucy?" Tyson asked behind me, making me look over my shoulder at him. I felt tears brim and spill over, realizing that they would think that little of me to sleep with a teacher. That they would take the word of another over mine.

"Believe what you want. You will anyway," I told him before shoving past Ace and heading to the bathroom.

Chapter 18

Lucy

Walking into the bathroom, I grabbed the pants I had on yesterday, and pulled them on. They were slightly damp from the wet floor, the room chilly from the tiles, and the window cracked open.

I then grabbed my jumper, tugged it over my head, and pulled my hair into a ponytail. That day was replaying in my head on repeat. The smell of his cologne, the weird prickling sensation of my hair standing on end when I realized his intentions, the fear that paralyzed me, making me freeze up while I tried to figure out what I did that would make him do this to me. That sense of dread, the coldest feeling in the world, before I felt my breathing become shorter. I clutched at my throat, trying to catch my breath as I started to hyperventilate, fear gripping me in its confines, suffocating me excruciatingly slowly.

I needed my pills, needed something so I could breathe. Yet, it became harder and harder to catch my breath. My vision blurred with panic from my inability to calm myself before everything went dark, and I knew I was falling into the depths of my tortured memories. My body hit the tiles with a thud, yet I couldn't feel any pain. I felt nothing. I couldn't feel anything when I was pulled back to that fateful day. Watching my own torment like it was a movie. Like it had happened to someone else. Only, I recognized the girl in it, because she was me.

Flashback

I used to like Mr. Tanner. How foolish and blinded I was, thinking he was one of the cool teachers at school. He had busted me and Josey ditching class multiple times and always stuck up for us. Caught us smoking weed in the bathrooms, and defended us to the principal.

We thought he was one of the good ones, easy-going, friendly, always willing to bail us out when we got ourselves in trouble. If only I had known there was a price for it, if only I had known what he really was. If only I had never closed that classroom door. He was a predator, and we were too blind to see we were his prey.

"Lucy, can I have a word with you for a second?" I heard Mr. Tanner's voice behind me as I packed up my school equipment.

Josey paused at the door looking at me. "I just need a word with her, Josey. Go to your next class. She will be there soon," Mr. Tanner said to her. She smiled and nodded.

"I will see you in class then," Josey said before walking out the door. I zipped my bag up after dumping my pencil case in it.

I then grabbed the strap and tossed the bag over my shoulder. Just as I was walking to the front of the classroom to see what he wanted, Mr. Tanner spoke.

"Shut the door, Lucy," he said, and I furrowed my brows but did as he said, not thinking anything of it. It was Mr. Tanner. He was our friend; why shouldn't I trust him? Not trusting him had never once occurred to me.

"Pull the blinds down, too," he said, making me look over my shoulder at him.

"Excuse me, sir?" I asked, confused.

Suddenly, he was right beside me. "I said pull the blind down, Lucy," he said before I heard the lock on the door click. I saw him pull his hand back, making me gulp.

Fear coursed through me as I stared at him.

"The blinds, Lucy," he repeated, and I looked at the little blinds on the door that would cover the glass.

"I should go. I am going to be late for class," I told him, becoming uncomfortable. I reached for the door handle only his hand gripped it.

"I told you I needed to speak to you. Now, pull down the blinds," he said, smiling at me.

Terror made my blood run cold. Mr. Tanner was a demon, not just in a sense, but an actual demon, just like Aamon. Demons were perceived as bad, but most weren't. Mr. Tanner was though, his eyes flickering black, and I saw my own fear-filled face reflect back at me.

I didn't want to close the blinds, yet fear made me do it as my shaking hand gripped the cord, tugging it down. His hand was still on the doorknob, and my entire body started to shake, my stomach sinking when he moved his face closer to mine.

"That wasn't so hard, was it?" he said before leaning back. "Come, I want to show you something," he said, smiling and waving me forward as he walked back toward his desk. He picked up some papers, and I felt relief flooding me. I was being irrational. He just wanted to show me some homework, I thought, trying to push the unease away. I saw him return to his normally bubbly self, making me wonder if I had just imagined it. I let out a breath, walking over to him as he stacked the papers in a pile.

"You okay, Lucy?" he asked, and I chuckled.

"Yes, sorry. I am not sure what came over me," I told him, shaking my head as I approached his desk. "Is it about the assignment due on Friday?" I asked, recognizing the papers on his desk.

He grabbed them, dropping them in the drawer under his desk before closing it. He then moved his laptop, putting it on the table beside the desk, which I thought was odd as I watched him clear his desk without saying anything. He then patted his desk with his hand.

"What did you want to show me?" I asked him when I felt his hand run up my thigh and under my skirt. I jerked away from him, and his eyes flickered.

"I should go," I told him, stepping back only for him to vanish in thin air before feeling his breath on the back of my neck, and I knew he was behind me. Knew my first instinct was right.

The hair on my neck stood up, his cold breath making me break out in a cold sweat, which chilled me to the bone. Leaving me paralyzed in my own fear. I couldn't move, I was completely frozen.

The room was so quiet that I could hear my own heartbeat and my shaky breath, along with that stupid song playing softly from the PA system in the halls. I felt his hands grip me, shoving me toward the desk as he tried to bend me over it. Only then, something snapped in me as I tried to struggle to get out from under him, my face jammed against the cold wooden desk as I thrashed trying to get out of his grip. His knees pressed between mine, forcing my legs open as he started ripping at my clothes.

My underwear ripped from my body painfully, his nails digging into my face as his hand pinned my head to the table. The smell of burned almonds permeated around me. My vision blurred with my tears as I begged him to stop. I felt my bra strap snap, the back of my shirt being ripped open as it fell down my arms.

I tried pushing off the table with my hands, only to be forced back down before feeling something hard hit the back of my head. My teeth bit into my tongue from the force as the room spun violently, my head pounding, and my ears ringing as I clawed frantically at the desk.

My fingers came in contact with something made of glass that was wet, and I turned just enough to smash the glass on him. Yet, he didn't stop as he pushed my skirt up. His hand went to my mouth, his thumb pinching my nose, making it difficult to breathe.

I felt his cock press against my ass and thigh, panic coursing through me, and I tried to reach behind me, clawing at anything I could. Trying to keep him away, when he gripped my hair, ripping my head back before slamming it into the desk. My head bounced off the wood, making me see black for a second. But his grip waivered, and I managed to turn, kicking my legs, trying to reach his laptop on the small table beside his desk. My fingertips grazed it as I struggled to keep him back before he pinned my legs to the desk just as I gripped the laptop. I swung it, smacking him in the side of the head, making him clutch his face. That momentary distraction was enough, and I jumped off the desk, racing for the door.

I didn't get far before he misted in front of me. Adrenaline coursed through me, I was so close to the door. He grabbed my arms, ripping me toward him, my hands going to his face as I dug my thumbs into his eye sockets, feeling the gooeyness of his eyes, making him let go as he clutched his eyes, screaming. I shoved past him, fumbling with the door lock before opening it, and I ran, not looking back.

"Lucy?" I heard a muffled voice.

Chapter 19

"Lucy, open the goddamn door and stop ignoring us!" Ace yelled, forcing me back to my surroundings. My hair stuck to my face as I broke out in a cold sweat, goosebumps covering my arms.

I was on the cold, gray, tiled floor. I shakily got to my feet before trying to compose myself, trying to convince myself they weren't my memories as I shoved them away, back in my box, locking them away where they couldn't get me. I opened the door to find Ace and Tyson in the hallway. Ace looked livid, while Tyson looked concerned, standing behind him. Ace towered over me as he glared down at me, taking up nearly the entire door frame.

"Lucy, come here," Tyson said, waving his hands forward, wanting me to go to him. I was tempted until Ace spoke, his arm blocking the doorway when I tried to move through, effectively blocking me. I looked up at him. I only reached up to his chest as he stared down at me intimidatingly.

"Explain! You hate me being with Melana, yet we are supposed to be okay with you lying to us and sleeping with your teacher? A FUCKING TEACHER?" he screamed at me.

"I never lied. Now move, so I can leave, Ace," I told him, becoming sick and tired of the accusations, everyone always pointing the finger at me. *Haven't they realized I usually own up to the shit I do by now? But that, I won't own up to that! Because that wasn't me.* It was amazing how carefree and blinded you were before something like that destroyed your world, turning everything on its axis, showing you with brutal clarity how easily you could be destroyed. How vulnerable you could become. The shame that came with it, the what-ifs, the guilt when you realized how powerless you were, shoving the blame inward. I questioned every action, every word I ever said, wondering if I had somehow asked for it. I didn't need others doing the questioning and accusing me of something I never dreamed could have happened.

In the facility, they broke our bodies, killed my wolf. But it was nothing compared to breaking your own tormented mind, sharp edges pricking and slicing at your memories, constantly waiting for something to trigger it back to the forefront of your mind. The anxiety that came with trying not to remember when it did, certain scents, certain noises. Shit, even in my adrenaline-filled fear, I still remembered the song coming through the PA systems softly as I escaped the classroom. A body can be fixed, but a mind? Not so much. That remains tortured, looming over you, tearing at you piece by piece until there is nothing left but hopelessness and despair. A mere longing for who you used to be before your world turned upside down.

"No! Not until you tell me who it is! I want to know who my mate was fooling around with! You come home and attack Melana when you are just as bad! Shit, not even I fucked my teachers, Lucy! Have you no limits?" Ace snapped at me.

Yet I was stuck on one word, one that was supposed to signify your other half, signify safety, *mate*.

"What did you just say?" I asked him, needing him to repeat it. Surely I didn't imagine it.

"You heard me, Lucy. Now tell me who he is! I won't have our mate lying to us!" Ace screamed at me.

"I never slept with my teacher..." I tried telling him when he cut me off, grabbing my arms, and ripping me closer to him. I finally realized what the sparks were and why I got them when they touched me. But that just infuriated me. If this was what mates were, I wanted no part of it. *You don't declare someone to be your mate, then hurt them.*

"Don't fucking lie to me!" he screamed, his claws sinking into my arms as his canines elongated, his face twisting in his anger. Tyson grabbed him, only for Ace to move quickly, elbowing him in the face. Tyson's blood from his busted nose sprayed across my face while Ace was on the verge of shifting, his entire body trembling with rage.

"I never fucked him, Ace..." But yet again, he cut me off, growling at me. His grip tightened, and I lifted my hands, shoving him with all my strength and making him stumble backward.

He smacked into Tyson, and I ran for the door, only for him to try to grab me.

His arm snaked around my waist as he jerked me backward, but I threw my head back, feeling it connect with his jaw. He grunted, and I turned on him, my fangs slipping from my gums as my vision turned red.

"I never slept with my teacher, you mutt! He tried to rape me!" I screamed at him as he regained himself. Tyson shoved him off, trapped beneath him.

Ace just stared at me. My breathing was heavy as hot tears of anger rolled down my cheeks.

"I never asked for it! Never seduced him, you sick bastard! That's why I burned his classroom down! That's why they kicked me out of school. Not because I was a disobedient bitch like you think! But because I had a pedophile for a teacher! But thanks! You truly showed me how little you think of me. What a great mate you will be." I told him before gripping the front of his shirt and shoving him back on the ground as he tried to stand.

"Lucy, no!" Tyson yelled, trying to get to his feet.

"I, Lucy Anneliese Black, reject you, Ace Kasen Black, Alpha of the Blackmoon Pack!" I told him.

Ace growled, and I shoved him back, letting go of his shirt, my chest heaving painfully as I felt something within me falter. My heart was aching and thumping rapidly when Ace suddenly lunged at me. I tried to step back but instead fell and hit the floorboards as he tackled me, landing heavily on me.

"I, Ace Kasen Black, reject your rejection." he growled before sinking his fangs into my neck. I screamed, feeling his teeth tear through my skin, his canines embedded in my flesh hitting bone, when he suddenly got ripped off me, his teeth tearing from my neck. I clutched my neck, trying to get to my feet, when I felt the bond snap into place. The room tilted as I tried to hold myself up using the wall before suddenly seeing the floor rush toward my face, my eyes rolling in the back of my head as I was swallowed by darkness.

Chapter 20

Tyson

She rejected him. And Ace, blinded by his own ego, launched himself at her, knocking her down. Tyrant was pressing beneath my skin as he watched him attack her, forcing me to my feet. I tried to get him off her when he sank his teeth into her neck. I grabbed him, ripping him off her, her scream making me enraged, and I punched him.

He growled at me, but he just fucking hurt her! He hurt her. He took away her choice. This was never meant to go down like this. She was never meant to find out like this, and he ruined everything, making me hate him for it. Ace tackled me, slamming me into the wall. I punched him in the ribs, making him grunt, letting Tyrant forward to help me shove him off.

Tyrant wanted to kill him. We accepted the fact we had to share her, but I did not accept what he had done, as I repeatedly rained blow after blow down on him. How could he? She was our mate! How could he hurt her like that?

Hearing her gasp, I looked up to see she had gotten to her feet, she was swaying, clutching her neck where his mark now lay on her delicate flesh. I watched as her eyes rolled into the back of her head, and I tried to reach her before she hit the floor when Ace gripped my ankle, ripping me back and making me fall face-first on the floorboards. I turned, using my other foot to kick him in the face, making his head snap back as he clutched his bleeding face. I heard the sound of her body hitting the floor with a hard thud, the sound of her head bouncing off the hard floor.

"Lucy!" I gasped, rushing over to her, her head bleeding where she'd hit the corner of the wall and spilling onto the floor. I turned her over, pulling her into my lap, and Ace came over still full of rage. He tried to grab me before stopping as he peered down at Lucy bleeding everywhere. She was healing, but damn. That gash was deep, her blood smeared down the wall and all over my legs and chest. I glared up at him.

"I didn't mean to," he gasped, reaching for her, but I pulled her away from him and tucked her against my chest, her body completely limp in my arms. I watched as he swallowed, his Adam's apple bobbing in his throat.

"She shouldn't have rejected me," he said, looking away and tossing the blame on her. I growled at him. Was that all he had to say? All he could think about after what she'd said?

"You selfish prick!" I told him, and his head whipped back to me while I glared daggers at him.

"She fucking rejected me! What else was I supposed to do?" he screamed at me.

"Not take her fucking choice! How could you? After what she just said! How the fuck could you believe Melana over her? You don't deserve her." I told him. He growled, stepping toward me, his eyes falling on her for a second, and he paused.

"Get out!" I told him. I was disgusted with him. He was just as bad as her teacher.

He didn't move. "You don't mean that. You are just angry," Ace said.

"I fucking mean it! Get the fuck out of here before I ring Ryker and have him remove you." I told him.

"She isn't just your mate, Tyson."

"You're right. But I wonder what Ryker and Reika will say when they find out you forcefully marked her. She just told us she was nearly raped! And then you go and take her choice? You are just as vile as him!"

"I am nothing like him!" Ace screamed.

"No? Because taking her choice wasn't something he did? You are right though, you aren't like him. What you did was worse! Because she is our mate. Ours, Ace! Ours to keep safe! And you just showed her you don't care for what she wants if it goes against what you want! Luckily she escaped him. But now she can't escape you," I told him before pushing my arms underneath her limp body and scooping her up.

"Get out. I don't want you here when she wakes up." I told him before stepping past him and heading back to my room. I kicked the door shut before placing her on the bed. I heard something break before the front door slammed as he left. Walking into the bathroom adjacent to my room, I wet a cloth before walking back out to her to clean her up, wiping the blood from her face and neck. She stirred but didn't wake.

I opened the mindlink, searching for my brother. Ryker opened it, allowing it to connect.

"Busy Tyson, can't talk now," he said, about to cut the link off.

"It's about Lucy," I told him and hesitated before opening the link completely.

"What happened?"

"You need to get a hold of Avery and Aamon."

"They won't let her back in, Tyson. She blew her chances. I already tried," Ryker told me.

"She is never going back. It has nothing to do with her wanting to go back to school, Ryker. Can you come over, please?" I asked him.

"I am in a meeting. It will have to wait."

"Cancel it."

"What's going on?" he asked, and it became startlingly clear to me that not one person who was supposed to care for her had ever asked her why she did it. I felt like a fool for not questioning it myself. Not demanding an answer from her. Lucy would never endanger other people, her pranks had a limit. Yet, I never bothered to ask.

"Did you ever ask her? Did Reika ever ask her why she burned that classroom down?" I asked him, and he paused.

"Tyson, I know she has problems with the students, but that doesn't give her the right to damage school property," Ryker said.

"You may just change your mind on that. It was never anything to do with her not liking school. Just come over. I will explain."

"Explain what? Nothing you say will change the fact that she burned down a classroom, Tyson. You always defend her actions instead of letting her own up to her mistakes. I will come to see you after work."

"You know she was homeless, right? She was living in the forest until I found her yesterday. I thought she was at home until Rayan told me he had been sneaking out to see her. For once, just bloody do as I ask," I told him.

"I thought she was staying at your house?" Ryker said.

"No. And you would have known if you hadn't kept blocking us out. I only found out because I picked up Rayan from school."

"Fine. I will be over when the meeting is over. I am having issues with Alpha Jamie," Ryker said.

"Fine. But bring Aamon with you. He needs to know this," I told him.

"Whatever it is, I can handle it, Tyson. I am not going to pull him from work because Lucy wants to go back to school when I already know the answer."

"Lucy is not going back to school. Nor is she leaving my side. Just get Aamon here, or Avery. I don't care which one," I told him.

"You are being a pain in the ass. Just spit it out, Tyson, so I can get back to work!" he snapped at me through the link.

I wanted Lucy to tell them, but now I was wondering if I had no other choice. None of them were going to take her seriously.

"Her teacher tried to rape her. That's why she burned the classroom down." I told him. He growled, the mindlink vibrating dangerously, almost cutting off.

"What did you just say?"

"He tried to rape her." I repeated, feeling sick just saying those words. No wonder she changed. No wonder she became distant.

"I'm on my way." he said, cutting off the link. I refocused on the room and looked down at my mate passed out on the bed. Getting up, I grabbed one of my shirts from the drawer before pulling her jumper off, leaving her in her singlet before pulling my shirt over her head. I then walked the blood-soaked jumper into the laundry before chucking it into the washing machine. Just as I turned around, Aamon misted into my hallway, scaring the crap out of me.

"Ryker said to come here. Something urgent?" he said, looking around. The smell of burned almonds flooded my senses, and I scrunched up my nose when I heard a car speeding up the long driveway before skidding to a stop.

"And that would be Ryker," Aamon said, walking to the front of the house.

I followed Aamon, Ryker stomping up the porch steps before nearly ripping the door from the hinges as he forced it open.

"Where is she?" he said, and Aamon looked at him, confused.

"She is asleep. Ace marked her," I told him, and he opened his mouth before closing it.

"She figured out she was your mate?" he asked.

"No. They had an argument, and Ace blurted it out. He marked her when she rejected him," I told him. He growled, his eyes flickering dangerously as his canines protruded. Good! Ace deserved what was coming to him.

Chapter 21

Lucy

I awoke to the sound of voices. My head was pounding, and my neck was stinging. Groaning, I got up, rubbing my eyes as I swung my legs over the side of the bed. I found myself in Tyson's room. The door was cracked open slightly, and I could hear the murmurs of people talking somewhere in the packhouse. Getting up, I clutched my neck, the movement making my mark sting. Tears brimmed in my eyes that he marked me. I hated him! I hated him with everything in me! I felt betrayed by him. Now, there was no escaping the bond.

Walking to the door, I opened it. The door creaked, and the house suddenly fell quiet.

"Tyson?" I called out, hoping Ace wasn't the one that was home. I heard footsteps before seeing Tyson suddenly appear in the hallway, and I rushed toward him. Throwing my arms around him, as he hugged me, and I breathed in his scent, sparks rushing over my skin as he pressed his lips to my head. Hearing voices again, I looked up at him.

"Who is here? Is Ace here?" I asked, not wanting to see him.

"No, he isn't here. But, come on," Tyson said, grabbing my hand and tugging me down the hall when the smell of burned almonds overloaded my senses, and I knew a demon was in the house. I froze, my entire body locking up, and Tyson stopped before cupping my face and brushing his thumb over my cheek.

"You are safe, I promise. Ace isn't here," he said, tugging me to him before walking me out into the living room. If I was scared before, it was nothing compared to how I felt now seeing all their faces. I felt bile rise in my throat, and I ripped my hand from Tyson's. My heart raced in my chest so hard I could hear it. My stomach dropped as I stared back at my stepfather, Aamon, Avery, and last of all, my mother. I stepped backward. *This can't be happening. Why were they looking at me like that?*

I hated being in the spotlight, and suddenly, all eyes were on me. The pity in their eyes made me feel pathetic, and I knew they knew. I looked at Tyson and stepped further toward the front door, my stepfather stepping in front of it before I could make a run for it.

"You told them?" I asked, horrified and humiliated, looking at Tyson.

"They needed to know, Lucy." I shook my head. How could he? How could he do this to me?

"Lucy?" my mother said softly, making me look at her and her huge swollen belly, tears running down her cheeks as she tried to get up.

"No. No, you don't get to care now! None of you do." I told her before looking at Tyson.

"How could you? You are supposed to be my mate." I told him.

"That wasn't a secret I could keep, Lucy," Tyson said.

"It wasn't yours to tell either!" I screamed at him, tears running down my face at the complete and utter embarrassment of this situation. This was the last thing I wanted, for everyone to know, everyone to judge me.

"They can help. Avery and Aamon needed to know Lucy. What if he does it to someone else? Could you live with that? Knowing you could have stopped it." Tyson said, stepping toward me.

"Well, they know now, don't they?" I told him, turning back for the bedroom, realizing I had no chance of escaping out the front door.

"Lucy, stop!" my stepfather commanded, my feet becoming suddenly glued to the floor, unable to take another step. His Alpha aura rolled over me, sending a wave of pain through me as I gritted my teeth, a whimper leaving my lips. I could hear Tyson growl.

"Drop it, brother! King or not, I will hurt you." Tyson growled, walking over to me where I was frozen. The command dropped, and I gasped, sucking in a breath. Tyson wrapped his arms around me, his hands running up and down my arms before resting his chin on my shoulder. I relaxed against him, leaning into him, sparks running over me, making me want to step closer and live in his warmth. Not that I could get any closer to him, when he was already pressed against me.

"You have nothing to be embarrassed about, Lucy. What he did is wrong. No one deserves that. But you have to tell them," Tyson murmured.

"I don't want to tell them," I whispered, horrified at the thought, my biggest shame, my weakest moment. *Tell them how pathetic I was? What if they blamed me?* I shut the door. I could have run, but I stupidly shut the door. I didn't want to tell anyone that, have them look at me differently.

"You don't have to say it, Lucy. Just let me look, let me in your head." came Avery's voice. I shook my head, and she got up, walking toward me, her emerald green eyes sparkling back at me as she stood before me. She always looked so regal, so strong, and I could see why she was the demon witch high priestess. She truly was a remarkable woman and had done so much to help us mutations. She helped save us, helped free us. She cupped my face in her hands, her auburn hair hanging over one shoulder to her waist as she gazed down at me.

"You don't have to tell anyone, okay? Just let me see. I need to see Lucy. I can't convict him if I haven't seen the truth."

"Convict him?" I asked. She nodded, her thumbs rubbing under my eyes when I suddenly got an idea. I touched the mark on my neck, knowing she was the only person to exist that could remove a mate bond. She was half-succubus, her father, Asmodeus, was the prince of hell, and her mother used to be the queen of the Faewood Coven before Aamon murdered her. Everyone had heard the stories of Avery and Aamon's tragic past, yet she still loved him and brought him back from the dead after killing him for his betrayal. I envied that she loved him enough to bring him back, but I hated Ace and his mark on my neck.

"You let me see, Lucy. I promise you will never have to see him again."

"What will happen to him?" I asked.

"I will send him back to the pits of hell where he belongs. My father will make sure he burns every day for what he did for the rest of eternity." she said, her voice never wavering, and I knew she would do just that. I nodded, and she smiled softly.

"I will also do what you want to ask but can't bring yourself too," she said knowingly.

"What's that?" I heard Tyson ask behind me.

She didn't answer him, facing me instead. "Sometimes you gotta destroy them, to make them see the error of their ways. If he doesn't, you will always have Tyson. He won't go anywhere."

"Will it be permanent?" I asked, wondering if I would regret it. Mate bonds were sacred, and even though I was not a werewolf anymore, I still didn't want to shun the Moon Goddess.

"No. I am just giving your choice back. Something he should never have taken," she said, and I nodded, a tear slipping down my cheek that she brushed away.

Her eyes burned brighter, and her hands warmed up before I was plunged into my memories, Avery going through and filtering through them. I watched them flash past in snippets before stopping on the worst day of my life. The memory played out, and despite knowing I was safe and it wasn't happening, I felt fear grip me in its deadly vice, tearing me apart once again as I was forced to relive every terrifying moment. I felt myself start to panic, my breathing getting harder and harder before I was suddenly struggling to breathe.

Hands were moving up my arms, and I heard Tyson's voice next to my ear. "I'm right here. Calm down, babe. I won't let anyone hurt you," he said soothingly, his hands warming me. I focused on his scent while the image flashed by before I suddenly saw Avery's face smiling sadly at me.

"Thank you, Lucy. He will pay. I can assure you of that," she said before her eyes flickered black. "Now, let's take care of this. We will have company soon." Her hand went to my neck.

"Will it hurt?" I asked.

"It won't hurt you, child, but he will feel it," she said.

"Lucy?" Tyson said, but I didn't answer. Avery did.

"It isn't permanent. But now she can choose whether or not to let him mark her again," Avery told him, and I looked up at Tyson. He pressed his lips in a line but nodded.

Avery looked back at me before I felt her hand on my neck go spine-tingling cold. I shivered before I gasped, feeling the teether snap. A cold feeling settled over me, but it wasn't painful, just empty, numb.

She pulled her hand away. "The foreign feeling will ease, I promise. But it will linger until you either let him mark you again or reject him," she said, and I nodded, swallowing before looking at Tyson. Hearing a roar outside, I jumped, and Avery's eyes darted to the door.

"And that would be Ace," she said, her eyes flickering dangerously. The door was suddenly thrown open, smashing into my stepfather.

"What did you do, Lucy?" Ace screamed before marching over to me. Ryker growled behind him and went to rip him back, but Avery stepped forward with her hands going to his face. He clutched her hands as they locked onto the side of his head before his eyes rolled into the back of his head.

Ace's body started to tremble, his canines protruding before his breathing became ragged. She suddenly let him go, and he staggered backward. Ryker grabbed his arm to steady him before his eyes locked on me. I stepped back into Tyson, his hand around my waist, and Ace looked at Avery.

"Did you do that, really?" He shook his head, his face twisted in anger.

"I gave you her memories. Maybe next time, you will make better choices. Never pick anyone over your mate," Avery told him before walking over to Aamon.

"It wasn't a lie?" Ace gasped, and my heart hurt at his words. He really thought I would lie about something like that. He believed Melana over me. It hurt, and I glared at him. Disgusted that he still didn't believe me even after I'd told them.

"I will take care of Mr. Tanner, but we will be leaving now," Avery said, and I nodded. She truly was a good woman. She and

Aamon misted out of the room, the smell of burned almonds getting stronger, and I cringed.

"Lucy?" my mother said from where she was sitting on the couch. I looked at her, smiling sadly.

"I'm sorry, I didn't know. You can come home if you want," she blurted as I turned to leave the room.

"Lucy, don't upset your mother," Ryker said behind me, and I turned back to face the room.

"Yet she has no problem upsetting me. The moment you had Rayan, you forgot about me! I get it. I was created from a bad past, one you wanted to forget. A constant reminder. So don't worry, mother, you don't have to worry about me corrupting your real children," I told her before turning on my heel and walking off.

"Lucy?" she called, and my heart clenched at her voice.

"Just let her calm down. She has had a rough day. I will bring her back over during the week," I heard Tyson tell her, but I just walked back to his room, shutting the door. I wanted nothing more than to curl up and go to sleep and forget this day ever happened, along with the rest of the days that tormented me.

Chapter 22

Ace's

I FELT GUTTED KNOWING EVERYTHING she said was true. I didn't know why I doubted her. Maybe it was my guilt, or maybe I was just too blinded by my anger after what Melana had told me that I didn't see sense. But now, I felt like a piece of shit for not believing her when she had never given me a reason to question her before. Lucy usually owned up to her wrongs, and now I was going to have to do the same.

Lucy stormed off to Tyson's room, and I didn't blame her; she hated me. I hated myself for what I did, but I never expected her to have the bond removed, and now I had to face her rejecting me all over again. Leaning on the veranda wall, I tossed my smoke. Ryker came out with Reika, and he opened the car door for her. A growl escaped him when he spotted me leaning on the wall. I watched as he shut her door before walking over to me. I knew what was coming; I could see it a mile away as he stalked up the steps toward me. I faced him head-on and didn't even flinch when he raised his fist.

My head whipped to the side as his fist connected with my face. My blood trickled down my chin, where he split my lip open.

"You knew she was your mate and fooled around on her. Then, to make it worse, you forcefully marked her," Ryker growled at me, raising his fist and punching me again.

I spat blood on the ground, knowing I deserved it, but it still angered me. He was no fucking saint either.

"If she rejects you again, you will not mark her," he snapped at me. "Ace?" he screamed in my face, grabbing the front of my shirt.

"I won't, okay? She rejects me again, I will leave," I told him. He growled but nodded reluctantly before shoving me away. Tyson came out, looking at me from the door. He pressed his lips in a line but said nothing. I knew he was angry at me. He had always been the more selfless one out of us. He waited for her and would have continued to wait until she'd figured it out. I ruined things for him, and now it has put a strain on our relationship.

Ryker nodded to Tyson, clapping his hand on his shoulder before heading to his car. I watched them leave before turning to Tyson, who was blocking the doorway.

"I'm not going to do anything," I told him. I just wanted to speak to her. He stepped out of the way, and I walked inside, about to head toward his room, when he called out.

"Leave her be," he said, and I stopped, a growl escaping me before I shoved it down.

"You must be loving this? Loving that she hates me because you can keep her to yourself?" I snapped at him.

"I didn't hurt her. You did! I may not like having to share her with my brother, but I would never do anything that would hurt her. If she keeps you, I won't try to stop her. I accepted the fact we had to share her, understood it, but I won't sit back and watch you destroy her more than she already is."

"And if she rejects me again? You understand she can now."

"She doesn't want to reject you, Ace, but you forcing her will make her. Stop being selfish for once in your goddamn life, and let her decide instead of taking her choice away from her."

"So, you expect me to sit back and watch you two cozying up together?" I growled at him.

"Yes, I do. Don't make things worse, Ace. You didn't just put your bond with her at risk; you put mine at risk too. This was never a normal mate bond considering she was raised alongside us, making it already more difficult enough than you screwing around with Melana. What did you expect to happen? Then to top it off, you mark her and choose Melana over her. You messed this up, not me. And I won't be punished for your misdoings," he said before walking off down the hallway toward his room. I watched him close his door. Jealousy coursed through me before I stalked off toward mine, slamming the door. I really made a mess of things.

"Just mark her," Atticus told me, and I growled at him.

"Shut up. You have been no help at all," I told him, shoving him back.

Lucy

Everyone left while I hid in the room. Tyson came in, and I could hear him arguing with Ace, but he said nothing of it when he stepped back inside the room.

"Do you want to watch a movie?" he asked, lying on the bed beside me.

I shook my head. I didn't feel like doing anything; I just wanted to get away from everyone, away from the drama. Yet being here that would never happen, and going home wasn't an option either.

Not yet, at least. Sitting up, I wanted to leave and see Mitchell but didn't know how Tyson would take that.

"What's wrong?" Tyson asked.

"I wanted to go see Mitchell," I told him, needing my friend, my only friend. Tyson growled but said nothing. Instead, he got up, walked over to his closet, grabbed a jumper out and pulled it on.

"Where are you going?" I asked him, suddenly worried.

"I will drop you off," he said, tossing me a jumper.

"Are you letting me go?" I asked, a little shocked.

"Yes. I am not happy about it, but I trust you Lucy. Just let me drop you off and pick you up," he said, and I nodded, pulling his jumper over my head. I mindlinked Mitchell, who said he was about to catch the bus home from school, but instead, Tyson told me to tell him we would pick him up. Pulling up out the front of the school, Mitchell was standing there, and he looked nervous as he approached Tyson's car.

Tyson had a tight grip on the steering wheel, and I opened my door and climbed out, and Mitchell gave me a hug. "So, why is one of the Alpha's of Black Moon picking me up?" he asked.

I opened the back door for him before climbing back into the passenger seat.

"Alpha," Mitchell said out of respect, even though technically Tyson wasn't his Alpha; my stepfather was. Tyson nodded to him and started driving.

"So, what are we doing?" Mitchell asked.

"I am dropping Lucy off at your place. I will come to get her later," Tyson said.

"Okay, am I missing something? Did I do something wrong?" Mitchell asked nervously.

"No, of course not. Tyson is just a little weirded out with me hanging out with you," I told him, looking over the back of my seat.

"And why is that, Lucy?" Tyson said, and I knew he wanted me to tell Mitchell he was my mate. I sighed, it was going to come out anyway.

Mitchell was watching him, trying to figure it out. "Tyson and Ace are my mates," I told Mitchell, who opened and closed his mouth a few times before he let out a breath.

"Okay, then," Mitchell said with a nod, processing that information. Tyson glanced at him over his shoulder.

"Well, at least mom will stop pestering me about you," Mitchell said, and Tyson growled at him. Mitchell put up his hands, shaking his head.

"I'm fine being friends, Alpha," Mitchell said, and I sat back in my seat. The drive wasn't long to Mitchell's place. Getting out of the car, Tyson hopped out before walking over to me. He pulled me to him before pressing his lips to my head.

"Mindlink me when you want me to pick you up," Tyson said, and I nodded. Mitchell and I spent all afternoon playing video games, and surprisingly, nothing changed with him knowing I was Tyson's mate. He didn't seem to care but was just glad to be spending time with me.

Mitchell told his mother, who seemed genuinely happy, and I stayed for dinner before we went back up and played more video games before watching a movie. I must have fallen asleep because the next thing I remembered was being woken by someone carrying me. My eyes fluttered open before I snuggled closer to Tyson, feeling cold air brush over my skin, and I knew we were outside.

"Mitchell rang me and said you fell asleep," Tyson said when I looked up at him as he put me in the passenger seat before pulling my seatbelt across me. I leaned back in the chair and saw Mitchell come over.

"I will see you later, Luce," he said, shutting my door, and Tyson nodded to him before climbing in the car and starting it.

"Why didn't you mindlink me to come to get you?" he asked, reversing out of the driveway.

"I fell asleep."

"I would prefer it if you didn't fall asleep in another man's bed, though," Tyson said.

"I'm sorry, I didn't realize how tired I was," I told him.

"It's fine, Lucy. I am not mad. I know everything must be confusing for you, and Mitchell isn't as bad as I thought. At least he rang me," Tyson said, pulling onto the highway.

"Ace?" I asked, and he growled.

"Feeling sorry for himself," Tyson said, and I nodded, resting my head on the window.

When we got home, the house was dark, no lights were on inside, and I hoped that meant Ace was asleep. Tyson parked his car before hopping out, and I followed him to the front door and watched as he unlocked it, pushing it open for me.

I yawned, wanting to go back to sleep, but I also knew Tyson wouldn't like smelling Mitchell all over me, so I walked back to his room, grabbing a towel from the linen cupboard on the way to his room.

"I will get you some clothes," Tyson said as I stepped into the bathroom, flicking on the light. I turned the shower on, waiting for the water to heat up. Tyson knocked on the door.

"Clothes, Lucy," he said, and I opened the door.

"Why didn't you just come in?" I asked him.

"Because I didn't know if I was allowed."

"You're my mate, and it's just skin Tyson," I told him, stripping off, but he looked away, turning his back to me.

"You are so much like your mother," he muttered.

"You have seen me naked before Tyson, geez."

"Yes, before you knew we were your mates, Lucy. Tyrant wants to claim you. I just don't want to be put in a situation where he might when you don't want to be marked yet."

I hopped in the shower, wetting my hair before grabbing the soap and washing myself, ridding my skin of Mitchell's scent.

Tyson remained near the door until I finished showering and talking about random things. Getting out, I dried myself and slipped on his shirt and some shorts.

"I'm decent," I told him, and he turned around while I rolled my eyes at him.

"Are you sleeping in here?" Tyson asked.

"I wouldn't have come in here if I wasn't planning too. And Ace won't come in here with you with me," I told him.

"He would, but I wouldn't let him mark you." I nodded before stepping past him and into the room.

I climbed onto his bed, getting comfortable before he changed quickly and climbed into bed with me.

I rolled over, resting my head on his bare chest, and he reached over, flicking the lamp off. The slightly open bathroom door allows light to filter in.

"What do you want, Lucy?" Tyson asked, his fingers playing with my hair.

"I want things to go back to normal."

"What is your idea of normal?"

I wasn't sure anymore either. "Back to before when I used to come back for the holidays."

"Before you knew we were your mates, before Mr. Tanner?" Tyson asked. I nodded, and he sighed.

"You know that's not possible. I don't want to be your friend, Lucy. Tyrant wouldn't let me even if I tried. You are mine and Ace's, just as I am yours, but I can wait," he said.

I didn't say anything, but at least I knew I was safe with Tyson.

Chapter 23

Ace

I COULD HEAR THEM TALKING, and it infuriated me to listen to their banter before the room fell silent. I was sick and tired of being compared to Tyson. Ever since we took over this pack, it had always been a competition, but it wasn't supposed to be like this with her. She belonged to both of us, yet he would toss me away from her, and that pissed me off. We agreed that we would share her. *Share, not one keeps her for himself.* It made me wonder if it had been his plan all along, but I knew that was just my jealousy talking.

I sat staring at the ceiling. I wanted to be with her, wanted to apologize, wanted to make up for what I had done, but I couldn't if she wouldn't let me near her. Atticus was frantic at the thought of losing his mate, frantic that she would reject us again. I was restless, and she was so close yet so far out of reach for me right now.

"Will you stop that?" Tyson's voice said, flitting through my head.

"Stop what?" I asked, annoyed. *I was staying away, like he'd wanted.*

"The scratching," he snapped at me. I looked down at my hands, not realizing my claws had slipped out, and I was tearing apart the side of my bed.

"Sorry. I didn't realize," I told him.

"Are you okay or not?"

"Like you care. What do you think?" I told him.

"She is asleep. You can come in but don't wake her. And you try anything…"

"I won't. Atticus is annoying me."

"I mean it, Ace. You try to mark her, I will lose it. You can come in, but hop out before she wakes," Tyson told me.

"I won't. I just want to be close to her," I told him, already climbing out of bed. I opened my bedroom door before creeping down the hall, creeping around my own damn house, but I felt better knowing Tyson still wanted me to be her mate. It put me at ease a little that he wasn't trying to shove me out.

"He is our twin," Atticus told me, making me realize how silly my jealousy was. He was just protective of her, we both are. Only I was the one that fucked up.

I pushed open his bedroom door, and he was watching TV. Lucy was asleep with her head on his chest. He pulled her closer, giving me room on the bed so I could lie beside her.

"Don't wake her. She will be pissed off," Tyson mindlinked, and I nodded before carefully lying down beside her. I shuffled closer to her, draping my arm over her waist. I buried my face in her hair, inhaling her scent. My wolf instantly relaxed, and so did I.

"If she accepts us, we will have to get a bigger bed. No offense bro, but I don't want you touching me," he said, and I chuckled, and she stirred. I froze, and Tyson did too before looking down at her. She rolled, both of us frozen before she turned into me. I knew she was reacting to the bond and not me, but I liked it all the same as she snuggled closer.

Tyson flicked the TV off before snuggling closer to her.

"Fine, you can stay. But if she wakes up and is angry, you are taking the blame."

"Deal." I replied, kissing her head and pulling her closer to my chest.

Lucy

Waking up, I was surrounded by warmth. Sparks rushed everywhere, all over my body, and I stiffened when I picked up Ace's scent. My hand darted to my neck, and I let out a breath of relief when I realized he hadn't marked me while I was asleep. I stared at him. Besides their scents, the only difference between them was Ace had a scar through his eyebrow and across his eyelid while Tyson's face was scar-free. Though Tyson had a rather large cut across his inner thigh from taking on a bear when we were camping when I was a kid. It had stumbled into our camp, trying to get in our tent.

It woke us up when it clawed through the canvas, and he barely had time to shift before it dragged him out. Poor thing was hungry. Tyson fought it off and scared it away, yet it tore into his thigh pretty badly, and I had to hold his thigh together while it healed, leaving the scar, while Ace went to get Ryker. I ran my fingers down his eyelid tracing the scar with my finger. His eyes instantly flew open at my touch.

"I'm sorry," he whispered, gripping my hand. He kissed my fingertips before holding them to his chest. "I know you hate me. I know I shouldn't be in here, but Atticus was restless," he said, closing his eyes again and going back to sleep.

"I am not forgiving you, Ace," I told him.

"Just don't reject me. I can live with you hating me, but don't reject me," he said. Now that I had calmed down and wasn't so emotional, I didn't think I could even if I wanted to. I still hated him, yet some part of me all along knew they were mine. I just didn't know it without my wolf. I didn't say anything, knowing I was too hot-headed to promise anything, but I knew I would stick with it when I truly decided. I felt movement behind me and looked over my shoulder just as Tyson sat looking over at us.

"Everything good?" he asked worriedly, and I knew he thought I would be losing it at Ace being there.

"You knew he was in here, didn't you?" Tyson looked away guiltily. I watched his Adam's apple bob as he swallowed.

"Yes, Lucy. I said he could come in, I won't lie to you," he said, resting his chin on my shoulder.

"He is my brother and your mate," Tyson said, looking at his brother. I felt bad because I knew I was coming between them. They were always inseparable, we all were growing up. It saddened me that it would never be like that again.

"You don't seem mad?" Ace said, drawing my attention back to him.

"Give me a chance to wake up. I am working up to it," I told him, and he chuckled.

"You know you can't stay mad at us long," he said cockily, and I raised an eyebrow at him.

"You have slept with Melana for five years, Ace. Knowing I was your mate," I told him. Just the thought of him being near her was enough to make the anger and hate return. He sighed before nodding.

"I will go then," he said, and I swallowed, feeling bad. *Fuck him! He should feel bad.* He accused me of lying and screwing around.

I didn't know what I wanted. I wanted them, yet my brain was telling me I was being stupid by accepting him, that he would only hurt me again. Yet the bond pulled me the other way, needing him close like they were both my safety blanket.

"Stay. Just a little longer," I told him, wanting to soak up his scent before I had to turn into the heartless bitch I knew I could be again. He laid back down before pulling me closer.

"I have loved you since before I knew you were our mate, Lucy. Melana was just a distraction. She means nothing to me. Never has, never will."

"But you picked her side over mine."

"I was angry. I thought you lied about being a virgin. Then Melana said all that, and it pissed me off. I should never have doubted you," he said.

"Even if I wasn't a virgin, you have no say in that anyway, after what you did!" I told him angrily. I couldn't believe that he expected me to wait, but he couldn't, knowing full well I was his mate.

"I am sorry. I should have waited like Tyson. But I can't go back and change what I did, Lucy. I can try to make up for it if you let me."

"Tyson waited," I told him, and he nodded, looking at his brother.

"And I won't ask for anything except you not to reject me. Tyson deserves you more than I do. I get that, and I understand if you want to be with him. I won't rush you, and neither will Tyson. But please don't reject me, Lucy."

I knew it was hard for him to apologize, he wasn't one to apologize. Neither of them was, but I felt like an apology just wasn't enough. It wasn't enough for what he had done and to accuse me of being a slut when I was the one hurt. I'd never expected that from him.

"I will leave you two alone. I need to get to work anyway," Ace said, hopping up. I didn't stop him this time. I just needed time to think. Yet that was impossible with both of them around.

"What do you want to do since Ace will handle pack business?" Tyson asked.

"I think I want to go home," I told him, unsure. I needed to face my mother, but I also wanted to see Rayan. I missed my room. I missed my old life. I missed myself.

Chapter 24

We waited for Rayan to finish school, and Tyson told Ryker he would pick him up. I was too chicken to face my mother, but I knew I could do anything with Rayan by my side. Rayan was my go to when shit hit the fan. He never judged me despite what my parents thought. Rayan was quiet, an observer, and my parents didn't realize how much he truly knew, he was smart.

Rayan knew information was the key, and by always playing in the shadows, he saw a lot of things my parents didn't know. But most of all, he saw me, saw me for who I was. He didn't see me as a problem child, didn't see me the way they did. He only saw me as his sister.

"Hey, sis," Rayan said, climbing in the back of Tyson's car. He leaned over from the back seat, wrapping his little arms around my neck, nearly strangling me against my chair, or at least that was what it would look like for anyone looking in the windshield.

I patted his hand before he kissed my cheek. "Are you coming home for a while or just dealing with mom?" he asked, sitting back and clipping his seatbelt in.

"Not sure yet. It depends on mom. Did you get in much trouble covering for me?"

"Eh, don't worry about it. Mom should be fine. Feels terrible for not listening to you." He laughed humorlessly. "Like anyone could get a word in even if she was listening," he said with air quotes.

"What about Dad?"

"Mom and dad have been fighting like cats and dogs. Mom even asked for a divorce. Like that would happen," he said, and he was right. They were mates. Dad would lock her in the house under guard if she tried to leave him, not that she would. Mom had a tendency to speak before thinking.

"How was school?" I asked him as Tyson pulled onto the highway, heading toward the packhouse.

"Good. I got an A+ on my history paper today." He laughed before rummaging through his backpack and handing me his assignment. I read it and laughed at what it was on.

"Hybrid mutations? Seriously? We have made history books now?" I asked, handing it back to him.

"Yep. It was easy for me seeing as I am partially one and you and mom," he said, and I snorted.

"Don't worry, got another one on the Hybrid Queen. Thinking of asking grandma to come in, be like a show and tell. Can't ask mom. She will probably go into labor from the stress of being in front of everyone or turn up naked. The assignment will change to how to deliver mutation babies," he chuckled.

"She would if you asked. She is always looking for an excuse to come visit. Mom would love it," Tyson added in for the first time.

"So, what's going on with you two and Ace? Sorted this mate's business out yet?" Rayan asked.

"Kind of," I told him, and he leaned forward in his seat, sticking his head between us.

"I'm still punching Ace in the face," he said, and my lips tugged up. Tyson smiled.

"You do that, little prince. I will even pay to watch you smack him one," Tyson said, pulling up out the front. He parked the car, and I stared at the packhouse.

"Want me to come with you?" Tyson asked when I didn't get out.

"Nah, she is good. She's got me," Rayan said, climbing out before coming over to my door and opening it.

"If you want to come home, ring me or mindlink me. I will come to get you."

"It will be fine," I told him, not even believing my own words. Rayan tugged my hand, and I looked at him.

"Come on. You can use me as a shield if she starts throwing shit," my brother told me.

"Yeah, right, like I would do that," I told him, and he shrugged.

"Come on. I am sure Tyson will sneak in tonight anyway," Rayan said, and I raised an eyebrow at my brother.

"What? He used to do it all the time while you were on holiday here. I thought you knew," he said, smiling deviously, and I looked at Tyson, whose face turned a little red.

"Oh. You really did?" I asked, shocked.

"Yeah, used to watch you sleep, not stalkerish at all. It was creepy as fuck," Rayan said.

"If you knew, why didn't you say anything?" Tyson asked him.

"I knew you wouldn't hurt her. Besides, she would have freaked out if I said anything." Rayan shrugged.

"How long have you known?" Tyson asked.

"A few years. I thought it was odd but figured you had your reasons. At first, I thought about saying something, but she always slept better and wouldn't be screaming in her sleep about the shit they did to her in the facility, and I thought you just missed her."

"I did miss her. and just so we're clear, I didn't watch her sleep. That sounds like I am a creep."

"Yeah, because crawling in her bed sounds better?" Rayan teased back before tugging on my hand. I climbed out of the car, a little shocked that my brother was more observant than me. Not that it was surprising.

We waited for Tyson to leave before Rayan led me inside, and we went to the kitchen. He started rummaging through the pantry, bringing out bread while I grabbed ingredients from the fridge, just like we used to do everyday after school when I attended the schools here.

"Pickles?" I asked him, and he nodded as I held up the jar. "Mom still likes chutney?"

"Yeah. She ate a jar the other day with peanut butter," he said, making a disgusted face.

We made sandwiches, and Jacob came in, grabbing one before pecking my cheek. "Lucy," he commented, biting into my sandwich. I started making another before looking up when I heard movement upstairs.

"She was napping," Jacob said. I felt bad for him. He got her worst sides constantly as he was always assigned to watch my mother. I grabbed more bread, smearing peanut butter on it before Jacob nudged me out of the way and smeared more on it before grabbing the chutney and spreading some on it too. He then sent me a wink, and I cut it in half, putting it on a plate. *That is disgusting*, I thought. I was just about to bite into my salad sandwich when mom stepped into the kitchen. I could feel my brother and Jacob watching us while we awkwardly stood there staring at each other.

Chapter 25

"You're home?" she asked, and I nodded before handing her the plated sandwich, her plate of grossness. She took it, placing it on the bench. I flinched and saw Jacob about to move out of his chair before relaxing when she finally hugged me. She wrapped her arms around me, and it felt odd. I couldn't remember the last time she actually touched me while not angry. It took me a second before I hugged her back, patting her back gently. Her huge belly made the hug even more awkward, like hugging someone over a table.

When she let go, she nodded once and grabbed her plate, walking to the table. She would pretend everything was peachy and that she didn't turf me out, and I was okay with that. Better than her wrath. We ate in silence, and Jacob was on his phone, ignoring us or pretending to anyway. When I was done, Rayan tugged my hand, wanting me to follow him. I got up, and my mother spoke.

"Are you staying or going back to your mates?"

"Staying if I am allowed," I answered, and I saw Jacob watching her again, waiting to see what she said. She nodded, and I realized that was the only answer I would get before Rayan tugged my hand. I followed him upstairs and walked to my room when he pulled me toward his. I frowned, wondering why, when he pushed his door open.

"I saved what I could," he said, and I saw one side of his room was full of boxes. He stared at his feet awkwardly.

"When she kicked you out, she went on a rampage and destroyed your room. After I brought you the clothes to school, I came home, and your room was destroyed. This is what is left, and what I could save from the bin," he said.

I walked over to it and saw my sketchbooks and a bag of clothes, plus the school bag that I'd left in the car when I arrived. I rummaged through it, grabbing my wallet, to find my cards gone.

"She cut me off too?" I asked him, and he grabbed his bag to hand me the card that dad used to transfer his allowance. I shook my head.

"No, it's fine," I told him, though it hurt that she would cut me off completely out of everything, knowing I had nothing to begin with.

Rayan pulled out the trundle under his bed while I rummaged through to see what else was in my bag. I found my school books and my make-up bag, but my heart sank when I didn't find my pills, until Rayan rummaged in his underwear drawer before tossing me the bottle.

"Was worried mom would come in and rummage through your stuff and throw them away. Figured you needed those when I found them. Why didn't you tell me you were on antidepressants?" I shrugged. *Not something I would tell anyone anyway.*

"I can give you some money to get more. I noticed you were nearly out," he said, but I shook my head.

"It's fine. I will ask the pack doctor at Tyson's pack. He will get them for me. I don't want mom knowing, and she will ask questions if I go to our doctor's anyway." Rayan nodded before placing his hands on his hips.

"Oh, and by the way, I threw out your dirty box of secrets. No way I was salvaging those for you, but I got rid of them before mom saw them. You owe me big for that one. Some things I don't need to know about you, sis."

"What box of secrets?" I asked him.

"They are the buzzing type that live in your panties drawer," he said before gagging. I laughed and threw his pillow at him before sitting on his bed.

"So, what are you going to do then? You have no school, or are you thinking of going back?"

"I don't think I have a choice. I will enroll tomorrow at the high school across from you. At least I can finish the year out and see you during the breaks," I told him, and he nodded.

"I will ask Jacob to enroll you or dad. Probably best if mom doesn't go in, she might tell you not to bother. But you should finish. You are smart, smarter than half the morons at that school," Rayan said. I nodded.

"Only a few months left anyway. I will just coast through the middle and be invisible," I told him, and he chewed his fingernail nervously while nodding. *Yeah, there is no coasting through the middle when you are a freak mutation like me, especially when you have no wolf.*

Rayan helped me set up his room because he wanted me to share it with him. He said he was worried mom would lose it again, and he was right. *I shouldn't get comfortable here, nothing goes right for me even when I try,* and I knew it would only be a matter of time before she found another reason to kick me out.

At dinner time, Rayan and I were playing video games when his bedroom door opened. My stepfather walked in.

"Hey kiddo, come here," he said, and I rushed to him, wrapping my arms around his huge frame. He kissed the top of my head.

"How was mom?" he asked.

"Fine, I saw her earlier," I told him, and he nodded before reaching into his pocket. He handed my keycards back that he must have stopped mom from cutting up. I shook my head.

"Lucy, take them. Please," he said, but I refused.

"Having somewhere to stay is enough," I told him. I wanted nothing from them and was nearly tempted to go live back in the woods just to get away from the guilt and pity in his eyes.

"You will need…"

"Leave her be, Dad. I already tried to give her mine. She doesn't want them," Rayan said. My stepfather pressed his lips in a line but nodded.

"You sort your room out?" he asked, still looking at the boxes.

"Yep. She is staying right here," Rayan said, tapping the trundle next to his bed.

"You do realize your sister is a woman, not a kid, Rayan? Most teens don't want to share with their baby brother," Ryker told him.

"Yeah, but she is my sister, and I have a bathroom to get changed in, nothing weird. You saying that makes it weird," Rayan said. Ryker gave him a look I couldn't decipher but nodded, leaving the room.

"What is up with you?" I asked Rayan. I wasn't used to him talking to our parents like that.

"Nothing. I am just sick of the way everyone picks at you when they know nothing. Sick of them thinking I am some good child while you are the bad one."

"You are a good child," I told him with a laugh.

"Yes. In a sense, but I am sick of everyone thinking you would somehow corrupt me. I am capable of making my own choices.

And I am not staying away from you just because they are worried. You're my sister. You could kill someone, and I would help you bury the body because you would do the same for me," he said, folding his arms across his chest. I smirked. He had a point, but I didn't want him getting in trouble because of me.

Chapter 26

Lucy
THE NEXT DAY

Why did I think this was a good idea? I knew I needed to finish school, but this was torture as I walked the halls to my next class. On the plus side, not one person said anything, but I figured that was more to do with Jacob being with me most of the morning while he helped with my enrollment. I needed an adult to sign my papers, and I wasn't asking my mother or stepfather. I probably could have asked Tyson or Ace, but they would have suggested I go to the one on their territory.

Walking into English, the teacher nodded to the chair up the back of the room, the only seat left. I was happy to be at the back, no one could see me. Pulling out my English book from my last school, I found a blank page. I would need to find a way to get new books as mine were almost full. On the plus side, I wasn't behind in classes because I always used to be in the advanced classes at my boarding school and being in the mainstream classes, I found most of the work I had today I had already done.

During the lunch break, the first thing I did was race across to the park so I could meet Rayan. Sitting on the swings, I waited, hoping they would let him out when someone sat beside me on the other swing. I looked over and saw Jacob.

"You alright?" he asked.

"Yep. Why are you still here?"

"Well, if the prince is leaving to meet you at lunch every day, I kind of need to be here."

"Oh, sorry. I didn't think of that. It is fine. I can tell Rayan not to come out so you can go back to mom," I told him, reaching down to grab my bag.

"It's fine, Luce. It's sometimes good to get away from your mother, and she can survive with Pat for an hour a day," he said, grabbing my hand and stopping me. I nodded, sitting back on the swing, but now I felt terrible, knowing I was once again interrupting everyone else's routine.

Rayan walked out before running across the road. He waved before sitting on the other side of me. Jacob got up, walking to his car before returning with a paper bag. He handed me a sandwich. I took it, looking at him questionably, while Rayan pulled his lunch from his bag.

"Notice you didn't eat this morning or make yourself lunch," Jacob said, giving me a wink.

"Yeah, I could hear mom in the kitchen," I told him. I wasn't avoiding her exactly, but I was trying to stay out of her sight. *Out of sight, out of mind, right?*

"She will calm down once she gets back on her meds. Hopefully. If Ryker can get her back on them," Jacob said, making my brows furrow. Rayan shot him a look.

"What do you mean?" I asked, I never knew my mother was on medication.

"For her wolf," Rayan answered.

"Huh? I don't understand," I told him.

"Dad didn't want you to know. Amanda is unstable. Always has been, but apparently, after I was born, mom was put on medication. She has been off her meds for two years now. Dad has been trying to convince her to go back on them, but Amanda guilts him out of it. Don't tell dad you know. Jacob wasn't meant to tell you," Rayan said. Come to think of it, she had changed over the last couple of years, turned distant, and then we started clashing majorly.

"Why is it a secret?" I asked. *Why would they hide this from me? Was I not trusted with this information?*

"Doesn't matter, Lucy, just forget he said anything," Rayan said, glaring at Jacob, who shrugged.

"What do you mean that Amanda is unstable?"

"She isn't controllable. The doc said it is to do with PTSD from being raised in captivity and everything that happened after she escaped," Jacob said.

"I still don't get why this is a secret? One kept from me."

Rayan frowned. "It doesn't matter, Lucy. Just drop it," he said, tearing off a piece of his sandwich and eating it. I was always going to be an outsider. The fact they wouldn't tell me was just another reason I would never be comfortable here. We ate in silence and chatted about classes until the bell rang, and I had to go back to class.

The first day was horrid. No one spoke to me, yet I heard the whispers and snickering about being a mutated freak, but I shrugged the comments off. They were not game enough to say it to my face, so they weren't worth my time. Jacob picked us both up from school and dropped us home before going to tend to my mother. All day, my mind tried to guess why I wasn't allowed to know about mom.

I was sitting on the floor in Rayan's room, helping him do his homework, when my father called out from downstairs. We both looked up before realizing he had to be calling us to dinner.

"Come on. We can eat in the room," Rayan said as we both hopped up. We walked downstairs to grab our dinner when my stepfather called out from the dining table.

"No! At the table. I am sick of you both hiding in the room," he said, and we both turned, walking to the table. Dinner was silent, and I could tell my stepfather was in a bad mood.

"How was school?" he asked. I nodded, stuffing pasta in my mouth to find my mother staring at me. I put my head down, focusing on my food, yet I could feel her gaze on me.

"You enrolled back at school?" she asked.

"Yes, I need to finish," I told her, and I was surprised at how weak I sounded.

"Why?" she asked, and her words shocked me, making me look up at her.

"Because I am nearly finished. I only have three months left before graduation," I told her. She didn't say anything, but I could see my father watching her. She also noticed his gaze, and she looked away back down at her food. This was so awkward. I could feel the tension sizzling.

"How was work?" I asked my father, trying to make small talk. I wasn't good at this shit. I wasn't good at being forced to sit at a table with my family. I was used to holiday breaks where I could get away with huge family gatherings and go unseen, or just stay with my aunts, or Ace and Tyson.

"Do you actually care?" my mother asked, and I clenched my fork, a lump forming in my throat. *Why would she say that?*

"Work was fine, Lucy," my father said, and I heard my mother growl at him, making my eyes dart to her. She had a feral look on her face. Rayan was watching her but looked back at his plate, eating quicker, and I did the same before asking if I could be excused. My father nodded to both Rayan and me, and we escaped back to our room. I grabbed a towel and my pajamas before heading to the bathroom attached to his room to shower.

While in the shower, I felt the mindlink open up.

"How's home?" Tyson asked before I felt Ace also force the link through.

"It's fine," I replied.

"You can always come home to us," Ace said.

"No, I want to be near Rayan. And mom is due any day now, so I am sure she will need help with Rayan," I told them, though Rayan was more than capable of looking after himself.

"Why are you avoiding us?" Tyson asked.

"I'm not. I will come and stay on the weekend, if you want," I told them, knowing it was hard for their wolves to be away from their mate. I don't have that issue, but I did miss them. I was more comfortable with them than being here, but I just couldn't wrap my head around being their mate. Plus, I was worried Ace would run back to Melana. I didn't know how they kept it secret for so long while waiting for me to grow up. It kind of made me feel guilty.

"Please, make sure you do. I miss you, Lucy," Tyson said, and I nodded before cutting the link off. I finished my shower before brushing my teeth and grabbing a glass of water to swallow my pills. Looking into the bottle, I only had one left. Rayan had a mini-fridge in his room with drinks and snacks. Besides having to go downstairs for the main meals, we could just stay in the room.

Chapter 27

Tyson

"Do you think this is her way of rejecting us without rejecting us?" Ace asked me after she cut off the mindlink.

I had no idea what was going on with her anymore. She was always so guarded, always putting on a front, and it was hard to get her to drop it. She didn't need to hide from us, we would love her anyway.

"She said she would come to see us on the weekend," I told him, and he nodded, sipping his beer. I wanted to give her space, but it was killing me, knowing she now knew what we were to her. Now she knew it made the time away from her a bigger struggle. It was easier when she was oblivious to the bond because I used that as an excuse to remain calm, reminding myself she didn't know. But now she did, and it was eating away at me and Tyrant that she kept her distance.

The next three days went by quickly, and I was becoming fed up. She said she wasn't avoiding us, yet she always blocked us out or made excuses. I was about to mindlink her when I felt Rayan force the link instead, opening it up to me.

"Hey, buddy, what's up?" I asked him.

"Nothing, but can you do something for me?"

"Depends. Why aren't you asking Jacob or your father?"

"Lucy doesn't want them to know. She keeps saying she was going to ask you, but I noticed she hasn't, and I am tired of her keeping me up at night."

"What do you mean?"

"Doesn't matter, but can you meet at school today? I will sneak out early," he said.

"Fine. Text me what time, and I will be there. Is Lucy okay?" I asked him.

"Lucy is coping," he said.

For some reason, that wasn't the answer I was hoping for. What the heck did he mean by it? Before I could ask, he closed the link before I got a text message telling me where to meet him. I kept mindlinking her all day, but she always said she was busy, making me wonder what she was busy doing?

"Ace, I am going to meet Rayan. Do you want to come?" I asked him. I heard him grab his keys before walking toward me.

"I'm driving," he said, and I growled. He drove like a maniac. I hated it when he drove but followed after him anyway. We arrived at the school, and Rayan was waiting in the park across the road.

"How do you get out all the time?" I asked him.

"Alpha's son has its perks," he said before handing me something. I looked at them and found them to be antidepressants.

"Lucy ran out two days ago. She won't go to the pack doctor to get more because she's worried mom would find out. I would have gotten them for her, but the pharmacist isn't going to give me a class A drug, seeing I am just a kid," he said, and I could tell it irked him that he couldn't sway a doctor to his will.

"Okay, I will get them for her," Ace said, grabbing the bottle from my hands before pulling his phone out to ring the pack doctor, as he walked back to the car.

"What did you mean earlier, when you said she was coping?"

"That every night she is awoken by nightmares. I usually end up jammed on the trundle with her, and I noticed she has a tendency to sleepwalk without her meds. Probably not the best thing when mom is off her meds," Rayan said.

"Your dad still had no luck?" I asked him, and he shook his head.

"Jacob told Lucy she was on medication," he said.

"Lucy is her daughter. She has the right to know," I told him.

"Yeah, but if she finds out she is the reason why mom went off the deep end, I worry for Lucy. She isn't in the best place."

"What do you mean?" I asked him, confused.

"Nothing. It's just… Amanda, she was always nuts. It doesn't matter. Can you bring her pills tomorrow, please?" he said, yawning. "I better go, I have to meet Lucy soon, and I don't want her to know I gave you those. She would be embarrassed."

"She is coming to meet you?" I asked him.

"Yeah, she goes to school across the road. Didn't she tell you?" he asked, and I looked at the high school.

"No. She didn't," I told him before nodding. I wondered why she kept that from us.

"I will see you tomorrow. Maybe you can stay at ours on the weekend? Lucy might actually come over if she knows you will be there," I told him, and he nodded.

"Sounds good," he said as the bells rang. He ushered us to leave, and I saw Jacobs's car pull up as we were reversing out of the parking lot. He waved, looking confused, before sitting on the swing beside Rayan.

"I have a feeling there is a lot we don't know," Ace said, and I had to agree. We stopped and picked up Lucy's medication on the way home.

For the majority of the night, I tried to get a hold of her, but once again, she shoved us out after a few words. When it hit midnight though, I could sense Rayan was up. The buzz of the teether when I reached out to him was alert before I pushed forward.

"Why are you up?" I asked him.

"Lucy's sleepwalking again. Did you get her pills?"

"Yeah., I will come over," I told him. He was silent, and I could tell he was trying to figure out whether to agree or not.

"Dad is trying to walk her back to bed without waking her. She attacked me last night when I accidentally woke her up, trying to get her back to her room," he said.

"Be there soon," I told him, cutting the link. She never sleep walked when here. It made me wonder if she was stressed being back home. It took me twenty minutes to get there, but Ryker was waiting out the front. Rayan must have told him.

"Finally. You're here. I need to go to bed. Don't wake her, she isn't lucid when you do," Ryker said, yawning.

"Where is she?"

"Back in bed. I got her to lie back down, but for how long, I don't know. Between her and Reika, I am exhausted, and so is Rayan," he said, pushing the door open wider. I walked in, heading for her room when Ryker pointed at Rayans. It was the old room I shared with Ace when I lived here.

"Don't ask," he said, walking upstairs to his room. I stepped inside to find her asleep on the trundle. Rayan yawned, and I placed the bottle of pills on his bedside table before lying down next to her.

"You told your father," I whispered.

"Not about the pills. He helped me yesterday when Lucy freaked when I woke her," he said, fluffing his pillow. I tucked the blanket up around her, and she rolled over, picking up my scent. Even in her sleep, her heart was racing. Her hands went underneath my shirt, seeking the bond, so I pulled it off before tucking her against me. Her heart rate slowed, and her breathing evened out. Tyrant relaxed inside me, finding her closeness soothing.

"I want her home. Where she belongs," Tyrant told me, his longing and sadness slipping into me despite her being in my arms.

"I love you, Lucy," I whispered to her, kissing her forehead. But she remained asleep, and I snuggled closer, enjoying the warmth her skin provided.

Chapter 28

Lucy

I woke up and instantly knew I was not alone in my bed. Tingles spreading everywhere, and Tyson's scent filling my senses. I moved, pressing my face into his neck and inhaling his scent. How I missed his scent. Missed him being close. He felt like home.

"Lucy, we have to get ready for school," Rayan whispered, shaking my shoulder. I looked up to see him dressed before moving away from Tyson.

"When did he get here?" I whispered, not wanting to wake him.

"Last night. You were sleepwalking again," Rayan said and sighed. Usually, I just climbed in with Rayan, but now I was starting to worry it was disturbing him.

Rayan tossed me a bottle, and I saw my medication, but the bottle was full.

"Tyson?"

"Ace," Rayan told me, and I nodded.

I quickly grabbed my uniform, changed, and rushed downstairs. The kitchen was quiet, and I decided to risk making lunch. Walking out, I froze when I saw my mother.

"Morning," she said, all chirpy.

"Morning, mom," I said when she suddenly walked over and hugged me. I stiffened and saw Jacob watching her before she let go.

"I made your lunch. Rayan, come grab your lunch," she called, turning and flicking the kettle on.

"Coffee?" she asked, and I looked at Jacob, who shrugged before sliding into the stool.

"Morning, mom," Rayan said, handing me a paper bag with my lunch. *She actually packed me lunch.*

"It's not peanut butter and chutney, is it?" I asked, and she laughed.

"No. A salad sandwich and some fruit," she said, passing me a mug of coffee.

I sipped it, wondering why she was being nice. She almost seemed normal, like when I was a kid.

"Can you wake Tyson up later?" I mindlinked Jacob. I saw him nod out of the corner of my eye.

I watched my mother as she cleaned the kitchen, her giant belly getting in her way. She smiled, rubbing it, as she wiped the bench near me before stopping.

"Wanna feel it?" she asked, looking at me. I looked at it and saw her beaming down at me before she grabbed my hand, placing it on her belly. Her belly was hard before I felt a kick. I smiled, knowing it was my baby brother.

"Picked a name yet?" I asked.

"Hmm…" she hummed, and I placed my other hand on her belly, liking the feel of my brother moving around in her. I loved rubbing my mom's belly when she was pregnant with Rayan.

"I like Ryden," she said, and I nodded. I felt him kick again and smiled, looking at Rayan. "Feel, Rayan," I whispered to him, but he was staring at my mother oddly, not taking his eyes off her. I smiled up at her before it slipped off my face, and I jerked my hands away from her, when I saw her glaring at me. I swallowed, and she growled before looking at Rayan.

"Time for school, son," she said, looking at Rayan, and I recognized the change in her voice instantly as her wolf, Amanda. Jacob hopped up, and so did I, grabbing my bag. Rayan grabbed my hand, tugging me with him, and mom grabbed his face giving him a kiss before turning away from me.

"Love you, mom," I told her, but she said nothing. I swallowed, walking out after Jacob and Rayan.

"Don't take it personally, Lucy. She doesn't mean it." Yet she didn't look at Rayan like that.

Jacob took us to school. My day was fine until I bumped into a boy in the hallway. I had avoided everyone's radar all day until then. I knocked him down by accident, not seeing him as I turned the corner. I offered my hand to help him up and apologize, but he slapped my hand away. He stood, his blond hair falling in his eyes before he growled at me.

"Must suck being the bastard of the Hybrid Queen," he said. I ignored him, about to walk past him when he grabbed my arm, shoving me into the locker.

"What? Nothing to say, Lucy? Or do you only answer to the teachers you fuck?" he said so loudly that the students around overheard and laughed.

"Whatever," I told him, wondering how the hell that rumor got around the school.

"Josie said you fucked half the teachers there. Is that why your grades are so high in English? You sucking off Mr. Clay too?" he asked. *That's why he was being a prick.* I remembered him as the kid that glared at me when I scored higher on the pop quiz. I clenched my fist and willed myself not to react, about to walk off.

"You fucking the principal? Is that why they let you back in?" he asked. I saw red, my gums tingling before I punched him. His head snapped back, blood spurting from his nose, and he shrieked just as the deputy walked around the corner. *Fuck! Why didn't you just ignore him?* I mentally scolded myself.

"Lucy Black, my office! Now!" she shrieked. I sighed, grabbing my bag, and he smirked, knowing I was getting in trouble. Not like I actually hurt him, it would heal instantly anyway. I hoped it would heal crooked. I smiled at that before trudging to the office.

"Not even a week, and you are already in trouble."

"He was picking on me," I told her, sitting down when she pulled a chair out, telling me to sit.

"Words can't harm you. You overreacted. Now, I need to call your mother Lucy. This will be a suspension," I groaned.

"What about him?"

"Did he hit you?" she asked, peering at me over her glasses.

"No!" I sulked.

"What did he say then that would deserve a smack?" I didn't bother telling her, instead folding my arms across my chest. The last thing I needed was for the teachers to start gossiping too. Bad enough Josie spread shit to the kids here. If only Mitchell was there, he wouldn't have been game enough to say shit.

She looked my name up to get my mother's details.

"You're not living at home, Lucy?" she asked, and I furrowed my brows.

"Pardon?" I asked.

"You have Jacob and Ace listed as your contacts."

I smiled, hoping she would call Jacob, then I wouldn't have to worry about my mother.

"Go sit in the hall while I call your guardians," she said, and I snatched my bag off the floor, storming out.

I was sitting in the corridor when Jacob mindlinked me.

"Lucy, what did you do? I can't come in. Your mother has gone into labor." I perked up at the news.

"Really?" I asked excitedly. I was about to grab my bag and rush out of the school to meet her at the pack hospital.

"I will go get Rayan," I told him.

"Ryker already did. But I can't come till he gets here," Jacob said.

"Rayan is already on his way to you?" I asked.

He paused. "I will come to get you when I can," he said.

"Okay, let me know how mom is. I could walk home if you told the school. Then I could ride my bike over to the hospital," I told him, wanting to meet my new little brother.

"Maybe it's best if you don't. Amanda has control, Luce. I will send Ace," he said before cutting the link. My mother didn't want me to come. Jacob was just too nice to say it outright. It stung.

I grabbed my history book and started reading my notes. I didn't know how long I stayed there before I heard footsteps and looked up to see Ace walking down the corridor. He stopped in front of me, and I looked up at him.

"Come on," he said, holding his hand out. I took it, and he walked me into the office to sign me out, and the deputy principal came over to him.

"Jacob said you were picking her up. Lucy will be suspended for four days for violence. Can I ask why her mother or father aren't listed in her contacts?"

"Because she doesn't belong to them," Ace said.

"Sorry, I am confused, Ace," she said.

"Alpha Ace. And what happened to the boy who was picking on her?"

"I sent him to class. She broke his nose."

Ace smirked, looking down at me. "And?" Ace asked her, and she looked confused.

"I am not sure I know what you are saying, Alpha."

"She broke his nose, but what punishment does he get?"

"I think a broken nose is punishment enough, Alpha," Mrs. Geld told him.

Ace turned to me and bit his lip. This was so embarrassing.

"Next time, Lucy, break his jaw. And if he still doesn't stop, I will remove his tongue for you," Ace said before glaring at the deputy.

"Alpha, I am afraid I can't have you threatening students. If it continues, I will have to bar you from school grounds," she said, but I heard her voice get softer and softer as she continued to speak, looking away from him.

"Do you think your Alpha would tolerate someone speaking shit about his Luna?" Ace asked her.

"She may be the Alpha's step-daughter, but she is still a student here, and we don't condone violence, Alpha."

"No, but a student talking shit and slandering her name is okay. Now, if Ryker heard someone talking about his Luna like that, student or not, what would he do?"

She swallowed. "But Lucy has no title, Alpha."

Oh my god, he wouldn't? Judging by the smirk on his face, he would. And, he did.

"See, that is where you are wrong, Tina. Lucy has got a title because she is my mate. Therefore, my Luna," he told her, and his eyes darted to me.

She went to say something, but he growled, and she bared her neck to him before nodding.

Ace then grabbed my hand, signing the book before shoving the door open and pulling me out after him.

"How did you know?"

"I mindlinked Mitchell to ask what happened. He saw it, but you ran off before he could get to you," Ace said, squeezing my fingers. "He wouldn't tell me his name, though," Ace said, but I shook my head.

"Lucy?" Ace said, but I ignored him. "If you wanted to go to school, why didn't you tell us? This wouldn't be an issue at our pack school."

"I don't want people to be nice because of who I am mated with, Ace," I told him. He sighed, tugging me closer and draping his arm across my shoulders before kissing my head.

"Looks like I will get you for a few days," he said, and I looked up to say no. "What excuse you got this time? You won't be busy," he said, and I closed my mouth before nodding.

"Mom is in labor," I told him.

"I know. Ryker rang this morning when he was picking up Rayan, and asked if you could stay with us," he said. *Was I the only one that didn't know?*

And why couldn't I go home just because Amanda was out? We walked out to his car in the staff parking lot. I groaned when I saw Tyson leaning against Ace's car. He looked like the god he was. Well, both of them did, though, Tyson was wearing a white shirt with jeans while Ace wore a black one, both drool-worthy, and I found myself excited to go with them, especially after this morning and mom's weird mood.

"Not happy with you. Jacob woke me up. Why didn't you wake me? I would have taken you to school."

I shrugged.

"Come on, then. We will run you home to grab some stuff, then you are staying with us for a few days," Tyson said, and I nodded before opening the back door and climbing in.

Chapter 29

I couldn't remain still. Rayan had sneakily left the mindlink open to me so he could tell me what was going on. He also confessed he didn't tell me straight away because dad and mom were watching him like a hawk. I didn't get it, and Rayan didn't either. Neither of us could understand why I wasn't allowed to come.

"I don't get Amanda anymore. She is different and doesn't even want me here. They nearly had to sedate mom to get her to the pack hospital," Rayan told me.

Mom hated the hospital, I knew that much. She refused doctors or anyone in a lab coat. "Let me know when she has him," I told him.

"Of course, Lucy. You will be the first person I tell," he said, just as excited, but I could hear his worry.

"I will let you go. It has been hours, and you must be getting tired, holding the link open for so long," I told him.

"Okay, I will mindlink as soon as I know what's going on," he said before cutting the link.

"No baby still?" Ace asked, watching me pace. I shook my head.

"Lucy, sit down. Rest for a bit," Ace said, patting the spot next to him. I looked at him.

"Lucy, come sit. Sitting down with me doesn't mean you have to forgive me. Just rest. Rayan will tell you when your brother is born," Ace said just as Tyson walked out of his bedroom, his hair still wet from having a shower.

"Any news?" Tyson asked, though I couldn't tear my eyes away from his exposed chest, abs and the deep V-line that escaped into the waistband of his sweatpants.

"Lucy?" Tyson said, and I shook my head.

"What?" I asked.

"I said, is there any news?"

I shook my head, looking away from him to find Ace smirking at me before he shook his head. My cheeks flushed, knowing he'd just busted me checking his brother out, while Tyson seemed oblivious, thank god.

"Hungry? What do you want to eat?" Tyson asked, walking past me and into the kitchen.

"Pretty sure she wants to eat you," Ace said, and I turned to glare at Ace. "What? You were the one eyeing him like he was a piece of meat," Ace said before shrugging.

My face got hotter with embarrassment.

"Leave her alone, Ace." Tyson snapped at him behind me, and Ace growled at him. I watched his eyes glaze over and knew Tyson was probably arguing with him through the link. I sat down on the couch before grabbing my bag and rummaging through it for my pills. I had to take them with food, so it would be best to take them now since Tyson was cooking.

Finding them, I got up and grabbed a bottle of water from the fridge before taking it. Tyson eyed me, and I sat up on the counter, watching him get ingredients to make whatever it was he was making.

"How long have you been on those?" Tyson asked, looking at the bottle.

"Um.. since I went to boarding school," I told him.

"So, you have been taking them for six years?" he asked, and I shrugged. I heard movement behind me before looking over and seeing Ace lean on the counter behind me. He grabbed the bottle, looking at them.

"These are mood stabilizers and sedatives. Who would give these to a twelve-year-old without parental permission?" Ace asked.

"You forget, the moment I went to school, my parents signed guardianship over to the school. Avery took me," I told him.

"Avery did?" Tyson asked.

"Well, she does own the school, and she said it would get worse. Said they would help."

"What would get worse?" Ace asked, and I shrugged, trying to find a way to explain it.

"The pain. It's hard to explain. It wasn't really pain, just debilitating, I don't know. Anyway, I started sleepwalking, and my bloodlust got worse because of it. I attacked Aamon one night. Demons do not taste very nice," I told them.

"You bit Aamon?" Ace said before chuckling.

"Yeah, apparently I was sleepwalking. He woke me, not realizing. Anyway, I came to with my teeth in his arm. He tasted burned," I told him, remembering the gross taste. I shook the memory away.

"Speaking of bloodlust, when did you last feed?" Tyson asked, while Ace seemed deep in thought for a second as he scratched his face.

"Two days ago. Mom doesn't keep blood in the house."

"Yeah, because your parents feed on each other. Who did you feed off then?" I bit my lip, not wanting to say.

"Rayan?"

I shook my head.

"Who then? Better not have been Mitchell." Tyson growled.

"No, it wasn't Mitchel. It was Jacob," I told them, and I saw Tyson's eyes flicker.

"Don't look at me like that, Tyson. Either that or I would have to go catch poor Bugsy."

"You could have called one of us," Tyson said, but Ace was still staring at the pills.

"You have been on these since you were twelve?" Ace said, his brows furrowing.

"Yes. I said that," I told him, turning back to face a pissed-off Tyson, who was now staring at his brother.

"What is it?" Tyson asked him when Ace stood up.

"Nothing. I will be back tomorrow," Ace said, pocketing my pills.

"Wait, where are you going?" I asked as he grabbed his jacket, pulling it on before reaching over the counter next to me. He grabbed his keys from the fruit bowl before pecking my lips. I jerked away from him.

"Shit. Sorry, Lucy," he said, shaking his head, realizing what he had done. "I will see you tomorrow," he said, walking toward the door.

"Ace, where are you going?" Tyson called after him.

"To see Avery," he said, walking out and not bothering to explain.

"Wait! He took my bloody pills!" I sighed, turning back to Tyson, who was staring at the door.

"He will be back tomorrow. You don't need them until then, anyway."

"Why does he want to see Avery?" I asked him, and he seemed puzzled.

"No idea, but don't change the topic. Why didn't you ring one of us?" I rolled my eyes at him. It wasn't a big deal, Jacob was gay.

"I don't understand why you're upset. Jacob is gay, not like I marked him," I told him.

Chapter 30

"I'm not upset. I just prefer you to drink from blood bags or off us, not some random person," Tyson said before sighing.

"Jacob isn't some random person, Tyson. He is family. I have known him just as long as I have known you," I told him, not seeing the big deal about it.

"That may be so, but if your mother wasn't stocking blood bags, you could have rung. Or why didn't you tell Ryker? He would have made sure there was some there for you," Tyson said, yet I felt like I was intruding by being there, let alone asking for anything.

"It's fine. You just need to feed, Lucy. Do you want to feed on me, or I can go get you a blood bag," Tyson said. My face heated up, but I could see he didn't really like the idea of a blood bag. I didn't think I would be able to bring myself to bite him. It was one thing in the forest, I was ravenous. But now, being faced with it, I suddenly felt embarrassed that I was a vampire. I felt dirty for needing blood.

"Stay here. I will be back soon. I will grab dinner on the way home," he said, grabbing his keys and pulling a hoodie on. He walked out, and I jumped off the bench, putting everything he pulled out away and doing the few dishes in the sink. I walked into the living room and changed the channel. I watched TV and waited for him to return. I tried to mindlink Rayan, but I could feel he was asleep because the link was dead, and I couldn't force it as he could.

Feeling for Ryker, I pushed on the link before he opened it.

"Hey, Luce," he said, yet he sounded exhausted.

"How is mom?" I asked him.

"Sedated. They are taking her in for a C-section soon."

"Is everything alright?" I asked, worried.

"Yes, she isn't coping with the doctors. I will come to get you tomorrow and bring you home to meet your brother," he said, and I fell silent. I was excited about meeting my new brother and seeing Rayan's face knowing he was now a big brother. Yet I felt left out.

"Dad?"

"I know you have questions, Lucy. Your mother is sick. I will come to see you tomorrow. You deserve answers. Maybe once you have them, you may understand, but it isn't your mother, Lucy. She loves you, but she is unwell, and I can't keep this from you anymore," he told me.

"But is she going to be okay?" I asked him.

"Yes, Lucy. She's not physically sick. All that time in captivity and everything that happened afterward, have taken a toll on her. She is no longer the woman I first met. And please understand, but I may have to hurt her to fix her. So please don't hate me for it."

"What do you mean?" I asked. *What does he mean to hurt her? Why would he need to hurt her?*

"I promise I will explain. Rayan has been pestering me to tell you, but I didn't know how. I will come to get you tomorrow. I love you, Lucy," he said before cutting off the link.

I felt sick. I wanted to know what was going on, yet I was also too scared to ask. *Why was Rayan allowed to know when I wasn't? Why would Rayan keep it from me?* I knew the answer to that though, because Rayan and I had no secrets. So, if he was keeping it from me, it was to protect me. But from what?

Hearing the door open, I looked over the back of the couch to see Tyson walk in with McDonald's. He walked over and placed the food down before coming over. He leans over the couch before wrapping his arms around my shoulders with a blood bag in his hand. He placed it in my hand, and I could feel that it wasn't as cold as it should have been.

I sniffed the air before looking at him.

"This is your blood, isn't it?" He kissed my cheek before walking off back to the kitchen. I punctured a hole in it while Tyson brought dinner over and placed it on the coffee table. A growl escaped me when his blood flooded my mouth. He tasted as good as he smelled! Better even, and I could feel my vision changing, the room turning red.

Tyson sat back, eating his burger, not even fazed by me drinking blood, as if it was a can of Coke I was holding and not his blood. They drank blood too, but they could go without it for months if they wanted to. Their bloodlust was tamed by their wolves when they hunted, and they were only half-vampire. Bloodlust seemed to be a big issue for the females in their bloodline, like his sisters and mother, but the boys picked up more of their father's traits than their mother's.

I drained the bag rather quickly, and Tyson looked at me.

"Do you want more?"

I shook my head, my cheeks heating, and I got up, unable to be in such close proximity to him. I now smelled like him, which was doing strange things to me, making me crave his scent. Tyson pulled me back down on the couch.

"Don't feel embarrassed, Lucy," he said, grabbing the blood bag from my fingers and chucking it on the coffee table before he pulled me closer, wrapping his arm around me and making me lean on him.

"I like that you smell of me. Don't be embarrassed because you like it too. It's okay to want to be with us, Lucy," he said, pressing his lips to my head.

"Don't you find it weird, though? You watched me grow up. Saw all my awkward phases."

"No. You got to see ours too. You're mine. I like knowing everything about you. Why? Is it weird to you?"

"Not really, just everyone will think it's odd," I told him.

"No, they won't. We don't choose our mates, Lucy. And even if we did, I would still choose you. Have Ace and I not shown you, we have always loved you, Lucy? From the moment we found you, we have been attached to you," he said.

"Yeah, but that was the bond. You just didn't realize it," I told him.

"Maybe. But before the bond kicked in, we still could have chosen to be away from you. We could have gone back to our mother. We stayed because we loved you, and your mother and our brother. I think I always knew you were going to be ours, even before we realized it. That is why I waited."

"You were with Tara for a while, though," I told him. She was actually a nice girl. I thought for sure they would have been mates.

"Yes, but it never felt right, so we never did anything. Ace was a dick for not waiting for his mate, but I am glad I did," he told me.

Chapter 31

Ace

I parked out the front of Avery and Aamon's house, it was a cottage-style house. She had three houses, but this was the main one she lived in with Aamon. From the moment I found out Lucy had been on these pills since she was twelve, it had been eating at me. Now that I was standing out the front of the witch hybrid's house, I couldn't bring myself to knock on her door and ask her.

I didn't want to be to blame for her depression, yet Atticus grew silent within me. He wholeheartedly believed we were at fault too. It was too much of a coincidence that we found out she was our mate when she was twelve, and she went on these pills at the same age.

"Do you plan to sit outside and admire the house, or are you casing the joint?" Aamon said, misting beside me and sitting in the passenger seat. I jumped when I heard his voice, the smell of burned almonds filling my nostrils.

"You know you could have just tapped on my window."

"Hey, You are the one out here moping like the little lost pup you are. Avery has made tea. She has been expecting you," Aamon said before disappearing again.

I sighed, tossing my door open before shutting it. The front porch light flickered on, and the gardens came into view. Avery had a green thumb. Being a witch, I suppose she would, but her gardens looked more like an exotic forest as I walked the stone path to the porch. The door was open already, and I walked inside. I could smell burning incense and salt across the entryway.

"Don't break the salt line!" she called out from the kitchen. I stepped over it carefully, walking down the long hallway to the back of the house and passing the dining room and living room.

"Conjured up some bad voodoo the other day. Just a precaution till dad gets here to summon it back to hell for me," she said as I stepped into her huge kitchen.

"Cookie?" she asked, setting them out on the stove. It was so weird seeing her baking. She looked like a normal woman, a housewife. Yet I knew she had the power to end the world if she wanted to. I sat at the island bench on a stool next to Aamon. He suddenly misted before returning with a hot cookie in his hands, Avery smacking him with her tongs.

"You impatient devil spawn!" she snapped at him, and he smiled at her, biting into the cookie. She raised an eyebrow at him, her eyes sparkling back at him before turning to me.

"You are here about Lucy's pills and the teacher." she said, grabbing some cups and making tea. She put some cookies on a plate before setting them down in front of Aamon and me. He instantly grabbed one.

"Share, Aamon." she warned, and I smirked at the demon being scolded by her. He was putty in her hands. It was clear who wore the pants in their relationship. Yet, it was known he was her antidote for her craziness, he had a calming effect on her.

When he first met Avery, my father told me she was crazed with power. Absorbing everything and everyone she could touch until her father, Asmodeus, The Prince of Hell and a gatekeeper, told her she'd punished Aamon enough and brought him back to try to subdue her. It worked, and without Aamon Avalon City might have ceased to exist.

My father was introduced to her when he was a kid. His father came to see her about the hybrids that were hunting people down, then he died and my father took over the pack. He got back in touch with her through my grandfather, Abel, when he went looking for a cure to help Lily control her wolf. He took Ryker with him, and they have been best friends for years now.

"Go on. Ask your questions, Ace. I have known your family too long. Don't be shy," Avery said, placing the tea down in front of me. I picked it up and sipped it. I hated tea. I was more of a coffee drinker. But she made good tea, and I always felt buzzed leaving her place. Making me wonder what she'd put in it.

"Is Lucy on these pills because of me?"

"Not just because of you. She was raised in captivity, Ace. The blame isn't all yours, but did you have a big impact? Yes. Yes, you did."

"How, though? She has no wolf?" I asked, resting my head on my hand.

"You forget she was forced to shift. Her wolf died, or so I thought, yet she still technically shifted. The bond would have kicked in when yours did, Ace. She was just too young to realize it, and to understand it."

"So, she could feel it every time I was with Melana?"

"She couldn't feel it like we do. But yes, she had some sense of it. It caused her pain. She thought it was to do with the experiments from the facility, her bloodlust. I wasn't going to be the one to tell her it was because her mate was fooling around. But that is why I wanted to speak to you. I was glad when I sensed you coming," Avery said.

"Why?"

"Because I noticed something when I saw Lucy the other week. That other issue has been dealt with, by the way. My father has taken great pleasure in torturing him. But back on topic, I don't think Lucy's wolf is dead. I think she is trapped, dormant."

"You think her wolf is dormant? Why would you think that? She should have shifted by now if that was the case," I told her.

"I thought her wolf was dead. There have never been any signs over the years. Well, until I saw her with both of you. Her aura shifted, reacting to you both. Vampire auras are usually black. Hers had always been black until I came to see her. Her aura shifted, changed, reacting to you both, as if her aura had been drawing on you both. When I removed her mark, it turned back to black, but I could see it flickering. Like something was trying to break through. The color her aura changed to I have only seen in hybrids and werewolves."

"I don't get it. What are you saying?"

"I'm saying you and Tyson are bringing something to the surface. And I think it is her wolf. I don't think she died. I think she is comatose inside of her," Avery told me.

CHAPTER 32

Tyson

I LOVED MY SCENT COMING off her skin, Tyrant purring in my head having her here. Though, I was concerned for Ace, wondering what was up with him. He left so quickly, but I knew he would return. So, instead, I just spent time with Lucy.

Rummaging through my DVDs, I found one I knew she'd always liked. A little girlie for my tastes, but she enjoyed it. I popped it in the DVD player before walking out of my room to the kitchen and hearing the microwave ding. The smell of popcorn filled the house before walking back to the room. Lucy stepped out of my bathroom, drying her hair on the towel, and sat on the edge of the bed.

"You don't have to watch it just because I like it. Pick something else. I know you hate this movie," she said.

I shrugged, sitting back and watching her dry her hair before she got up and hung the towel on the bedroom door.

"Dad mindlinked while I was in the shower. They just took mom in for a c-section. He was going in with her, and said he would let me know when he arrives."

I nodded to her, pulling the blanket back for her, and she climbed in before rolling on her side and propping her pillow up.

I placed the popcorn in front of her before molding around her and tugging her closer. She stiffened for a second before relaxing against me, and I kissed her cheek before grabbing some popcorn from the bowl. She pressed play before jamming her feet between my legs, making herself comfortable.

Nothing felt more right than this right here. I watched her, trying to go unnoticed, so she wouldn't think I was some kind of creep. Yet I noticed her stealing glances at me too. She wasn't oblivious to the bond.

My body was definitely not oblivious to the bond, as her ass pressed tightly against my front. Every time she moved, I had to fight back a groan as she rubbed her ass against me. I rolled onto my back, trying to hide how badly her being this close affected me. Yet she sat up, placing the bowl on the bedside table before rolling into me and chucking her leg over me. I swallowed, praying she didn't notice or lift her leg any higher.

Lucy

I snuggled against Tyson, placing my head on his shoulder before pressing my face into his neck. I always felt safe with him. I trusted him, and it felt good knowing he was mine. Knowing I wasn't some mateless freak. Knowing he didn't care that I had no wolf.

"You alright there?" he asked when I pressed my nose against his neck again, inhaling his mouth-watering scent. I also loved the tingling feeling that raced over my skin, and the warm feeling in my belly at his closeness.

"Yep! Never better," I told him, and he turned his face, pressing his lips to my cheek. I moved when he suddenly gripped my knee before pushing it down slightly. And moving over like he was trying to get away from me.

"What?" I asked him. I sat up on my elbow, looking down at him, his cheeks turning slightly red. He turned to look at the movie, I knew he hadn't been watching. "Tyson?"

"Lie back down," he said, and I chewed my lip, wondering why he kept moving away from me.

"I can sleep in the other room if you want," I told him, suddenly feeling like he didn't want me close to him. Maybe I was annoying him when I was inhaling his scent.

"No! Of course I don't want that," he said, tugging me back down. I nestled against him, trying to get comfortable, yet he kept moving away.

"Tyson, just say it if you don't want me in here. You won't hurt my feelings," I said, though that was a lie. I would feel gutted if he asked me to leave, as well as embarrassed at his rejection.

"Lucy, I don't want you to leave," he said, looking away, But I could tell something was wrong with him because he wouldn't meet my eye.

"My body is reacting to you being close. I just don't want you to get the wrong idea," he said.

"Pardon?"

"Lucy, I have an erection, okay? You haven't done anything wrong. I don't want you to leave, but I understand if now you want to," he said, pinching the bridge of his nose and squeezing his eyes shut. He looked ashamed, though I thought it was funny and couldn't stop the laugh from leaving my lips as I tried to stifle it.

"That's why you're moving away from me and wriggling like you have ants in your pants?" I chuckled, lying back down.

"Don't laugh. I didn't want you to think I was some perv Lucy, or feel pressured to do anything."

"Tyson, I have known for like the last hour. I could feel it against my back. Don't be embarrassed. I know how the bond affects you. It affects me the same way," I told him, putting my leg back over his waist. This time he didn't shove it off, instead, he pulled me closer, his hand rubbing my thigh down to my knee. Sparks flew everywhere, and I felt my stomach clench and shiver at his light caress. He chuckled, realizing the bond did affect me.

"We don't have to do anything. I just want to make sure you feel comfortable. I didn't mean to be short with you," Tyson told me.

I nodded against his chest, feeling better knowing he wasn't rejecting me.

"It's fine, Tyson. I thought I was annoying you, and you wanted me to go," I told him, and he sat looking down at me.

"You couldn't annoy me even if you tried. I like having you close, but you can always tell me to go or back off if you are uncomfortable."

"I don't feel uncomfortable with you. You have never done anything to make me feel uncomfortable." I chewed my lip nervously, yet I was too embarrassed to say it outright.

Chapter 33

*W*HAT IF HE SAID no? But if I had to choose between them, I would choose Tyson to mark me first, if he wanted to. Ace, I couldn't trust him, not after everything he did. Not after Melana. But would Tyson hate me if I didn't let Ace mark me?

"What's wrong?" Tyson asked, moving his hand and tugging my lip from between my teeth, making me realize I had actually torn the skin.

"Lucy, you won't hurt my feelings. Just say what you want to say. I can see you are worried about something." I shook my head, suddenly embarrassed.

Why did I have to be so awkward when it came to relationships? Probably because I had never been in one. But still, the thought of him saying no hurt, and I didn't think I could handle that rejection, and then have to go home to deal with my mother's rejection too.

If he said no, I would have to go home, and I didn't want to be stuck there while my family played house. and I was expected to watch them happily and pretend it didn't kill me, knowing I was the unwanted one. The burden on their perfect family, an intruder.

"Lucy?" Tyson chuckled, making my eyes dart to him, his lips tugging up slightly while his thumb brushed my cheek, flaming with my shame.

"I'm worried you will say no," I told him.

"You won't know unless you ask, whatever it is, Lucy. Yet, I don't think I could say no to you," he said, leaning down.

Tyson pressed his forehead against mine, his breath fanning my lips. I squeezed my eyes shut before blurting it out like word vomit.

"I want you to mark me," I told him, and he pulled back.

"You want me to mark you?" he asked, like he was making sure he'd heard me right.

I nodded, licking my lips, unable to form words at the look he gave me. His eyes darted to my lips for a second.

"Why would you think I would say no?" he asked, and I looked away from him, knowing he was going to be angry, when he suddenly sighed, making me turn back to him.

"You don't want Ace to mark you," he said with a groan, and I knew I was right. This would cause issues between them.

"Lucy, he is your mate too," Tyson whispered. "But if you don't want him, that's okay too. But please, give him a chance to make things right before you decide on something permanent. Are you thinking of rejecting him?"

"I don't know. I don't want to, but I will. After what he said and did? I am not sure I can forgive him, Tyson."

"Lucy, if you reject him, it will kill him. Can you just wait a little longer before deciding? Please? If you still want to reject him later, that's fine. That's your choice, but I don't want you to rush into anything. Ace loves you, Lucy. He is a dick, but he would do anything for you."

"Yeah? Like keeping his dick in his pants? Or did he stumble and trip into Melana's vagina? Then he called me a slut and took her word over mine."

"I know what he did, and he made the wrong choices, Lucy. And now, he is paying for all those mistakes. I'm saying you have to forgive, and if you choose not to, I will be fine with you rejecting him. But give him a chance is all I am asking," Tyson said, pushing my hair off my neck. His eyes lingered there for a second before moving back to mine.

"You don't want to mark me unless Ace does, too." I sighed. *Exactly like I thought.*

"I want to mark you, Lucy. I just don't want my marking to sway you over more to reject my brother," he said, running his index finger down my neck, and I shivered. He smiled at my reaction to his touch.

"How about you wait until after your birthday in three weeks to decide, and until then, you can mark me?"

"What if I reject him?" I asked, worried he wouldn't want to mark me, yet I would have marked him.

"I will still mark you, Lucy. You are mine and always will be. No matter what you decide to do about Ace. He is my brother, but you are my mate." His hand moved to the back of my neck. I shivered at the touch of his fingers moving into my hair when he leaned his face closer to mine before hesitating to see if I pulled away.

I didn't. Instead, I closed the distance pressing my lips against his, and his grip tightened. His fingers tangled in my hair, tilting my face up. My lips parted when I felt his tongue run across the seam of my lips, and he groaned before I felt his tongue brush mine.

I wrapped my arms around his neck, tugging him closer as I deepened the kiss, loving how gentle he was. Loving how safe I felt with him. Tyson moved slightly before his arm hooked under my waist. He moved back, leaning against the headboard and pulling me onto him, his lips not leaving mine when I found myself straddling him.

His hands ran up my thighs to my hips, and I could feel his erection beneath me, yet he didn't move. Didn't grind himself against me. Instead, his lips moved down my chin and jaw to my neck, before he pressed a kiss to where his mark should lay, branding my skin.

I pressed myself against him, and I could feel his canines had protruded, yet he didn't sink them into my skin, even though I wanted him too.

"I promise, no matter what you decide, I will mark you. I will always want you," he whispered against my neck before he turned his face offering me his neck.

"You sure?" I asked him. Once I marked him, the only person that could remove it was Avery, if he changed his mind.

"Yes, Lucy. I have waited six years for you. You are all I want and need," he said, cupping my cheek.

"I only want you," he whispered, erasing all doubt, and I nodded. I pressed my lips to his neck, and he exhaled. His body shudders beneath me, and I felt my fangs slip from my gums grazing his skin, aching to be embedded into his skin.

Tyson pulled me closer, and I let out a breath before sinking my teeth into his neck. He shuddered as I felt my teeth push through the layers of tissue and muscle. His blood flooded into my mouth, and he groaned, his hand slipping into my hair before I felt the rush of the bond.

A warm feeling spread over me as I felt the bond snap into place. His emotions rushed into me like a tidal wave, making me gasp, and tears blurred my vision when I felt nothing but love and acceptance, and his own happiness at me marking him. I pulled my teeth from his neck, running my tongue over his mark to seal it.

"I love you, Lucy," he whispered against my collarbone as he pressed his face against me. I pushed his head back so I could see his face.

"I love you too," I told him before pressing my lips to his.

Chapter 34

Waking up to Ryker's voice in my head, I rolled onto my back to find an extra body in the bed, as Ace had curled up beside me, pushing me to the middle of the bed.

"Hey, Lucy. Ryden was born at 00:01 AM last night. Your mom wants to know if you want to come over?" Ryker asked.

"Of course! I can ask Tyson to run me out if you want?" I replied through the link.

"That would be good. I am exhausted."

"How is mom?"

"Good, she has asked for you a few times," he said, and excitement took over at his words. *Maybe I could have my mom back in my life.*

"Okay, I will be over as soon as possible. I will get dressed now," I told him before cutting the link. Sitting up, I wiggled out from between the pair of them without either of them stirring, making me wonder what time Ace had come home during the night.

I shook Tyson's shoulder, and he mumbled something before I leaned down and kissed his cheek. His eyes opened groggily before his lips tugged up slightly.

"Mom had baby Ryden. Can you run me home?" I whispered to him.

He nodded, yawning before tossing the blanket back and standing. He stretched his arms above his head before turning around to point to Ace. His brows furrowed, and it was clear he also wasn't aware Ace had come home during the night.

"When did Ace get back?" he asked, and I shrugged, unsure.

"I woke up, and he was here." I could feel Tyson's nervousness through the bond, and my eyes darted to his neck, where my mark lay on his skin.

"Let me shower first to wake up. Then I will take you to meet your brother," Tyson said before walking to the ensuite. I tried to move off the bed when Ace's arm reached over, grabbing me and pulling me back to him. His eyes opened as he pulled me down to face him.

"What time did you get home?" I asked him.

"Couple of hours ago," he said, closing his eyes again. He buried his face into the crook of my neck.

"Just stay for a few minutes," he whispered when I tried to pull away from him. I sighed, lying there and letting him breathe in my scent. His wolf was purring, making the sound rumble out of him before he cleared his throat, trying to get Atticus to stop.

"Please don't punish my wolf for what I did," Ace finally said as I lay there awkwardly.

"Your wolf could have stopped you from doing the things you did, Ace. He is just as much to blame as you," I told him. Ace shook his head but didn't say anything.

"Can I get up now? I need to get dressed," I told him, and he rolled on his back, releasing me from his grip. I climbed out of bed before rummaging through my bag of clothes. I really needed to buy some more clothes. I was alternating between three pairs of pants, a shirt, a tank top, a jumper, and Tyson's clothes. Crouching on the ground as I pulled out what minimal clothing I had, I pulled Tyson's shirt off before slipping my tank top on.

"Why do you torture us like that?" Ace grumbled, making me look over my shoulder.

"It's just skin," I told him before pulling my jeans on and buttoning them up. I then looked for a hairbrush before realizing I didn't have one here, and settled for tying my hair in a messy bun. Knocking on the bathroom door, I heard Tyson sing out.

"You can come in, Lucy," Tyson said, and I quickly slipped in, grabbing the spare toothbrush from the holder and rinsing my mouth before brushing my teeth. Jumping onto the basin, I turned to face Tyson, who was showering.

"Perv," he said.

I shrugged, not caring in the slightest I was gawking at him. And through the bond, I could tell he wasn't the least bit self-conscious of my gaze, nor did he seem to mind. My eyes roamed over his body as I soaked him in, before nearly choking on my spit and gagging on my toothbrush ,when I saw what lay between his legs.

Tyson chuckles, shaking his head at me. "Bite off more than you can handle, Luce?" He laughed, not even bothering to cover himself as he stood watching my burning face.

"Pretty sure that's more than what most can handle. You must have got all the dick in the family," I told him, rinsing my mouth.

"You can't judge that yet, Lucy. You have only seen him," Ace said from the doorway.

"I was assuming yours would be the same. You are Identical twins, after all."

"Not everything is identical," Ace said, his eyes flickering as he looked me up and down.

Tyson threw the wet loofah at him, and Ace caught it, tossing it in the sink. I handed Tyson a towel, and he shut the water off before wrapping it around his waist and stepping out. Ace's eyes instantly went to Tyson's neck before his eyes moved to mine. He swallowed, his lips pressing together slightly before ducking his head and leaving the room. I looked at Tyson, who was staring after him, and I could feel Tyson's guilt, yet he also didn't regret letting me mark him.

"You okay?" I asked him.

"He will get over it," he said, walking to his dresser. As he got dressed, I sat on the edge of the bed, not wanting to leave the room and face Ace again. Tyson dressed in some jeans and a black shirt before slipping his runners on.

"Come on," He said, holding his hand out to me, and I took it. We started walking down the hall when Tyson stopped suddenly, and I looked up at him. His eyes glazed over, and he growled. Ace came out of his room, looking annoyed, as Tyson refocused on the room before looking down at me.

"What's wrong?"

"Alpha Jamie is at the border requesting I meet him," Tyson said.

"I can go," Ace said, leaning on the doorframe of his room with his arms folded over his chest.

"No. Last time you ended up in a fight with him. I will go. You can run Lucy home and meet me out there," Tyson said, and Ace nodded.

"I will get my keys," Ace said, walking out and toward the kitchen. Tyson kissed my head.

"I need to go but will see you later this afternoon," he said, walking off, leaving me in the hall as he stripped his shirt off. It had to be serious if he was shifting and running there.

"Come on, Lucy," Ace called to me, and I finally moved to catch up with him as he walked outside.

Chapter 35

$\mathcal{A}$CE BARELY SAID ANYTHING the entire car ride home. It was tense and silent as I stared out the window, watching the scenery go past. We were nearly all the way home before he even spoke.

"So, did you and Tyson…" He didn't finish, yet his grip on the steering wheel tightened. I knew what he meant.

"Did we have sex?"

He said nothing, but I knew I was right with the way he swallowed, and his eyes flickered for a second.

"No, we didn't. Not that it would be any of your business if we did," I told him. He nodded, turning at the cross-section.

"Would you really be mad if we did?" I asked him, shocked at his strange reaction, all this because I had marked Tyson.

"No, Lucy, I wouldn't. I was just curious." He paused for a second, looking at me before looking away. "Tyson waited, I get it, and you should be with him. You didn't let Tyson mark you?" Ace said, pulling up in the driveway of the packhouse and stopping the car.

"No, I asked him too, but he wouldn't," I told him, and Ace pulled the keys from the ignition before turning to face me.

"What? Why?" he asked, confused.

"Because I haven't marked you. That's why," I told him, a little pissed off. Ace looked out the windshield and nodded.

"But you want him too?" he asked, and I chewed my lip nervously but nodded.

"I'll speak to him. He shouldn't feel guilty for the mess I made of everything," he said, opening the car door and getting out.

I opened my door and got out of the car.

Ace walked to the front door with me. "Are you excited?"

"Yes, but nervous about how mom will be," I told him, and he reached over and grabbed my hand before squeezing my fingers.

"You can always come home, Lucy. Whether or not you decide to let me be with you, it is your home," Ace said before letting go. I was just about to knock when the front door was thrown open, and Rayan tackled me. He squeezed his arms around my middle, and I kissed the top of his head.

"God, this place is boring without you," Rayan said, squeezing me tighter. I hugged him back, excited to have him close again.

"How's mom?"

"Good. Better." he said before noticing Ace next to me. Rayan turned and folded his arms across his chest, staring him down.

"Rayan?" Ace arched a brow at the glare Rayan was giving him. If he hadn't only come up to Ace's stomach, I would have actually been worried by the deadly glare Rayan was giving him.

"If I were Alpha, I would banish you from the pack for what you did to Lucy." Rayan told him, and I snorted before muffling my laughter.

"Good thing you're not Alpha. What are you going to do, Pipsqueak?" Ace asked.

"I should punch you in the mouth for just being in her presence." Rayan growled at him.

"If you could reach, short stuff," Ace said when suddenly Rayan punched him in the nuts. I choked on my spit when Ace dropped to his knees, clutching his balls, his face turning red. And Rayan pulled his arm back before punching him in the face as hard as he could, which probably wasn't hard, but he definitely showed Ace he could punch him in the mouth.

Ace growled at him and reached for him, but I pulled Rayan back to me before Ace smacked his nephew's ass.

"That's for my sister!" Rayan spat at him before walking inside like he was the king of the world. I chuckled before offering my hand to Ace. He growled but took it, and I pulled him up.

"I think the little shit just popped one of my nuts out of my ass," he said, adjusting himself just as Ryker came out.

"Lucy?" he said, shocked, like he hadn't realized we were there yet.

"Your mother was just asking when you would get here," he said, chucking his arm across my shoulders and pulling me toward the stairs.

"What was it you had to tell me?" I asked him, but he shook his head.

"Doesn't matter. Everything seems better now. She has been good, Lucy. Like when you were a kid," Ryker said as we walked up the steps. Ace followed us up, and we stopped out the front of my parents' bedroom door.

"Lucy, she is good. I promise. I think she is getting better," Ryker told me, but yet I still didn't understand. *Better from what?*

He opened the door, and I saw my mother sitting on the bed with my brother in her arms, bundled in a blanket. Her eyes lit up when she saw me, and a grin lit up her face.

"Lucy!" she said excitedly, waving me over, and I moved toward her, sitting on the bed beside her. I tucked the blanket back to look at his little face. He looked so much like Rayan, with his dark luscious locks of hair and silver eyes. It was definitely a family trait among the males in the Black family.

"You want to hold him?" my mother asked, and I nodded eagerly. I held my arms out, making sure to support his little head when she passed him to me.

"Hello, Ryden," I whispered to him. He yawned, his eyes fluttering shut as I held him. Ace came over to look at him. He stroked the back of Ryden's hand.

"Reminds me of Rayan," Ace said, and I nodded.

"How do you feel?" I asked my mother, turning to look at her.

"Tired, but better," she said, looking at my stepfather. He nodded to her and my brows furrowed in confusion.

"Your birthday is next week. Are you staying home? I can help you set up your room," She said, yawning.

"I will stay, but I will just stay in Rayan's room," I told her.

"You sure, Lucy? I can have a few people fix your room," Ryker asked, but I shook my head.

"I'll stay a few days, but I want to go home to Ace and Tyson's," I told him, and he nodded. I looked at Ace to make sure he meant what he said, and he leaned down, kissing my head. This was no longer home. Home wasn't meant to be uncomfortable, and being here, I felt like I was walking on eggshells. Home was with them. As much as I denied it, they were home.

"Can Ace have a hold of him?" I asked my mother, who nodded. I could tell Ace was waiting to get his hands on him. He loved kids, and the moment I asked, he already had his hands out for him. I passed the Ryden to him, and he looked tiny in Ace's arms.

"Hey, little man," Ace said, sitting next to me with Ryden in his arms.

After a few minutes, Ace said he had to go and gave Ryden back to mum. I walked him downstairs to the door.

"Mindlink if you want to come home. One of us will come to get you," Ace said, hesitating before turning back to me. He tugged me to him, hugging me, and I let him before hugging him back. "I will speak to Tyson for you," he whispered, but I shook my head.

"No, Lucy. He doesn't need to feel guilty for me," Ace said before pulling away and walking back to his car. I watched him leave before walking back up to see mom and spend time with her and my brothers.

Chapter 36

The first three days were great at home. Mom was in a great mood, and it reminded me of when Rayan was born. I was joined at her hip, always wanting to help, and I was glad to see mom let me spend time with Ryden. Rayan was just as excited, and for three days, everything was like when I was a kid. We were one happy family. I was excited to have my mother back, and I could tell Rayan was too. That excitement dimmed though, when I walked into the kitchen. Waking up a little earlier than I normally do, I walked into the kitchen to find Rayan crushing pills with a spoon on a piece of paper before I watched him slip them into a cup of coffee. Mom had been complaining that the coffee tasted funny, and I thought it odd that Rayan was getting up early every morning to make her morning coffee. Now I know why.

"Rayan!" I whispered to him, snatching the bottle of pills off him. He pressed a finger to his lips, pointing to the roof.

"Does dad know you are doing this?" I asked him, and he shook his head.

"She isn't breastfeeding. And I heard the Doc tell her she could take them while pregnant, so they wouldn't harm Ryden."

"What if she caught you? You don't just go around drugging people, Rayan. How long?" I asked him.

"I had no choice, Lucy. Amanda is a monster, and dad… dad…"

"Dad, what, Rayan? What aren't you telling me?"

"Dad and the doctors were talking about killing mom's wolf off. Making her dormant."

"What? How does that make sense?" I told him.

"By commanding Amanda never to shift. Never to come forward again. Unless dad calls upon her, mom won't be able to shift or speak to her wolf without dad. But the pills are working. They didn't work before, but they are now," Rayan told me.

"So, dad thinks she just got better? What are you going to do when you run out of pills?" I asked him, and I knew instantly from how he looked at me.

"You were going to get me to get them off Tyson," I told him, and he nodded. I sighed, and looked at the bottle and saw they were the same as mine but a way stronger dose.

"You need to tell dad, Rayan. He will go ballistic if he finds out you've been keeping this from him for too long," I told him, and he nodded.

"I will tell him tonight. I promise. I just wanted our family back together. I wanted mom back," he said, tears brimming in his eyes, and I pulled him to me. He wrapped his arms around me, and I kissed the top of his head.

"I know, buddy, so do I," I told him before grabbing a teaspoon and putting an extra teaspoon of sugar in it. Rayan looked at me.

"I heard mom say yesterday the coffee tasted funny to dad," I told him, and he nodded before taking the mug and the plate of toast up to her.

I followed him up and watched as he gave it to her. She thanked him and asked if I could take Ryden and change him. I nodded, picking him up out of his cradle, and Rayan slipped out of the room. I changed Ryden and turned around to find her passed out asleep. I quickly moved to remove the mug from her fingers before she tipped the scolding coffee on her lap and placed it on the bedside table with her toast. Using one arm to cradle Ryden, I pulled the blanket up under her chin before grabbing his bottle and walking downstairs.

"Did she drink it?" Rayan whispered.

"She fell asleep before she could," I told him, and he appeared to be worried. I knew those pills had to be taken at the same time every day, but if I woke her and insisted she drank it, she would be suspicious.

"Tell dad when he gets home." Rayan nodded, and I walked into the living room and settled on the lounge, deciding to let mom sleep while she could. I knew she was exhausted. I heard mom and dad up during the night constantly, sleep wasn't something they were getting much of.

Mom must have been tired because she slept nearly all day. Rayan and I both watched Ryden taking turns feeding him while I did all the nappy changes, because Rayan gagged when he tried to change a dirty diaper. I laughed before taking over. Hearing movement upstairs, Rayan looked up.

"Mom is up," he said, pausing the movie we were watching. He got up.

"I will go let her know Ryden is down here and see if she needs anything," Rayan said. I nodded to him. Ryker mindlinked us earlier, saying he was bringing dinner home and should be home soon. I heard Rayan walking up the steps before his feet stopped, and I could hear the worry in his voice as he spoke.

"Amanda?" he said, and I got up with Ryden in my arms. I heard a growl, making me move quicker, when I heard Rayan running down the stairs. Mum's voice carried through the house.

"You took him!" she growled at him just as I reached the corner of the living room and turned into the foyer. Rayan almost ran into me.

"Mom, you okay?" I asked her. Rayan was right. This wasn't mom, but Amanda. She stopped, her head cocking to the side as she looked at me before her eyes darted to Ryden in my arms. Her claws slipped from her fingertips.

"Get dad here! Or Jacob!" I mindlinked Rayan as she took a predatory step toward me.

"You would betray me like this son?. Give your own brother to them After what they did!" Amanda snapped at Rayan, who cowered behind me. I swallowed. This was not my mother, and I had never seen Amanda like this before.

"Mom, what are you talking about? I have Ryden right here. See? He is safe," I told her, trying to calm her down, but her eyes were wild, her aura slipping. I fought the urge to whimper, when I felt Rayan's hand on my back, his own aura was so much weaker than hers but it was keeping me up as I became trapped between.

"Give him to me!" Amanda snarled at me.

"He is safe, mom. I have him. Look," I told her, not wanting to give him to her while her claws were extended and canines protruding. Her entire body was raging with anger, and she could hurt him. Rayan must have had the same thought when his voice flitted in my head.

"Give me Ryden. Dad and Jacob are on their way," he said.

"You are exactly like your father. I knew you would be like him, A fucking monster, just like him! I won't let you take him from me!" Amanda growled, and I passed Ryden to Rayan just as my mother lunged at me.

Chapter 37

Mom tackled me before I even turned back to her. Rayan screamed, jumping out of the way as I crashed into the wall.

"Mom, it's Lucy. I am your daughter," I screamed at her when she slapped me. My face whipped to the side before she got up.

"You're not my daughter. You're his," she said, and I crawled to my hands and knees.

"Now, GIVE ME MY SON! YOU WILL NOT TAKE HIM FROM ME!" she screamed at Rayan. Rayan stepped away from her just as I got to my feet. Amanda growled at him and raised her arm back to hit him, but I caught her wrist, ripping her backward.

"Run!" I yelled to Rayan, and he darted off.

Mom's hand connected with my cheek, her claws slicing down my face. Her other hand twisted in my grip. She raised her hand again to hit me when I punched her. I couldn't tell who was more shocked, her or me, but I still did it, and her head snapped backward. She growled at me before attacking me.

"I hate you! You are a monster! Just like him!" she screamed, hitting me wherever she could.

"I am not him, mom. I am yours, Not his!" I yelled at her, and she stopped shaking her head, pulling her hair out. She was manic, and I could tell whatever she saw looking at me took her back there, yet I couldn't understand it. I was not my father.

"I am your daughter, Amanda, Yours, Not his. I would never take him from you," I told her, but she scratched her face, clawing at herself and hitting herself.

"You are like him. Every time I look at you, I see him. You are him; You look exactly like him!" she screamed, her chest rising and falling heavily.

"I am not him." I told her, tears streaking my face. Did I make her this way? Was that what she saw every time she looked at me?

"YOU ARE!" she screamed at me, and I shook my head.

"Every time I look at you, I remember what they did. Remember what he did to me." Her words angered me. How could she? How could she see him and not me?

Getting to my feet, I growled at her. "I am not my father."

"You... you... you!" she rambled. "You did this to me! You let them do this to me!" she said, and I could see she'd lost it. She wasn't of sound mind, She was erratic, and Amanda was the dominant one now, more dominant than her human counterpart.

"I didn't do shit to you. You think you were the only one trapped in that place?!" I yelled at her, and she growled, stepping toward me, but I shoved her, shocked by my own strength and the anger behind it.

"You weren't the only one in that place. They did the same shit to me. The only difference is, you got out with all of you still intact. They killed part of me. You think you're the only one that suffers with what they did, What they put us through, Amanda?" I screamed at her.

"They destroyed me!" she screamed just as the door burst open. Yet she didn't notice.

"You! Every time I look at you, I see him, See that place."

"And every time I look at you, I am reminded how I will never be good enough for you! Never be the good child! You say I am like him, but look at the monster you turned into!" I snapped at her. Her claws slipped into my arms as she grabbed me.

"Amanda, let her go!" Ryker said behind me.

"She was trying to take him from me!"

"You aren't stable to have him. You are taking him from her. You are taking him from mom. Not us," I told her, pushing her back, her claws slipping from my skin, but I barely registered the pain. Rayan came in, tears streaking his face, and Jacob pulled him behind, motioning for me to come to him. I turned to go to him.

"This is your fault!" Amanda screamed before charging at me.

Ryker grabbed me, shoving me behind him and taking the brunt of her attack when I felt his aura slip out, and Amanda whimpered, dropping to the floor, wailing. I, too, was forced to my knees, my head felt like it was about to explode when Jacob's hand wrapped around my wrist before jerking me toward him. Rayan's hand fell on me, and I wondered how I never noticed his aura before. His aura got stronger each time I felt him use it, making me wonder how my brother was able to hide it so easily. But it explained how he was always able to get out of school.

I turned to face my mother, who was on the ground at my stepfather's feet. She whimpered, and Ryker looked over his shoulder at Jacob. Tears were running down his face, and it was the first time I had seen my stepfather on the verge of breaking down. His voice stuttering as he spoke.

"Get them out of here. They don't need to witness this," he said to Jacob, and he nodded, pulling Rayan and me out of the house. Rayan held Ryden, and I took him from him. I heard mom scream, and my heart clenched as the cool night air brushed over us. I knew they would be battling out Alpha auras. Making me wonder how much of his aura Ryker would have to use, to make Amanda shut down completely. Judging from my mother's screams, he would have to exert all of his power to break her like that. Rayan whimpered beside me, and I tugged him closer when Jacob's hands slipped over his ears as mum's screams grew louder. Tears slipped down my cheeks listening to her agony like she was being tortured, but I knew he had no choice. This was the only way to help her.

Listening to her screams was a form of torture on its own, and I could feel my heart break for her. I knew exactly what it was like to have that part of you die. It was the loneliest feeling when you lose yourself. Ryden started crying, and I tried rocking and covering his ears from her deafening screams. While Jacob shielded Rayan's, who I could tell was focusing on breathing and counting. Suddenly, I felt warm hands slip over my own, and I was tugged backward against a warm body. Tyson's scent floated around me, and I buried my face in his chest, soaking him in my tears. I could tell he ran here because he only had shorts on.

"Ace!" Ryker yelled through the link, and I turned my face to see a shirtless Ace walk inside the house, closing the door behind him. I looked up at Tyson, and his voice moved through my head.

"Your mother is stronger. And can endure more pain than most. Pain is something Amanda is familiar with. Ryker is having trouble breaking her will. So Ace is helping him," Tyson said, and I knew Ace would also be helping torture Amanda into submission. Her screams got louder when I felt Tyson open up the link to Jacob, Rayan, Ryden, and me and filled it with the pack chatter to drown out my mother's screams. Tyson kissed my forehead before tucking the blanket around Ryden, up a little more to cover him, before pressing closer to me and using our body heat to keep him warm.

Chapter 38

Ace's

Ryker was a mess as Amanda finally gave into our commands. Her screams made my ears ring, and I had never been so sickened before. I had a new respect for mental torture. My stomach turned as she collapsed on the floor at our feet. Both of us were torn to pieces by her wolf fighting the commands. Amanda was somehow unaffected because she was Ryker's mate. Yet the pain he was enduring, not only doing it, but feeling through the bond was heartbreaking.

Reika laid in a huddled heap on the floor at his feet, his chest rising and falling heavily, and he was sweating profusely. Tears streaked his face as he bent down with shaky hands to grip the tops of her arms.

"Get away from me!" Reika snapped, her voice trembling. She slapped his hands away and started sobbing. I couldn't imagine having my wolf forced into submission like that. Forced to go dormant and have the sudden chatter stop. The loneliness in her own head had to be a form of torture on its own.

Ryker fell to his knees beside her, pulling her to him, his fingers gently brushing her hair. "I had no choice. I won't let her destroy you," he whispered to her. Reika's hands clutched his shirt in a fist as she clung to him.

"I'm sorry. But we talked about this. She was hurting you. She was hurting our kids," Ryker told her, and she nodded, yet it was obvious she had just paid the ultimate sacrifice for her family. Not only did she lose her wolf for them, but she basically just tossed all her free will away. Something I knew had been holding Ryker back from doing this earlier.

Ryker could just command her now, and she would be unable to defy him. Effectively stripping her of her title, even though she would remain Queen and by his side. He had the ultimate control. And against him, she would be a mere puppet on some strings.

"I know," she cried, pressing her face into his chest. The amount of trust she must have had in him, to allow him to take her free will was obvious. She trusted him to make the right choices. Trusted him completely. I hoped one day Lucy could trust me the way Reika trusted Ryker wholeheartedly.

"Lucy?" she asked, looking up at him.

"She is with Ryden and Rayan."

"She must hate me. She must hate me for everything," Reika told him.

"She knows it wasn't you. She knows Amanda was unstable and suffering."

Reika shook her head and started crying again. "I hurt her. The things Amanda said to her," Reika said, crying harder, but Ryker pressed his chin on her head, tucking her to his chest.

"She knows it wasn't you," Ryker told her before he looked at me. I nodded to him, turning and opening the door to let them know it was safe to come in. I wondered if Lucy would hate me for participating in her mother's torture. But it needed to be done. Amanda had become more estranged and more unstable, and the PTSD was uncontrollable and ruined not only her family but also her mother.

Tyson nodded to the door, and Lucy turned to see me standing there. Jacob was trying to calm down an upset Rayan, while Lucy cradled her brother in her arms.

"Rayan, it's over. We can see her," Lucy told him, and I could barely just make out her voice. Rayan looked at her, and she nodded toward the house, and his eyes darted to the open door before rushing to it. He stopped next to me, and Lucy came up behind him, giving him a nudge when he didn't enter. Both of them stared at their mother on the floor in Ryker's arms, and Reika looked up at them before sighing in relief when she spotted they were okay.

"Mom?" Rayan asked, looking at his father for confirmation that it was her. Ryker nodded to him, and Rayan threw himself in her arms. She kissed his face, clutching him and stroking his face with her hands. Lucy chewed her lip, and Ryden stirred in her arms, making her look down at him. He sucked his fingers, and Jacob stepped inside.

"I will go make him a bottle," he said, kissing Lucy's head on the way past, as he walked toward the kitchen.

"Jacob?" Reika called out to him, and he stopped looking at her. "Thank you," she told him, and he nodded to her.

"Anytime, Luna," he said to her before walking off. It was no secret that he was specifically assigned to Reika, because she shouldn't be on her own. The number of times he had taken the brunt of Amanda's anger was nearly as much as Ryker did, trying to protect his kids from her unstable wolf. Jacob was always willing to throw himself in harm's way to protect Rayan, and to protect Reika from herself.

Ryden cried out, and Lucy rocked him, tapping his bum before looking at her mother and stepfather. I could see she was wondering if it was safe to hand him over. I had no doubt Lucy would die before letting her mother hurt her brothers, but she need not worry now. Reika looked up at her, and I watched her lip tremble, the guilt on her face for what she had done over the last couple of weeks obvious.

It was one thing when Lucy was away most of the time. But Lucy came home while Reika was struggling the hardest, because she was pregnant, and if she wasn't, I doubted it would have gotten to this level. Reika and Ryker had always been careful to hide this from her, though. I don't know why they kept it secret, but we all knew something was going on with Reika. Everyone saw the change in my brother, but it only showed that nobody truly knew what went on behind closed doors.

"It's okay, mom," Lucy told her, walking over to her. She bent down, placing Ryden in her mother's arms before kissing her mother's head and stepping back.

"I messed everything up, didn't I?" Reika asked, looking up at her, and Lucy shook her head.

"I know it wasn't you," Lucy told her, but I could hear how destroyed she was. I could see she blamed herself for her mother's psychosis.

"Amanda is me. A part of me. But I think things will be better now," Reika said, and I believed she was also telling herself that. Like saying it out loud would fix everything.

"I know you will get better," Lucy told her, stepping away and toward us. It was weird watching Lucy with them, and I could truly understand why she felt like such an outsider. Looking at

Reika and Ryker with both boys in their arms, despite looking like crap, they looked like the perfect family, and Lucy was the odd one out. She didn't look like them, except for sharing her mother's eyes and hair color. You could tell she wasn't Ryker's daughter, and you could tell she took after her father because her facial features were nothing like her mother's. Lucy's were softer and not so stern-looking. Reika was beautiful, but Lucy was different.

"You can come home now. It will be safe for you to come home," Ryker told her, but Lucy shook her head.

"This isn't my home," Lucy told him, and I could tell by the look on her face that she'd never really felt at home here. Or anywhere. The facility was the only true home Lucy had ever had. And the one place she'd spent the longest time in, to call home. Even after we got her back, she went to boarding school when she was twelve. So, she had spent more time in school, and in the facility, than she ever did at home. No wonder nowhere felt like home to her. There was no sense of belonging because she never belonged anywhere, just existed. And the three places she called home had only destroyed her, taking that sense of belonging from her.

"Lucy…" Reika said, hurt shining in her eyes.

"It's okay, mom. You have the boys to look after. You don't have to worry about me," Lucy told her, smiling sadly.

"Lucy, this will always be your home," Ryker told her, but Lucy shook her head, and I knew what she was going to say. I could see she really felt that way too. Like she was a mistake.

"This was never my home. I don't have a home. I belonged here as much as I belonged in that facility. I was never supposed to exist. In a perfect world, only those in your arms would. I was never meant to be part of this. I was just chucked into the picture by a mad man."

"Lucy, you are our daughter. Of course, you belong here. I would never have survived that place if it weren't for you. You kept Amanda going," Reika told her.

"But that's the thing, mom. You didn't survive that place. You just thought you did. And I was just the reminder that sometimes slipped through, telling you you didn't survive. Not really, not completely," Lucy told her. Reika hung her head, shaking it.

"Are you leaving me, Lucy?" Rayan asked just as Jacob came out. He handed a bottle to Ryker, who then took Ryden from Reika.

"No. I will never leave you. But I can't stay here, Rayan," she told him, and he nodded.

Chapter 39

Lucy

"Lucy?" Tyson asked as I closed the bathroom door. I couldn't wait to get away from there. I was the reminder. The pain that broke my mother and, in turn, broke myself. I couldn't stand the guilt on her face. I couldn't stand the guilt I felt toward her. Knowing everyone knew I was to blame, sucked. I hated that they all hid it from me. If I had known, I never would have come home at all.

"I'm fine, Tyson. I just want to shower and go to bed," I told him. Ace had been silent all night since we left. No one knew what to say or think. *What do you say when you know you are the reason someone is so mentally unstable they literally had to kill off a piece of themselves?* Sorry didn't seem like a good enough word.

I heard him still hovering near the main bathroom door, his weight creaking the floorboards.

"I'm fine. Go to bed, Tyson," I told him, and I heard him sigh before walking off. I turned the shower on and hopped in. I washed quickly, wanting to go to sleep so this day would be over and done with. Forget that my life wasn't some huge disappointment and overall fuck up. Getting out, I quickly brushed my teeth before rinsing my mouth. I chucked on my panties and Tyson's shirt to wear to bed before towel drying my hair. When I was done, I sneaked into one of the guest rooms before climbing on the bed and crawling under one of the covers.

Everyone lied to me. They all pretended nothing was wrong and kept it from me. Rayan even kept it from me. I made sure to lock the door. I just wanted to be alone, alone with my thoughts. I wondered if I would ever build a relationship with my mother again. *How do you build on that when all we seem to do is cause each other pain?* We were each other's punching bags and each other's guilt.

My eyes felt like sandpaper and burned from my tears, but I eventually succumbed to sleep. I was woken up by a loud banging. I waited for one of them to answer the door, but I hauled myself out of bed when the banging got worse.

Tossing the door open, someone was pounding on the door. I saw a post it stuck to the bench, picked it up, and read it.

"Got an urgent call to the borders. Mindlink when you wake."

I placed the post it down, and the banging on the door got worse.

"Hold your horses. I am coming," I yelled out, rubbing my eyes from sleep. My eyes felt so dry and itchy. The banging stopped, and I opened the door only for it to be shoved in the moment it unlocked.

"Good morning to you too," I snapped at her. She waved me off while walking in and placing her hands on her hips.

"Ace isn't here," I snapped at her rudeness as she just walked in like she owned the place.

"I'm not here to see Ace. I am here to see you," Melana said before walking into the living room and flopping on the couch.

"Seriously, Melana, leave. Ace told you to stay away, now leave," I told her, walking into the kitchen. I flicked the kettle on and grabbed a coffee mug.

"Two sugars," she said, walking over and sitting on a stool at the bench.

"Did you not hear me tell you to leave?"

"Oh, I heard. But like I said, I am not here to talk to Ace. I am here to talk to you. Now be hospitable," she said.

I rolled my eyes, grabbing another mug and making coffee. "Fine, what is it you want to talk about?" I asked her, plastering a fake smile on my face. *Fuck. If being Luna means smiling at dumb bitches all day, I don't want to do it.*

"I want you to reject Ace," she said, reaching for her cup and taking a sip. I felt like tossing mine in her face. I didn't know what was going on with Ace and me, but I sure as hell didn't want Melana to have him.

"Look, I get you were with Ace for years, but you aren't his mate. I am," I told her, and she frowned, looking down at her cup.

"You have Tyson. Why do you need Ace? You don't need both of them. Either way, you will be Luna," she said.

"I don't give a fuck about being Luna, Melana. Ace is my mate, and I am not giving him up because you have a stupid crush on him. Get your own mate. Better yet, maybe beg the one you rejected to take you back," I snapped at her.

"I gave up everything for Ace, only to be tossed aside when you come back. I love him. You had no right to come in here and stake a claim on him when you don't even want him," she said, standing up and placing her hands on the bench. I sipped my coffee.

"He is my mate, Melana. I am not rejecting him," I told her, still unsure of that answer when Melana decided to get petty.

"Must really grind your gears knowing that while you were away at school, I was keeping his bed warm. And he had no care for you at all. Bet it really sucked knowing he was screwing me for five years, not caring you were his mate. That's how little you meant to him."

"Yep. The same way it must suck for you that he tossed you aside after five years because he was only fucking you to pass the time, not because he actually wanted you," I retorted, downing the rest of my cup and placing it in the sink.

"Is that all you wanted to speak about, Melana? Because I really haven't got the time to listen to you whine about my mate," I told her, opening the door. When I did, I saw her car wasn't empty. I stared shocked as I looked at her, my blood boiling in my veins. Josie was sitting in the passenger seat of Melana's car.

Chapter 40

I walked out, and she spotted me, a grin splitting on her face. She opened the car door and got out.

"Lucy!" She smiled like we were best friends, and she didn't try to destroy my reputation by making me out to be some whore.

"How fucking dare you show your face here after what you did!" I told her, walking down the steps. She stopped in front of me, and I pulled my arm back and punched her. She squealed, clutching her nose before pulling her hands away that were drenched in blood just as my head was suddenly jerked back by my hair.

"That's my sister!" Melana screamed, but I twisted in her grip before punching her in the stomach. She gasped before letting go, and I stood upright, only for Josie to punch the side of my head. I growled at her.

"You are a fucking bitch! A bloody whore, Lucy! It wasn't bad enough you took him from me, Now you are taking Ace from Melana. Is no man safe around you?" Josie screamed at me before wiping her nose.

"What the fuck are you talking about?" I snapped at her.

"You know Avery and Aamon sent him off, And now he will spend the rest of his life burning and being tortured by her prick of a father! Just because he told you he didn't want you and you were jealous of me!" she screamed at me.

I tried to piece what she was saying together before it finally registered. I snorted. *This is fantastic! It now makes so much sense.*

"Mr. Tanner? Are you fucking serious, Josie?"

"Don't deny it, Lucy. I saw you running from his office, and then to say he tried to rape you," she scoffed, shaking her head.

"You have no idea what you are talking about, Josie. I was not sleeping with Mr. Tanner. He was a predator. A fucking predator! And you and I were his prey. I can't believe you were stupid enough to fall in love with a monster like that," I told her.

"He loves me," Josie said, shaking her finger in my face.

"Loves you? Is that what you think? Josie, he was grooming you. He didn't love you. Did you sleep with him?"

"He does love me. You just had to go and ruin it, like you ruined everything. You destroy everything you touch, Lucy!" she screamed at me, tears streaking down her face. I could hear car tires in the distance, and Melana looked down the driveway before looking at me with a smirk on her face.

"Josie, you are wrong. Mr. Tanner was not a lover. You are supposed to be my friend. How could you say those things about me? What the fuck did I do to you?" I asked her. Like how could she not see Mr. Tanner was just using her? He didn't love her. He was a sick, perverted freak.

"He is a sick bastard, is what he is." I told her.

Her face twisted in anger before she lunged at me and tackled me. I hit the ground, landing on my elbow before I slapped her. Rolling her off, I climbed on top of her and tried restraining her arms beside her head.

"Josie, he doesn't love you. Why can't you see that?" I asked her when I suddenly choked on my breath. I felt something cold slide into my body between my ribs, making me gasp before I sputtered and choked on my words. I felt something warm soak my shirt, and I looked down to see a knife jammed in my ribs. I looked at it and pulled it out, wondering how it got there, when I looked up and saw Melana slicing herself to pieces with her claws.

I feel my lungs filling with blood, making me cough blood all over Josie's face just as I heard a car stop, and suddenly Ace stepped into view. Melana was screaming frantically that I had attacked her and was trying to kill Josie. Josie was sobbing beneath me, and I actually wondered if I'd stepped into an alternate reality. Shit like this just didn't happen. *How could I be this unlucky in life?* As if I didn't have enough going on, I now had to defend myself against my own mate from his psycho ex.

Ace growled, and I looked up at him, his face twisted in rage. I gulped, yet I was finding it easier to breathe as I slowly healed. Melana was soaked in blood from her self-inflicted injuries, and Josie was thrashing beneath me, trying to get me off her.

Ace grabbed my arm, pulling me up and off Josie, and I saw Melana fight back from smiling out of the corner of my eye.

"Lucy, are you alright?" Ace asked. Melana's face fell, and I looked at him, shocked.

"She just attacked us, And she was going to kill Josie! Just because Josie told her some home truths. She is a fucking psycho, Ace! A danger to the pack!"

"What truths are those?" Ace asked, looking down at Josie. Josie cowered away from his glare but didn't answer. Instead, Melana did.

"That she is a homewrecking lying whore, that's what. And then she attacked us." Melana feigned innocence.

"This is un-fucking-believable," I muttered, shaking my head.

"No, it is very believable," Ace said, and my stomach dropped. Melana grinned triumphantly.

"I now realize the extremes you would go to to try to hurt my mate, and I will not tolerate that. I told you to stay away, Melana. You had no right to come here, let alone attack my mate and your Luna!" Ace yelled at her.

Melana flinches at his anger, yet not even I was prepared for what left his mouth next.

"I, Ace Kasen Black, Alpha of the Black Moon Pack, banish you, Melana Addison Parker and Josie Claire Parker, from the Black Moon Pack and hereby declare you both rogues." he said firmly, his aura rushing out.

"Wait, Ace! You can't," Melana gasped as she was stripped from the pack, her scent instantly changing. I heard Josie gasp, and she glared at me with such malice I was surprised I didn't catch on fire.

"I can, and I did. I warned you to steer clear, Melana. I won't have you attacking my mate because you are jealous of her. I told you all along that nothing would ever come of us," Ace told her.

"You will regret this, Ace. She doesn't love you like I do. What if she rejects you? You and I both know Tyson is the better choice between the two of you. She doesn't give a fuck about you! Only about titles."

"If she rejects me, that is her choice. Lucy doesn't care about titles, Melana. Unlike you. The only fucking regret I have, is getting involved with you in the first place! Now get the fuck off my pack territory!" he screamed at her.

Chapter 41

Ace didn't wait for her to leave, instead he turned to face me before gripping my shoulders and turning me toward the house, and pushing me toward the stairs. I could hear Melana crying and begging for his attention, but he ignored her, and I looked up at him over my shoulder as I opened the door. He must have been quite confident in his Alpha aura just to turn his back on her like that. But they were Pure Hybrid, so I suppose it would be a first if anyone could withstand the pressure of their auras.

I heard her car leave, and Ace shut the door before walking over to me. I thought at first he was mad by the angry look on his face, but he grabbed my hips, and placed me on the counter. His hand lifted my shirt to look at where Melana had slid the knife between my ribs. It felt more bruised than actual pain, as it had all but closed up. Besides, thanks to the facility, my pain tolerance was higher than most people's.

"Does it hurt?" Ace said, running his thumb over the small neat line that was almost completely closed.

"No, it just feels bruised," I told him, looking down. The shirt was ruined and soaked in my blood. Ace cursed under his breath before tugging it down and stepping closer, moving between my legs and effectively trapping me. I could think of worse places to be than trapped in my mate's arms.

Ace pressed his face in the crook of my neck, inhaling my scent, and I shivered when his hands moved to my ass, tugging me closer to the edge of the countertop. "Tyson is on his way home," Ace whispered against my neck.

"What happened at the borders?" I asked him, and he shrugged. I could tell he was reluctant to tell me.

"He wants land on this side of the river that runs between packs."

"Why, though?" I asked him, and he pulled back his hands, running up my thighs. For a second, his hands were all I could think about. I had to force myself to remain on topic and focus on Alpha Jamie. It seemed pretty stupid to start a war over land that wasn't his to begin with.

"Tyson and I have a few theories as to why he wants it. More reasons not to give it to him," Ace said.

"Like what? What could he possibly want with it? He could always get more land from his other neighboring pack." Ace nodded, but I heard Tyson's car pull up out the front, my eyes darting to the door before going back to Ace. He watched me carefully, and I could see he wanted to say something and held back. I wondered why he was hesitant to tell me about Alpha Jamie.

"Lucy, there is something I should tell you," Ace said, looking away guiltily. I felt my confusion spread across my face. Maybe it was to do with me stepping over the border of Jamie's pack without permission.

"What is it?" I asked him, slightly worried. *Did I start a pack war?*

"I went to see Avery and Aamon about your pills," Ace started when the door opened up. Did something happen to Mr. Tanner? Did Avery not believe me even after what she saw? Yet, I could tell she did when she was here last. Tyson walked in, and Ace sighed before stepping away. I grabbed his hand, pulling him back.

"What's wrong? Say it, Ace," I told him, needing to know, my anxiety was through the roof.

Tyson stopped, assessing the situation before slowly emptying his pockets into the bowl that sat on the stand by the door.

"I am the reason you take those pills. Not the entire reason, but it is mostly because of me."

"No, Ace. I have depression. Depression isn't blamed on a person or any one thing," I told him. How could he blame himself for my pills? I had been on them since I was a kid. Ace grabbed my face in his hands, and I saw Tyson move out of the corner of my eye like he was about to jump his own brother if needed.

"No. Lucy, think. Think about it. I knew you were my mate when you were twelve. You have been on those pills since then. Avery told me it was the aftermath of me ..." He didn't finish, but Tyson growled at him, stepping toward him and Ace looked at him.

"I didn't know. You know I would never deliberately cause her harm," Ace told him. Tyson's eyes flickered to Tyrant, and Ace turned his attention back to me. I was confused, trying to piece together what he was saying. I was twelve, so what? He found out I was his mate when I was twelve. It took a few minutes to piece together what he was saying, and my eyebrows shot up as recognition slipped over me. I stared at him, blinking back tears. Avery had convinced me that the pain I was feeling was due to the PTSD of the facility. Nearly all of us suffered from it. The things they did to us there were not easy to get over.

But Avery said the pain would worsen and that the pills would help stop it from being unbearable.

"Lucy?" Ace breathed, his hands still cupping my face. "I swear I didn't know. I would never have been with her. I... I was stupid and selfish. Please understand. I wasn't trying to hurt you."

"Let me go," I whispered to him. His lips parted like he wanted to say something, but I just wanted to get away from him. The number of times I had thought about ending my life just to make the pain stop. And it was because he was fucking her, because he was being untrue to the mate bond.

"Lucy, please. Just ..."

"Ace. Let me go," I told him, and he nodded, dropping his hands from my face and stepping back. I jumped off the countertop. I started walking down the hall, my eyes burning with unshed tears, when I felt warmth pressing against my back as I stopped at the spare bedroom door.

"No. I am not sleeping without you again tonight. My room, Lucy," Tyson said behind me, his hand on my hips, steering me toward his room.

"Be mad at him all you want. But please don't hide away from me," Tyson whispered below my ear before opening his bedroom door. He pushed it open before pushing me inside.

Chapter 42

Tyson

She was angry at Ace, but I refused to let her hide away again. She could be angry all she wanted. She could throw shit, break shit, but not run and hide from me. I hated it when she suffered in silence. There had been enough silence, and I couldn't handle her silence anymore. She stumbled forward as I pushed her into the room. I managed to grab her before she fell over, jerking her back against me as I closed the door with my foot.

"Did you know?" she asked, looking at me over her shoulder.

"No. I didn't. But it does make sense," I admitted. I wanted to kill him, but he was my brother. I just hoped this wasn't the tipping point that would make her reject him.

"I'm not rejecting him. I am just mad," she states, and I almost forgot she could feel my emotions now and sense what I was thinking.

"You are allowed to be mad. You have every right to be, Lucy," I told her, turning her around in my arms. She wrapped her arms around my neck, standing on her tippy toes, and I smiled, leaning down so she could kiss me.

"Going out," Ace said through the mindlink.

"Where?"

"Avalon City," he said before cutting off the link, and I heard the front door slam. .Lucy pulled away, looking behind me.

"We have the house to ourselves," I told her, wondering if that would bother her.

"Is he mad?" she asked, and I shrugged, not sure what was going on with him. Though I knew it was killing him seeing Lucy and I get closer while he was pushed out.

Lucy sighed before stepping away and walking into the bathroom. I followed, watching as she stripped off before turning the shower on.

"Ace was talking to me earlier. Did you say something to him?" I asked her, and I saw her confusion as she looked over at me.

"Say what to him?" she asked while checking the water's temperature with her hand. I looked away from her, my cock twitching in my pants at the sight of her plump ass, heavy breasts, and small waist. She was perfect and curvy in all the right places, yet not completely smooth. I liked that she wasn't all hard and toned like most she-wolves. Lucy was still soft and not as skinny and athletic looking like most of the pack's she-wolves, who spent most of their lives training.

"Ace asked why I hadn't marked you," I told her, and she looked at me, chewing her bottom lip.

"He may have mentioned it," she said, stepping into the shower and closing the door. I moved further into the bathroom.

"What did he say?" she asked, wetting her long golden hair. I watched her breasts jiggle and groaned at the sight of her before readjusting myself. I then looked up to see her watching me with an amused smile on her lips, while I tried to stop my dick from pitching a very obvious tent in my shorts.

I cleared my throat, folding my arms across my chest and looking at the ceiling. "He said I should mark you, even if you haven't marked him."

"And you obviously don't agree," she replied, and I could hear her annoyance.

"It's not that. I just don't want to be the one that forces your hand."

"You think if you mark me, I will just toss Ace aside and give up on being with him?" she asked, and I nodded, looking back at her.

"I won't reject him," she answered, though she didn't sound so sure herself.

"What bothers you the most? The fact he was with someone? Or that it was Melana he was with?" I asked her.

"Both. It being Melana was just the fucking icing on the cake. He knows how much I hate her," she said, and she was correct. I warned him when he first got with Melana that it wasn't a good idea.

She and Lucy used to get along until Lucy caught them together when she was eleven, and suddenly a switch flipped, and they became enemies overnight. Making me wonder if that was the first sign of the bond kicking in for her. Even though she was underage for a wolf, she instantly turned on Melana when she walked in on them fooling around. Yet when I was with Tara, Lucy didn't seem to have an issue. But in saying that, we never really did anything together. But now I was wondering if the bond kicked in first for her with Ace.

"What bothers you most?"

"She had her hands on him from the moment we got out of the facility," Lucy said with a growl, and my lips tugged up slightly.

"When did it bother you?" I asked her.

"When I caught them together in your room," she said, confirming what I thought, just before she left for boarding school.

"Why did it bother you then, though?"

"Because he was mine, and she was touching him," she said before realizing what she'd said.

"You were jealous?" I asked her, and she seemed to think before shrugging.

"You were both always with me, and then he started hanging out with her," Lucy said.

"But you weren't like that with Tara," I told her.

"She didn't reek of you, and you didn't reek of her. I knew Ace was with Melana back then," Lucy said, and I realized Avery was right and that everything Ace said was correct. Lucy had been able to feel the bond from the moment we met her. She just wasn't sure what it was, yet she had always been drawn to us and us to her. Yet it was only recently that she realized what it all meant.

I tugged my shirt off before undoing my pants. Here we thought we were waiting for her when in reality, she waited for us longer. She was just unaware of what it was she was waiting for. But that left another thing to think about. Avery told Ace that she thought Lucy's wolf was dormant, not dead. Now the question was, how were we going to wake her wolf?

Opening the shower screen, Lucy moved over, and I smiled down at her, pulling her to me. Her hands moved to my chest, her breasts squashed against my abs. I gripped her thighs, lifting her and wrapping her legs around my waist. She smiled before wrapping her arms around my neck and pressing her lips against mine. I felt her smile against my lips, and I pressed her against the cold tiles earning a shriek from her. As I nipped at her chin she sighed.

I used one hand to turn her face, exposing her neck to me. She shuddered, and her nails dug into my shoulders where she was holding me. I ran my tongue over her neck, and she moaned, making me chuckle.

"Tyson?" she whispered, and I felt bad that I didn't mark her right away after hearing the desperation in her voice. She was after the same assurance that I wouldn't toss her away.

My canines grazed across her skin, and I felt the sharp points press against her delicate skin, and she shivered against me. I sealed my lips over her neck before sinking my teeth into her, my canines embedding into her flesh. She made a strangled noise that sounded pained before turning to a moan as I pulled her closer, letting my teeth tear through the tissue and muscle until I felt them hit bone.

I felt relief rush into me from the bond as it formed and snapped into place, followed by exhaustion and an overwhelming urge to sleep. I slowly pulled my teeth from her neck, and she slumped heavily against me, going completely floppy. I felt silence through the bond and knew I'd knocked her out. I shut the water off before hoisting her up and scooping my arms under her legs that had fallen down my sides.

"Maybe we should have marked her in bed. Now we have to figure out how to dry her and hold her upright," Tyrant told me, and I rolled my eyes at him before snatching the towel off the towel rack. I dried her back while I leaned her against me before scooping her up and laying her in bed. Then I dried the front of her and tucked the blanket around her.

"Man, you really want to torture us, don't you?" Tyrant whined at me when I didn't bother to dress her, and I found myself repeating what Lucy had always said.

"It's just skin," I told him. I quickly dried myself before slipping some boxer shorts on and climbing in beside her.

Chapter 43

Ace

I drove all night for Avery to turn around and say no. I thought she would be happy, it was the most selfless thing I could do. I let her go, letting her be free of me and all the pain I had caused her. Yet Avery turned me down, refusing to remove the mate bond. Still, she took Lucy's mark when I marked her. I hoped to plead with Aamon, but he wasn't home. She removed the bond for Lucy, but now she wouldn't take the bond for me, saying it was for Lucy to decide. Decide what? She fucking hated me, and I knew the only reason she hadn't rejected me was her fear of upsetting Tyson.

Her being mated to me was making her miserable, and my brother too. Walking out of Avery's house, I got back in my car. This was fucking bullshit. She didn't want me, so I didn't see the issue with Avery snapping her fingers and relieving us both of the bond. She was not only punishing Lucy but Tyson by leaving her tied to me.

"Ace?" Avery said, chasing after me as I slammed my car door shut.

"Bloody hybrids. Aamon, where are you?" I heard her say just before I started my car. I tore out of the driveway before racing down the street toward the highway. Atticus wasn't even talking to me, convinced I'd fucked everything up, and he was right. *I fuck everything up. Anything I touch becomes ruined.* I refused to be the reason they both suffered. I refused to be the one that ruined their lives. I didn't deserve her, and now realizing that, I'd just made my mind up completely.

Driving along the highway leaving Avalon City, I knew there was a bend with a sheer drop. If Avery didn't save Lucy from the bond, I would save her myself. I floored it, pressing the pedal all the way to the floor, listening to my car rev as it picked up speed for the sharp bend. I unclipped my seatbelt just as I smashed through the barrier, and the car was suddenly falling. It smacked the side of the cliff and tipped, and I was suddenly looking up the cliff as it started somersaulting when burned almonds invaded my senses. *Great! I am going to hell!* I thought, knowing that usually meant a demon was near. Demons came from hell, and I was sure that was where the Moon Goddess would send me for hurting Lucy. I saw the ground coming toward me at an alarming speed and closed my eyes, bracing for impact, when I felt a hand touch me.

"Fucking idiot!" I heard Aamon yell at me, before feeling a whoosh motion and a vacuum-like suction rush over me. My eyes opened to see Aamon standing in front of me while I was sitting on the hard ground near the busted barrier. I touched myself, shocked that I was alive. Then I heard the loud boom of an explosion, and a billow of smoke and flames filled the sky behind where Aamon was standing.

"I didn't believe you would be so stupid. Do you have any idea how fucking stupid that was? You could have died," Aamon snapped at me. It was the first time I had seen him angry at me.

"That was kind of the fucking point," I growled at him, getting to my feet, only for him to shove me to the ground. I growled at him before feeling his fist connect with the side of my face. My head whipped to the side. Black dots danced in front of my vision, and I shook my head to clear it before glaring at him.

"How fucking dare you. Do you have any idea how many people that would have destroyed? Your brothers, Your mother, And what about Lucy?" Aamon screamed at me.

"They would be better off without me. Lucy doesn't want me. I am just stopping her and Tyson from being together," I told him.

"Is that what you think? How do you think Lucy would feel knowing she was the reason you killed yourself? How would Tyson feel knowing his twin fucking killed himself? You think you are saving them? You nearly just fucking ruined them, Ace! Lucy loves you! Your family loves you. And you doing stupid shit like this will only cause them pain while ending yours," Aamon said.

"Avery wouldn't take the bond. This is the only way to free her from me," I yelled at him. *How does he not see that?*

"Yes, because Avery can see the bond is worth fucking saving, you idiot! If she wouldn't take it from you, it's because she saw something worth keeping. Not because she is punishing you, Ace."

I thought over his words, yet I saw no way to fix this. Lucy hated me, and it would only be a matter of time before Tyson did too.

"Get up. Get home. And fix it. Stop being a coward. And for once in your god damn life fucking fight for something! Instead of letting Tyson deal with everything for you." Aamon said before reaching down and grabbing the front of my shirt and jerking me to my feet.

"You ever do something like that again, I will burn your ass in hell for all eternity!" Aamon said, gripping my arms. I felt the suction sensation of him misting as I was pulled through space, before appearing out the front of my packhouse.

"Go back inside to your mate." Aamon ordered, and I looked around. I could already feel the bond pulling me toward her, knowing she was just inside the house. Atticus clawed in my head to be near her.

I looked at Aamon and nodded, suddenly realizing how stupid trying to kill myself was. I stopped realizing I now had to explain what happened to my car.

"You aren't going to tell them, are you?"

"No. As long as you get your ass inside and promise never to do anything like that again." Aamon said, and I nodded. I turned, looking back at the darkened house before turning back to Aamon, only now he was gone. I sighed, heading inside and hoping the front door was still unlocked. Thankfully it was.

Chapter 44

Lucy

I woke in the middle of the night to this overwhelming feeling of dread. Sitting up, I found myself naked, and Tyson was fast asleep, pressed against my back. I tossed the blanket back before rummaging through the dresser, I grabbed one of Tyson's shirts and slipped it on before walking out of the room toward the kitchen. My stomach turned violently, making me wonder what was going on. My mind was racing and somehow kept going to Ace. I just had a terrible feeling something was going on with him.

I poured myself a glass of water before picking up Tyson's phone and seeing it was a little after 2 AM. I drank the glass of water before rinsing it and placing it on the sink upside down. I then slipped down the hall, stopping out the front of Ace's bedroom door. I gripped the door handle and twisted it open. His scent was faint, and I couldn't see him in the room. I flicked the light on and confirmed that he still wasn't home. I sighed, shutting the light off and closing the door.

I wondered where he was. Maybe he was with Melana, and that was the feeling of dread that was consuming me. But then again, he now knew I could feel them together, so I doubted that he wouldn't be that stupid. He would also know Tyson would lose it, and I would reject him if he did. Yet the feeling got worse, and I couldn't place it. I just knew it had something to do with Ace. Walking back to Tyson's room, I climbed back into bed. I tossed and turned, trying to get back to sleep, but the sinking feeling in my gut was making me nauseous.

"What's wrong?" Tyson asked sleepily, yawning as he rolled into me before tugging me flush against him.

"Have you heard from Ace?" I asked him.

"He still isn't home?" Tyson mumbled, and I shook my head.

"He will be fine, Lucy. He will come home when he is ready," Tyson said, kissing my shoulder when I suddenly heard the front door open.

"See. He is fine," Tyson mumbled, and I heard the front door close before hearing footsteps walking down the hallway. I heard him stop at his bedroom door for a second before he continued, and I felt myself relax when I sensed a whiff of his scent seep into the room before the door was pushed open more. Ace walked in and leaned over the bed. I turned my face to look up at him, and he jerked back.

"Sorry. I didn't realize you were awake," he whispered, standing upright. Yet I couldn't explain the immense relief I had upon seeing him. The sickly feeling in my stomach settled now that I could see him.

"Why didn't you come home earlier?" I asked him as he turned around to leave.

"My car broke down. I only just got home," Ace told me, and I nodded.

"Were you in my room?" he asked, and I realized that had to be why he came down to Tyson's room. He could smell my lingering scent in his room when I went to check if he was home yet.

"Yes. I didn't touch anything. I was only checking if you were home," I told him.

"You can touch whatever you want, Lucy," he said, turning around again. The moment his back was to me, the sick feeling returned.

"Ace?" I whispered, and he stopped, turning back to me. "Will you stay? Please."

"In here with you?" he asked, confused.

"Just for tonight. I just want you close. Something feels off," I told him, and I saw him bite his lip before he nodded. Ace sat on the edge of the bed and removed his shoes and shirt. I moved over, pulling the blanket back, and he laid down. I moved closer, needing to feel his skin. I suddenly felt worried about letting him go, like he would disappear. I couldn't explain the feeling, but something about Ace scared me, like he was leaving me. Or maybe it was because Tyson and I were talking about Ace in the shower. I wasn't sure. Ace turned his face, pressing his nose into my neck.

"Tyson marked you?" he asked, though I could tell he already knew. I didn't say anything, not wanting him to get upset and leave.

"Good," he said, rolling over and tugging me closer. He kissed my forehead.

"I love you, Lucy," he whispered, hugging me tighter. I draped my arm over him, snuggling against him and inhaling his scent. Nothing felt more right than being between both of them. Feeling both of them next to me like this was how it was supposed to be, and a part of me was sick of denying it.

Ace's hand moved down my side to my hip before moving underneath Tyson's shirt, his hand moving back up, and he stopped at my ribs. Ace's hand was warm against my skin, and he kissed my forehead, pulling me closer when I felt Tyson move behind me. Pressing closer and pushing me impossibly close to Ace. I felt Tyson's hand run along my thigh before he lifted my leg, draping it over Ace's hip. Ace pulled me closer when I felt Tyson's breath on my neck as he moved, before hearing his voice below my ear.

"I know you want him, Lucy. It's okay to want Ace. I want you to want him too," Tyson said, kissing my mark before sucking on it and making me moan. I felt my eyes roll into my head when Tyson's hand moved under his shirt, stopping on his brother's hand. He moved Ace's hand to my breast, and I felt Ace hesitate before palming it. I wanted them, wanted both of them. Tyson knew that through the bond, but he also knew I wouldn't do anything about it.

Tyson's hand slid across my stomach before moving between my legs. I felt his erection pressing against my ass, his fingers trailing along the lower half of my stomach, yet he didn't move them lower. I knew he wanted permission despite being able to feel my reaction to him through the bond, and I grabbed his hand, moving it between my legs. He groaned when he felt how wet I was, completely intoxicated by their scent and my senses overloaded as my arousal spilled onto my thighs. They barely touched me, and I felt like I was about to combust on their closeness alone.

Chapter 45

A DELIGHTFUL SHIVER RAN ACROSS my skin as Tyson's fingers brushed over my slit. He glided his finger between my wet folds, making me moan at his teasing. My hips bucked against his hand, and Ace suddenly gripped my hip holding me still, but I gripped his hand, moving it back to my breast.

"Lucy!" Ace growled when I rolled my hips against Tyson's hand, and I realized I'd made Tyson's hand brush up against Ace.

Tyson's hand jerked away when he accidentally touched his brother, and I ground my hips against Ace's erection wanting the friction back. Tyson's hand went to my neck as he squeezed my throat, turning my face and bringing my lips to his. His tongue invaded my mouth as he tasted every inch, making me moan into his mouth when he suddenly let go of my throat. His hand moved to my waist, and he gripped the shirt.

I sat up, letting him peel it off. Ace also sat up on one elbow. I watched him before feeling Tyson sit up behind me, his lips going to my neck and my eyes closing as he continued leaving open-mouth kisses along my neck and shoulder. Tyson's fingers played with my nipple, making it harden, and I leaned back against him.

"Let him touch you, Lucy. He wants to touch you. And I know you want him to," Tyson whispered below my ear before sucking my earlobe into his mouth.

I nodded, a breathy sound leaving my lips when Ace suddenly moved, and his lips locked around the nipple Tyson wasn't teasing. I gripped Ace's hair, his hot tongue flicking over my hardened nipple before he bit down on it, making me flinch at the sudden pain before his tongue soothed it.

My grip on his hair tightened as I pulled him closer. He growled, his tongue vibrating against my breast as he nipped and sucked on it. Ace moved his face higher, nipping and sucking my skin before nipping at my neck, and I tensed, having him that close to my marking spot.

Ace pulled back, watching my face for a second, when I felt Tyson move, and he pulled me onto his lap. Ace's hands ran up my thighs, and I shivered. Gripping Ace's hair, I brought his lips back to mine, and he made a satisfied noise in the back of his throat when I kissed him. His tongue tracing across my bottom lip, wanting entry. I let my lips part, wanting to taste him. Tyson's relief through the bond hit me when I kissed Ace back, like a weight had been lifted off his shoulders.

Tyson's hand moved between my legs, and he rubbed my clit in circular motions, making me move my hips against his hand.

"Fuck! She's so wet," Tyson groaned below my ear, before kissing my jaw and shoving his finger inside me. I squirmed at the sudden intrusion, and he stilled his movements for a second before withdrawing his finger slowly. My juices spilled onto my thighs and coated his fingers.

I felt him slowly work another finger inside me, stretching me. I rolled my hips against his fingers and cried out when he forced his fingers deeper inside me, wiggling them and curling them upward.

Ace's hands moved to my hips, and he tipped my hips forward, giving Tyson easier access as he slid his fingers in and out of my soaking wet heat. Ace watched Tyson's fingers move in and out of me before he suddenly moved off the bed, and pulled me toward him. Making Tyson's fingers leave my body as I was pulled to the edge of the bed, my feet touching the soft carpet.

Ace kissed my knee, and my eyes darted down to him kneeling between my legs. Tyson moved behind me, pulling me back against him.

"Let Ace taste you," Tyson purred against my mark, enticing a moan from my lips as sparks rushed over my body. He chuckled against my skin, and I felt Ace's hands slide under me as he gripped my ass, jerking me closer to his face before his hands went to my thighs, opening them wider for him. He drapes my legs over his shoulders, his hands sliding up and down my thighs while he trailed his lips and tongue along the inside of my thigh, making me shudder. I felt his breath on my core before he pressed his lips against my slick folds.

His tongue flattened against my folds, licking a straight line to my clit before sucking it into his mouth, and I relaxed against Tyson, a moan escaping my lips. Ace's grip on my thighs tightened, and my legs trembled, wanting to close them around his face as I squirmed, but he held them open. His tongue ran between my folds before he slipped it inside me.

He growled, the vibration making me buck against his mouth before he held me still, his hot mouth devouring me as he licked and sucked. I felt my body heat up, and goosebumps rise on my arms, and all I could think about was his hot mouth devouring me, and the pleasurable feeling that was growing within me.

Tyson brushed my hair off my shoulder before sucking on my mark, making me moan loudly as pleasure rushed over me. I became lost in the feeling of them touching me, consumed with their touch. Tyson's mouth moved up my neck, and I felt his canines graze my skin before he nipped at my chin.

I turned my face toward his. Tyson's lips crashed against mine, swallowing my moans as Ace continued relentlessly flicking his tongue over my clit. I felt my stomach tighten, my hips moving against his mouth when I felt my eyes roll into the back of my head, my toes curling, and my entire body tense before letting go.

I cried out at the sudden intensity of my orgasm washing over me and my walls clenching as my orgasm pulsated out of me. Ace was licking up my juices as they spilled out of me as I rode out my orgasm, leaving me breathless. My body went limp, and I leaned heavily against Tyson.

My body was completely relaxed yet exhausted, like I had run a marathon. Ace moved, kissing the inside of my thigh before sliding my legs off his shoulders, and they fell heavily on the bed when he sat up on his knees. I yawned, and he chuckled before gripping the back of my neck and bringing my lips to his. Ace forced his tongue between my lips, his tongue tasting every inch of my mouth, and I could taste myself on his lips and tongue, making me moan softly when he pulled away and pressed his lips to my forehead.

Tyson lay back down, tugged me against him, and pulled me back down. I sank heavily into the bed, my hand tugging Ace's, not wanting him to leave, and he climbed back on the bed next to me before tucking my hair behind my ear.

"Sleep, Lucy," he whispered, pressing closer, his arm draped across my waist while Tyson's was across my ribs. I let my eyes close, loving them being so close, feeling at home, and for once, I felt like I actually belonged somewhere.

Home. They were home, I thought to myself as my eyes fluttered shut. For once, I didn't question anything, letting my mind go blank as I started to drift off. Knowing no matter what happened, I would always have them, that they would always be in my corner, and I in theirs.

Chapter 46

Waking up to hands shaking me, I squinted up at Ace.

"Morning," he said as he smiled down at me. My lips tugged up slightly, and I felt for Tyson behind me, but he wasn't in bed. His side was cold like he hadn't been in bed for a while.

"He is at work. You have your end of suspension meeting this morning, unless you want me to pull you out?" Ace said, sounding hopeful, and I groaned, stuffing the pillow back over my face, hating the idea of going back to school. But at least I could see Mitchell, and soon I would graduate, so I figured I would just suffer through it.

"No, I should go. What time is it?" I asked him.

"In that case then, it is time to get up," he said, gripping my hips, making me squeal before I was flung over his shoulder as he marched into Tyson's ensuite.

"Shower. I will make you some breakfast," Ace said, placing me on my feet, and I instantly shivered from the cold tiles.

"We leave in thirty minutes, so shower quickly," Ace said before walking out. I quickly showered before digging through my clothes and finding some jeans, a blue tank top and hoodie.

"Lucy?" Ace called from the kitchen.

"I am coming!" I screamed back to him while stuffing my shoes on my feet before grabbing my school bag. Walking down the hallway, I tossed my bag near the front door before turning into the kitchen, and tying my hair in a messy bun on my head because I couldn't be bothered to brush the knots out.

Ace placed a coffee on the bench in front of me before sliding a plate of peanut butter toast over to me. I sipped my coffee before picking up a piece of toast and biting into it. My tongue was sticking to the roof of my mouth from the peanut butter.

"Well, that defeats the purpose of brushing my teeth," I told him, seeing as he smothered the poor toast in so much peanut butter that I might as well have been eating it straight from the jar.

"Too much peanut butter?" Ace chuckled as I tried to swallow it down with the dry toast, having to wash it down with my coffee.

"Just a little. What's going on with Tyson? He always seems to be working these days?" I asked him.

"Nothing. Just Alpha Jamie's pack causing problems. We have had a few issues within the pack because of him."

"What sort of problems in the pack?"

"Mate problems mostly. Three pack members from our pack found their mates."

"Why is that a problem, though?"

"Because they are from Alpha Jamie's pack."

"You don't want them to leave the pack?" I asked him, and he shook his head while sipping his coffee.

"No, we said they could go. It's not us. It's Jamie, he's using his pack members as hostages. Refusing to let them leave and denying our pack members time with their mates," he said.

"Well, that sucks. All for a piece of land? Why not just hand it over to him?"

"For starters, we had plans for it, but that isn't the only reason. Alpha Jamie wants the river to send his shit across pack borders. He knows if he steps over our packs', or the other packs' borders with his drugs, he will be strung up. The other packs bowed down and gave in, so the river running along the back here belongs to him. Except the piece that backs onto our land. Unless we give this side, he can't run his drugs up and down it to get it out of the city without crossing into someone's pack territory."

"Why doesn't Ryker do something about it?"

"Because he needs proof and reason to step on his land for him to intervene. Sure, he can walk in there and search his pack, but it would cause an uproar with him just walking in. And that may cause problems with the other packs."

"How was he getting it out before this then?"

"Planes from what we gathered. Ryker shut the airport down, which was on Alpha Jamie's territory, and had a new one built on the other side of the city. Then all this shit started," he said, looking at his watch.

"Come on, time to go," he said, finishing the rest of his coffee. I quickly did the same, dropping my plate and cup in the sink before following after him. I grabbed my bag and rushed out to his car, which was parked out the front of the packhouse. Only it wasn't his car, but a new silver one.

"Where is your car?" I asked him, and he scratched the back of his neck.

"Motor blew up. and Aamon has a friend who owns a dealership. He had this sent here this morning for me," he said with a shrug. Hitting the button to unlock the doors, he smirked. I huffed, walking over to the passenger side.

"You don't like it?" he asked.

"No. I preferred your old muscle car. This one is too… too…"

"Pretty and girly looking?" He chuckled, and I nodded, looking at the sleek Audi that Aamon had sent him.

"Well, lucky for you, I am not keeping this. I'm only borrowing it until I find another car," he said before climbing into the driver's seat. I climbed in before putting my seatbelt on.

"You don't have to go to the meeting thing, you know?"

"Well, Jacob is busy, and I am down as your guardian on the paperwork. So I kind of do have to go."

"Because that doesn't sound creepy at all. Mate and guardian," I told him. He shrugged, pulling out of the driveway and onto the highway.

"I don't mind. I like it. They will ring me if you need anything or if something happens," he said. We drove listening to the morning radio show for about twenty minutes before crossing the border into my mother's territory.

"Are you sure you want to come? I know you hate my principal," I told him as we got nearer.

"Lucy, I am going to the meeting. Now stop asking. I am not dropping you off and leaving. Besides, I already told them I would be going."

"But technically, I don't need a guardian. I am eighteen now," I told him.

"Yes, but for school, you do. Also, Tyson was pissed off you wouldn't let us come see you on your birthday," Ace said, and he didn't sound too happy about it either.

"I hate birthdays. Besides, I was busy helping mom with Ryden," I told him. He growled clearly, not happy.

"Well, it doesn't matter. Tyson still has something planned anyway," Ace said, and I rolled my eyes at him.

"My birthday was a week ago," I told him.

"I know when your birthday is, Lucy. I use it as my password for everything," he chuckled.

"Really?" I asked, a little shocked.

"Grab my phone out of my pocket," he said, and I leaned over and dug through his pants pocket. He lifted his hips, letting me get my hand into his pocket, and I pulled his phone out. Clicking on the screen, I saw a picture of me with Tyson from a few years ago at Christmas as his screensaver.

Chapter 47

Swiping up on his phone, it asked for a password, and I typed my birthday in as an eight digit number before his screen unlocked.

"See? Tyson also uses it for everything, too," he said.

"Sweet! Now I can snoop," I chuckled, and he held his hand out for his phone, but I pulled away, going through his shit on his phone.

"Lucy!" Ace said, leaning over and trying to take it from me.

"What are you hiding, Ace?" I taunted, flicking through his messages, but they were mostly Tyson, Jacob, and his mother. I clicked out of his messages and snooped through messenger and a few other apps but found nothing, before checking his browser history, which also was boring as fuck.

"Don't understand why you got your knickers in a knot. There is nothing bad in here," I told him, and he growled, holding his hand out for his phone.

"Though now I have to change my phone password. I wouldn't want you to see the nudes I sent to Mitchell a few months back," I teased when he suddenly jerked the car to the side of the road before slamming on the brakes

"You better be joking," he said, snatching my bag off the floor from between my legs. I rolled my eyes at him.

"Nope. Not joking. I even sent a few videos," I taunted as he rummaged through my bag. *Bloody idiot*, I thought to myself, *he should know me better than to do something stupid like that.*

"Ooh, I wonder if you have nudes?" I asked Ace, going into the camera roll on his phone as he grabbed mine and unlocked it. His eyes darted to me before he lunged for his phone, making me laugh as I turned in my chair and shoved him back with my feet.

"So, this is why you didn't want me snooping. Will I find dick pics?" I told him, praying there weren't nudes of Melana in there as I clicked on it. Ace tried reaching for his phone, but I kept shoving him back, and a laugh escaped me. He tried taking it from me with no luck. My face fell when I saw they were photos mostly of me, a few of Tyson, and one of Ryden with Rayan.

"Stalker alert," I shrieked as he tried to snatch his phone.

"It is not stalking! You are my mate."

"So, you take photos of me sleeping with your brother?" I told him.

"When you say it like that, yeah, it sounds creepy. But you wouldn't let me near you," he said before scrolling through my phone. I handed his phone back to him.

"You don't seriously think I would send nudes to someone, do you Ace?"

"No. But I would like to see what you talk to Mitchell about," he said, reading my messages.

"We will be late," I told him.

"Why will we? How many messages have you sent him?" I shrugged, not knowing because there were too many to count.

"If you want, just keep my phone, if you want to read my messages. I will take yours to school," I told him.

"Or, you can drive while I read," he said, still scrolling.

"No license. And this is manual. I can't drive manual," I told him. I also sucked at driving in general, but didn't want him to know I made no use of the driving lessons Tyson had paid for last year. He huffed before sliding his chair back, patting his lap. I raised an eyebrow at him.

"You can steer then," he said.

"What if I crash?" I told him, looking at this posh ass car that didn't suit him.

"Then it looks like I brought it. You will be fine. I will be controlling the pedals," he said, patting his lap again, and I could see he was too busy snooping through my phone. I sighed, climbing on his lap.

"Fine. But if we get pulled over, you are taking the blame. I am not losing my license before I even get it," I told him.

I turned the ignition on, and Ace moved his legs and put the car into gear, his hand on my thigh while he rested his chin on my shoulder, looking at the phone and also watching the road, making sure I didn't kill us. I pulled back on the road, and my hands started sweating instantly. I never wanted my license and hated the idea of driving.

"Slow down, Ace," I told him, my heart racing as the car picked up speed.

"Lucy, we still aren't even at the speed limit yet," he said, changing gears again, and the car picked up more speed.

"Ace!" I squealed. He tossed the phone in the passenger seat.

"You didn't do the driving lessons Tyson paid for, did you?" he said, remembering last year's birthday present from Tyson.

"Nope, I don't like driving," I told him, and one of his hands gripped the steering wheel, the other pulling me back against him while he sat up a little.

"Pull over so I can get in my seat."

"We are nearly there. Besides, you have the best seat," he said, thrusting his hips up, and I could feel the bulge in his pants.

"Ace," I said through gritted teeth, and he chuckled, pulling onto the road toward the school. I sighed, leaning back against him while he drove. My phone started ringing, and I glanced over at it and saw Mitchell's face pop up on the screen. I reached for it when Ace turned sharply, the phone sliding into the footwell out of reach.

"You did that deliberately," I told him, knowing that the corner wasn't that sharp.

"Yep," he admitted, kissing my cheek when it started ringing again. Ace pulled up at the school, and I looked at the dash to see we were five minutes late for the principal meeting. Yet many kids were still walking around just inside the gates when I knew the bell had rung ten minutes ago.

I shook my head and reached over, grabbing my bag and phone off the floor before climbing off Ace's lap when he opened his door, thankful no one was actually looking this way to catch me sitting on his lap. Ace climbed out before grabbing my hand. He tugged me toward the school, and I dropped his hand. Ace arched an eyebrow at me before draping his arm over my shoulder and pulling me beside him.

"Ace…" I whispered when I saw a few kids staring, but he just tugged me closer, ignoring me trying to escape him. My phone started ringing again as I entered the gates, and I retrieved it from my pocket, glancing at it to see Mitchell's face pop up again.

"Do you usually get this much attention?" Ace asked, making me look up from my phone, wondering what he was talking about. People were staring at me everywhere we turned, and at first, I thought it was because I was with Ace, but the whispers got worse as we entered the building. My phone started ringing again, vibrating in my hand, and I answered it.

"Yes, Mitchell?" I said, annoyed.

"Don't come to school," he said in a frantic, rushed voice.

"And why wouldn't I come to school, Mitchell? Besides, I just got here," I told him, seeing a few people whispering and pointing before Ace glared at them, and they scampered off. *What the fuck is going on?*

Chapter 48

"Lucy, turn around and leave the school Now!" Mitchell demanded.

"I have a meeting. I am just about to ..." I stopped talking and froze as I reached the doors that led to the quad in the center of the school. The principal's office was at the back of the school, and cutting through the quad was the fastest way there. It was also the main hangout spot for students.

Tears burned my eyes as I looked around, horrified. My stomach dropped, and my heart felt like it was lodged in my throat. I took a step back, praying this was some kind of nightmare I was yet to wake up from.

A growl tore out of Ace, and everyone ran as Ace started ripping the pictures down while I stood there in shock. Mitchell came racing over with a handful of papers like he was trying to pull them down himself, and I also noticed staff members trying to rip down the numerous pictures stuck to the walls.

"Lucy! Lucy!" Mitchell said.

I shook my head, words failing me as I looked around at every wall covered in pictures of me. Writing covering every wall in red paint. *Homewrecker! Whore. Slut*! Absolutely vile words, along with the pictures of that day. I just couldn't figure out how anyone got these photos or who took them, but I knew it had to be Josie as I felt my heart sink, twisting painfully in my chest.

Teachers were rushing around trying to rip them down along with janitors as I looked horrified at a picture of me running down the corridor barely dressed after Mr. Tanner tried to rape me. I knew it was that day from the fact I was clutching my torn shirt to my chest, my bra strap was broken, and just the look of pure horror on my face.

There were three different photos: one of him with me shoved over his desk, my skirt shoved up, and my face turned away from the person who took the photo. Mr. Tanner was standing behind me with his hand pushing my head into the desk. Looking at that particular photo, it looked like a porn scene from a movie. Only I knew it was actually him trying to rape me, and I also knew if the camera were on my face, it would see I clearly was not liking what he was doing to me as I struggled to get out of his clutches.

"Why?" It was all I could muster to say. How could she get photos from inside the classroom? Yet, I could see the photo was taken from the door and the gap where the blind didn't cover the window fully as I could see part of the blind. I swallowed when I saw one of me leaving the classroom, and my entire boob was exposed, my mascara all streaking my face, and my hair a mess.

I felt sick. And bile rose in my throat. Everyone had seen them. There were hundreds of prints stuck to the walls and glass windows surrounding the quad.

Mitchell was trying to steer me out of the quad, but I was frozen in place, and I suddenly fell deaf to my surroundings as I looked around. Everyone stared with judgmental eyes, seeing their lips move as they whispered. The worst day of my life was on display for everyone to see.

How could Josie take such photos and then say I was lying about what he tried to do? How could she see it as anything other than attempted rape and then photograph it and put it up for everyone to see? I blinked a few times. I could see Mitchell standing in front of me, trying to block me from seeing what she had done.

Was this payback for Ace banishing them? Doors swung open all around the quad. Ryker walked in, and shame smashed into me. It was one thing for everyone to see this, but my family? I looked around and saw Jacob and a few other close members in the pack rush in and start ripping them down, and I knew Ace must have mindlinked them. Students completely disappeared as Ryker growled at them, and I felt his Alpha aura rush out in a burst. Mitchell nearly dropped to his knees, and I didn't even feel the pain, having gone completely numb.

"School is over. Get the fuck out!" he boomed, making everyone run, including the teachers, leaving only four of Ryker's pack members, including Jacob and Tyson, who had rushed over.

Mitchell was still clinging to me, and I realized Ryker hadn't commanded him to leave, though he looked pale from Ryker's aura smashing into him.

"Get her out of here!" I heard my stepfather bellow before Ace and Tyson looked at me, about to come over to me. Realizing they were walking in my direction, I felt my heart twist painfully in my chest, suddenly facing them after having them see all this. I was mortified, ashamed, and never had I ever felt so disgusting and weak now that everyone had seen it, including my mates. Now everyone had witnessed my horror, witnessed my darkest secret and my most shameful moment. Now everyone knows.

I turned around and ran, not seeing the glass door was closed with my blurry vision as I ran flat out. I crashed straight through them, glass cutting into my hands, face, and chest, as I hit the ground with a thud, my teeth biting into my tongue as my chin smacked the ground. Yet, I still felt no pain but could taste my own blood filling my mouth, smell the bleeding from my cuts, yet no pain. Just shame, Just humiliation that cut so deep I suddenly wished I would just drop dead so I wouldn't have to face them.

"Shit! Lucy!" I heard Mitchell shriek, but I got up and continued to run. Unable to face any of them. Not wanting to face the judgment at how I could be so stupid to get myself in that situation. How weak I was. But most of all, I didn't want to see their pity. It was one thing for them to know what happened, but having a glimpse of it sickened me.

"Lucy, wait!" I heard one of them call, but I didn't stop and ran straight out of school.

Chapter 49

Tyson

I DIDN'T EVEN MAKE IT to work before Ace's voice boomed across the mindlink. What I wasn't prepared for was rushing to the school to see such a vile act against Lucy. Ryker, Jacob, and a few other pack warriors from Ryker's pack arrived at the same time I did, and we all froze as we looked around the quad. Hundreds of pictures of Lucy hung on the walls, and I froze in shock. It was one thing to know what that man tried to do, but to see it? I suddenly wished I hadn't. I Wish I could remove this memory from my head. Remove the images from my mind. It was one of those horrific scenarios you just couldn't unsee. The pure fear on her face as she ran out of that classroom. Teachers were racing around, trying to pull them down while students lingered and whispered.

Ryker started screaming orders and shut the school down while I scanned the quad looking for Lucy. Her horror in the photos was the exact same mask she was wearing on her face when I spotted her. Like she was reliving that day, like she was no longer here but trapped in her memories. Mitchell was gripping her arms, shaking her, but she was frozen in place, her eyes looking around at pictures exposing her. She looked devastated, vulnerable, but most of all, like she was about to break. Her eyes were glassy as she fought back the tears, and I couldn't decipher any emotion through the bond, like she had just shut down.

"Get her out of here!" Ryker yelled at no one in particular. Ace turned, tossing the pictures in his hand in the bin, and I turned back to look at her. Yet as her eyes darted to us, her face was morphing, and I couldn't decipher the look on her face when she turned around and ran. Running for the doors, Mitchell moved to chase after her, but she was running like her life depended on it. No. She was running like she was running from her teacher. Running from the man that nearly destroyed her. But this might just finish her off. As she approached the glass sliding doors, I could see she was too stuck in her head, and I screamed out to her.

"Lucy!" I choked out, but it was too late as she burst through the doors, tripping on the lip of the door and falling through the glass. The doors burst like an explosion, and Mitchell jumped back just in time as the glass shattered, covering her in its sharp shards and cutting her to pieces. She crawled to her hands and feet, and everyone held their breath as the glass crunched under her.

A few lingering students were snickering to themselves, and Ace growled, making them dart off like their asses were on fire. She stood so quickly that I almost missed the movement before she took off running from us.

"Lucy, wait!" Both Mitchell and Ace screamed after her, but she was gone in a blur. Leaving behind a trail of blood as she ran through the school's corridors while we chased after her.

The moment we were out of the school gates, Ace shifted, and so did Mitchell, their clothes shredding as they gave chase. But Lucy was fast and running on adrenaline. I could almost feel it coursing through her veins through the bond. We stood no chance of catching her. Hybrids were fast, but Lucy was more vampire than hybrid, making her quicker as her vampire DNA was strongest.

After losing her in the forest that surrounded the high school and primary school, we had to follow the scent of her blood, which was easy. Blood dropped, leaving a clear path after her.

"How the fuck did this happen?" I mindlinked Ace and Mitchell, who were running off my side.

"The quad doesn't get opened till the first bell. As soon as the janitor noticed, he went to retrieve the principal. But Lucy was already at school," Mitchell explained, but that still didn't explain how the person responsible got into the quad.

When the blood trail started to become more obvious, we realized she had started to slow down, and so did we. We stood there, listening for movement, but with the stream running alongside the forest, it was hard to pick up any movement. When I realized we were getting close to Ryker's packhouse.

Breaking through the treeline, we slowed as the front of the packhouse came into view. Lucy was still running toward the packhouse when the most heartbreaking guttural scream left her. You could hear her devastation. Feel her breaking as she starts to come apart at the seams.

"Mom!" One word, but the way it was screamed was gut-wrenching, soul crushing and filled with the torment swirling within her like a tornado. Lucy didn't stop, jumping clear over the boundary fence surrounding this side of the property. I saw the front door of the packhouse open, Reika rushing out the door in a panic, and my heart faltered for a second at her reaction, wondering if she would be mad.

"Lucy?" Reika said before spotting her daughter running toward her. Reika's face was panic stricken before she took off, running toward her daughter. Lucy ran straight into her arms with so much force they both tumbled toward the ground, Reika catching her and crushing her against her chest while Lucy wailed.

"What's wrong, What's wrong, baby?" Reika said, her voice panicked as Lucy clung to her like she was her life support. Reika also clung to her as we approached. All of us slowed down as we gave them space. Lucy was crying hysterically, wailing as her mother tried to soothe her, rocking her back and forth in her arms as they sat in the dirt.

Reika hissed, and I realized there was glass still sticking out of Lucy's face and arms and was cutting into her. Yet she didn't let her go, realizing her daughter needed her. Reika's eyes darted to us questionably, and I realized she was unaware of what had happened at the school. I could hear Ryden inside crying, and Reika looked back at the house when Mitchell suddenly shifted back, covering himself with his hands.

"I can go get him, Luna," he said, and Reika nodded to him. Mitchell rushed off to the packhouse, and Atticus approached Reika and Lucy on the ground. I also approached them and kneeled beside them, pulling the glass from her arms and hands. Atticus, Ace's wolf, was licking her wounds, yet I couldn't get to her face as it was buried in Reika's chest.

"Lucy. Honey, let your mates heal you," Reika said softly, pulling Lucy's face from her chest with her hands. She had glass jutting out of her cheek, and another large shard piercing through her chin.

Chapter 50

Her entire body was shaking, yet she didn't even flinch as I pulled the first three pieces of glass from her face. When she started shaking her head and pushing my hands away instead of letting me pull the rest out.

"Lucy! Stop! Let them," Reika said, gripping her face in her hands.

"What's wrong? What happened, baby?" Reika said, tears falling down her cheeks at seeing her daughter so frantic. Lucy tried to talk yet couldn't seem to catch her breath as she started to hyperventilate, gasping for breath. Tears continued to pour from her eyes, when she suddenly started flailing, ripping handfuls of her hair out and clawing at her face. I watched as Reika frantically tried to stop her hands from ripping herself apart, while Lucy started screaming.

My stomach twisted at the sight of her. Ace shifted back, trying to grip her hands and hold her still while Reika tried to soothe her, but she was way past soothing. She was turning manic. This was what broken looked like. When someone was pushed to close the edge, leaving them dangerously close to the brink of insanity. She was losing it. And nothing we did would calm her as she tore at her face, her scalp bleeding as she tore her hair from her head. You could only push someone so far before it became too much. And Lucy had hit her breaking point, and break she did.

"Do it!" Reika said, her eyes going to Ace and me. Ace fell back, shaking his head.

"I can't. I can't do that to her. Not again," he said, shaking his head, and Reika's eyes darted to me, and so did Ace's.

"Remark her," he choked out, looking at me. I hesitated, knowing that if I remarked her, not only would I knock her out, but it would reinforce the bond. I knew that from Lana, and her being marked repeatedly over the years. Both her mates had to rebite her as the bond strengthened more one way.

Ace hadn't marked her yet. Me marking her before both of us mated her could completely remove her bond to Ace.

"Ace?" I looked at him, panicked.

"It's okay, brother. I won't mark her again, not without Lucy's permission," he said.

"Ace?" I looked at him while Reika was still trying to restrain her.

"One of you needs to do it, And fast!" Reika snapped at us while Lucy screamed and flailed.

"It's fine. Just do it, Tyson," Ace said, moving her hair off her neck. I hesitated, when Tyrant forced control, sinking our teeth into her neck. She screamed, and I choked on her emotions as they slammed into me full force like they were mine and not hers. My teeth hit bone, and her movements slowed and became weaker.

"It's okay, baby. Momma's got you," Reika whispered before she went still. I pulled my teeth from her neck as she slumped forward onto Reika. I quickly pulled the rest of the glass from her wounds, and she started healing when Ace suddenly stood, making me look up at him. My stomach dropped at the dark expression on his face, yet he said nothing and bent down, taking her from Reika, and hugging her close to his chest.

"I fixed her room up the other day. We can put her in there," Reika said, standing up. Her chest and neck were covered in blood, but her cuts had already healed. Ace nodded to her before walking toward the packhouse silently. Yet his aura was potent as it rushed out of him, and I wasn't sure if he was mad at himself or me.

"It will be okay, Ace. She won't reject you when it comes time to mark her," I told him through the mindlink as we walked toward the house.

"I can't feel them, Tyson," he said.

"Pardon?" I asked.

"The tingles. I can't feel them."

"It may only be temporary," I told him.

"I hope so," he said as he continued toward the house.

Walking inside, Mitchell was standing in the foyer with a towel around his waist and Ryden in his arms while he gave him his pacifier, rocking Ryden in his arms.

"I didn't know how much formula," he said, but Ryden seemed fine as he sucked on his pacifier. He handed him to Reika, who took him.

"I will be up in a minute," she said to Ace, who started climbing the stairs toward Lucy's old room. Reika walked toward the kitchen.

"I should go," Mitchell said, and I shook my head.

"You can stay if you want," I told him, and he nodded, looking down at the towel around his waist.

"I will just duck home and grab some clothes," he said, and I nodded.

"I will come back soon," he said, walking toward the front door.

I walked upstairs to Lucy's bedroom, pushing the door open. I found Ace lying beside Lucy on her bed. The entire room had been transformed back to the way it was. Reika had even managed to reprint all of Lucy's photos that hung on the walls and replaced them. Ace had tucked her purple comforter under her chin, his head propped on his hand as he watched her, and brushed her hair from her face.

"This is all my fault," he said, and I shook my head.

"No, Tyson, it isn't. This all started because I was with Melana. And when Lucy wakes up, she will realize that and want nothing to do with me."

"It's not your fault, Ace. Lucy will see that."

"Will you stop it? Stop covering for me, Tyson. You don't have to fix this. I know what I have done. If Lucy wakes up and doesn't want me, you let her walk away. I won't cause any more damage to her," Ace said, sitting up.

"That won't happen, Ace. Lucy loves you. Loves both of us. You can't just walk away from the mate bond."

"What mate bond, Tyson? She won't feel it. And I won't have you making her feel bad if she doesn't want me anymore."

"You are being ridiculous. This changes nothing. You don't get to walk away. If you loved her, you would fight for her."

"No. It is because I love her that I would let her go. Let her be free of me. Let her be happy, with you. Everyone is right, Tyson. You are the good twin. You did everything right from the start. I don't deserve her. And Lucy deserves better than me, and that is you," Ace said before walking out of the room.

"Where are you going?" I called after him, yet he didn't answer. Instead, he ran down the steps, leaving the house.

Chapter 51

Lucy

My head was pounding when I woke up. I wished I didn't wake up at all, the numbness wore away, leaving fear and humiliation. The moment I did, everything smashed into me like a ton of bricks, threatening to suffocate me, restricting my ability to breathe. I was never going to escape him. Even now, when he couldn't get to me, he still haunted me, still lingered at the edge of my mind. Opening my eyes, I found myself lying beside my mother, who was asleep beside me on a bed that resembled my old one. It even had the same matching comforter I had before my room was destroyed. I sat up on one elbow, looked around, and realized I was in my old room. Everything was back to the way it was before I left for school in Avalon City.

It was like I'd stepped back in time before everything went to shit, a glimpse into my old life, to the person I once was. Now, though, I saw my old life differently. I found the darkest parts of it looming over me, and I realized how naive and young I truly was nearly a year ago. Pictures of me having fun with Mitchell when we went to the beach and bowling hung on the walls. Mom had blown those up and framed them. Photos of Rayan and me. Some of Ace and Tyson, it all seemed like a lifetime ago as I spotted each one on the walls.

It's funny how it only takes one thing to ruin your essence. One thing to burn the light out of your soul and dim the spark of life within you. Spending my early childhood in the facility was tough, horrific, and a brutal place to grow up in. But once I was freed, I thought that would be the end of my suffering. I had hopes and plans and was excited about my future and getting to experience the world to its fullest. The pictures held hope while I now felt nothing but hopeless and exposed.

Growing up in that place meant solitude, loneliness, and hopelessness. Stepping out was experiencing everything for the first time. The way fresh air smelled, how the breeze felt on my skin, and the feel of the earth under my bare feet was all new to me. And I was ecstatic at my newfound freedom. Sure that place sometimes haunted me still, the memories forever ingrained in my head. Yet I could disassociate them from the life I had now, separate them from me, and allow myself to feel safe for once.

But Mr. Tanner ruined that sense of safety. It took years of counseling and occupational therapy during the first few years of my freedom. Even just learning to adjust. That place made me institutionalized, and I struggled without the constant routine. Always looking over my shoulder and on edge, waiting for the doctors to come in and poke and prod us. Then everything went down the drain again, all that time gone, and I was finally free and happy within myself, and I felt safe.

Only to have the blindfold ripped off and be shown that even out here, monsters still existed. Showed me that they were lurking in the shadows, only now I was older and the horrors more real because I knew how dangerous they were. I was at the age when

I should have been able to understand and pick up the signs of what a monster looked like. How could I be wrong and blind to it when I was raised in a facility full of them torturing us?

You would think I would be able to recognize them instantly. Yet no one tells you the biggest monsters are those we put our trust in. Those we blindly trust because they have sworn to protect and teach us. Now looking back, the signs were there. I just missed them. But now, they were startlingly clear. And I feared I would never be able to go back to the comfortable bliss I lived in before he tried to destroy me.

The way he used to hang around us students, us girls in particular. The way he would help us get away with things and bail us out. I thought he was just one of the good teachers, a friend even. An adult that saw us for who we were, instead of just pitying the mutated freaks. But I learned everything comes with a price, I just didn't see it then.

So, does it make it my fault because I missed the warning signs? Even when he asked me to pull the blind down, something was screaming at me that something was off. Yet I shoved it aside, stupidly trusting the devil in disguise. So, now I find myself questioning everyone's intentions, looking for anything to warn me away. I missed how I was carefree, invincible, and free of my own tormented mind before it all.

I missed my innocence when the world looked colorful and beautiful. Now, I only saw the darkness in everything, the things that could go wrong. Now I worried about how I dressed, how I talked, and how much of myself I put on display. That worried me. Besides, couldn't they all tell? Could they not see how disgusting I was? Couldn't they see how much I hated what he tried to do? How much I hated myself for almost letting him succeed? But the biggest burning question was, do they blame me the same way I blamed myself for not seeing the warning signs? Did I ask for it? And was it my fault?

Looking at my mother, I truly saw her for the first time. Saw why Amanda snapped. I was the nightmare Amanda kept living. The memory ingrained in her mind like he was in mine. Tragically broken and left with only the broken pieces. No matter how much glue, how much force and strength you used to hold those pieces together, it only took one trigger to shatter them all over again and dissolve the little safety you'd once felt.

Hearing movement, I looked down between us and found Ryden stirring before feeling movement behind me, making me look over my shoulder to see Rayan curled up and jammed in my back as he snuggled against me. Turning to face my mother, I found her eyes open, staring back at me.

Chapter 52

I watched as she pressed her lips together, and my breathing hitched, wondering if she knew what Josie and Melana had done. It was the only explanation for how those photos got out. Even banished, we no longer cast rogues out, they were still allowed to join other packs. They just had to get off the turf of the pack they were banished from. I couldn't see my mother or Ryker accepting them into the pack, making me wonder how they got into this territory unnoticed, let alone on the school grounds. Judging by the look on my mother's face, she knew exactly what they did as her eyes softened and turned teary.

She reached over, gripping my hand that was by my face before kissing it and holding it tight. Her hand was warm as she brushed her thumb over my fingers softly.

"You don't let them win. What happened, happened and it's not who you are. You are not the things that happen to you Lucy. So don't keep giving them control," she whispered. A lump formed in my throat as emotion tried to choke me.

"Everyone knows, mom. Everyone saw it," I told her. Shame crushed me. Everyone knew now. My secret was out, and my agony was on display for them all to judge and see.

"Let them see you survived what they couldn't. People break for less, Lucy. You learned to live. You will learn again. You know what I see?" she asked, her eyes holding mine, and I swallowed, wondering if she saw the same sharp shards of my soul that were jutting through my flesh and slowly killing me. I wondered if she saw me the same way I saw myself, disgustingly weak and naive. The foolish girl that walked into a monster's den and let him almost destroy her.

"I see my daughter. I see the little girl who grew up in a glass cage surrounded by people who tried to break her but couldn't. I watched you die, but then I watched you live. It was hard, but you did it. You rebuilt yourself to become the woman that you are. You fought so goddamn hard to put that place behind you and live a normal life. If they couldn't break you in that place, don't let one man do it. You survived hunters as a child. You survived your own death. And you will survive this, because I know my daughter, and I see you, and you will not break. So don't give them that satisfaction. A lesser person would break, but not my Lucy. My Lucy is a survivor," she said before wiping my tears.

I sniffled and nodded, trying to force myself to believe her words. This was the woman I missed. Even when everything happened, even when I knew we weren't on the best terms, all I could think was that I needed my mom. Mom could fix this, she would make it go away. Now I realized she couldn't, but she wouldn't let me fall either. She would hold me up when I no longer could because she was my mom, the woman who tossed away a huge part of herself for me. The woman who chose me over her wolf and still forgave me for almost destroying her.

Ryden stirred, crying out, and I reached over with my other hand rubbing his belly in a circular motion before looking up at my mother.

"Where are my mates?" I asked her.

"Tyson is downstairs. But Ace went with your father. Mitchell went home. I had Jacob drop him off."

"Where did dad go?"

"He is tearing the city apart with Ace, looking for Josie and Melana." I swallowed and nodded. How could someone who used to be my best friend cause so much destruction to my life? It didn't make sense. She was a woman too. How could another woman do that to another? Brand their soul with such cruelty, and put them on display like that? I could never do what she did, no matter how much I hated her. How much pain she caused me. I could not do that to another woman and live with myself.

"Your father said it will be your choice what becomes of them," my mother told me, but I didn't want that choice. I didn't want to be the monster. I dealt with monsters my entire life, I wasn't going to become one.

"I can't," I whispered to her. I just wanted to understand why she would hurt me this way. We grew up together, lived the same nightmare, and were bonded by it, yet she still did this.

"You can't do what, Lucy?" my mother asked me.

"Decide their fate," I told her. I couldn't do it. I hated them, and I knew that would taint my judgment, and I wouldn't stoop to their level. I didn't need to destroy them the way they tried to destroy me. I knew how that felt, and banishment wasn't enough. Still, I couldn't take their lives because that would be on me. I couldn't have their deaths on my hands.

"Then I will do it," she said, making my eyes dart to hers. "No one messes with my children and gets to keep breathing afterward," she said, and I gulped at her words, seeing the determination in her eyes. She meant every word she said, I would never doubt that.

Yet could I let her do this? Would it be the same as me signing their death warrant?

"Mom?" I whispered.

"I know you, Lucy. I know you don't want to do it but they will pay. You don't have to live with their deaths on your hands. But I would wear their blood happily on mine. There is no bigger monster than a mother's wrath. And I will make them pay with their lives," she said. I knew this was a promise she would keep.

They would pay, and I felt sorry for anyone that got in her way because she would destroy them. She wasn't just the Queen, she was my mother, and I feared my mother more than her title as Queen. As Queen, she ruled fairly, but as my mother, she would destroy them until there was nothing left but a hollow corpse of despair. One thing my mother did best was to switch from diplomat to warlord. Josie and Melana had no idea who they had just signed up to war with. And my mother didn't fight fair.

Chapter 53

Ace

We searched everywhere, even split off to a few different territories, searching for Melana and Josie. Yet we came up empty. For the most part, the other pack Alphas gladly accepted us on their territories, leaving only one territory left unsearched. Which I knew was either going to be a flat out refusal or a pain in the ass to convince.

Ryker could demand entry onto Alpha Jamie's territory, but he would receive backlash from the other packs for abusing his power. The last thing we needed was to go to war with the five packs surrounding ours, though two of the smaller new packs were less likely to give us trouble and my family's packs outnumbered them. I knew that the other three were itching for a chance to take on the Alpha King, and with a new baby and his family to protect, I also knew that wasn't something Ryker was willing to risk right now.

Ryker pulled up at the bridge crossing between the two territories and got out of the car.

"Stay here. And keep your mouth shut!" Ryker snarled at me when I took my seatbelt off. I folded my arms across my chest, glaring out the windshield as Ryker approached the boundary line. Alpha Jamie, the smug bastard, was leaning against the bridge's barricade, like he had no care in the world.

He smiled brightly as Ryker approached and bowed his head slightly to Ryker, but in no way was he about to bow down to the Alpha King. Alpha Jamie had called in reinforcements to witness this showdown, and I knew as soon as we pulled up, and I spotted two of the Alphas from rival packs standing on Jamie's side that they were here to see if Ryker would force entry onto Jamie's territory.

"Fuck this," I muttered to myself, tossing the door open. Ryker looked over his shoulder at me, his lips pulling back over his teeth and his canines slipping out before his voice boomed through the mindlink.

"Get back in the fucking car, Ace!" His command rolled over me, and I faltered but grit my teeth through it. Alpha Jamie's taunting, knowing smile irritated me as I fought the urge to turn around and get back in the car.

"Run along, boy. Let us adults handle this," Jamie taunted, setting my blood on fire.

"Step over this side and say it. See how cocky you are then," I spat at him, forcing Ryker's command off and taking a step forward. Pain radiated and coiled around my muscles, but just them witnessing me fighting off his aura was enough to make Jamie stammer. Ryker might be King, but we had the same blood running through our veins.

"Ace, get in the car. I will handle this," Ryker told me.

"Exactly what will you be handling? The answer is no. And if you step on my territory, I have witnesses, Ryker. You're a smart man. Would it be worth angering the packs if you storm into my territory?"

"You are harboring rogues that committed treason against the Alpha King's family!" Ryker bellowed, and Jamie shuddered as his aura rushed at him, forcing him to his knees as he bared his neck. The two other Alphas glanced nervously at each other.

"She isn't blood, therefore not treason. Just normal schoolyard bullying, and unless you have proof of them being on my territory, you have no right to ask for entry. Especially for a mutated freak," Jamie grit out through clenched teeth. Ryker stepped toward him, a growl escaping him, and Jamie laughed sadistically while the two Alpha looked on the verge of wetting themselves.

"Go on, my King. Step over the border, but make sure you smile for the camera," Jamie said, and Ryker froze, looking toward the parked car and blocking the bridge. I could see the blinking red light and knew they were recording this, and no doubt would be live streaming it to the surrounding packs. Yet Alpha Jamie wasn't someone to mess with lightly. His drug connections not only had humans on his side but also other supernaturals that were part of his organization. Ryker had been trying to get him shut down for years, but somehow, he managed to get himself out of trouble every time with the help of the supernatural society pulling strings for him and the human government.

Pack wars were one thing, but a flat-out war with other supernaturals was another thing entirely. I knew if it came down to it, Avalon City's occupants would come running if their High Priestess Avery stepped forward and declared war. Which I had no doubt she would if our family was threatened but war was something we tried to avoid. The casualties among the humans and our own kind would be damaging, and the humans would cause a headache with their armies, which outnumbered the supernaturals ten to one. No one wanted to go to war; it was not worth the risk of causing World War III.

"When I get proof Jamie, you better run for the fucking hills for getting in my way," Ryker warned him.

"Well, until then, Alpha King, get the fuck off my territory," Jamie grit out. Sweat was now rolling down his face and neck, drenching his shirt as he tried his best not to cry out. I knew he had to be in agony. If Ryker really wanted to put on a display, I knew he would be screaming and begging Ryker to let the command go, but with witnesses and laws sanctioning all supernaturals now, it wasn't worth the headache it was causing him.

Ryker started walking back to me and dropped his command over Jamie. I could tell he wanted to rip him apart, but the laws had his hands tied.

"Get in the car. You just had to get out?" Ryker growled at me. I wanted to argue with him, but the look he gave me had me shutting my mouth and obeying.

I got in the car before hearing the mindlink open up to all five of our family packs, which were all interlinked.

"Alpha Jamie crosses into any territory, I order you to kill on site. Do not grant him entry or try and talk to him," Ryker snarled through the bond. His aura was so violent and potent in the car, I was trying to stop my hands from trembling as I fought against him.

A chorus of "Yes Alpha" and everyone asking what was going on slipped through the link, but Ryker was much too angry to explain as I heard my sisters, aunty, and brothers-in-law's voices slip into the mindlink. My mother frantically tried to get an answer, but Ryker cut the link shutting them out.

"I will explain later," he told me, and I nodded as Ryker started the car.

"He will slip up. Those girls won't be able to resist hiding for long, and when they come out, I will show them what nightmares are made of," Ryker growled.

"So, what now? I just go home and tell Lucy she has to deal with it until we find them?" I asked him, annoyed that we couldn't just finish this shit once and for all.

"Yes, That's exactly what you will do. Keep her safe and at home until then." I growled, annoyed at his words, but I also knew there was nothing else we could do for now.

"If she still wants me," I muttered to myself.

"Well, you should have thought about that before you stuck your dick in someone that wasn't your mate," Ryker told me.

"You think I don't wish I could take that back?" I snapped at him, sick of everyone throwing it in my face.

"You knew she was your mate and still did it." Ryker said simply.

"You know the bond is gone, right?" I told him, and he nodded.

"Tyson told me. She will come around. She knows you are her mate. Why didn't you just mark her again? She would have forgiven you?"

"Yes, but I don't think I would forgive myself. She has had enough people hurt her. I have hurt her. I won't make that mistake again," I told him as we headed back to the packhouse.

"And if she doesn't want you? Then what?"

"Lana said I could move to their pack."

"You're going to leave?" he asked.

"If she doesn't want me, I won't be the one to cause conflict between Tyson and her."

Chapter 54

Lucy

Rayan eventually woke up, and mom had to leave to make a bottle for Ryden. I didn't want to leave the little bubble of my room, but I missed my mates too, and I wanted to go home. As much as I loved being here, it was no longer home anymore. Getting up, I grabbed a bag just as my mother came back in with Ryden in her arms, feeding him a bottle.

"You're leaving again?" she asked, and I nodded.

"Well, I can help you pack. I replaced almost everything. Ryker kept a detailed list of everything I destroyed, thank god but a lot of it I found was in Rayan's room," she said, and I could see the guilt on her face as she placed Ryden down on the bed.

"Lucy, I am sorry for everything. I should have told you about Amanda. I should never have—"

I waved her off. "It's fine, mom. I get it. I really do. I know that wasn't you, and even if it was, I understand it," I told her. She nodded before opening some of the drawers, pulling my clothes out and putting them in a duffle bag.

"Is Tyson still here?" I asked her, and she nodded.

"Yes, he hasn't left except to get his car," she told me, and I felt relief flooding me.

"What about Ace?"

"Ryker is dropping him home now. He wants to give you some space," she told me, and my brows furrowed.

"What do you mean?"

"You will figure it out. Not really my place to explain. Your relationship is between them and you. I will be here no matter what you choose, Lucy," she told me, making me more confused.

I gathered a few things and placed them in my bag before finding an old photo album and tossing it in with my things. I zipped the bag up, and my mother grabbed it, so I grabbed Ryden before following her downstairs to the living room. Rayan came over to me before spotting the bag in my mother's hands.

"You aren't staying?" he asked sadly, and I felt my heart clench.

"No, but maybe you can come for a sleepover on the weekend," I asked, looking at my mother. She nodded, and Rayan smiled sadly before agreeing and wrapping his arms around me. I passed Ryden back to mom, and I hugged him close before kissing his head.

Leaning over the back of the couch in the living room, I found Tyson asleep, his mouth wide open as he snored. I jammed my fingers in his mouth, and he choked, jolting upright, and I laughed at him.

"What the fuck?!" he choked out before noticing me. "Lucy?"

I smiled at him before he jumped off the couch in a blur, racing around it and engulfing me in a hug. Tingles rushed everywhere so much stronger than before, and my mark tingled, making me shiver as I leaned into him.

"You're okay. You made me worry for a bit." I nodded, hugging him back. I was far from okay, but I had my mates and my family.

"Yeah, I am fine. I just want to go home," I told him, pressing my nose into his neck and inhaling his scent.

"You don't want to stay? I don't mind staying here," Tyson said, but I shook my head.

"No. Besides, Ace is at home," I told him, and he pulled away, looking at me oddly.

"So, you spoke to him?" Tyson asked, and I shook my head.

"No, but I want to go home with my mates," I told him, and he nodded, looking at my mother, who shook her head at him.

"Why are you being strange? What is going on?" I asked them.

"Nothing, but we should head home before it gets too late," Tyson said, taking my bag from my mother. The tension in the room was so strong that I could almost taste it. I could feel worry eating at Tyson through the bond as he grabbed my hand, heading toward the door.

"What's wrong? Didn't they catch Josie and Melana?" I asked, now worried. Tyson tensed before stopping and retrieving his keys from his pocket.

"No, but we will. We won't let them get to you, Lucy," Tyson assured me. Knowing they were out there doing god knows what sickened me. Those girls were never going to stop until they broke me, and I wasn't sure how much more I could take. What else could possibly go wrong?

We said goodbye to everyone, and Tyson put my bag in the trunk. Just as we were leaving and pulling out, my father's car stopped beside us. Tyson wound down my window, leaning across me, and my stepfather did the same.

"I just dropped Ace off. We will keep searching tomorrow," he told Tyson, who nodded before my stepfather looked at me.

"We will find them," he assured me, and I knew he would do everything in his power to do exactly that.

"I will talk to you tomorrow. Let me know how Ace goes. Fair warning, though; he is in a mood," my stepfather told Tyson.

Tyson sighed. "I will deal with him," Tyson told him, and Ryker nodded before winding his window up and parking his car. We headed home, and the entire drive, we barely spoke. I could tell something was on Tyson's mind, feeling it eating away at him. His grip on the steering wheel was a clear giveaway of how tense he was. I felt like everyone was hiding something from me, but with everything going on, I was too caught up in my own tumultuous thoughts to pry too much just to get answers.

"When we get home, please try not to freak out," Tyson suddenly said.

"Huh, what do you mean?" He didn't bother to elaborate, and I gave up trying to understand. When we pulled up at the packhouse, the porch light was on, and I could see Ace's car in the driveway.

"I will grab your bag. Are you hungry? I can cook dinner or order out."

"No need. I am already cooking," Ace said as I stepped out of the car. I smiled up at him, and he watched me nervously before taking my bag from Tyson and walking inside. I looked at Tyson, wondering why Ace didn't approach me. Did he believe Josie's and Melana's lies? Did he think the pictures were true to what they'd said? I followed them inside, my stomach growling hungrily at the smell of food, yet Ace's strange behavior made me nervous. Ace placed my bag in Tyson's room, and I made my way to the kitchen to see what he was cooking.

"Something smells good," I told him, looking in the oven.

"Yeah, pasta bake," Ace said, leaning on the other side of the counter. I walked around to him, and he stepped away from me, and Tyson cleared his throat awkwardly.

"Come on. Let's go find a movie to watch," he said, grabbing my hand and pulling me away from Ace. I shook his hand free.

"Wait, I just want to speak to Ace," I told him, ignoring him. I walked over, wrapping my arms around his waist and inhaling his scent. Ace's entire body tensed, and I looked up at him, wondering why he was acting weird. When it suddenly hit me. I sniffed him, his scent the same, yet it wasn't as intoxicating. Where were the sparks and the weird magnetic pull I usually felt toward him?

"It's my fault," Tyson blurted out, making me look over at him.

"Pardon?" I asked him, letting Ace go.

"The reason the bond is gone. It can be fixed," Tyson rushed out.

"Our bond is gone, completely gone?" I asked, looking up at Ace. His jaw was clenched, and he wouldn't meet my eye, and I stepped back. *Is that why he was being weird?*

"Yes, Lucy, it is gone," Ace said, and I felt my stomach drop and my face heat up at his words. So, he was acting like this because he didn't want me anymore? I was so confused by this situation and now understood why everyone was acting strange. I didn't even think it was possible without rejecting someone.

"How?" I asked, looking over at Tyson.

"I marked you again. It weakens the bond when you have multiple mates. Lana told me about it. Ace hasn't marked you, so it forged our bond to become stronger. Apparently, it wears off but takes time."

"How much time?"

Tyson shrugged, and I could see he didn't know.

"So, you don't want to be my mate anymore?" I asked Ace. He finally looks at me, his head whipping to the side.

"No, I do, but you can be free of me if you choose to. I won't stop you, Lucy," Ace said.

"Is that what you want?" I asked him, suddenly unsure. Ace also looked uncertain. Was he second-guessing the mate bond now that he wasn't tied to me? Everything was so straightforward before. The bond made it nearly impossible to reject each other, but with it gone, did that mean he no longer felt as strongly about me as I still did about him? Bond or not, he was still mine.

Chapter 55

"It's okay if you don't, Lucy. I am giving you an out. I will walk away and let you live in peace with Tyson. I know I don't deserve you after everything I put you through, after what I have done."

I let his words sink in for a second; he was giving me an out. But I didn't want an out, we were all paired together for a reason, and if the Moon Goddess believed it would work, I had no reason to doubt her, right? It was unconventional to be destined to two mates, yet I knew it would work with them being twins. It worked for Aunty Lana and so many others. Tyson might agree that the choice was mine, only it wasn't. It was up to the Moon Goddess, and if I were to be paired with anyone, I was now glad it was two people I knew, two people I loved anyway. Two people who loved me just as much as I loved them.

"Just let me gather a few things, and I will go," Ace said, mistaking my silence for rejection. *Why does he think I would just toss him aside after everything?* Yes, Ace fucked up, but he couldn't be blamed for Josie and Melana. He thought he was doing the right thing by banishing them; he had the right intentions, and it wasn't his fault they retaliated by trying to ruin me.

"What? No!" I told him in panic. That was the last thing I wanted. The entire time at home, all I could think about was coming home to my mates; that meant both of them. Ace stopped and turned around to face me, his eyes moving to Tyson, but Tyson didn't interrupt or add anything. He just watched us, though I could feel his worry loud and clear through the bond.

"You don't have to say yes because of Tyson, Lucy. I know Tyson is the better choice," Ace said, stunning me. I shook my head, stepping closer to him, and I could feel Tyson watching us, but he remained quiet, and I realized they were really giving me a choice to turn him away.

"There is no better choice, Ace. If I can't have both of you, then I would rather have neither of you," I told him. His eyebrows pinched together before he looked at Tyson behind me. I couldn't choose, and I didn't want to, and it would destroy both of them if they didn't have each other. It would also destroy me not to have them. I marked Tyson already, and he had marked me, but that didn't mean I felt nothing for Ace. Yes, the bond was gone, but I had always loved them. I just didn't realize it.

"So, you want me to stay?" Ace asked, scratching the back of his neck and looking down at me. I ran my hands across his chest to his shoulders, stepping closer to him. He needed to understand that this decision was what I wanted, that Tyson didn't influence it in any way. I just needed him to stay.

"You're mine, Ace. Nothing changes that. You are mine just as I am yours," I told him.

"You're not just saying that for Tyson, are you? I can't feel you, Lucy, so I need to be sure. If you don't want this, I understand. Don't feel guilty or pity me. I made mistakes, and I will live with them no matter what you decide." The look on his face told me he really thought I was saying this for Tyson's sake.

I reached up, wrapping my arms around his neck. His arms wrapped around my waist, and he dropped his face into my neck, inhaling my scent before he sighed, pulling back to look at me. Before he could say anything or question me further, I jumped up, wrapping my legs around his waist and sinking my teeth into his neck. His grip on me tightened, one of his hands going under my butt, the other pulling me closer and crushing me against his chest like he was afraid to let go, and this all had been a mere trick of his imagination. His blood poured into my mouth, and I moaned at the taste of him.

The tingles returned, making me shiver, and Ace made a noise in the back of his throat. I felt the bond solidify and snap into place with so much force that it made me jerk back. My mark now lay on his flesh, forever marking him as mine. I leaned down, pressing my lips to his mark before running my tongue over it to seal it and stop the bleeding. Ace let out a shaky breath, and I looked at him to see tears rolling down his face. I clutched his face in my hands, his silver eyes glowing back at me.

"You're mine, Ace. Just as I belong to you. I want to be yours too," I told him. I pressed my lips to his before turning my face and baring my throat to him, where Tyson's mark lay etched into my skin. I felt heat press against my back as Tyson wrapped his arms around both of us, his lips pressing to my cheek softly when I felt Ace's teeth sink into my neck above Tyson's mark.

My entire body ignited in sparks, and goosebumps raised all over my skin. Ace pulled his teeth from my neck, running his tongue over his fresh mark, and I felt the heaviness of the bond creeping in and trying to suck me under as I pulled back from him.

"And now I'm yours," I whispered, my eyes growing heavy when Ace clutched my face staring at me as I fought to remain awake, my muscles becoming heavy and my face falling forward against his hand.

"Tyson, her eyes," I heard him whisper before losing consciousness, wondering what he was talking about.

Chapter 56

Josie

The creaking of the cell door had my head snap up to see Alpha Jamie walk into the cell I was put in. Melana said we would be safe here, but the moment we stepped over the pack border after Ace had banished us, we were dragged to the cells and separated.

"Where is my sister?" I asked, looking at the man that had ruined her life from the moment we left the facility. Recruiting kids to run his drugs on the street, he was as low as they came. Melana never stood a chance when he took us in. Only to send us off to Ace's pack a year later as a spy, under the excuse he didn't want mutations breeding with his pack.

"You don't ask questions, mutt. Now get up and follow me," he growled, and I got off the concrete floor. My back cracked as I stood up. I had no idea how long I had been stuck down here, but the tightness of my muscles meant I had been here for at least a few hours already. Walking up the steps, I stepped outside of the bunker. Alpha Jamie shoved me toward the packhouse, and I nearly stumbled.

"Get moving. She should have let you die; it would have saved all this drama," Alpha Jamie snapped at me. I felt my stomach sink. He was right; this was my fault. My sister was the only reason I was still alive. I walked toward the packhouse, keeping my head down when I picked up my sister's scent, making me move quickly as I stepped inside. The polished floorboard made my sneakers squeak.

Turning into the living room, I saw my sister sitting in the armchair by the fireplace. Her lip was split but already healing, and she had a huge black eye. Tears brimmed in my eyes at the sight of her, knowing it was all my fault. I rushed to her side, and she opened her arms up, instantly embracing me in a hug and checking me over.

This was my fault. She was hurting because of me. I put my trust in the wrong person. I thought I could trust him. How was I supposed to know he would keep Alpha Jamie's shipment for himself? He said he would do the job; he was my mate. I had no reason to think he would do that to me. Mates were supposed to love us. Clearly, that was a lie.

"Both fucking useless. You were supposed to convince Ace to hand that land over, not fall in love with him. Is that why you rejected him, Melana? I will fucking kill him. Is that what you want?" Alpha Jamie snapped at her. Melana shook her head.

"No, no, please. You know that's not why. I don't know what you expected. I told you Lucy was their mate. Leave him out of it. We can work something out. I will get you your money back," she begged him with tears rolling down her cheeks. Alpha Jamie laughed cruelly.

"You got 500 thousand, Melana. The deal was you would convince Ace to sign that land over, or I would kill your sister.

So since I don't own that piece of land, looks like it's going to cost you your sister," he said, taking a threatening step toward me.

Melana jumped to her feet, shoving me behind her and onto the armchair behind her. Alpha Jamie punched her, and I screamed as blood spurted from her nose, and he grabbed her hair.

"Stand down, Melana. We had a deal, but I am open to negotiations," Alpha Jamie growled at her.

"She was meant to have nothing to do with this. Keep her out of it. I told you not to involve her. If it is anyone's fault, it is yours for putting your shipment in a seventeen-year-old girl's hands. There is no way she could move that amount in a fucking school," Melana snapped at him. Despite bleeding and being in pain, she still fought for me, still defended me fiercely.

"I will get the money. I will speak to Ace—" Melana said, but Alpha Jamie laughed in her face before shoving her backward onto me, her entire body shaking, blood drenching the front of her shirt.

"You haven't heard? There is a bounty for both of your heads after your little school incident."

"What school incident?" I asked, confused. Alpha Jamie walked into the office attached to the living room, and I looked at Melana, but she was just as clueless as me. Alpha Jamie returned with my phone and a handful of papers. He tossed them on my lap. My phone lit up, and I saw the photo of Lucy and me at a football game three years ago pop up on the screen.

I looked at the papers, and my stomach dropped. "What did you do?" I gasped, shocked, when I saw the photos of Lucy running from the classroom after he tried to rape her.

"I made sure both of you are as good as dead." He laughed. Melana ripped the papers out of my hand.

"I... what did you do, Jamie? This isn't funny. How—" Melana said, and I saw the hurt on her face; it matched mine when I took them.

I was devastated when I took them but also pissed off, the mate bond making me blind to what I was truly seeing. I hated calling her names when I saw her last, hated what we did, and so did Melana. She always knew about Lucy. Ace told her as soon as he'd found out she was his mate, but Melana still fell in love with him. Still, she knew she had a mate out there for herself too.

When she found him, Alpha Jamie used him as a tool against her, forcing her to do his bidding and get information from Ace. It caused major problems so he wouldn't suffer if she had rejected him, but he refused her rejection and said he knew why she was doing it, and he wouldn't accept her rejection even if the bond was severed already.

What we weren't expecting was for Mr. Tanner, who is my mate, to run off with a shipment of drugs I had in a storage locker that Alpha Jamie had given to me to sell around school and in Avalon City. Melana was going to walk away and leave it at that when Lucy turned eighteen. But once Alpha Jamie found out my mate stole his drugs and I couldn't get them back, he told Melana to convince Ace to hand that stupid block of land over.

She almost had him convinced, too, but then Lucy came home early. She was so close to freedom, and she would have gotten her mate back from the bastard, and everything would have been fine, but Lucy came home early. I didn't blame her after what Nathan had done to her, but it was really shitty timing.

"I have my ways, and I had a heap of flyers made, decorated that school for her. Now you have the entire city looking for you, girls. You are as good as dead unless—" He laughed, but Melana cut his words off.

"You fucking sick bastard, how could you do that to her? She has nothing to do with this," Melana screamed at him. He growled at her, but she didn't back down.

"I will go to them and tell them it was you, you sick fuck. Josie isn't taking the blame for this!"

"Is that so? Don't forget where your mate is, Melana. I will kill him. Do you want to see your precious mate die because of that little bitch?" he asked, pointing at me.

Melana looked over her shoulder at me and hung her head. She was caught between me and her mate. We were in this situation because of a debt I owed. Alpha Jamie whistled loudly, and two men walked in. I shrank back, recognizing them to be the guards from the cells.

"So I have another deal for you. Do this one job successfully, and I will set you both free, including your mate," he offered, and Melana's shoulders slumped.

I gripped her arm and shook my head at her. "It's fine, Melana. I did this," I told her, accepting my death. If it meant she would be free, I would happily accept my death.

"So, which is it, Melana? Josie or one last job?" Alpha Jamie asked her.

"Don't do it," I whispered to her, clutching her face in my hands, pleading with her to let me go.

"I won't lose you. You're all I have, and I promised mom I would keep you safe, Josie," she said. I tried to protest, but she grabbed my face in her hands.

"I won't lose you. This life has taken enough from me. I won't let it take you too," she said before letting go and turning to Jamie. I hated this man, hated him more than anything on this earth, hated him as much as I hated my mate for what he did to Lucy.

"What is the job?" Melana asked, standing up.

"I want Lucy, you bring her to me, and I will get you both out of the City and free of this place."

"What do you want Lucy for?" I demanded.

"As a bargaining tool," he answered simply.

"For some fucking land?" I screamed, outraged. He stepped forward, and the two guards did too. Melana blocked him, and he smirked before chuckling at her actions. My sister would throw herself in front of a bullet for me. Alpha or not, she would fight back even if it meant her death.

"Not just the land. I want Ryker to give me his son."

"But he is a kid," I told him.

"He won't be for long, and I want his son, promised to Emily when she turns eighteen," Alpha Jamie said with a shrug.

"Emily is six," Melana said. I was shocked that Alpha Jamie could so easily marry his daughter off. The thought sickened me. *Take her choice away before she even understood what it meant.*

"What about her mate? She won't want to be married off. She will want to be with her mate," I told him.

"I will take care of any mate she has," he said with a shrug.

"Don't do it, Melana," I told her, and even she wasn't sure about this idea. It was one thing kidnapping the Alpha King's step-daughter, another to then threaten him with her and demand his son.

"Exactly how do you plan on getting him to agree to this? He will just back out and refuse to marry your daughter when he is older."

"Not if they are blood-bound," Alpha Jamie said. My face scrunched up, having never heard that term before.

"I only need his son's blood. I won't be here forever, and I need to ensure she is taken care of. She isn't made for this business, and unfortunately, I don't have any sons to pass it on to. This will ensure her future."

"You're sick. It will never work, and Ryker will never agree to this," Melana said.

"Ryker doesn't need to agree. Only his son does. It will work. I have a witch that will ensure they will be tied to each other, and my daughter will be the next Queen of Alphas."

Chapter 57

Tyson

"Tell me you saw that too," Ace asked me, and I nodded. Lucy's head was resting on his shoulder as she passed out from his bite.

"I saw something," I told him, not sure what to make of it. Lucy had never had a wolf, yet her eyes flickered black, as if her wolf had come forward for a second.

"It's impossible. Her father killed her wolf when he killed her," I told him, but Ace shook his head.

"Avery said something to me about it. She thinks Lucy's wolf is dormant, not dead."

"Then why hasn't she come forward before?" I asked him yet if Avery believed that maybe it was possible.

"We will have to wait and see, I guess, but—"

"You're not sure if we should tell her," Ace finished for me, and he sighed but nodded his head.

"You know how much she hated not being able to shift when everyone else could, how depressed she got when every other mutation shifted but her," I told him. Lucy struggled when she was younger. All the other mutations had wolves and survived the transition; hers didn't, making her feel more out of place because she knew she was different.

"Come on, we should put her to bed," Ace said, and I reached down to grab her bag. Ace started walking toward my bedroom, but I stopped by his bedroom door.

"No, yours. Your bed is bigger, and we can all fit comfortably in it," I told him. He stopped looking at me, and I pushed his bedroom door open. Ace also had a bigger room, and I didn't think Lucy would like bed-hopping.

"You're okay with all this?" Ace asked me, following me inside. I flicked the light on.

"Of course I am. Why would you ask?"

"Because of what happened. I know this isn't normal for brothers to share a mate, and you could have had her to yourself." I nodded at his words.

"Good thing we know how to share then. She is your mate too, Ace. I never wanted to take her from you," I told him, placing her bag next to the bed. Ace gently laid her down, tucking her in while I started unpacking her bag.

Ace opened some drawers, clearing them out, and I handed him her clothes before finding a photo album tucked down the side of the bag. I pulled it out, and Ace looked over at me.

"What's that?" he asked, sitting beside me on the edge of the bed.

"Her photo album," I told him, opening it to see what was inside. I was shocked to find that most of them were of us growing up together. Ace pulled a smaller one out, which was full of family photos. He flicked through it, but the album I was holding was mostly of Lucy and us.

There were heaps of us camping together and at the lagoon, her first day of school. Flicking further into the album, I found some of when we first rescued her from the facility. How small she was and underweight. I looked over my shoulder at her sleeping. She was not this little girl anymore but a woman. Yet the sadness in her eyes in these photos, the hollow look, I had seen over these last few weeks, and I hated seeing that fear in her eyes again.

"I remember that day," Ace said, pointing to the picture of both of us in lab coats sitting next to Lucy in the doctor's office. Lucy had the same fear as her mother when she first got out. Took us six months before she would get checked out by the pack doctor. Yet when they wanted to run tests, she freaked out and refused, instead running from us. Ryker had to chase her down. Reika's fear didn't help, though, as she always waited in the car, refusing to set foot in the place; she still had that fear.

"I spent two weeks learning how to take blood," Ace said, and I laughed at the memory. When Lucy refused to get blood taken, the doctor even tried with no lab coat on, but Lucy knew what she was and refused. Ace spent two weeks off school at the pathology lab learning how to take blood samples.

We didn't think it would work, but Ryker was willing to try anything, and he excused him from school until he was comfortable doing it. I managed to convince her to go back to the doctor's office, holding her down while they checked her over. When it was time for the blood tests, though, she freaked out again, and the doctor left the office only to return with Ace in a lab coat.

Flashback

"Lucy, calm down! Stop kicking," I told her as she thrashed in my arms.

"Okay, Lucy. I won't take your blood," Doc told her. Lucy slowly calmed down, yet her heart was racing a million miles an hour. I dragged her back up so she was sitting on my lap, my arms locked around her. Ryker hated bringing her, and this time Ace and I offered to try and pin her down. Seeing her scared always angered Ryker, making him want to smack the doctors trying to help her.

"I want to go home, Tyson. Take me home, please," Lucy cried, looking up at me. We tried to explain everything. The doctor wasn't even wearing her coat this time, but nothing helped; she wanted nothing to do with them once she knew they were doctors.

"They just need to do some tests, Lucy. I promise they won't hurt you," I told her, but she started crying, shaking her head.

"No! No!" she started screaming when the doctor once again tried to approach her.

"Calm down," I told her, but she didn't.

"I will be back, okay? I have a surprise for you, Lucy," Doc told her.

"I wonder what it is?" I asked her, knowing it was Ace. Lucy looked up at me, but only fear shone in her mutated eyes.

"I won't let anyone hurt you. You trust me, don't you, Lucy?" She nodded, chewing her nails, and I kissed the side of her head.

"Do you trust Ace?" I asked her, and she nodded again.

"Where did Ace go?" she asked, and I pulled her fingers from her mouth when she started making her nails bleed. She was terrible for it. She would chew the tips of her fingers until they bled sometimes. I didn't even think she realized she did it half the time. It was a nervous reflex she had, same as chewing on her shirt sleeves. The door opened, and I heard her heart rate pick up, and she started thrashing when the figure stepped into the room in a lab coat.

"Stop, Luce. Look, it is only Ace," I told her, holding her tighter. She stopped thrashing, looking over at my brother in his lab coat.

"You're not a doctor," Lucy laughed.

"I am. I have a badge, see?" he said, tapping the badge on his coat that said Doctor Awesome. I rolled my eyes at him.

"No, you're not," she giggled, and the doctor stepped in behind him, her eyes going to the doctor. But she sat down in her chair, observing.

"I am today. I get to be your doctor," Ace told her, pulling a stool over and sitting in front of her.

"See? It is just Ace," I told her, and she nodded, looking over at the doctor who handed a tray to Ace. He placed it on the bed beside Lucy, and she looked at it.

"So, can I be your doctor today, Lucy?" asked Ace while grabbing some gloves and putting them on.

"Are you going to stab me?" she asked, looking at the needles on the tray.

"What about if I stab Tyson first to show it doesn't hurt?" Ace asked her, and I glared at him. He knew I hated needles, and Ace smirked at me. Lucy nodded, looking up at me expectantly, and I fought back a growl, but Ace didn't wait for an answer and instead shoved my shirt sleeve up as Lucy watched.

"You scream or flinch, I will kick your ass," Ace mindlinked me.

"You couldn't have volunteered Doc as your test subject?" I mindlinked back.

"No, I want to watch you sweat. Now hold still. I would hate for the needle to snap off in your arm." He laughed. "Don't worry, that only happened once," he added through the link, and I turned my face away, staring at Lucy instead of what he was doing.

Surprisingly, he was actually gentle—well, as gentle as a needle could be.

"See? He didn't cry, and we know what a baby Tyson is," Ace told Lucy while handing the vial of my blood to the doctor. She turned around, putting a label on it while Ace told Lucy to hold the cotton bud on my arm, and she did.

"Now, which band-aid should Tyson have?" he asked her, and she picked a little pink one. Ace stuck it on my arm.

"See? Didn't hurt, did it, Ty?" Ace asked me.

"Nope, not at all," I told her, and she nodded, bouncing on my lap before offering her arm to Ace. He rolled her sleeve up before putting the strap on her arm and grabbing a fresh needle.

She jumped when he pushed it through her skin and then relaxed before watching the small vial fill up with her blood. He took four vials of her blood, handing each one to Doc, who labeled and bagged them. He unclipped the strap and gently removed the needle, placing a cotton bud on it when he was done.

"Hold that," he told her, and she pressed her thumb on it while he picked her a purple band-aid. "See? All done. That wasn't so bad, was it, Lucy?" Ace asked her, and she shook her head.

⁂

I shook the memory away. "Yeah, and you stabbed me, you jerk," I told him, and he laughed.

"But it worked. She got over her fear of doctors, didn't she?" he said, and I smiled.

"Yes, she did." Lucy got over a lot of fears. She excelled in school despite being severely behind. Every night we helped her with her homework, and every night Ryker would read to her and Reika before bed.

"We should tell her about her wolf. Even if she doesn't ever get her wolf back, she has a right to know," I told Ace.

"Yeah, I don't like keeping secrets from her," he agreed.

"I have pack patrol tonight. You can take her back to your room if you want," Ace told me, but I shook my head.

"No, but can I move my crap in here?"

"You're serious about sharing a room?" he asked, getting up and putting the last of the other things away.

"Yep, I don't plan on sleeping without her. You?"

"Me neither. If she lets me sleep near her," he said.

"She let you mark her, and she marked you," I told him, wondering why he was still second-guessing her.

"Yeah, I know, she may forgive me, but that doesn't mean I forgive myself," he said, and I nodded to him before lying back on the bed.

"I need to go, but I will be back in the morning. Let me know when she wakes up," he said, leaning down and kissing her cheek.

Chapter 58

Lucy

My body felt like it was vibrating as I woke up, the tingles moving over my skin, making my eyes fly open to find Tyson fast asleep beside me. His face pressed into my neck, and I rolled into him, running my fingers through his hair. I could feel him becoming alert to his surroundings as he rubbed his stubble across my neck and chest. Looking around, I noticed we were in Ace's room, yet I didn't see him anywhere.

"You're awake finally," Tyson said, and I nodded my head, his hand brushing gently up and down my arm.

"What time is it, and where is Ace?"

"Ace is on patrol, and I have no idea what the time is," he said, his eyes opening, and he pulled back and looked at me. I loved the silver color of their eyes and the way they glowed in the dark, making me remember the last thing I heard was Ace talking about my eyes.

"What's wrong?" Tyson asked.

"Nothing. Did something happen when Ace marked me?" I asked, wondering if my memory was wrong. Tyson sat up on one elbow before reaching over me to grab his phone off the bedside table. He looked at it, and I glanced at his phone to see it was nearly 11 PM. He dropped his phone behind me on the bed before reaching over and flicking the lamp on the bedside table beside him.

"Something happened, didn't it?" I asked him, feeling his nervousness.

"I don't want to get your hopes up, in case it was just you responding to the bond," Tyson told me.

"Well, you have to tell me now," I told him. He sighed before nodding his head and sitting up.

"When Ace marked you, your eyes turned black like a werewolf's, Lucy."

"But I don't have a wolf," I told him, chewing my lip.

"Avery said something to Ace that she believes your wolf isn't dead but dormant."

"Dormant?" I asked, but I couldn't wrap my head around what he was saying. I felt no presence of a wolf, nothing.

"It could just be you reacting to the bond. We weren't going to tell you but decided last night we didn't want any more secrets between us. Things are hard enough without us all hiding things from each other." I let out a breath but refused to get excited about the possibility of having a wolf.

"Are you upset?" Tyson asked, but I shook my head. I wasn't upset; I wasn't anything. I was feeling rather neutral about the idea of having a wolf. I hadn't had one, so it wasn't like I could miss it if it were just a reaction from the bond.

"I'm fine. I just wasn't expecting you to say that," I told him, and he nodded, leaning back on the headboard.

"When will Ace be back?"

"Early in the morning," Tyson said, closing his eyes. I moved closer, resting my head on his chest. He pulled me closer before pressing his lips to my head.

"Are you hungry? You haven't had dinner yet?"

"No, not for food anyway," I told him, and he looked down at me before pulling me higher and on top of him. I straddled his waist, my hands on his stomach, and he tugged his shirt off over his head before sitting up straighter.

"You can feed on me. There aren't any blood bags here," he told me, and I felt my gums tingle as the bloodlust started to take over. His hands went to my hips, pulling me closer to him, and I felt his hands trail up my sides, sparks rushing over me. I moaned softly before being able to stop myself. My bloodlust turned to arousal. Tyson's eyes flickered at the noise I made, Tyrant pressing forward for a second before his eyes returned to their normal silver.

Tyson cleared his throat, though the sound was more like a growl, and his hands moved lower away from my skin, but I grabbed them, pushing them back where they were. My breathing hitched as I felt the sparks ignite on my skin again, making me shiver. I held his hands there for a second before letting him go. Tyson stared at me questionably, but I knew he could feel my arousal through the bond, yet he was still unsure about touching me.

His hands gently trailed up and down my sides, and I closed my eyes at the feel of his touch, loving how gentle he was when his grip tightened suddenly on my hips, making my eyes open to see Tyrant had forced his way forward.

"Tyrant, give Tyson control back," I told him. His look made a shiver run down my spine when he leaned forward, kissing me harshly. His hand tangled in my hair as he tilted my head back, nipping and sucking on my skin; his wolf was not gentle. My scalp burned as he pulled my hair, and I pushed on his shoulders, pushing him back, reminding myself this wasn't Tyson but his wolf.

"Tyrant, give Tyson control, please," I breathed out before hissing as his canines grazed my shoulder before he ran them over my mark, making me moan. His arm around my waist was crushing me as he drew me closer to him. I could feel Tyson fighting for control back, but Tyrant was relentless, and I could feel his need to complete the mating process through the bond.

"Tyrant, don't do this to Tyson," I snapped at him, becoming annoyed at his wolf. I knew Tyson was a virgin like me, and it wouldn't be fair for his wolf to take this from him.

Tyrant whimpered and pulled away. His grip on my hair let go, and I looked at him. Tyson's chest rose and fell rapidly with each breath he took. Yet the demonic look in his eyes told me Tyrant was still in control.

"I want you, you mine," Tyrant growled menacingly, possessively, which stunned me. Before realizing he was jealous Ace would take me. Tyson wasn't the jealous type; clearly, his wolf was, though.

"Ace isn't here. Now give Tyson back control, Tyrant." I told him. He growled, but I watched him recede before Tyson's eyes returned to their normal silver. He let out a breath, his cheeks burning, and I found it cute that he was embarrassed by his wolf's actions.

"Lucy, I'm sor—" My lips cut his apology off when I kissed him. After a few seconds, Tyson kissed me back, his hand cupping the back of my neck as he deepened the kiss, his tongue playing with mine. I rolled my hips against him. I could feel his erection through his boxer shorts pressing against me, and Tyson pulled away.

"Lucy, we can wait. Don't let Tyrant get to you." But I shook my head, pecking his lips.

"I don't want to wait," I told him.

"You want to?" he asked, unable to hide his shock or mask his expression; he almost looked scared.

"Lucy, maybe you should let Ace," he said, but I shook my head, realizing he was just as nervous as I was, which was okay by me because I had no idea what I was doing either.

"No, Tyson. Ace can wait. I want it to be you," I told him, and his gaze softened.

"Are you sure?" he asked, and I leaned down, pressing my lips to his softly.

"Positive," I whispered against his lips. He groaned, his tongue slipping into my mouth as he pulled me closer before flipping us so I was on my back, Tyson's lips not leaving mine.

Chapter 59

Tyson's weight pressed down on me, and I could hear his heart rate jackhammering in his chest. I felt his nervousness seep into me, and I was glad I wasn't the only one filled with this much anxiety. Tyson's hands glided over my skin, and I could feel the tremble in them, feel his hesitation which removed all my discomfort, knowing he was trusting me as much as I was trusting him, making me content, knowing I was making the right decision.

I pushed on his shoulder, and he sat up, kneeling between my legs. Sitting up, I tugged my shirt off over my head when I felt Tyson's hand grip the waistband of my pants. I lifted my butt so he could remove them, and he dropped them off the side of the bed before staring down at me, his eyes flickering. I knew he was struggling with his wolf.

"Maybe it's better if you wait for Ace, Lucy. He knows what he is doing," Tyson said, his hands running from my knees to my thighs softly.

I leaned forward, pecking his lips while unclipping my bra. "Why are you so nervous?" I mumbled around his lips.

"Because I don't know what I am doing. Well, I do, but Ace has more experience. I don't want to ruin your first time, Lucy, and for it to be a disappointment," he breathed out.

"The fact that you said your brother has more experience is exactly why I want to be with you, Tyson. Stop worrying about me. It's your first time, too. I don't expect it to be some magical experience. I am not unrealistic, but I want it to be you. It feels right, but if you want to wait, we can," I told him.

"No, I do, but are you sure you wouldn't prefer Ace?" he asked. Suddenly, both of us were pulled into the mindlink at the same time.

"You're awake, Lucy?" Ace's voice flitted through my head, making me jump. I saw Tyson's eyes also glazed over, feeling his vibration through the mindlink that Ace had connected to both of us.

"Yep, woke up not long ago," I told him, and I could feel Tyson's anxiety through the bond, like he was worried his brother would find out what we were planning on doing.

"What are you both doing? I can feel your nervousness through the bond," Ace asked, and my eyes flicked to Tyson as he started waving his hands at me, not wanting me to tell him, but I rolled my eyes.

"He will be able to feel it through the bond anyway, Tyson. No point in lying to him," I whispered to him.

"Hello, are you both there?" Ace asked.

"Yes, sorry, I was talking to Tyson."

"You didn't answer when I asked. What are you both doing? It's bloody boring out here tonight," Ace told me.

"Nothing because Tyson is too nervous," I laughed before seeing Tyson's horror at what I said, making my lips tug up slightly.

MY TWO ALPHAS | 295

Tyson rubbed a hand down his face, and he sighed. "Bro, you are being awfully quiet," Ace told him.

"I am just listening. I am here," Tyson answered. Ace sighed through the bond before I felt recognition hit me through the bond. Ace laughed through the mindlink. "Did I just cock block you?" he laughed, and I snorted.

"Yep, we're kind of busy," I admitted.

"How busy?" Ace asked, and I felt arousal hit me from him. It was strange feeling Ace so clearly now; Tyson I was used to, but it took a little concentration to pick up his emotions and what they meant.

"Not that busy because Tyson thinks I should wait for you."

"What, why?" Ace asked him, but Tyson didn't answer him.

"Look, it's simple. Penis goes in the vagina, and that's it. Besides, I have heard you rubbing one out in the shower. The stamina of Mrs. Palmer and her five daughters is quite impressive. You should have an arm on you like Popeye," Ace said, and I laughed while Tyson face-palmed himself, shaking his head.

"I am well aware, Ace. Thanks for pointing that out and making shit awkward," Tyson said, and I laughed at him.

"Wait, are you still in my bed, dude? I swear if you blow your load near my damn pillow, I will gut you with a butter knife," Ace said though he didn't seem mad we were in his bed; he seemed more amused at the situation.

"Okay, well, that just killed my mood," Tyson mumbled, his face heating up.

"Your pillow is safe," I told Ace with a chuckle.

"Speaking of safety, Tyson, there should be condoms in the top drawer beside my bed."

"You are not seriously giving me a sex talk right now," Tyson told him.

"Hey, just helping a brother out, or have you got some?"

"Why would I have condoms, Ace? I have never had sex."

"Well, good thing your brother's prepared then. Just help yourself. There are even flavored ones," Ace told him. I knew Ace wasn't a virgin, and I hated that, but at the same time, I found their conversation amusing and found what he was saying didn't really bother me as much as I thought it would with Ace talking about his sex life. I knew that marking him meant I had to push the past behind and leave it there if we wanted this to work.

"Oi, you should leave the mindlink open. I could rub one out. I'm sure Jacob won't mind."

"Definitely not. You are not listening to us have sex, Ace," Tyson snapped at him, and Ace laughed.

"What? It would be like phone sex, only it would be mind sex," Ace said, and I giggled.

"I am your brother, just no! Don't you have work to do?"

"Yeah, not much happening right now. Jacob has been on the phone with his boy toy. I am bored, and how is it gross? We're practically the same person. It'd be like listening to myself. Hey, want me to talk you through it? I could add running commentary like at the races."

"Pretty sure I will pass on that idea," Tyson said with a sigh. His face turned red, and I rubbed my foot against his thigh, and he smiled, grabbing it.

"Okay, are you done? Little busy here," Tyson told him.

"Such a Debbie Downer. Relax a little, Ty."

"Okay, we are going now," Tyson said, his tone almost bored.

"Condoms are in the top drawer. Maybe a little big for you, but I am sure you will manage," Ace said with a chuckle, and Tyson growled through the link at him.

"Fine, fine, I am going but stay away from my pillow, and if you change your mind about the mind sex—"

"Nope, bye Ace," Tyson said, cutting the link off and shoving him out of our heads. I laughed at Tyson's face, and he chuckled softly.

"Well, that was awkward," Tyson said.

"Which part? Him trying to give us a sex talk, or him wanting to mind sex? Poor Jacob would have been horrified," I told him, and he laughed. I used my legs to tug him closer. Tyson ran his hands over my legs to my hips before leaning down to kiss me, yet I could feel he wasn't so nervous now as he moved over me and pressed his weight against me. I gripped his hip, tugging him closer and deepening the kiss. My legs wrapped around his waist when Tyson chuckled against my lips before pulling back.

"What?" I asked him when he reached over, grabbing Ace's pillow.

"Lift up," he said, tapping my hip with a devious smile on his lips.

"What are you doing?" I chuckled.

"Looking after his pillow he loves so much," Tyson said, shoving it beneath my butt.

"He is going to kill you," I told him.

"Serve him right for interrupting," Tyson teased, his lips moving back to mine as he settled between my legs.

Chapter 60

Tyson kissed me gently, his lips moving against mine, and he sucked my bottom lip in his mouth. Sparks rushed over my skin when he ground his hips against mine. His erection was pressing against me, and I gasped at the feel of the sparks rushing over my skin straight to my clit.

His lips were devouring mine as he tasted every inch of my mouth, his tongue demanding as it fought mine for dominance which I let him have. Tyson's hand moved down my side, and he growled against my lips when he palmed my breast. Arousal flooded me when his thumb brushed over my nipple, making it harden under his touch. I rolled my hips against him, my hand moving down the hard muscles of his chest and down his abs to the waistband of his boxer shorts. I tugged on the waistband, pushing it down a little, and Tyson pushed them down, his cock springing spree out of its confines before he removed them completely and kicked them off.

My hand shook as I wrapped my fingers around his hardened length, and Tyson groaned, thrusting into my hand as I stroked him. His lips trailed down my neck to my mark before he sucked on it, his teeth grazing against it, making sparks dance across my skin. I clutched him to me, loving the feel of his hot skin against mine, loving the feeling the bond had been flooded with.

Tyson gripped my hip, tugging me closer. I moved my hand, and he ground himself against my pulsating core. Anticipation made my stomach flutter as arousal flooded me. His cock pressed against my lips before running between my folds and brushing against my clit, making me moan softly.

I rolled my hips against him, his lips moving to my breast before he sucked my nipple in his mouth, his teeth tugging on it when his hand moved between my legs. He rubbed his fingers against me, rubbing my clit, and my hips bucked against his hand as the friction built. My arousal spilled onto my thighs when I felt his fingers move between my wet folds before he pushed a finger inside me. I squirmed at the sudden intrusion, but it wasn't painful, like I was expecting, as he slowly moved his finger in and out of me.

Tyson growled, pulling back slightly before looking down. He watched his finger slide in and out of me. I moved my hips against it when he pulled it out, adding another and sliding it in, and I tensed slightly, the feeling fuller as my body stretched around them.

"Am I hurting you?" Tyson asked, his fingers stilling inside me.

"No, I'm just trying to get used to the feeling," I told him, and he pulled his fingers out slowly before pushing them back in. His fingers, slick with my juices, slid in easier, and he curled them, making me buck against them before rubbing my clit with his thumb. My walls tightened at the friction he was building, my walls clenching around him, coating his hand in my juices and making me cry out. Tyson leaned forward, kissing me and swallowing my moans as I moved against his hand, the friction building. I clutched him to me, wanting more than just his fingers, wanting all of him.

Tyson groaned, his fingers slipping from me, and he ground himself against me, coating his cock in my juices before I felt him move. He tugged on the top drawer of Ace's bedside table, opening it before pulling out a foil package and tearing it open with his teeth. I rolled my hips against him, his lips devouring mine as he rolled the condom down his length before pressing closer, his hand cupping the back of my neck as he deepened the kiss. I felt him position himself, his cock running between my folds and pressing against my entrance, and my stomach fluttered. I moved my hips against him, and his hands ran up my thigh to my knee as he wrapped my leg around his waist.

"Tell me if I am hurting you," he whispered against my lips, and I nodded, chasing his lips with mine. I felt pressure as he pressed the tip inside me. My walls stretched around him; the feeling was uncomfortable but not painful as he slowly sheathed himself within my walls before he stilled when I gasped at the foreign feeling. It hurt, but it didn't hurt more like pressure within my stomach as my body stretched around him.

"Are you okay?" he asked, pressing his forehead against mine when I wiggled slightly, trying to get used to the feeling of being so full. I nodded my head, and he kissed my cheek.

"I'm going to move now, Lucy. Tell me to stop if I am hurting you." Tyson breathed next to my ear, and I moved, wrapping my other leg around his waist, my hand moving to his chest when he pulled out of me and before pushing back in. His cock stroked the insides of my walls slowly as he moved. Tyson reached between us, rubbing my clit with his fingers, and I moaned, moving my hips against him, loving the feeling building within my stomach. The feeling of him stretching me as he picked up his pace. I moved my hips meeting his thrusts, my walls clenching around him as the friction built, his pelvis brushing against my clit, making me cry out.

Tyson's grip on my hip tightened, and he thrust in harder, his cock hitting my cervix painfully, but the friction of our bodies connected overrode the pain, making me moan, pulling on his hip to go faster as I felt the pressure building, my skin heating up, and he slammed himself into me.

"I'm not hurting you?" Tyson breathed.

"No, just don't stop," I told him, feeling myself reach the precipice. My back arched off the bed when his lips crashed down on mine, pushing me back. His hand tangled in my hair as he kissed me, his tongue invading my mouth before he bit down on my lip just as he sent me over the edge. My entire body clenched, and I cried out when my orgasm washed over me in waves, making me writhe beneath him, my walls clenching and pulsating around his length.

"Fuck!" Tyson groaned when my pussy gripped him, his movements becoming erratic before he stilled inside me. His breathing was heavy when he collapsed on top of me. Both of us were trying to catch our breath. I felt his lips press to my shoulder before he moved, pressing his lips to the edge of my mouth. His weight lifted off me as he pulled out before rolling and falling onto his back beside me. My entire body felt completely relaxed, but I was also exhausted.

We lay there for a few seconds before Tyson got up and walked into the bathroom before returning. I rolled on my side as he lay back down, resting my face on his chest. He kissed my forehead before tilting my chin up with his fingers so he could kiss my lips.

"I love you, Luce," he whispered, and I ran my fingers down his chest.

"I love you too," I told him while yawning. Goosebumps rose on my arms, the ecstasy and high leaving my body, making me shiver. Tyson tucked the blanket up to cover us, and I shut my eyes, listening to the sound of his beating heart as I slowly drifted off to sleep tucked in the warmth of his arms.

Chapter 61

Melana

We watched Jacob and Ace from the shadows, making sure we remained far enough away where they couldn't pick up our scent. We needed to find a way to get across the borders without being noticed as we sat among the trees, high up in the branches out of sight. Ace and Jacob had been patrolling the river all night. This damn river caused so many problems for us, yet not as many as that bloody demon my sister was mates with.

Watching Ace, though, killed me and gave me doubts about what we were doing. If only I had gone to him when Josie got in trouble, we could have avoided this mess. If only Ace was my mate instead of Nathaniel, Alpha Jamie would have nothing to use over me, and Josie would still be at school tucked safely away and never would have got involved in this mess.

Looking at Josie, where she was perched next to me on the branch, she seemed stuck in her own head. So much pain behind her eyes, and I knew she was struggling the most. Lucy had been her best friend for years, and I was the one person that caused a rift between them, or so I thought. I was angry when I found out she kept the knowledge of her own mate from me. If I had known he was a teacher and a demon, I would have kept a closer eye on her, maybe even pulled her from that damn school.

Leaning back on the tree trunk, I watched her. Something had changed within her; gone was the sweet girl she used to be. Now she was bitter and angry and broken.

"So, Mr. Tanner, huh?" I asked her, trying to get a reaction out of her.

"Hmm…" is all she answered, her eyes darkening slightly. I could see the conflict in her eyes, yet she hardly spoke of him when I had asked. Maybe it was what he did to Lucy? I wasn't sure, but she kept him a secret until he got locked up. Only then did she say she had something on Lucy and offered to help. That was how I found out about him.

"Why didn't you tell me?" I asked her.

"He was a teacher. He could have gotten in trouble," she answered.

"That's bullshit, and you know it. He is your mate. He may have been told to steer clear of you until you finished school, but no one would have stopped you both being together since you are fated mates," I told her, and she chewed her lip.

"It's not that simple," she said with a sigh.

"How isn't it, Josie? He is your mate, is he not?"

"He didn't want me. Demons don't have mates, Melana," she said, and my brows pinched in confusion.

"So he rejected you?" I asked her, feeling sick to my stomach.

"No!" she said before shifting over to sit next to me and lean on the trunk.

"Well, he must have wanted to be with you," I told her, thinking of my own mate. He was locked up god knows where and out of reach. The last time I saw him was to reject him, but he refused to accept my rejection. I knew I had put him through pain over the years; I knew he had felt the things I had done, and that sickened me and also confused me because I didn't understand how I was still able to feel the way I did about Ace.

"He wanted Lucy," Josie whispered, shutting her eyes.

"That's why you hate her?" I asked her.

"I don't hate her. I… I don't know, Mel. It's hard to explain. Lucy was my friend, but every time I see her, I remember how he wanted her over his mate. He wanted Lucy and not me. It was different with her. The others he wasn't so obsessed with."

"What do you mean the others, Josie?"

She placed her head in her hands. "I didn't think. I just thought once he got them out of his system, he would come back to me, choose me but then he asked me about Lucy."

"What are you talking about, Josie?" I asked her. Did Mr. Tanner try to rape other girls too?

"Did he try that shit with others?" I asked when she didn't answer.

"No… yes… I don't know exactly. He just asked me to bring them to his office. That was all I did. I told myself that he would be with me once he got them out of his system, so I did what he'd asked but then he asked about Lucy, and I got angry because he promised." I stared at her, appalled by her words.

"Josie, please tell me you had nothing to do with luring those girls to him." She looked away guiltily, and I knew she did. How could she do that to another woman?

"You let your mate rape them?" I asked, disgusted by her.

"He may not have. I didn't stick around to see but he wiped their memories. He wanted to do the same with Lucy."

"How many? And how could you, Josie?" I asked, standing up and walking along the branch, needing to put some distance between us.

"Don't judge me, Melana. You can't talk. Look at what you are doing to your mate."

"That's fucking different, and you know it. I have no choice here," I spat at her.

"Whatever. You knew Ace had a mate, knew you had one!" she growled.

"I didn't believe him, though. He was fucking drunk, and it was years ago on his birthday. He mentioned it once and never again. It wasn't until she came back that I realized he meant it. It's not like they both shouted she was their mate from the fucking rooftops."

"Yeah, but what about your mate? At least I didn't reject mine. Ace always said nothing more would ever come between you. He told you he was waiting for his mate. He made that damn clear when you first got involved with each other but you still rejected your mate?"

"Don't try to turn this back on me. What you did was worse. You lured his fucking victims to him and let him rape them. But hey, no harm done, right? Because he erased their memories," I spat at her, disgusted she was my sister, disgusted I had thrown everything away for her only to find out she was just like her despicable mate.

"He said he couldn't help it, that the urges were too strong, and once he got them out of his system, he would stop and come back to me."

"You are not defending him right now. What is wrong with you? Are you really that stupid, Josie? He used you, used you to get to them."

"You think I don't know that now?" she yelled, and we both froze, gazing out the branches to see if anyone heard her. Ace and Jacob were further up the river, now thankfully out of hearing range with the wind blowing in our direction.

"I threatened to tell. I told him no more and..." She looked away without finishing.

"That's why he sold you out, isn't it? You told him to stop, and he stole the shipment." I groaned; it all makes so much fucking sense.

"I didn't think he would do that. I didn't think he would cross me like that. He said once he had Lucy, he would give it back, and we could be together. We were going to run away and leave everything behind."

"So, you sold out your best friend?"

"What? No! I tried to help. I was going back for her, but I knew no one would believe me, so I took the pictures, but I was going to intervene. I wanted to help her but—"

"But what?"

"You have no idea how hard it is to go against your mate, Melana. When I saw her with him, it enraged me. I felt betrayed because he didn't want me. He wanted my friend. It's always Lucy everyone wants, always her side they choose even my mate chose her over me," she said, tears streaking down her face.

"So, you were going to walk away because you were jealous of her? Jealous your bastard mate wanted to rape her?" I snarled at her.

"It's not my fault, and she fought back. She got away, so no harm done. I can't help how the bond makes me feel. I know what he did was wrong, but it was like she was the one that betrayed me for making him want her over me."

"I can't believe you. Mom would have been disgusted with you. We were nearly free, Josie. I was nearly free, and then you had to fuck things up by trusting that leech and handing shit over to him. This is exactly why I told you to stay off Jamie's radar. You just had to get involved," I told her.

"I wanted to help, Mel. Do you know how hard it is knowing I am completely dependent on you? How hard it is knowing you were caught up with him because you promised mom to watch over me?" she said.

"And that was my choice. You should never have gotten involved. Now we are both trapped."

Josie hung her head and rubbed her eyes.

"I'm starting to think we should have walked away," I whispered to her.

"What about your mate?"

"I don't know, Josie, okay? I don't know. We dug ourselves a fucking huge ass hole, and I don't know. I don't know how to get us out of this, not without losing everything," I admitted.

"Wait, I think they are going," Josie said, looking out at Ace and Jacob. My heart pinched at the sight of him leaving when he stopped sniffing the air, and I realized the wind's direction had changed. Could he pick up our scents from way back here?

Chapter 62

Melana

*J*osie glanced at her watch. "I think the shift change is about to happen," she said before she suddenly started climbing down. I reluctantly followed, grabbing the bag on my way down that was hanging from a branch. When we got to the ground, we hid in shrubs, looking at the bridge. The patrols have been tighter than ever, and we needed to get across to set the plans in motion, but we also needed to be smart. If anyone was alerted to us stepping across, we would find ourselves in deep shit.

"Okay, once the new shift patrol takes over, you take out one, I will take out the other," Josie said, pulling the dart guns out.

"That will give us six hours before the next shift comes on, and we can drag them out of sight," Josie told me, and I nodded. We watched the patrols talk. Ace was speaking with them along with Jacob when he turned to look in our direction. We managed to duck down out of sight before he spotted us.

After about twenty minutes of them messing around, we retrieved the darts, pulling them out when my fingers suddenly started burning, making me drop the dart. I looked at my fingers before sniffing them as Josie went to grab one out, and I stopped her.

"What?" she asked.

"These aren't tranquilizers," I told her, wondering how we hadn't noticed before. Pulling my phone out, I held the dart under the screen light, instantly recognizing the contents to be wolfsbane. Josie gasped.

"But he said we only had to knock them out," Josie said, horrified. I looked out to see Ace had left, and two new warriors had taken over the patrol. I recognized both of them; one of them was Floyde, and he was one of their Betas. The other was Floyde's son, Daniel; we were the same age, and I went to school with him for a bit.

Nausea welled inside me at what we were expected to do, knowing shooting them with these darts could kill them. I had had a fair amount of run-ins with Floyde over the years, but that didn't mean I wanted him dead.

Josie took aim, and my heart hammered in my chest. Would she really do it? Would she really kill someone? Yet I knew she would as I watched her finger move to the trigger. I would do anything for her; she was family. But to destroy another's family? The thought sickened me.

I put my hand on the barrel, ripping it toward the ground.

"What are you doing?" she hissed at me.

"You really want that on your conscience? Another thing to taint you?" I asked her.

"We don't have a choice."

"Yes, we do. We will find another way," I told her.

"What other way? We need to get across. What about your mate?" Josie asked, and tears burned my eyes at the thought of what I had already put him through, what Alpha Jamie would do to him.

"No, it's not right."

"Nothing about this, right" Josie snapped.

"You're right, but I'm not a murderer."

"Then I will do it," Josie said, and I looked at her.

"What, no, no. We will scope out somewhere else, follow the river. No one needs to die, Josie," I told her.

"You don't know they will die. They have hybrids for Alphas. You know that gives the pack members extra abilities."

"So what? Just because it might, doesn't mean it won't kill them," I told her, yanking the gun from her hands as she went to raise it.

"Get it together, Melana. We have to do this," she snapped. I shook my head, wondering what the fuck had become of her. She used to be the one telling me not to do stupid shit, but now she was willing to kill someone?

"We go back without Lucy, you are signing both our death warrants."

"Hours ago, you were the one begging me not to agree to Jamie's terms and to walk away. You wanted to help Lucy and warn her," I told her.

"We are so close, so fucking close, Melana. We get this done and bring her back here, and you get your mate, then we are free," she said.

"No, what has gotten into you?" I asked, confused by her actions. Mine had been solely based on her and my mate, but Josie was only begging a few hours ago for me to not agree with Alpha Jamie and to let him kill her, saying she wouldn't hurt Lucy anymore, practically begging me not to go through with it. She went quiet before trying to take the gun back from my hands. What happened in the few hours in the cells that she had a change of heart?

"No!" I told her, and she growled at me, but my hand whipped out, and I slapped her face. She seemed shocked for a second, tears brimming in her eyes when her face twisted in anger, and she tackled me, trying to wrestle the gun from my grip.

"I won't fucking lose him again," she snarled, her fist connecting with the side of my face while I tried to make sense of what she said. I shoved her off, only for her to attack again, but I sidestepped, kicking out the side of her knee and making her scream. I quickly dropped on her, covering her mouth and muffling the sound. Looking out toward the warriors, I could see their heads whipping from side to side. *Shit! They heard her.* Josie was thrashing on the ground underneath me, trying to shove me off.

"What did he promise you? What the fuck did he offer you, Josie?" I asked, pinning her down.

She growled at me and bit into my hand, making me jerk it back. "You may not have the balls to do it, but I fucking will! Now get off me!" she spat at me.

"No, we aren't doing this. I will take the punishment. I accept my fate, but I won't kill someone, not for my mistakes," I told her. She snarled at me, glaring daggers before trying to toss me off her again.

"He did, didn't he? He offered you something. What did the Alpha offer you, Josie?" I asked her. I saw movement out of the corner of my eye and looked back between the shrubs to see them pacing up and down the river, looking for the person responsible for the scream.

"Answer me!" I told her, gripping her shirt and slamming her down on the dirt again. She laughed, and I suddenly didn't recognize my own sister anymore. She was unhinged; she wasn't the girl she was when she came home during the break last time.

"One last job, Melana, then I can get him back. Lucy will be out of the picture, and I will get him back."

"Who?" I asked when it suddenly clicked.

"No, you can't be serious. Your mate? How the fuck could you want him back after what he did?" I screeched at her.

"Once Lucy is gone, he will want me back after what she did to him. We could finally be together. He will see that," she said, and I was stunned. Did she really think he wanted her? The man was sick, fucked in the head. How could she claim to be Lucy's friend but also go through with this for her stupid rapist mate?

"You're disgusting. It's not Lucy, Josie. It's your mate. He doesn't want you. Why can't you see that? No, I am telling Ace. This has gone on too long. I should never have let it get this out of hand. Jamie kills me, then so be it, but I am not killing anyone, and I am not helping you get that monster out," I told her, shoving her back and standing.

I would hand myself in, walk over the bridge and hand myself in. Hearing a clicking noise, I froze as I went to pick up the tranquilizer gun.

"I can't let you do that," Josie said, and I turned to face her. She had the other gun pointed directly at me.

"I am your sister," I told her, appalled that she would even threaten me after everything I had done for her.

"But he is my mate. Jamie's witch will get him out for me. He promised he would. I am not losing everything because of that slut," she yelled too loudly, and I hoped to see Floyde, but they had run off down the river.

"You have lost it, Josie. This isn't you."

"You may not be willing to help your mate, but I won't lose mine."

"He doesn't want you!" I screamed at her.

"He does. He fucking does want me. I just need to get rid of her first. She is the problem," Josie spat at me. The hatred in her eyes, her manic behavior—nothing made sense. One minute she wanted to be friends with Lucy, the next, she wanted her dead.

"Josie, stop, think about this for a second."

"I am thinking about it, Melana," she said, reaching down and grabbing the cuffs out of the front pocket of her bag that were intended for Lucy.

"Put them on," she said.

"No!"

"Put them on, or I will fucking shoot, Melana," she said, but I shook my head. She growled before smacking herself in the side of the head with her palm.

"You, why are you making me do this?" she asked before she started rambling, and I slowly reached down for my gun when she spun back around.

"Put them on, Melana!"

"I can't do that, Josie. Something is wrong with you. Can't you see how wrong this is?" I told her when she shot me in the leg. I looked down at the dart sticking out of my leg before pulling it out. I gasped, the wolfsbane spreading through my system, and I stumbled forward, gasping for breath. My veins felt like they had been set on fire, my blood boiling, and my throat felt like it was swelling shut. Josie shrieked, racing to me.

"I didn't mean it. I didn't mean it. I'm sorry," she gushes, patting my face. "You are alright. I will get help."

"Get Floyd," I choked out, and she dropped my head from her lap.

"What? No, no, Mel. I will get the Alpha" I shook my head, and she glared at me.

"Leave, Josie. Just go and be free of him. Forget your mate, forget everyone," I told her, but she growled, pulling her phone out and dialing a number. I was slipping out of consciousness, the wolfsbane burning like acid, and I knew I just needed to ride it out. Wait for it to subside or get to a blood source.

I didn't know how long had passed, but I awoke to voices. I tried to force my eyes open, feet coming into view.

"Well, hasn't this been an interesting change in events?" Alpha Jamie's voice said, reaching my ears.

"Good girl, Josie. I knew you wouldn't betray me. Now, what do we do with you?" I heard him say.

"Just don't kill her. I will get the job done. Just don't hurt her," Josie said, and I growled at her.

"Well, looks like we have to go to plan B or is it or D? I don't know, but you keep on fucking up," Alpha Jamie said.

"I just need a little more time, a bit more time, and I will have it done. I just need to find a way to get across." Silence ensued, but I could cut the tension with a knife.

"What about your person on the inside? Maybe he can get me in?" Josie asked.

"They aren't one of their members. He would have no reason to be over this side." He paused for a second. "But maybe he could get you in, further up the river on his territory."

"His house isn't far from the river there, and they wouldn't expect you to breach from Ryker's side. It may work. I will call him."

I felt hands grip me and put me over someone's shoulder.

"So, how far up do I need to go, and is it anyone I know?" Josie asked, determined to get her mate back. *Why she would want that piece of shit back is beyond me.*

"I am not sure. You didn't go to school with him. Maybe."

"Okay, what's his name?"

"Mitchell. He is part of Ryker's pack. He is the one that put the pictures up in the school for me."

"Yeah, I know him. He was friends with Lucy," Josie said, and I couldn't help but think how unlucky with friendships Lucy was.

"Put her in the cells," I heard him say before the person carrying me started walking, and their voices started to fade away. Now I just needed a way to warn Ace and pray he wouldn't kill my sister.

Chapter 63

Ace POV

Something was nagging at me the entire time I was patrolling. Jacob also felt something was off too. Just that eerie feeling like someone was watching us, something lurking in the shadows. No doubt, Jamie would have had his men watching, and I put the feeling down to that.

Shifting as the packhouse came into view, I walked up the steps, not even bothering to put my shorts back on, needing a shower desperately to wash the night away. The house was quiet, and I knew they were still asleep, being it was so early. I checked my phone quickly to see a message from Ryker asking if anything had happened on patrol. I quickly answered, telling him it was uneventful, before placing my phone back down and heading to the bathroom.

I showered quickly, exhaustion seeping into my bones, but I was also nervous. Should I go back to my room or go crash in Tyson's? I knew what they did while I was on patrol but did Lucy want me there with her? We still hadn't cleared everything or asked her what she wanted. I know we have marked each other but doubt still crept into me about whether or not she truly forgave me for everything.

Walking down the hall toward the bedrooms, I hesitated to decide whether or not to go in there, knowing what I would find. They were in there together. Would it be awkward to disturb that? I had so many questions running through my head.

"It's our room. Just go in there," Atticus growled at me. He just wanted to be near his mate. I wanted the same, but knowing they were probably in there both naked, I wasn't sure whether it would be appropriate for me just to be climbing in bed beside her.

"Oh for the love god, open the door or I will," Atticus snarled, and I growled at him before reaching for the door handle and opening it. My room smells heavily of them, every inch of the room drenched in their scents, and I found it oddly comforting, like it was supposed to smell this way. Even Tyson's scent mingled with hers was oddly comforting. Stepping into the room, I found them tangled in each other. Lucy was asleep with her head on Tyson's chest, her leg over his waist. I moved to my dresser, pulled a pair of boxer shorts out, and slipped them on before moving to the other side of Lucy.

Pulling the blanket back, I lay down excited for sleep. When I rested my head back on my pillow, I was suddenly assaulted with both their scents so strongly that I jerked upright, grabbing my pillow and sniffing it. A growl escaped me when I could smell Lucy's scent and her bodily fluids and not just hers, my nose was raped by my brother's scent. *That motherfucker.* I looked over at Tyson, sleeping peacefully before whacking him with the pillow as hard as I could. He jumped before I ripped his pillow out from under his head, stealing it. Lucy also awoke when Tyson jumped and groaned from the impact.

"What the fuck, Tyson? What did you do to my pillow?"

Lucy giggled before closing her eyes and going back to sleep. Tyson looked around tiredly before he smirked, also closing his eyes and turning my pillow over before using it, not a care given...

"You owe me a new pillow," I told him. He smiled, rolling as Lucy turned to face me and drifted back to sleep. I growled at him, not wanting to know what he did with it. Lying back down and trying to go to sleep, pissed off about them fucking on my pillow. That was the only explanation for how her scent could be so strong on it. Lucy moved as Tyson tucked her against him. I sighed, unable to be mad, not that her arousal bothered me but knowing my brother probably had his nuts resting where my head slept made me shiver in disgust. It took me a good half an hour before I felt sleep trying to take me.

I closed my eyes when suddenly the mindlink opened up, and I groaned, praying to the Goddess to let me sleep and let the world end around me. When I felt it was my brother, though, I knew I couldn't shove him out, not without him coming over and kicking the door down and dragging me out to deliver the ass-whooping he would no doubt give me if I blocked him. *Please, don't make me have to leave*, I thought to myself.

"What, Ryker?" I asked, wanting to go to sleep.

"Is that any way to speak to your king? What is up your ass?"

"King or not, you're my brother and interrupting my sleep."

"Still doesn't explain your bad mood," he tossed back at me.

"Well, if you must know, I came home to find my pillow violated by Lucy and Tyson fucking on it."

"Argh, no, that's disgusting. Stop right there, or I will remove your bloody tongue. I do not want to know what you pair are doing to my step-daughter," he growled almost violently through the link.

"Well, you wanted to know," I told him, and I could feel the smile creep on my face.

"Nothing about Lucy. Keep that to yourself," he said, and I could almost feel how disgusted he was with that over-share of information.

"What's up?"

"Nothing, but I was wondering if you could check Lucy's phone for me because I am assuming she is asleep since it is only 3 AM," Ryker said, and I groaned, not wanting to get up but forcing myself nonetheless.

"You assume right. Want to know what she is wearing since I am about to violate her right to privacy by snooping on her phone?" I teased. *I think I have just found some new ways to torture my brother. It just may get me killed, but it would be so worth it.* His growls made me chuckle.

"One word, Ace. I mean it, your tongue will go."

"Yeah, whatever. You won't do it," I laughed at him.

"No, you're right, but I am sure Reika will if I told her of your oversharing about her daughter." I went quiet. She would remove more than my tongue and then would feed it to me.

"Fine, what am I looking for?" I asked him, and I could practically feel how smug he was, knowing he'd won that one.

"See if she has any missed calls from Mitchell for me."

"Why?" I asked, looking for her phone. When I couldn't find it, I looked at Lucy, knowing I would have to ask her where she had put it. I shook her shoulder gently, and she rolled over, her eyes fluttering open to look up at me.

"Where is your phone, Luce?" She mumbled, waving off in some direction.

"I can't find it. How important is it because I don't really want to force her awake?" I asked him.

"Just look for it. His mother said he rushed out of the house about an hour ago, and he is blocking her out. She said he has been acting strange lately."

"Strange how?"

"She said he has been depressed, and she is worried about him. That he barely sleeps or eats and hides in his room besides going to school. I did have a complaint the other day that he hadn't been showing up for training either." I sighed before shaking her shoulder.

"Luce, baby, I need your phone," I told her, and she mumbled something about her jacket, and I let her fall back to sleep. Walking out of our room to the kitchen, I saw her jacket on the back of the stool. I rummaged through her pockets, pulled out her phone, and turned the screen on.

Walking back to the bedroom, I gripped her fingers, so I didn't have to ask for her password and pressed her finger to the back of the phone on the fingerprint panel. The phone unlocked, and I lay down beside her.

"I got it, and there are no missed calls, but why would he ring her when he can mindlink her? All our packs are linked now?" I told Ryker.

"Doesn't matter. He will come home eventually. Hopefully, his mother has calmed down."

"Okay, so I can go to bed now that I am done invading Lucy's privacy? She has a go at me, you are taking the blame," I told him, placing Lucy's phone on the bedside table.

"Yes, I will speak to you tomorrow. If Lucy hears from him, let me know," Ryker said, cutting the link off before I could reply. But now he told me I was finding it hard to go to sleep. Mitchell was her best friend, and I was worried about how much it would affect her if something were going on with him. She had enough going on without adding more stress to it.

Lying down, I rolled toward her, my hand resting on her naked hip, and she moved closer to me, following the pull of the mate bond when she put her face into my chest. I rolled over onto my back, pulling her on top of me, and she snuggled against me, pressing her face into my neck. Tyson also moved with her, chasing her in his sleep as he pressed to my side, tossing his arm over, his hand resting on her ass and back of her thigh.

I stifled a laugh. Payback was a bitch, and I had no intention of waking him and letting him know he was pressing his face into my armpit. Instead, I tucked him closer to really get his face in there while my other hand ran up and down her spine. I sighed, relaxing while drowning in her scent when I heard purring. I looked at my brother, disgusted. He was getting his kicks in his sleep about being tucked in my armpit, and I was about to shove him away when I realized the noise was coming from Lucy.

The sound vibrated against my chest. The purring noise was not her normal one, not a vampiric growl, which was menacing and usually induced by anger or hunger, but like a cat purring, only deeper. It wasn't her vampire side reacting like that but her wolf. The wolf she apparently didn't have, making me think of what Avery had said as I let sleep take me.

Chapter 64

Josie

I waited at the meeting spot for hours for this idiot to show up. He was supposed to convince the border patrol he was meeting a friend. The sun was coming up, and I was becoming annoyed. Jamie called him hours ago, and he was supposed to be here by now.

Seeing a car coming up the deserted dirt road, I moved off to the side on alert in case it wasn't him. The car stopped beside me, and I recognized the boy inside to be him. I had met him a couple of times with Lucy while on school holidays, but I didn't like him much; he was always so greedy for her attention, and that used to irritate me.

He got out, popping the trunk and not saying a word to me, yet his jaw was clenched.

"Get in," he finally said.

"I am not getting in the trunk," I told him, and he growled at me.

"Stay here then. You can't be spotted when I drive over, so the trunk or find your own way in," he snapped at me. It was clear he thought very little of me. I glared at him before climbing in, and he slammed the lid down before I even lay down. The trunk door hit my head, and I punched it.

The car started moving, and this jerk wasn't even gentle, driving like a maniac, when I felt the car move off the dirt and onto the road. The drive took half an hour, and I swear he deliberately took every corner too fast. Then the car came to a halting stop, tossing me against the rear seats.

The trunk opened, and he glared down at me.

"Now, get out," he spat at me. I got out, glaring at him and wanting to rip the prick to pieces with the way he was acting. I looked around and realized he didn't drop me anywhere near Tyson and Ace's packhouse.

"You are supposed to drop me over there," I told him.

"No, Jamie said to get you over the border. I fucking did that, now fuck off."

"No, you are supposed to help me. What the fuck is your problem?" I demanded.

"Maybe I don't like betraying my best friend. I did my part. Now, get. Before I decide to alert patrols of you being here."

"Like you can talk, preaching about betraying friends," I told him.

"What the fuck are you talking about? Besides helping you over, I haven't done shit to Lucy, and I would never hurt her, not like you did."

"So, you didn't put pictures all over the school of her naked?" I taunted, and he growled.

"That wasn't me that wasn't me, that was the fucking janitor. I just gave him the phone. I didn't know what was on it, you bitch. Now fuck off away from me. You are nothing but a vile, disgusting bitch, to take photos of her like that and not try to help her. What the fuck is wrong with you?"

"Don't for one second think you know me, now help me get to Lucy, or I am calling Jamie. I don't know what he has over you, but it must be something good for you to be going against her and helping him." I watched as his expression shifted from anger to something else, something I couldn't decipher. He looked almost pained before he masked it, looking away.

"I did my part. I won't help you do whatever you were sent here to do," he said, and I realized whatever Jamie had over him had him conflicted. I knew Lucy and Mitchell were close, but I wasn't expecting him to be so defiant about Jamie's orders.

"So, you aren't going to help me?" He didn't answer and just headed to the driver's side door.

"I get caught because of you, I will tell them you were involved."

"Go ahead, Josie. Lucy is my friend. No one will believe you, and if they did, so be it."

"You really don't care, Mitchell. What about Jamie?"

"Fuck Jamie. He has taken enough from me, and I now realize nothing I do for him is enough. He always wants more. I am out," he said, getting in his car.

"You are best listening to him. When this all goes down, you want to be on the right side," I yelled at him, and he tossed the door back open, standing and looking over the roof at me.

"When what goes down?" I didn't answer. He slammed his door before walking over to me and gripping my arms so tightly that I felt his nails slice through me before I shoved him off.

"What has he got you doing over here?" Mitchell demanded.

"Help me, and I will tell you." His lips pulled back over his teeth, his canines slipping out.

"I can't wait to see your face when you witness her downfall," I told him, and he chuckled.

"You're here to kill her?" He laughed like he thought it was hilarious. Though that wasn't my intention right now, once Jamie tied his daughter to Rayan, I get to finish her. Something that made me feel sick but also excited. I couldn't understand the conflicting feeling I was having about it. She had always been there for me, so why did she have to get involved with my mate? Why did he want her instead of me? I wasn't going to lose him. I needed him, and she was getting in the way of us being together.

Mitchell was smiling like he knew something I didn't, and it was setting me on edge.

"What?" I asked, and he laughed, walking back to his car.

"Nothing, I was just taking one last look at you. Can't say I will miss you, but if you think Tyson and Ace will let you hurt their mate, you are delusional."

"By the time they realize, it will be too late."

"You keep telling yourself that, you are in for a rude shock because it won't just be them after you. Clearly, you forget who her parents are, who her family is. You are a mutation, and you think you can go up against her family? You are just as delusional as Jamie," he said before getting in his car and tearing away down the road.

I had one way to make Lucy comply; Jamie looked at it wrong. He needed Rayan. I wanted Lucy gone and my mate back. What better way than to kill two birds with one stone? Lucy would do anything for her brother, and he was the same. Now I just needed to get them in the same place at the same time. *Piece of cake.*

Chapter 65

Lucy

I woke up to the sound of my phone vibrating and ringing loudly. I groaned, not wanting to get up. Peering around the room, I found Ace beneath me and turned my head to see my phone on the bedside table. I vaguely remembered Ace asking for it, but I couldn't remember what he wanted it for or if he'd told me. Grabbing it, I saw it was Mitchell calling. The sun was barely up outside the window, the sky orange and pink as it rose outside my window. I sat up, straddling Ace's waist.

Ace woke up from the movement, and I answered the phone, yawning. Ace ran his hands up my thighs, jostling me around as he nipped at my neck. I pushed him away, his stubble tickling.

"Lucy, are you there?" Mitchell asked.

"Yes, I am here." I yawned again. Ace kissed my jaw, and I ran my fingers through his hair.

"Where are you? I need to see you. I need to explain. I fucked up, I fucked up, but I swear I didn't mean to hurt you. Are you home?"

"I am at Ace and Tyson's. What's going on?" I asked, and Ace straightened.

"Is that Mitchell?" he asked. I nodded, and he reached for the phone, but I pulled away.

"I will see you soon," Mitchell said, hanging up. I stared at my phone, blinking, trying to figure out what was going on.

"Where is Mitchell?" Ace asked. His eyes suddenly glazed over, and I could tell he was mindlinking. Tyson also jolted upright and also mindlinking with someone. I sighed, waiting for them to come back to their surroundings. Both their eyes glazed over, and Ace growled, making me jump and nearly fall off him; if his hands weren't quick to grip my hips, I would have fallen off the bed. He got up abruptly and placed me on the edge of the bed.

"Stay here," he snapped, the roughness of his voice sending a tremor through me. He was enraged about something, his deathly aura radiating out of him. Tyson jumped up, grabbing some shorts and slipping them on.

"What's going on?" I asked, also climbing out of bed and putting one of their shirts over my head.

"Stay here," Tyson said. I heard a car pulling up out front and a car door shut. Ace roared with fury, and Tyson jumped, rushing for the door.

"No, tell me what's going on," I asked Tyson, and he stopped.

"They caught Josie. I need to go," he said when I heard Mitchell's frantic voice.

"Let me explain, Ace," he said, and I rushed out, chasing after Tyson. I ran down the hall, looking out the door, when Ace slammed Mitchell on the hood of his car. I screamed, and Mitchell had his hands up, trying to block him as Ace repeatedly punched him.

"No! No! What are you doing?" I screamed, bursting through the screen door. Mitchell's face was bloody, and Ace turned his glare on me. Mitchell slid off the hood.

"Get her inside!" Ace screamed at Tyson.

"Let me explain! Please, Ace," Mitchell begged, and Tyson tried to grab me and put me inside. Ace kicked Mitchell in the face, his head snapping back.

"Let him go!" I cried, smacking at Tyson, trying to drag me inside.

"Stop, Ace! He isn't even fighting back! Stop!" I screamed, thrashing, and Tyson dropped me. Ace gripped the front of Mitchell's shirt, slamming him down on the ground. I jumped on his back, and Tyson tried to rip me off him.

"Let him go! Let him go!" I screamed, tears trickling down my face as Ace continued to beat him, his face swelling until he was almost unrecognizable. Blood everywhere but Ace wouldn't stop; he wanted to kill him.

I sank my teeth into his back, and he growled, jumping up. Tyson yanked me off at the same time, making me land on top of him.

I rushed off his lap, crawling off Tyson and over to Mitchell, who was choking on his own blood. My hands shook terribly as I held them in front of Ace, trying to get him to stop. His breathing was heavy as he glared down at Mitchell, who lay limp on the ground, his eyes flickering back and forth between him and Atticus.

"Stop, please!" I cried, trying to figure out what the hell was going on. Mitchell whimpered, the cuts on his face slowly healing. I bit my wrist when Ace snatched it in his tight grip.

"Heal him, and I will fucking kill him," Ace growled at me, yanking me to my feet. Tyson walked over, looking down at

Mitchell. Tyson's, I realized, was a different sort of anger. Ace was hit first, ask questions later. Tyson was deadly calm, his eyes calculating as he watched Mitchell try to sit upright.

Tyson crouched down in front of him. "I will let you explain, but if you lie, or I don't like your answer, you will die."

"What? No! He is my best friend!" I snapped at Tyson, but Ace yanked me back and away from Tyson and Mitchell.

"I'm so sorry, Lucy. I'm sorry. I tried to make it right. I called Ryker the moment I dropped her off and left. I told him where she was," Mitchell said, hanging his head.

"Where who was? Josie?" I asked. Mitchell nodded while I tried to put the pieces together. Mitchell tried to crawl over to me, but Tyson's hand closed around his throat, slamming him back in the dirt on his back, the air expelling from his lungs. His strength was shocking because looking between Ace and Tyson, that sort of strength you would expect from Ace, yet the calmness radiating off Tyson scared me more. Tyson was so much calmer, and it was weird seeing him so angry, feeling it coursing through him.

"You don't go near her. Not after what you did," Tyson growled, his voice menacing and cold.

"After he did what? Can someone tell me what the fuck is going on?" I asked.

"Mitchell helped Josie get over the borderlines last night. He also is the one responsible for the pictures at the school," Tyson said, but I shook my head. *Mitchell wouldn't do that.*

"No, I didn't know, I swear. If I had known, I never would have given the janitor the phone. Please, Lucy, you have to believe me. That's why I called you that morning. I gave him the phone like Jamie asked, that's it. When I came to school the next day, I saw what he did. I saw it, and I tried to call you and tell you not to come in. I tried to rip them down," Mitchell told me. I knew he was telling the truth. I knew Mitchell wouldn't destroy me like that.

Ace growled, and Tyson's hand tightened around his throat, his face changing color and turning purple under his grip. Mitchell clawed at his hands.

"Stop. He is telling the truth."

"I don't care," Tyson said.

"Let him go, Tyson, or I swear—"

"You swear what, Lucy? As long as he is dead, I can live with you alive and hating me."

"Can you live with me leaving you, too? Mitchell wouldn't deliberately try to hurt me," I told him; that much I was certain of.

We had been best friends from the day we met. Not once had he ever betrayed me like this. I knew he had to have a reason for it, and I trusted it was good enough. I had seen Mitchell go toe to toe with my mother for me, back me up and cover for me, no matter the circumstances, when I attended school before boarding school. He was there when no one else was. I trusted him, and I knew he had to have a reason for helping Jamie.

"Why? I know you had to have a reason for working with Jamie. I know you, Mitchell, and you hate him as much as everyone else."

"He has my mate. He has Hank's daughter. I thought it was just another drug run, that the phone was for his contacts. I bring the drugs to Hank. Hank gets them out of the city. I swear that's what I thought the phone was for. I just wanted my mate. Please, Lucy, you know I love you. You know I would never hurt you. My mate is the only reason, I promise," Mitchell pleaded.

"Let him up."

"No, he needs to pay," Ace said.

"He has paid enough. Jamie has his mate, and you just beat him for nothing," I snapped at Ace.

"He could be lying about having a mate," Ace growled.

"He isn't. Mitchell is a terrible liar. He gets eye twitches," I told him, and Mitchell chuckled.

"Mom said the same thing," Mitchell laughed. Tyson pinched the bridge of his nose and let out a breath.

"My brother caught Josie," Tyson said, and Mitchell's shoulders sagged with relief.

"Good, at least something came out of all this," Mitchell said when his eyes glazed over suddenly. He started shaking before he stopped, his eyes coming back into focus.

"Your parents want me to hand myself in," Mitchell said.

"I will come with you."

"It's fine, Lucy. One of them can take me," Mitchell said, and Tyson nodded.

"No, I'm coming with you," I told him, walking inside to grab my shoes and put on some clothes.

Chapter 66

Melana

I was taken to new cells and dumped on the cold concrete floor. I groaned, rolling on my back. I could barely move, and everything hurt. The cell door slammed, and I succumbed to the urge to pass out, sweating beading on every inch of my body. I shuddered, letting the darkness eat me up and offer the relief of feeling nothing.

Cold hands were what kept me awake though not letting me rest, gently tapping my face, and I blinked up at the ceiling. The fluorescent light made me squint as I tried to regain some form of focus when I felt blood trickle into my mouth. I swallowed, welcoming the taste. *Oh gosh, how I was starving.* I could feel the blood working through my system, awakening the hunger within me, and I gripped the wrist of the person feeding me and sank my teeth into them…

"That's it, Melana," said a soft feminine voice. I thought I was dreaming; it had to be a dream. I hadn't heard that voice for years. I let her arm go, turning my head, and my eyes widened at the sight of her. Hollow cheeks, and sad eyes were peering at me. She had lost a lot of weight, but there was no doubt it was her.

"Aliza?" I whispered before rolling and propping myself up on an elbow to look at her. I reached out to touch her, and she was indeed real. She was really here. She was a good woman, too good for Alpha Jamie. I had always wondered what had happened to her. Rumors said he'd killed her, but I knew that couldn't be true because he was crazy but not batshit crazy, like a severed-mate-bond kind of crazy.

"How? Why are you here? How long have you been here?" I asked, confused. Aliza had always been nice to Josie and me, and it was shocking to see her in this state, so malnourished and looking so weak. We all knew he beat her, knew she feared him, and I thought she ran, escaped him. I didn't think even Jamie was cruel enough to lock up his own mate.

"How is Emily? Did you see her?" Aliza said, gripping my arms with frail hands. I tried to shake off the shock of seeing her.

"She is fine. I have seen her a few times. She looks healthy," I told her.

"He was always a good father, unfortunately, not a good mate," she said, and I saw relief flood her as she leaned back against the cell wall. I sat up before sniffing the air, and my heart beat erratically when I picked his scent up, making my head whip from side to side, looking for him. I was in a room with four cells. Each cell had someone in it.

"Hey, baby," Nathanial's voice said, barely a murmur before he started coughing, and I ran at the bars flinging my arms through, the bars burning my skin. He looked terrible. His blond hair was longer now; it sat past his shoulders limply and drenched in sweat. His hazel eyes looked sad and bloodshot.

"I'm sorry, I am so sorry," I whispered to him, tears falling down my cheeks. He reached his hand out through the bars, trying to reach across to me and my heart broke at the sight of him and what he had endured. He was just as skinny as Aliza. I didn't deserve him but seeing him had sent the bond into a frenzy. Even though I rejected him, I could still feel it come to life with him this close, though it was incredibly weak and barely existent.

His fingers reached mine before his hand dropped to the floor. But that fleeting touch was enough to make my fingertips burn. "Nathaniel?" I sobbed. *I ruined everything. I ruined him.*

"Don't cry. I am alive," he said before coughing again.

"You didn't deserve this. I should never have rejected you," I told him, hating myself.

"We can fix it when we get out of here. If we get out of here. I know you had your reasons, Mel." I let out a shaky breath, looking around at the other cells; it was all the same. People in each one, all looking on the verge of death.

"Carla?" I asked, looking at her.

"Hey, Melana," she said, also coughing and rasping for breath.

"Does your father know you're here?" She nodded. I knew her father was a janitor from high school. Now making me realize who put the photos up of Lucy. I shook my head before hanging it when I heard another voice, a softer one, making me turn my head to the cell beside me.

"Is Mitchell okay? He was from the other pack, the Alpha King's pack," the girl said.

"Mitchell?"

"I don't know his last name," she said sadly, but I could tell by her scent that she was from Alpha Jamie's pack.

"He is our age, though," she said, looking at Carla.

"Mitchell Davis, Lucy's friend?" Carla choked out, and I realized whom she was talking about.

"Maybe. He is my mate. That's how I ended up here. Alpha Jamie killed my parents and took me," she said, her lip trembling. She looked around seventeen but was in better shape than the rest of the prisoners. But her question made me look at Aliza, wondering what she did to end up here.

"It's okay, Taylor. I am sure he is fine," Aliza tried to comfort her.

"Emily looks like you," I told Aliza, and she smiled. Her blue eyes filled with tears; she was skin and bones beside her fake boobs that now looked too big for her tiny frame. Her foiled blonde hair sat in the middle of her back, and her mousy brown hair had grown right out.

"How long has he had you in here?" I asked her.

"Since just after Emily's first birthday. I haven't seen her since. She probably thinks I abandoned her," she said, closing her eyes and resting her head on the wall behind her. *Has she been here for three years?* I gasped in horror that Jamie would do that to his own mate.

"After he found out what I did, he lost it. I was planning on leaving after I sent an anonymous letter to King Ryker about his dealings and the airport."

"You got the airport shut down?" I asked her. She nodded.

"His Beta caught me packing and told him," she said.

"I was planning on taking Emily and fleeing the country. He would never allow me to take her. He said I couldn't leave until I gave him a son, but Emily wasn't leaving. When he found out what I did, he put me in here." She chuckled.

"What do you mean?" I asked her.

"I had myself sterilized. I knew I was a breeding machine to him. After Emily, I refused to have any more. I wanted out, and

I knew it would be harder to leave with more than one child, so I went to Avalon City and met a surgeon there, had them take everything out. When I told him this, he threw me in here and said I could rot in hell," she said, shaking her head.

Chapter 67

Suddenly, I heard the vents shake, and everyone started whimpering, trying to get under the thin sheets.

"What is it?" I asked, and Aliza pointed to the vents. A second later, it hit me when I turned to look and sucked in a breath. Wolfsbane was being pumped into the vents. I coughed, covering my mouth, and Aliza offered me a piece of her sheet. I covered my mouth and nose. My eyes burned and watered, and my skin blistered and burned, but it didn't last long, and the vents stopped shuddering and groaning. It wasn't enough to kill anyone but enough to keep them weak. We needed to get out of here. I looked at the vents running along the roof, and they were pretty big, big enough to crawl through, but they were also pretty high up the roof.

I waited for my body to stop retching and hacking up on the wolfsbane. My breathing wheezed and burned each breath I took, and I used the wall to push myself upright, staggering as I looked for a join in the vents and at the brackets.

"What are you doing?" Carla asked.

"Do you know where the vents lead?" I asked her, and she shook her head.

"The laundry room in the packhouse. They are set on a timer. Every hour, they open the vents. You can't use them. Those vents are coated in wolfsbane. You would die trying to get out of them," Aliza said, and I shook my head.

"I need to get in those vents to get help," I told her.

"Did you not hear what I said? They are coated in wolfsbane, and if the vents turn on while you are in there—" She didn't finish and started coughing instead.

"It may kill you, Aliza, but I am not just a werewolf. I am a mutation. Wolfsbane affects me, but it would take a lot to kill me," I told her while looking around the cell. The cells were bare except for the steel sinks and toilets in each one. Looking around the other cells, I noticed a piece of bent rebar sticking out of the wall in Carla's cell.

"Carla, can you break that bar off?"

She shook her head. "I tried it won't budge," she said, and I nodded, looking back at the ceiling.

The cells were barred but painted red with wolfsbane. I gritted my teeth before walking to the corner of the cell where our cell met the other. I tugged off my jeans, leaving me in only my pink panties. If I could just get my jeans around the sprinkler system, it might hold my weight to get close enough to the vent. I could break the bracket where they joined, but would the vent hold my weight?

Gripping the bars, I lifted my leg onto the bar that ran crossways before pulling myself up. I tried to reach the sprinkler system, but it was too high, and my thighs were too wide to fit through the bars to climb them.

"Pass my jeans," I told Aliza. She staggered over, coughing, and handed them to me. Holding one leg, I tried to toss them over the sprinkler system. It took multiple attempts trying to hang onto the bar with one hand while tossing the denim jeans over it. As the gap was so small, they would fall each time I hit the roof, missing the bar, but eventually, I managed it.

I was eating up the hour already, and I didn't want to be stuck in those vents when the timer went off. I carefully jiggled my jeans, so the other leg would fall through the other side. Once it was through enough to grab, I looped my arm through the bars while I reached out for the other before grabbing both in one hand. I tugged on the jeans, and they held; the bolts holding the sprinkler system didn't budge. I tested my weight on it.

"Now what?" Carla asked, looking up at me curiously.

"Now I need to break the vent bracket at the joint," I told her, trying to think of how exactly I would do that. The brackets were not very big, but they were held with two bolts on each side. Leaning back with the pant legs clutched in one hand, I now had to try to swing over and hope it would hold my swinging weight.

The sprinkler system ran alongside the vent but higher up the roof, the vents hanging down a little lower, so I would be close enough to climb in if I could break the bracket or bust one side of the vent open. They joined in the center of the cell. A bracket on each side of the joint; if I could break one and pop the vent out, I should be able to climb into the side with the bracket attached still.

Testing that theory, I jumped, clutching the jeans with both hands. I spun for a second before climbing the denim like a rope and wrapping my hands around the sprinkler system. The metal was cool to touch but hard to grip. I kicked at the bracket to find it already loose. *Oh, thank the Goddess*, I thought to myself and checked how rusted the bolts holding it to the roof were. Instead of kicking the bracket, I started kicking the side of the vent crushing the wall inwards. I knew that by gripping it, the bracket would rip from the roof, and hopefully, my weight would separate the vents.

I kicked the side, denting it all in and the bottom of the vent using my toes. I hissed when my toes broke before healing, only to break again as I kicked the bottom of the vent when I heard a click, the vent popping out from its groove.

Adrenaline coursed through me, and I kicked the bracket a couple of times to make sure it was loose enough before reaching over and grabbing it. The moment I dropped my weight on it, this side ripped from the ceiling, and I barely hung on before dropping down and jarring my feet. I climbed back up, repeating the process, kicking the dented vent to knock them apart enough to get my fingers between them. When I managed that, I gripped the vent; my weight and the missing bracket on that side made the vent bend downward when it pulled out of the wall, and I hit the concrete on my ass. The piece of vent I was gripping fell onto me and knocked the air out of me.

"Are you okay?" Nathaniel coughed. I groaned, and Aliza helped me up.

"You should wait. We haven't got much more time until the timer goes off and pushes the wolfsbane through the vents again."

"Are you sure it leads to the laundry?" I asked her.

"Yes. One side would have to lead outside, the other to the laundry," she said, looking up at the vents. I didn't have a choice in which one to go through now as half the vent was on the ground, and I couldn't climb the brick. So, hopefully, the one I was going through led outside. *If not, laundry it is,* I thought to myself, climbing the bars to my jeans again.

My fingers were cut to pieces as I gripped the lip of the vent. I dangled there for a bit, trying to find a way to pull myself up, managing to get one arm in, and I used my elbow to help pull myself in. The wolfsbane residue on the vent was like acid on my skin.

I coughed and spluttered in the vent; my bare legs felt like the skin was being eaten off. Each second in there, I grew weaker and dizzy, having to stop. I made it to the bend in the vents, but now it went up. I felt like I was playing Tetris, moving my body at odd angles to turn on my back before pulling myself up to a sitting position. It went up a little over a meter before turning flat again. Bent over slightly, I slid into the other vent on my stomach. I groaned when I saw the fan and knew I was in the laundry. The other side went outside. The laundry, though, wasn't the worst option as it was on the back deck of the packhouse, so also outside the main house.

The grate on the side was covered to stop Wolfsbane from spilling into the laundry, but the covering on the side was thin, and after a couple of elbows, I managed to get one side to break just as the vents groaned and turned on. I gasped as I inhaled a huge breath of wolfsbane before holding my breath and slamming my elbow into the other side, shoving the grate covering the vent hole out. I was surprised no one came bursting in because it was hardly a quiet task breaking into the vents and crawling through. The grate fell to the ground with a clang, and I squeezed out, covering my mouth and nose, trying to find the switch for the fans to the vents. Looking out the window, I looked down to see our concrete prison underneath the back deck and check if anyone was lurking outside.

Luckily no one seemed to be around, making me wonder why no one was at the packhouse today and where Alpha Jamie was. I couldn't see a single person. Turning back to the laundry, I spotted the switch and shut it off before spotting a 2L bottle of wolfsbane sitting on top of the fan, a hose and funnel coming out of the motor from somewhere, which had to be where they poured wolfsbane in.

Despite this being a laundry room, it was empty. The last time I was out on the back deck here, I saw the washer and dryer on the back deck and thought it was a little odd but never questioned it. To think everyone had been trapped at the packhouse this entire time. That made more sense because the pack believed Aliza was dead, so his Beta must have been the only one to know of the cells under the deck.

Opening the laundry door, I sucked in a deep breath of unpolluted air. My face was burning from the wolfsbane, and I wasted no time rushing down the steps of the back deck to the ground. I looked at the door of the outbuilding that I always thought was for storage as it went the entire length of the deck. I snuck around and saw a huge padlock on the door and a digital key panel. I let out a breath. Now, I just had to throw myself over the borders and hope Ace and Tyson wouldn't kill me at first glance. Running across the rear lawn, I climbed the fence and darted into the trees.

Chapter 68

Lucy

Ace wouldn't even let me in the car with Mitchell, instead forcing me in his while Tyson drove off with Mitchell. I felt sick with nerves about what would happen to him. I had no doubt that my mother would unleash hell on him, but hopefully, my presence would deter her from hurting him. I knew Mitchell wasn't lying, knew without a doubt.

Ace mumbled under his breath when he suddenly veered off, going in a different direction from my parents' house.

"Ace, where are you going?" He didn't answer and just completely ignored me.

"Ace, the packhouse is that way," I told him, but he continued ignoring me until I grabbed the steering wheel and jerked the car. His growls bounced off the windows.

"You aren't going there. He deserves what he gets."

"Pull the fucking car over now!" I screamed at him, knowing he and Tyson were going to just hand him over to my mother and stepfather. They wouldn't ask questions; they would just kill him.

"He betrayed you. He fucking deserves to die," Ace snarled. His anger was out of control. I knew he was mad, but this? He wanted to hurt someone; he needed to hurt someone. His fingers white-knuckled against the steering wheel.

"That's not for you to decide. He is my friend. Pull over, Ace. Now, or so help my god, I will—"

"You'll what? Hate me? I can live with that, and so can Tyson," he bellowed. Fur started growing on his arms as his anger became worse.

"Pull over. You said I could go with him. You said I could help him."

"Yeah, and that was a lie. We don't want him near you. He deserves to die for helping Jamie."

"He did it for his mate."

"Bullshit, he's just trying to save his own skin, Lucy. Open your fucking eyes. Not everyone is your friend. He betrayed you, end of story."

I reached for the handbrake, ripping it up, and the car started sliding before Ace corrected it, undoing the handbrake.

"Let me out! Stop the car, Ace!" I snapped at him.

"No, you're staying with me," he said before flooring it. I was thrown back in my seat as he started driving at alarming speeds.

"Ace, slow down!" I told him as he hit a dip. My head hit the roof of the car, and it became airborne.

"Ace!" He laughed maniacally.

"What, are you scared, Lucy?" he asked as I gripped the seat.

"Yes, now stop!" I shrieked as he turned around a bend so sharply that the car slid out.

"Fucking stop!" I screamed.

"You scared?" he asked again.

"Yes, fucking yes, now slow down," I screamed, shutting my eyes.

"Please, stop!" I begged him.

"I will when you stop taking his side."

"He is my best friend!" I snapped at him, and he growled.

"He is a traitor! I hope my brother rips him to pieces for what he has done," Ace screamed before punching the dash. A crack ran across it, and his breathing increased in harsh breaths, but the car slowed down slightly.

"You took his side," he said, and I said nothing.

"You attacked me for him," he seethed. I shook my head. Mitchell did nothing wrong, not in my eyes. He was protecting his mate. Ace growled, and I could feel Atticus's jealousy simmering in him, urging Ace to kill Mitchell.

"Please, Ace, take me to my parents'," I asked him. I hated to think of what Tyson could be doing to him. I could feel Tyson's anger just as hot as Ace's.

"He won't be there," Ace said before cursing under his breath.

"What do you mean?" I asked, my heart jolting in my chest. I should have known better than to let Tyson take him.

"I said he won't be there. Tyson isn't taking him back to your parents. He was turning around after we were out of sight and heading back home," Ace said.

"Turn around. I won't let you hurt him!"

"It's done, Lucy. Mitchell won't be a problem anymore. You may trust him, but we don't," Ace said.

"Take me back, Ace."

"No!" he snapped, and panic rushed over me. Mitchell would be petrified; I wasn't going to let him die over something I would have done if our roles were reversed. Why couldn't they understand that? Would their decision be different if they were in his shoes? The answer was no. They would do what they needed to get me back, the same as Mitchell.

"Turn around," I told him one last time. I didn't want to throw myself from a moving vehicle; the gravel rash would be a bitch. But I would if I needed to.

"No!" he growled out, forcing my hand. I tossed the door open and unclipped my belt. Ace reached for me a second later, his fingers gripping my shirt, but he was too late. I tossed myself out of the car. The road tore at my clothes and skin as I skidded and rolled across it. I heard the screeching of brakes as I finally came to a stop. Groaning, I rolled on my back. *Ah, that hurt*, I muttered to myself, hauling myself upright.

"Lucy!" Ace roared in panic, and I forced myself upright, staggering. I started limping, and Ace growled.

"Stop, Lucy!" Ace snapped, but I ignored him. Sucking in a breath, I started running before hearing Ace roar behind me and hearing his bones snapping. Looking behind me, I saw Atticus, and I shrieked, taking off like my ass was on fire and heading back home.

Ten minutes, I could make it in ten minutes. I moved in a blur and hit a tree with my shoulder as I zipped through the forest. I was faster than a werewolf, but I was also pretty banged up, and I could hear Ace gaining on me, yet I kept running, refusing to look back as he chased me.

Atticus, fueled by his anger, launched at me just as I reached the driveway of the packhouse. I saw Tyson's car parked and could hear fighting and gurgling cries. My heart skipped a beat when I was thrown forward in the gravel. Atticus landed on top of me. I felt his teeth dig into my shoulder as he bit me, making me scream. I rolled, punching him in the side of the head. He shook his head, baring his teeth at me in warning, but I lifted my knees under him before kicking him off. He snapped at me, but I rolled quickly to see Mitchell's beaten and bloody naked body tossed into the side of Tyson's car. His body was lying limp, and I saw Tyrant stalking toward him. I screamed, slipping on dirt as I raced toward Tyrant and Mitchell. My scream was deafening, and Tyrant looked at me in surprise before turning back to Mitchell to deliver the lethal bite.

"NOOOO!" I screamed when pain rushed over me in my panic. I saw tan-colored fur erupt from my arms before I screamed in pain as I launched myself at Tyrant just as he went to tear into Mitchell's neck. My furry body collided with his, and we rolled, smacking the ground hard. Tyrant growled and snarled when I heard a voice in my head.

"I got this, Luce," echoed a feminine voice in my head that wasn't mine. I blinked to see I was no longer in human form but wolf form. No longer in control as the mystery voice shoved me back before tearing into Tyrant viciously. She shook our head as she bit into his flank, and he whimpered before tossing her off and biting our back leg. Mitchell lay unconscious, and I saw Atticus jump into the fray, but my wolf stood over Mitchell's limp body, and she growled, baring her teeth and snapping her jaws at them.

"Back off!" I bellowed through the mindlink, and Tyrant shook his head, cocking it to the side and staring at me. Atticus stepped too close, and she snapped her teeth at him when I heard the snapping of bones, yet she didn't take her eyes off Ace's wolf.

"Lucy?" Tyson's voice said, shocked, off to the other side of me. Atticus growled but shifted back, and my wolf stretched her sharp claws on the ground, moving the veil and letting me come forward with her. She sniffed the air and growled at them before licking the side of Mitchell's face that was between her front legs. He didn't move, no reaction at all.

MY TWO ALPHAS | 349

Both of my mates growled at her, and she snarled at them in return.

"Shift back!" Ace commanded at the same time as Tyson. She tried to fight their command and whimpered, having both of them force their auras over us and was forced to shift back. I cried out as my bones started snapping at an alarming speed.

"Sorry, Lucy," she said in my head in a pained voice.

"What's your name?" I asked her, thankful she had just saved my friend.

"Lucille."

I stood on all fours naked, covering Mitchell's body and panting hard from the transition.

"You shifted!" Tyson said, shocked and horrified. Ace reached for me, but I slapped his hand away.

"Don't fucking touch me unless you want to lose that hand," I snapped at him.

Chapter 69

Lucy

Mitchell groaned underneath me, and I became very aware of the fact that I was crouched over him, completely naked. Ace growled as he rolled, and as awkward as it would be for poor Mitchell to open his eyes to my breasts hovering over his face, I was too scared to move in case they attacked. I knew they wouldn't while I was positioned above him, so I wasn't willing to move just yet.

Mitchell sat up, completely oblivious to me hovering over him. Ace growled when Mitchell smacked his face into the side of my breast. Tyson stalked off when I heard Mitchell's voice.

"Ah, Lucy, why are you naked?" he asked, and I moved, so I was sitting in front of him between him and Ace. Mitchell sat up, and we must have been a strange sight to see. I had never shifted before, yet I was used to seeing other people naked all the time. But being naked myself, I felt extremely exposed. I heard the front door bang as it smashed against the wall. Tyson rushed out with a pair of shorts on and a handful of clothes. He tossed a shirt at me.

"Put it on," he snapped, and I raised an eyebrow at him.

"Lucy, put the fucking shirt on," he growled as he handed Ace a pair of shorts before tossing pants at Mitchell.

"Stop looking at her," Ace barked at Mitchell.

"I have a mate, chill out," Mitchell said behind me as I pulled the shirt on. I was half-tempted to leave it off as a big fuck you to the pair of them, but I wasn't comfortable being this exposed to the world, though Mitchell had seen plenty of my boobs before when we had sleepovers. No girl can keep their titties in a tank top while sleeping; he had seen plenty of nip slips or full-on boobage exposure.

"Not like I haven't seen her naked before," Mitchell muttered. Tyson stepped toward him, and a furious growl ripped from him.

"When the fuck did you see her naked?" Tyson growled, but I could hear the warning behind his voice if he answered wrongly.

"Relax, I am not interested in your mate. I used to be. Not since I found mine, though and to answer your question when she would sleep over." *Oh my god, Mitchell, stop talking. You are digging us a bigger hole to climb out of.*

"You slept at his house naked in his bed?" I facepalmed at his stupidity.

"No, he meant he has seen pieces of me. You all have long before you knew I was your mate. Hard to contain all this. I have known Mitchell just as long, he has caught glimpses of me before, and we always slept head to toe," I told them, wondering how the fuck their minds could go from wanting to kill Mitchell to this topic.

"Yeah, mom was always funny that way. Doors open and head to toe, so Lucy could kick me in the face all night," Mitchell chuckled.

"Pretty sure they still want to kill him," Lucille told me. It was so strange hearing a voice in my head that wasn't my own.

"Well, technically, we are the same person. Therefore, your own voice. I am just the more sordid unrestrained version," she told me.

"What a word choice to describe yourself," I told her when I heard a menacing growl snapping me back to the issue at hand. Tyson had moved closer and was about to grab me. I could see that having a wolf thing would be a distraction.

"You just need to learn to focus on your surroundings while talking to me instead of trying to find me to speak to me. Multi-task," she said. Tyson's hand wrapped around my wrist, but I twisted out of it.

Tyson glared at me, and Mitchell remained still behind me. He knew I was the only thing keeping them away from him.

"Lucy, come here," Tyson snarled, his lip pulling over his teeth slightly as he glared at Mitchell pressed against my back.

"No, not until you give Mitchell his car keys and let him leave."

"That's not happening," Ace said with a snarl as he folded his arms across his broad chest and glared down at me.

"Then we will remain right here. I am not moving because the moment I do, you will hurt him." Ace reached for me, but I slapped his hand, wondering if Lucille would shift again if needed. I wasn't sure how to force it.

"Right here, Luce. I have a bone to pick with him anyway. I don't mind delivering on that threat earlier or taking his hand. At least then the jerk will know to keep them off other girls," she said.

"Wait, you know?" I asked her, remembering to focus on my surroundings.

"Yep, I have always been here, Lucy. I was just blocked off. I still saw and felt everything you did though sometimes it was hard to see," she said.

"So, you know everything about me?"

"I am your wolf. We are one now. You will never have to fight a battle alone again, Lucy. I am sorry I failed you," she said, but I shook my head.

"Weird, huh, talking to a wolf?" Mitchell said behind me.

"The weirdest," I told him.

"Yeah, I spent two weeks talking out loud to myself. Should have seen the looks I got at school before I realized I was speaking my mind to the world." He laughed.

"Wait, was I doing that?"

"No, Luce, I could just tell by the distracted look on your face," Mitchell said. I let out a breath, but Tyson and Ace were observing us. Mitchell's phone started ringing on the ground behind Tyson, who turned and picked it up.

"It's his mother," Tyson said, and I held my hand out for his phone.

"No, not until you move off him. You are practically sitting on his lap, Lucy."

"I want his car keys," I told him, and his jaw clenched as his eyes darted to Mitchell before going back to me.

"That is not an option," he said when I saw his eyes glaze over. Ace did, too, and I reached over, snatching the phone from Tyson's grip and passing it to Mitchell. Tyson's claws slipped from his fingers, and he looked like he was about to do something. Ace, however, was still locked in a mindlink and by his expression, he looked pissed off before his eyes brightened to the normal silver color.

"Ryker is on his way," Ace said, looking at Tyson, and he cursed. Not even two minutes later, I heard a car on the gravel driveway. A few more minutes passed when I stood up, and so did Mitchell. Tyson instantly lunged at Mitchell to grab him as Ace ripped me toward him. A growl escaped me, and I elbowed him in the stomach, making him let go before elbowing him in the face. I then shoved Tyson and got back between Mitchell and him. The car stopped, and Ryker jumped out with Jacob.

My stepfather looked as murderous as Tyson and Ace, and I grabbed Mitchell's arm as he approached.

"Why is he still here?" Ryker snapped at Tyson and Ace.

"No one is touching him," I blurted out, and my father snarled at me.

"That's not for you to decide, Lucy. Grab him, Jacob," Ryker said, and Jacob rushed over. I growled at him, baring my teeth, and he stopped.

"Lucy, enough. Stop this," Ryker snapped at me.

"No! You don't get a say. He is my friend. I forgave him for his part. He handed Josie over, for fuck's sake. He isn't going to do anything."

"You're right, he isn't, because he is coming with me. Now, stand down, or I will make you," Ryker said coldly. Mitchell sighed behind me.

"Where is mom?" I asked Ryker.

"At home with Ryden and Rayan, now move."

"No!" I told him, and I felt Lucille come forward. Ryker blinked at me before his eyes darted down to realize I only had a shirt on before flicking back to my eyes. He stepped forward, cocking his head to the side and observing me, and I knew he could feel her.

"She has a wolf," Tyson told him. Ryker clicked his tongue before nodding to Jacob in front of me.

"No, you can't, Dad. He did nothing wrong."

"He betrayed the pack, Lucy."

"Like you wouldn't if it was mom."

"No, I wouldn't. I would have sought fucking help if our roles were reversed. He made a stupid decision that could have cost your life."

"I will go with them, Lucy," Mitchell said, touching my arm. Ace growled at him but didn't do anything.

"What will you do to him?" I asked.

"Avery is on her way. She will get in their heads and see who is telling the truth and who isn't. If what he claims is true, then I will think of letting him go home. Argue with me, Lucy, and I will banish him."

"Melana?" I asked.

"Josie said she left the City. We have no idea where she is," Jacob said, and Mitchell slipped out from behind me.

"It's fine, Lucy. Avery will see, okay?" Mitchell said, kissing my temple before stopping next to Jacob.

"You two, I will deal with later," Ryker told them, walking back to the car. Mitchell hesitantly got in, and I went to go with him when Tyson grabbed me, tossing me over his shoulder.

Chapter 70

"Not a chance. You are staying here," Tyson said, turning and heading for the house.

"Put me down. I can fucking walk Tyson," I told him, but he ignored me, and Ace glared at the car as it left. When he turned around, Tyson was climbing the steps, and Ace turned to look at me.

"I liked it better when you weren't an asshole," I muttered.

"I have always been an asshole, Lucy, just not to you," Tyson snapped before depositing me on the couch. Ace walked in, locking the door.

"What were you thinking?" Ace snapped at me while Tyson wandered to the kitchen and turned the kettle on.

"Helping my friend?" I snapped back at him.

"You chose your friend over us, you fought us for him, and you what? Tyrant fucking hurt you? Did you think of what that would mean for Tyson you jumping in like that?"

"He didn't do anything wrong, Ace. Like you can judge him. You would have done the same thing," I told him, stepping up.

"We were not judging him, Lucy. He betrayed you, that's it. Nothing to judge when he handed himself in. You are the worst judge of character. Think with your fucking head, Lucy. What is to say that he won't do it again, for this so-called mate?" Tyson bellowed.

"I know him, Tyson. Mitchell wouldn't hurt me."

"Just like Josie or your teacher. Your judgment of them was pretty fucking wrong too," Tyson said. I blinked at him, taking a step back. *He did not just say that.*

"Shit, Lucy, I didn't mean it like that."

"Then how did you mean it, Tyson? Because what you said can only mean one thing in my eyes. I have questioned that fucking day and my actions over and over again. I don't need you questioning me too," I yelled at him. He stepped around the counter, but I held up my hand, not wanting him near me.

"But you got one thing right. I am the worst judge of character because I thought you were better and knew better than that. Of all the people, you were the one I least expected to say something like that," I told him before storming out.

"Lucy, I didn't mean—" I ignored him, heading to the room to grab some clothes. Tears pricked at the edge of my vision. I blamed myself enough for everything that was going on, and that would have hurt less if he had just slapped me. *Do they think I don't know all this mess is because of me? And now they throw it in my face.* Emotion choked me as I headed to the bathroom.

"Lucy, I don't think he meant it," Lucille told me, and it was weird feeling her anger and hurt on top of mine. It felt heavy, oppressing.

"He still said it, and he was right. I knew something was off, and I ignored my instincts. I didn't think he would try to do that, though," I whispered to her as I turned the shower on.

Lucille whimpered in my head, and the sound was heartbreaking. "I am sorry I wasn't there to help you. I would have taken your place in a heartbeat if I could." Her guilt weighed heavily, and despite not knowing her all this time, I felt like I had known her my entire life and her guilt was seeping into me. Something I wasn't used to. It was one thing recognizing my own emotions, but feeling hers was overwhelming as tears slipped down my face.

Arms wrapped around me from behind, and I jumped, not hearing the door open, too consumed in my wolf.

"He shouldn't have said that. He knows that, but he didn't mean it the way it came out," Ace whispered, pressing his face in my neck. I inhaled and exhaled deeply.

"You know Tyson wouldn't do anything to hurt you. He is the good twin. I swear, Lucy, he didn't mean it, and if you bothered to feel through the bond, you would feel it," Ace said, but I refused. I block him out, too, angry. It didn't matter if he meant it; he still said it.

"We all say things in anger, Lucy. It's been a rough day."

"Never thought I would see the day when you were defending Tyson to me. Usually, it's the other way around," I told him.

"Like I said, it has been a rough day. Just don't be too mad at him. We love you. We just don't like the idea of someone possibly hurting you. Neither of us thought Mitchell would do that. We know how close you are to him. I am sorry for scaring you in the car earlier, too," Ace said before reaching down and gripping the hem of my shirt and lifting it off me. He placed his hand under the water before adjusting the temperature. He kissed the side of my neck and stepped back.

"Hop in while I check on Tyson," he said, and I did. Ace left, shutting the door, and I washed the dirt and gravel sticking to my sweaty skin off. A few minutes passed when Ace returned, placing two towels on the sink basin and removing his shorts.

"Tyson?"

"Moping," Ace answered, stepping in behind me and reaching for the soap.

I kept my back to him, fully aware of his nakedness.

"Come on, just a quick peek. Let's see if he is as well-endowed as his brother," Lucille said.

"We just saw him naked," I told her.

"That wasn't looking, though. That was us trying to keep them away. You didn't even peek. Now be a team player and turn that pretty head of ours for a quick looksy," she whined.

"You really are the sordid one, aren't you?"

"I have been locked in your head for so long. I have nothing better to do than think of my mate. Well… mates, as it turns out," she said, and I rolled my eyes at her. Looking over my shoulder, Ace had his eyes closed, water streaming down his body as he washed his hair.

"See? He won't even know," she urged, and I chewed my lip before looking down. Lucille hummed in my head, and my lips parted slightly.

"Guess they aren't a hundred percent identical, 'cause damn girl, it's like a baby's arm holding an apple."

"A what?"

"Touch it."

"No!"

"Come on, just poke it a little," she said, and I went to look away only to find Ace smirking at me. All the blood rushed to my face.

"Oh, fuck!" I snapped at her, mortified.

"Oh, fuck is what you will be saying when he comes at you with that. That is the best monster deformity I have ever seen," Lucille said. Ace raised an eyebrow at me.

"It's rude to stare," Ace said before smiling.

"I wasn't… It wasn't my fault." I pressed my lips in a line.

"Because you didn't just turn to gape at my cock?"

"Lucille—"

"And what did Lucille say?" Ace said, pressing closer. His hand moved to the side of my breast, his thumb rubbing over my nipple.

Chapter 71

My breath hitched as sparks rushed south. My nipple hardened as he continued to brush his thumb over it, his other hand moving to my hip. I swallowed, my brain losing all train of thought at the feel of his touch, and his gaze made me squirm as I tried to regather some sense, but that flew out the window the moment his lips crashed against mine. His tongue delved between my lips, and he growled deep in the back of his throat.

His tongue was demanding. There was nothing gentle or sensual with the way he kissed me; it was hungry and hot-blooded, igniting a fire inside me that had my blood singing. His tongue tasted every inch with an aggressive desire that made my pussy clench air, forcing my thighs to slap shut to stop the throbbing between them.

My back hit the tiled wall harshly, making me gasp at the impact, and I kissed him back with the same intensity, loving the feel of his body pressed against mine when his hands grabbed the back of my thighs, making me squeak at the sudden unexpected movement. Yet also giving me a chance to finally be able to suck in much-needed air.

Ace's lips playfully bit my lips, cheek, and jawline before moving to my neck and collarbone as he bit and licked at my skin like he was about to devour me whole. My legs tightened around his waist when he moved his hand, fumbling to shut off the water, his lips not leaving my skin as he hoisted me up higher, only to bite the top of my breast before grazing his canines down my skin, making me moan and grip his hair.

My hips rocked against his pelvis, seeking out the friction, as my pussy pulsated and my arousal spilled onto my thighs and coated his rock-hard abs. The shower screen smacked into the tiled wall as he stepped out of the shower. My hands gripped his shoulders to stop me from falling back as his hands squeezed my ass.

A risqué dirty sound left my lips when he walked out of the bathroom, my lower back slamming into the dresser next to the bathroom door in his bedroom. The items on top rattled and fell off when my ass landed on the smooth, hard surface as he placed me on top of it. His lips moved lower, nipping at my ribs and sides. His hand gripped and squeezed my thigh as he forced one over his shoulder before burying his face between my legs.

"Ace!" I shrieked, worried about toppling off the dresser, then his tongue plunged into me, his mouth covering my pussy completely as he fucked me with his tongue. A growl escaped him as his tongue licked and tasted every part of me when I felt his tongue roll over the tight muscles of my ass, making me jump and try to pull away. The movement caused him to chuckle and dive his tongue back inside me before sucking my clit and making me cry out.

My hips rocked against his face, his hands pinning me in place as he continued his relentless licking and sucking. My skin heated, and my stomach muscles tightened as he shoved me over the edge, and I crashed hard, my hips moving against his face as his tongue continued to lap at my juices, making me shudder and collapse against the dresser. His hot mouth moved to my thigh when he bit the inside near the apex of my legs before he gripped my hips, dragging me off the top of the dresser and forcing my legs back around his waist as he grabbed me.

Quickly gripping his shoulders to stop me from falling back, he pulled me flush against him. His hand gripped the back of my neck, bringing my lips back to his, forcing his tongue into my mouth and making me taste myself on his tongue. His fingers slipped into my hair before he fisted it, knotting his fingers in my hair.

My back hit the mattress with so much force that I bounced beneath him as my legs unwrapped from his waist, as he pressed himself between my legs. His cock was pressing against my core as he rolled his hips against me, his massive length running between my folds, making me buck against him as his cock brushed against my clit.

I barely registered how much larger and thicker he was compared to Tyson until his tip pressed against my entrance, stretching me instantly around his head. I lifted my hips, wanting him to bury himself inside me. His lips sucked on my mark when Ace thrust his hips forward slightly, and I fisted the sheets at the stretching feeling, my insides stinging when he forced inside further, making me hold my breath.

"Fuck, you're tight," he groaned. His hand gripped my knee and pushed my leg flat against the mattress, opening me up wider, and I gasped as his pelvis hit mine, his cock plunging inside me as he sheathed himself within my tight confines. My walls clenched around him, and I felt overfull as he stilled, giving me time to adjust to his massive length buried to the hilt inside me, his cock pressing against my cervix. Ace rocked his hips slowly, his mouth biting and nibbling on mine when he pulled out and thrust back in, shoving me higher up the bed with force.

My hips rolled against him, trying to meet his thrusts as he brutally pounded into me. Obliterating my insides and making my cries turn to screams, I became lost in the feel of his cock rubbing my walls and building up fast friction that had me coming apart at the seams when he suddenly pulls out. He leaned back, kneeling between my legs before manhandling me and flipping me onto my stomach. His hands gripped my hips and pulled my ass into the air.

I was like a ragdoll in his hands as he pulled me around to how he wanted me. I felt his cock press against my entrance before sliding between my ass cheeks as he rocked his hips against my ass. His lips brushed my shoulder as he pressed closer. He kissed below my ear before flicking my earlobe with his tongue. His raspy, provocative voice below my ear made me moan softly.

"I'm going to fuck you now." His voice turned to a growl, and I pushed back against him when he pulled back. His hands gripped my ass cheeks and pushed them apart so he could watch himself slip in and out of me.

I felt his cock line with my entrance before he slammed into me. My walls instantly gripped him as he started to pound into me. This angle was so much deeper as he pushed me to the edge of pain. The intensity was so excruciatingly high my senses felt overloaded, and my blood pressure rose while my skin heated, making my entire body heat up as I pushed back against him.

The sounds of slapping flesh filled the room, along with my crying moans as I buried my face into the mattress, feeling like I was about to combust when I felt his thumb brush over the muscles of my ass as he pressed his thumb against it. His hand moved, dipping between us as he coated his thumb in my pussy juices before pressing it back against my ass. He groaned, shoving his thumb in my ass and driving into me harder. His movements became harsher and more erratic when I felt my stomach tighten.

My walls clenched him in a vice-like grip, and I shattered, feeling the intense rush of my release that made me scream as I came hard, making me writhe and convulse on his cock. He groaned, pumping into me one last time before stilling, his cock buried deep within me, and I felt his seed coat my insides, leaving me breathless and panting for air.

My legs collapsed under me, his hands on my hips, the only thing keeping me up when I felt him pull out of me slowly, letting me collapse face-down on the bed. Ace fell beside me on his back, also trying to catch his breath. My insides felt battered, but my entire body felt relaxed despite also feeling like I had run a marathon. I lay there, trying to catch my breath, my hair sticking to my face when he rolled on his side, his face hovering above mine when he dipped his face, pressing his lips to mine, his tongue running across the seam of my lips when the door opened.

Tyson walked in naked like he shifted and went for a run. He stopped in his tracks, his eyes moving to between my legs.

"Fucking hell, Ace, you didn't use protection," Tyson growled at him, pointing at me, and I sat upright.

"Shit!" I shrieked, scrambling off the bed, only for Ace to wrap his arms around my waist and pull me back to him.

"It's fine. I will go to the pharmacy and get the morning-after pill if you're worried."

"You should have been more careful. She is only eighteen, Ace. She won't want kids this early." Tyson scolded.

"What, did you ask her?" Ace snapped at him before squeezing my ass as he pulled me on top of him.

"Lucy?" Ace's voice rumbled next to my ear.

"Yeah, the morning-after pill. I am not spitting out pups yet," I told him, and Ace chuckled, kissing my forehead. I sat up, my legs straddling his waist, and he bucked his hips against me.

"Round two?" he asked, and I felt a stupid grin split onto my face.

"What's stopping you?" I asked, biting my lower lip before leaning closer to him. His hands gripped my ass tighter, grinding my pussy against his rapidly hardening cock.

"Lucy." He growled, my name slipping off of his lips like a warning. Tyson shifted behind us, and I looked over my shoulder at him.

"Well, are you coming?" I asked. His eyes widened at my question, his lips parting as he sucked in a breath. "Or are you planning to keep moping?"

The tops of his cheeks colored with a blush. "I wasn't moping."

"Sure you weren't." Ace chuckled beneath me, rocking his hips upward.

"Lucy," Tyson said. His eyes traveled over my naked body as I rocked my hips, letting the rugged ridge of Ace's cock stroke against my clit until my eyes closed at the pleasure of it all. It turned me on having him watch me with his brother.

"Well, are you joining us or not?" Ace asked. "Are you going to help me fill our mate up?"

Ace's words made heat build up in my lower belly, coiling tight like a spring. I knew that I was too young to get pregnant, but the thought of having both of them cum inside of me turned me on. It felt right, like it was always meant to be.

"Ace," Tyson growled, but I could feel his resolve weakening. It seemed he liked the idea as well.

I couldn't help but think about how it would feel to have them both inside of me, unsure of whether I should fuck back into the cock in my ass or the one in my pussy. Letting them both use me as each of us chasing our release.

My eyes slipped closed, and I rocked my hips faster, a moan slipping past my lips. There was a rustling of clothing behind me, and I knew that we had won. Tyson was stripping down. The bed dipped behind me, and my breath caught in my throat. Nerves tightened up inside of me.

I was nervous about being with the two of them, but I knew that it was what I wanted, what they wanted too. I could feel it pulling at my skin, feeding into my need like a drug.

Ace's hands relaxed, and I leaned back, trying to steady my racing heart. His hands moved to my breasts, cupping them and testing their weight in his palms before his thumbs stroked over my nipples. Working them into tight peaks before he leaned forward, sucking one into his mouth.

Tyson's hands moved over my hips. His touch was almost hesitant like he was worried about what he should do. His nervousness was almost tangible, but I knew that we were meant to be like this, the three of us.

I glanced back, locking eyes with him. "You won't hurt me, I promise. Just go slow."

Ace let go of my nipple, his mouth hot against my skin as he let out a growl. "The lube is in the top dresser drawer. Make sure you coat your fingers in that before you get her ready." Ace tells him.

"Get her ready?" Tyson asked, his voice hitching.

"Yeah, you've got to get her warmed up to take your cock, or else it will hurt." Worry bled through the bond from Tyson and I expected a witty reply or refusal, but instead, he listened to his brother. Ace bit at my flesh, sucking my breast into his mouth as his cock jumped against my sex. I didn't know if it was the thought of Tyson fingering my ass or if he was getting off at the idea of me being in pain.

Either way, it fed into something dark inside of me that filled me with need. My arousal grew heavy in the air around us, making Tyson let out a whimper behind me. He climbed off the bed, making his way over to the dresser.

Ace's hands gripped my hips, lifting me up so that his cock was notched at my entrance. "You ready for this, to be full of both of us?" he asked.

I nodded, dropping my hips to sink down onto his dick. Taking him inside of me inch by inch, letting him stretch me out until he was fully seated inside of me. "Oh, fuck." my voice an airy moan

"That's right, baby." He growled, lifting me up until just the tip remained before forcing my hips down as he thrust up into me. He hit something inside of me that made my body tense up and lightning shoot through my spine.

"Going to fill you up. Make it so you feel me deep inside of you." His words were said through gritted teeth, and fuck if they didn't turn me on more.

Tyson moved behind me, the bottle of lube clutched in his hand. He uncapped it, and Ace stilled inside of me. The cool drip of liquid slid over my ass and between my cheeks, making my vaginal walls flutter as he slicked me up before his index finger pressed inside of me slowly.

I stilled, my eyes slipping closed. Ace moved his hand between our bodies, his thumb stroking over my clit as Tyson worked his finger deeper inside of me.

"She likes that." Ace groaned low in the back of his throat. "Every time you do that, her pussy grips me tight. Like she's trying to suck me in."

Tyson let out a strangled sound before clearing his throat. "I'm doing it, right?"

"Yeah." I panted.

He added a second finger, his pace languid as my body adjusted to the intrusion. I concentrated on how it all felt, everything that was flowing through me with the bond that I shared with my mates.

"Open your fingers." Ace ordered, and Tyson went still behind me.

"Won't that hurt her?"

"No, it'll fit. When you're able to work in three fingers, she's ready." His lips moved over the side of my neck, sucking my flesh into his mouth.

Tyson took his time, scissoring his fingers inside of me. Letting my body relax until he could work a third finger into my ass and I push back against Tyson's fingers, chasing the delicious sensation that made my walls grip Ace.

"More," I moaned.

"Such a good girl." Ace growled into my ear, his hands moving to my hips. Shifting me around so that my knees were braced on either side of his hips, and my hands were braced beside his head.

"Ace." I whimpered.

"Go slow until she relaxes, then you can fuck her good." Ace ordered, and Tyson nodded, notching himself against the tight muscles of my ass.

His hand moved to grip my hip, the other one at the base of his cock as he worked himself into me. Past the tight muscles that made me burn.

"So tight, Lucy. Oh, goddess." Tyson hissed, his hand clutching at my hip as he held still.

"She's fucking perfect, isn't she?"

"Yes." Tyson groaned, thrusting deeper inside of my ass.

I wanted to push forward or buck my hips back. I felt full of Tyson, pleasure moving through me as Ace worked his fingers over my clitoris. Trying to take my mind off of the burning pain/pleasure that was building inside of me.

When Tyson was deep inside my ass, he went still, both of his hands moving to my hips. "Are are you okay? Is this okay, Lucy?" he groaned.

I nodded, gently thrusting myself back into him. His breath caught in his throat, and his fingers tensed on my hips, digging into the soft flesh hard enough that I knew I would have bruises.

He pulled out of me, and Ace thrust into me. The rhythm was wonky as they tried to figure it out. Soon enough, though, we all found our rhythm, and I lost myself to the pleasure my mates were building inside of me.

I didn't know where I began, and they ended. Wanton moans filled the room with the scent of sex, and I realized that the cries were coming from me.

Bracing my hands on Ace's chest, I pushed myself up, so that I was riding his cock. My back pressed tightly against Tyson's chest. His hands moved around my body to massage my breasts.

"That's right. You like taking us both. Don't you?" Ace growled from beneath me, his eyes growing dark as he got closer to the edge. His movements grew rougher with each flex of his hips.

"Yes," I keened, bringing my hands up to cover Tyson's hands. Making him squeeze my breasts harder.

"Then come for me, Lucy." Ace growled. "I'm going to fill you up with my come."

"Tyson," I moaned as he squeezed my breast.

His breath was hot against my ear. His hips stuttered, and I could feel the wave of his orgasm rushing through me, driving me closer to the edge. I gripped his hand, moving it down my body.

Showing him how I liked to be touched, how I needed him. I worked his fingers over my clit, feeling everything inside of me tense up. My eyes slipped closed, and flecks of gold painted across my eyelids as I came, my pussy and ass milking both of their cocks.

Tyson cried out behind me, his hand tightening on my breast as his movements grew frantic. My name fell from his lips as he came inside of me.

Ace followed, his cock twitching deep inside of me before painting my walls with his release. The three of us collapsed together onto the bed, each of us panting and trying to catch our breaths.

"Fuck, that was-" Ace started to say, but I cut him off.

"Amazing, fucking amazing," I said, opening my eyes.

"I hope it's always like this," Tyson asked, his voice quiet behind me as his penis grew soft inside of my ass. I rolled my hips, letting them both slip from my body.

"Only with her." Ace said, and my heart fluttered at his words. Rolling over, I went to look back at Tyson when I spotted a face at the window, making me shriek. Tyson's eyes darted to the window before he grabbed something, covering himself.

A growl ripped out of me as she quickly turned her face away. "Fucking Melana," I growled, climbing off Ace and stalking toward the window.

Chapter 72

Melana

I HAD TO WAIT HOURS before managing to sneak into the territory. I guess I had my sister to thank for the added security. I trekked through the forest surrounding the packhouse, careful to move quietly, knowing the patrols would listen for the slightest noise. Yet the further I moved into Ace's territory, the more my heart raced.

I hated knowing I had left Nathaniel back in the cells; I had no choice. I would have been caught trying to break into the out-building. This was the better option. I just hoped they didn't kill me before letting me explain. I needed to make things right, needed to fix this and save my mate.

Moving through the trees, the packhouse came into view, and I had a clear shot straight for the house. I could see Tyson's car and another I hadn't seen before in the driveway, an Audi. *Please be home, Ace.* I could be willingly walking into my own death. If Ace wasn't here, it was a guarantee, though I was nervous. Ace told me if he ever saw me again, he would kill me, but I stood a better chance of finding him than Tyson. Tyson wouldn't even blink before he killed me, no skin off his nose. He had wanted to do it for years; now, I understand why.

I tried to will my feet to move and step out of the shadows concealing me behind the shed. I had to do this. I had to do this for my mate and everyone else in the cells, for Emily, so she could get her mother back. Josie chose already, she chose wrong, and I was sick of digging her out of trouble. I resigned myself to her fate. I wouldn't seal my mate's, too, not when he was willing to forgive me for what I had done. I wouldn't risk losing him again.

Swallowing down my fear, I made a beeline for the front of the house. I rushed up the stairs before knocking on the door. No one answered, but I could hear movement inside. I knocked again, glancing around, worried about patrols spotting me. When there was no answer, I walked around to Ace's window. He usually left it unlocked. I reached up, gripping the windowsill and peering in.

I gasped, about to duck down and go to the front door, when I spotted Lucy straddling Ace, my cheeks redden and I was about to step away when I heard a feral snarl. "Fucking Melana." My head turned back to the window to see Lucy stalking toward me. She didn't even open it, and I didn't know what was more shocking, the fact that she dived through the closed window at me or the fact she shifted.

Her body crashed into mine and knocked me to the ground, her wolf tearing into my shoulder, and I was too shocked to react at first. Her teeth sank into my leg, and she viciously shook her head. I tried to push her face away. I knew that Ace and Tyson would kill me if I attacked her back.

Tyson launched out the window, ripping the entire frame out as his wolf barreled out, and Lucy's wolf grabbed my arm, flinging me across the ground like a rag doll. Gravel tore at my hands as I put them out instinctively. Lucy suddenly shifted back, stalking toward me.

"Wait, I am here to help."

"I will help you alright, help fucking bury you," she screamed at me. I looked at Ace, who was just staring at me with a disgusted look on his face when I felt Lucy's fist connect with my face. Blood sprayed the ground when she was suddenly straddling my waist.

"Fight back, bitch," she screamed angrily while I tried to block her blows. Her screaming anger was potent, her aura smashing against me, and I knew they had both marked her and could smell them all over her.

"Lucy, stop. Listen, please," I begged her as she pummeled me, becoming angrier when I didn't fight back. I felt my ribs break on the left side when her weight was suddenly gone. Her furious scream resonated through the air, and I put my hand up when Tyson stalked toward me.

"Wait, please."

"Tyson, leave her," Ace bellowed, and Lucy shrieked louder, shifting in Ace's grip.

"I am not defending her, Lucy. Stop," he said, refusing to let her go, even as she shifted and tore into him.

Tyson growled at him and turned toward Ace, who dropped to the ground. I could hear him trying to calm her down, whispering softly to her.

"She knew coming back here would be her death. I know Melana. She wouldn't risk her hide for anyone unless she is desperate," Ace said to her, and the wolf's wild thrashing slowed, her breathing still heavy.

I wiped the blood off my face with the back of my hand, the movement catching her eye, and she lost it again. I felt guilty. I could see how much my sister and I had hurt her. I would probably be the same if our roles were reversed, and Ace not letting her kill me must have been a kick in the gut.

"Lucy, enough," Ace snapped at her, his aura rushing out, and she quieted. The growl that left Tyson raised goosebumps on my arms as he stalked toward his brother, his fist connecting with Ace's face, and I saw Atticus come forward for a second.

Tyson reached down as Lucy started shifting back. He grabbed her, walking off toward the front of the house, her body drenched in cuts from the window and my blood. Ace watched them leave before pinning me with his glare. He stood covering himself with his hands, not that I was looking; I had no interest in him.

"I swear if you just ruined things with Lucy for some selfish reason, I will make Ryker look like a pussy with what I will do to you," he growled. He made no move toward me. Just glared.

"I need help." Ace scoffed, his canines slipping out and fur growing on his arms.

"Of course you do," he growled.

"Not for me, for my mate. And Aliza. All of them are trapped in Jamie's cells."

"Aliza? She left Jamie, don't come here and bullshit me," he said, taking a menacing step forward.

"I'm not, I swear. Please. Aliza, Nathaniel, Taylor, they are down there. Jamie threw me into the cells when I refused to help Josie. I swear, Ace. I would never come back here otherwise," I told him, begging for him to believe me.

"If you were in the cells, how did you get out?"

"The air ducts. Jamie pushes wolfsbane through the ventilation shaft, and I climbed through. They couldn't because—"

"Because they aren't hybrids," Ace finished for me, and I nodded.

"I swear if you are lying to me, I will skin you alive and tie you to an ants' nest." I swallowed, knowing he meant it, and quickly nodded.

Tyson and Lucy came out, this time fully dressed, and Lucy hesitated to look at Ace standing a few meters away from me. He opened his arms to her, but she turned her head away from him. She seemed calmer. Whatever Tyson did obviously calmed her enough to be rational.

"Why are you here? If it is to get your sister back, that isn't happening. Hopefully, my father strings her up."

"He caught her?" I couldn't help but ask. Ace growled, and I held my hands up.

"No, not like that. Did he catch her or not?"

"Yes, she is in the cells." I gasped. This was terrible.

"What?" Ace asked, recognizing my alarm, and Lucy's eyes flicked to him.

"If Josie was caught, that means she let you catch her."

"No, patrols found her," Tyson said, and I shook my head.

"What, they found her wandering around? If your brother has her, I am telling you it's because she wanted to be caught. You need to get hold of your brother and tell him to check wherever he is holding her. NOW!" I told them.

Chapter 73

Josie

They thought they beat me, that this was the end and all their problems were solved, but little did they know I was exactly where I needed to be. This was precisely what I intended. I fooled them all. Mitchell, so severely wanting to redeem himself, I knew he would toss me to them. I knew his loyalty lay with Lucy, and he was only a willing participant in Jamie's plans out of fear for his mate.

I knew nothing would come between him and Lucy once he found out what Jamie had planned; not even his mate would make him cross her. Their friendship was built on love, respect, and a deep understanding. Yet I managed to fool him, fool the King, fool everyone.

"Not long now, my love, and you will be back with me where you belong." I smiled, thinking of my mate. We would soon be together and free. This was the only way, and I didn't care what I needed to do to get my mate back.

Lucy stupidly thought she could take him from me, and I wouldn't retaliate, wouldn't get even. How wrong she was, and I planned on taking everything from her. Jamie was just the start of my plans. I would make her pay. She got us banished, got my mate taken from me, and now turned my own sister against me; she would pay for all she had done.

I listened to the sounds coming from above, waiting them out. I only had one person to fear, Avery, but my task should be done by then. Reika and Ryker were arguing as he tried to reason with her; I was a minor and a student, untouchable. They touch me, and the King would be breaking the laws he'd put in place to protect us hybrid mutations.

He enforced rules, and the only person reliable for my punishment was Avery, as she was my legal guardian. Nothing could be done without her input, but I didn't plan to be here when she got here. I clicked my tongue. *Tsk, tsk, tsk.*

"Should have listened to the wifey, Ryker. Should have let her kill me when you had the chance. You won't get another." I chuckled at my words before hearing him talk to Jacob; I couldn't stand him. He was a pet to Ryker, a minion. I knew they would be standing guard at the basement entry, expected it, yet I had a plan to get rid of him too.

"Reika, if you kill her, it will start a war. I cannot go against the laws I made. King or not, I am not exempt from the penalties, and neither are you. Until I speak with Avery and she gets here, she remains in the cell. The mutations are protected for a reason. We pleaded that their behaviors weren't entirely their fault. If I kill her, I am going against the laws we placed around them for their protection." I listened as they argued before he talked to Jacob.

"Don't let her down there. Reika, upstairs, now. You stay off the bottom floor and remain on the second floor until I return."

I felt the command from down here; he thought he was protecting his mate. How very wrong he was, but that made everything easier for me. They were too predictable. Ryker was a reformed man doing everything by the book and trying to redeem himself for god knows what, not that I cared. Reika was still just as unhinged but now without a wolf, quickly put in place by her mate and holding no actual authority anymore. Everyone only obeyed her out of respect. Respect won't help her now.

"I am leaving to head to Avalon City to meet with Aamon. Avery is visiting her father, and he will try to contact her. But he needs someone to watch over their bodies while they navigate the underworld. It should only be a few hours. Just keep an eye on Rayan. Ryden is upstairs asleep. Do you need me to send anyone else over to help keep watch?"

"No, she is a teenage girl, and she is passed out. We will be fine," Jacob told him, and I tried not to laugh. I heard Ryker give a few instructions before listening to his footsteps leaving the house. The door shut before I heard a car's engine and the tires on gravel indicating he was going. *Good riddance, now back to my plan.*

My arms were tied behind my back, the cuffs burning my skin, and I reached around and gripped my thumb before gritting my teeth as I broke it to stop from screaming out. I knew them thinking I was passed out would be an advantage. Fewer restraints and fewer guards. No one would suspect the small innocent-looking girl was putting up a fight.

My fake tears and begging when they found me clearly worked before dosing me. No one suspected a thing. Pain rippled through my palm as I was forced to break it and dislocate it to squeeze my hand through the cuff of my restraint. I rubbed my wrist, trying to get the blood flowing freely again. The burns from the wolfsbane started to heal, the sedative having no effects on me whatsoever.

"Idiots," I muttered, pulling my bobby pins from my hair. With a bit of fiddling, the ankle cuffs released. Burned rings wrapped around my ankles where the flesh melted off, but they were already healing. They fed me concentrated levels of wolfsbane and a sedative, enough to even take out a hybrid.

Beryl, Jamie's witch, made me an antidote, and I had been drinking the crap for weeks. My toxicity levels from the mysterious substance were through the roof; they could have fed me the entire damn plant, and it would not have affected me.

Thank the Moon Goddess that I took drama at school. A bit of fake illness, and Ryker believed I was down for hours; it helped a little that the initial effects did make me woozy until Beryl's concoction stabilized it in my system.

Getting up, I walked over to Ryker's torture table. Not that they left any instruments in here, they were in the next cell over. Washing my hands in the sink and drinking straight from the tap, I wiped my mouth on the back of my hand before zeroing in on the cell door. *Piece of cake.*

Jamming my fingers down my throat, I continued to heave until I emptied my stomach of its contents—the purple balloon full of Belladonna was thrown up and landed in the sink. The second balloon contained wolfsbane in a lethal dose. Pocketing them, I moved to the door of the cell.

I must say, their protocols for checking minors were a little out of whack. They really needed to work on that. Retrieving the bobby pins, I fiddled with the lock. It was more complicated than I thought. Every time I thought I got it, the pin would slip, but eventually, I got it to unlock. Cursing under my breath, I tried until finally, I heard the lock click, and I could turn the lock.

See? All that time lock picking and breaking out of the school came in handy. Thanks to my mate, I haven't found a lock yet that could beat me. Walking out of the cell, the door groaned as

I pushed it open, and I stopped listening for Jacob to see if he'd noticed.

The cell next door was wide open, and I walked over to the bench, jamming a knife in its pouch down the side of my pants on my hip before grabbing another.

This blade was thinner and razor-sharp, drumming my fingers on the steel bench. I had an arsenal at my fingertips as I looked over everything before finding what I was looking for. A needle and plunger. Quickly ducking over to the sink, I ripped the plunger out before pouring the syrupy liquid from the balloon into it, squeezing it out before using some hot water to melt it a bit more, and jamming the plunger back in. I shook the steel needle, watching the liquid change color and turn into metallic silver.

The pipes rattled inside the walls, and I could just make out the sound of the shower running upstairs as I stared at the ceiling. I hoped it was Reika and not Rayan, that little shit I needed to get my mate back. Creeping up the steps, I listened for any noise, trying to work out where everyone was located. The TV could be heard in the living room, and I gripped the door handle and pushed the door open just enough to see into the foyer.

I could hear Jacob talking to Rayan as they discussed Rayan's game in the living room. Slipping out the door, I made a dash for the coatroom. It was next to the hall beside the stairs and across from the conference room. Jacob returned to the basement door, and my heart raced as I slipped out of view just in time before he spotted me when taking his place by the basement door. He took his seat beside the door and pulled out his phone.

I was trying to figure out my next move and how I would get to Rayan on the other side of the house. Ryden cried out upstairs; I knew this place like the back of my hand, having spent so much time here with Lucy, her family was picture perfect. I was always a little jealous of how she would go home to them every holiday, and she always took it for granted. Whining and groaning about not wanting to come back here. The shower was still running before I heard Jacob sing out.

"I will get him, Reika," Jacob called out to her just as I heard the water shut off upstairs, only for it to turn back on again. This was my chance to catch him off guard. Jacob took the steps two at a time, and I quietly sneaked after him, the needle in my hand as I crept up quietly before sneaking up behind him and getting ready, my other hand clutching the knife.

Chapter 74

As I lifted the knife, Jacob whipped around in time, hearing my approach behind him. Still, I jammed my knife into his neck before he could mutter a word and alert Reika. Though, Ryker would notice when he eventually bled out and his tether died, but for now, I still had a few minutes to set my plan in motion.

Blood sprayed across my face as it spurted out of his neck, his life liquid spilling out violently and splashing the walls scarlet. His mouth opened and closed in shock as he stared at me, and I gave him a brief wave, and a smile spread across my face.

Jacob collapsed at my feet, gurgling and choking on his own blood, his horrified eyes staring up at me as he clutched his throat, trying to stem the bleeding. I stopped when I saw Jacob's eyes glaze over to the mind link. I would need to be quicker than I thought as I slapped him, making him break the connection. He choked and gurgled some more, and I plunged the knife into his temple. He died instantly, and his body went slack along with his face.

Not wasting any time, I rushed up the steps, following the sounds of the crying baby before walking into a bedroom; by the stench, I could tell it was Reika and Ryker's room. The scent was suffocatingly strong in this room, and the cries were louder.

Reika was humming in the bathroom, and I rushed over to Ryden's bassinet removing him from his bed, only to then rush out of the room and back toward the stairs. Walking down the steps, I hushed Ryden and stepped over Jacob's dead body, his eyes vacantly staring off at the wall as his blood seeped into the carpet.

I knew instantly when Jacob's tether was felt breaking; Reika screamed before rushing out. The noise immediately alerted Rayan as I reached the bottom step in time to see Reika look down at me from the landing above.

I waved and smirked when she spotted her son in my arms before holding him up for her to see. A growl escaped her before she rushed for the stairs, only to stop, a strained expression on her face that looked pained.

Ryker's command prevented her from leaving upstairs, and she was stuck without him there to remove it. I knew it, and she knew it, and she knew she could not help her defenseless children.

Her furious scream rang out through the house, and I turned to see Rayan staring at Jacob's dead body on the stairs before he turned to glare at me.

"Now, you little prince will be coming with me," I told him. He glared at me and went to take a step forward, and I continued down the last two steps toward him, his baby brother in my arms, babbling quietly and eating his hands, unaware of the danger he was in.

"Ah, ah, ah. You wouldn't want your sweet baby brother to get hurt now, would you?" I asked Rayan, and he finally spotted the needle in my hand resting gently on his brother's chest, the needlepoint at his neck.

"Try anything and bye-bye, baby brother," I warned him, and I saw his eyes dart to his mother and his lips part as he stared at her wanting to know what to do. Turning slightly, I looked up at Reika who was watching me in just her towel. The shower was still running, and she clutched the banister staring down at us helplessly.

"Mom?" Rayan called out behind me, and I smirked. *Not so big and scary now.*

"Do what she says," Reika told him before her eyes glazed over. Reika tried to command me, but her aura was easy to resist without her wolf, and I laughed. *Pathetic.* To think this was our Queen. It was laughable.

"You hurt my kids—"

"You'll what?" Reika screamed at me from the landing upstairs. "You and I both know you are in no position to make threats, but go ahead, alert your mate. We will be long gone before he finds us. Besides, you have more pressing things to worry about," I told her.

I nodded toward the kitchen. "Move, now," I told Rayan, and he growled before stalking off down the hall and standing next to the bench where I followed closely behind.

I used to love this kitchen. I had often sat around this dining table and enjoyed spending time with Lucy. It would be sad to lose those memories, but you have to do what you have to do. I grabbed the lighter that was always kept on the range hood above the gas stove. I then reached into the third drawer and retrieved the lighter fluid. Rayan was watching me, his eyes glaring daggers at me.

"Don't try to be brave, little prince. You will only get your brother hurt," I reminded him before nodding to go back the way we came. He did as he was told, and it was almost too easy.

Reika called out to Rayan, and I heard her sigh when he walked into view again.

I flipped the lid on the lighter fluid, squirting it on the drapes in the entryway and then the carpet on the staircase. Moving to the room adjacent to the foyer, I sprayed the couch with what remained in the bottle.

"What are you doing?" Rayan shrieked, reaching for the now-empty lighter fluid, but I shook it, showing him it was empty.

"Bonfire," I told him, and he reached for the lighter fluid again. Passing him the lighter, he looked at me and then back up at his mother.

"Light it up," I told him, smiling. He shook his head and took a step away from me. His heart rate intensified, beating rapidly with his panic.

"My mother is trapped up there. She can't leave," Rayan stuttered out.

"Exactly," I told him, and he stepped back, shaking his head like he was about to make a run for it.

"You will do it, or—" My fingers twitched on the needle, and I pressed it closer to Ryden's neck.

"Do it. Just do as she says," Reika called to him, but he shook his head.

"Now, Rayan. I will be fine. I will find a way. Keep your brother safe," Reika called to him.

"But mom," Rayan called out, his voice a choked garble. Tears brimmed in his eyes, and his lip quivered as he looked down at the lighter in his hand.

"Look after your brother. Your father will find you. He will find you," Reika told him, her eyes on my hand by her baby's neck.

"Now!" I told him, and he jumped before moving to the living room drapes. He flicked the zippo, and the flame ignited before he held it under the drapes before moving to the steps and stopping.

"Please?" Rayan begged me, tears streaking his face and dripping off his chin.

"Go on, or I will make you watch as she burns," I told him. Tears trekked down his cheeks as he tossed the lighter on the stairs before looking at his mother, who nodded to him.

"I will be fine. Look after your brother for me," Reika told him. Blue flames ran across the stairs before it set completely alight.

Rayan stared horrified at his mother, who was glaring at me.

"Say goodbye to mommy, little prince. You are now coming with me. You have a date with your future mate," I told him while pushing him toward the back of the house and away from the flames.

Chapter 75

Lucy

I HATED HAVING TO GET in the car with my mate's ex and the woman responsible for all the drama caused, but when Ace couldn't get a hold of Ryker through the link, we figured he was too far away.

Melana sat in the back with me, staring out the window and pressing against the door and as far away from me as possible. She seemed increasingly nervous, and she began to fidget the further into my stepfather's territory we got.

Was she worried for her sister? I couldn't see how her sister could escape or how she planned to. She was in the cells. There was no escape from them. She was under guard, yet something about her nervousness made me worry.

It wasn't until we were halfway to the packhouse that we were alerted that something was wrong when Ryker's voice boomed across the mind link, not only to his pack members but also to get to the packhouse immediately, screaming that my mother was in trouble.

I pressed my fingers to my temple as voices suddenly flooded my head, and Ace nearly veered off the road before jerking the steering wheel and pulling us back on the road. For Ryker to be mind linking, he had to be on his way back from wherever he went.

My heart jolted in my chest when he said the packhouse was on fire and my mother was trapped inside. I tried to mindlink Rayan before forgetting I wasn't a part of my family's pack anymore but Ace and Tyson's. We were no longer linked unless they opened it to me, and I glanced at Ace and Tyson.

"Mindlink Rayan," I told Tyson, knowing he could link anyone being a hybrid and not a mutation like me, knowing he could get in anyone's head. I watched as his eyes glazed over before they returned to their sparkling fluorescent silver color before he tried again, but it was the same result.

"Well?" I asked, and he shook his head.

"It's like he is too far away. I can't reach him or he is knocked out," Tyson offered, and I turned to look at Melana sitting beside me. She glanced at me, and her entire body tensed, and a whimper escaped her.

"What was Josie asked to do? What was she supposed to do for Alpha Jamie?" I asked her, realizing it was one question we had all forgotten to ask.

We were too busy trying to get a hold of Ryker. We never thought to get a hold of mom, and mom has had trouble mind linking anyone besides Ryker. The longer she went with Amanda suppressed, the more she turned vampire, and the fewer traits she had from her wolf side.

Her vampire side became more dominant, and I never realized what a disadvantage that was when she only had a direct link to her pack and mate now.

"He wanted to use Rayan for a blood bond to Emily, Jamie's daughter. It was a backup plan he had on the side. I didn't know until I disagreed with it, and he locked me up, but Josie didn't care. She wanted her mate, and she will do anything to get her mate back."

"You didn't think to mention that detail back at the house?" I growled at her. Fur started spreading across my arms, and my canines slipped from my gums as my wolf became just as enraged. Lucille wanted to tear her to pieces and watch her die slowly.

"Lucy!" Tyson snapped, turning in his seat to look at me as I fought Lucille for control. He reached over, gripping my hand and squeezing it.

"Lucy, get a grip of yourself. If you shift, you will hurt yourself while in the car. Kill her after we get your mother," Tyson said before he turned and looked at Melana.

"I suggest you shut up. I won't stop her if she kills you," Tyson snapped at her, and I gritted my teeth when Ace suddenly gasped. My eyes looked to the windshield to see the packhouse set ablaze.

I knew it was on fire but didn't expect the carnage before our eyes. Plumes of smoke filled the air, and warriors tossed water onto the burning building, trying to extinguish the inferno.

"My family!" I gasped, clutching my mouth with my hands in horror. Melana's eyes widened in horror as she leaned forward. The entire thing was engulfed except for two bedrooms on this side, and pack members stood outside trying to extinguish the fire. Ace skidded to a stop, dust and dirt spraying everywhere, and I was out the door before the car entirely stopped.

"Mom! Rayan!" I screamed when suddenly there was an explosion, and I was tossed backward. The gas cylinders at the side of the house exploded under the heat. The loud bang made my ears ring, and the ground shook.

I was slammed against Ace's car from the blast, and I dented the door as I crashed against it, but adrenaline was pumping as fear flooded me. Were my brothers still in there? A huge gaping hole was now where the gas cylinders were, flames were licking up the side of the packhouse, and a tree close to the house had now caught fire.

I felt blood trickle down my face, and I pulled a piece of metal from my cheek. I barely felt anything when I noticed my mother standing at one of the second-floor windows, warriors trying to climb up to her as she screamed at them to stop.

"Jump!" I screamed to her when one of the warriors looked at me in horror before rushing over. He was around Ace and Tyson's age, gangly looking and had a dark mop of hair, his face covered in soot. I noticed he had burns that were healing up one arm like he had tried to break in already to get to my mother.

"Mom, jump! Where are Rayan and Ryden?" I asked her, and she looked over at me.

"She can't. She was commanded to remain on the second floor."

"What?" I gasped in horror. The man shrugged, using the garden hose to try and extinguish the flames, but it was of no use. There was no putting out the fire as it burned my childhood, burned our home, a home that had stood for generations.

Papa Reid was raised in this house, and he raised his own children here before Ryker took over and raised me. It was all going to perish, and so was my mother if we couldn't get her out.

"Your brothers aren't in there. Josie took them. Your mother has been mindlinking. She sent warriors to find them, but no trace of them. It is like they just vanished."

"Please, tell me you can do something. Can you override your brother's command?" I asked desperately, and Tyson swallowed, looking back toward the window where my mother stared off blankly. I could see she was mindlinking and no doubt was either trying to contact Rayan or my stepfather.

"How far out is Ryker?" I asked, turning back to the man. The warrior from before glanced over at us, holding the hose through the burst living-room window.

"Twenty minutes. Same as the fire brigade. He said, when he gets closer, he will shift and run to get here quicker. It's also peak hour traffic in the city, and the bridge is still closed on the other side," the man answered. Warriors were running around everywhere. I could barely hear the sirens, but even I knew they would be just as far out coming from the city, and I could only faintly make them out if it was even them.

"She doesn't have twenty minutes," I murmured to no one.

Chapter 76

"It's okay, Lucy," my mother called out before choking on the smoke billowing out the windows. I shook my head, staring up at her. We bring her out, she would just run in, and if we held her down, it could kill her. The only option was hope for Ryker to get back in time but time was not on our side as the fire zeroed in, and I knew it would only be a matter of time before the floor she was on became engulfed in flames and collapsed.

"Tell Avery the witch's name is Beryl. Josie said her name was Beryl," my mother screamed down to us.

"We need to do something. We need to get her out of there," I told them.

"Maybe both of us can try to command her at the same time?" Ace suggested.

"Worth a try, but we will have to be close to her. She is under a King's command," Tyson said, looking around before pointing to the porch.

"Reika, get to Rayan's room," Tyson called up to her before he ran toward the shed with Ace following closely behind them. I watched them climb the side, and I chased them before climbing up after them.

"Lucy, no!" Ace snapped at me, but I ignored him, and he continued pulling himself up.

"Bloody stubborn woman," he growled before offering me his hand when he was safely on top of the garage roof.

"Watch your step and try to stay off the main roof in case it collapses. Use the sides. I can feel the heat from here," Tyson said before using the stonework to walk along the front of the packhouse to the porch roof. My mother pushed Rayan's window open and moved back, allowing Tyson to climb in the window before helping me through while Ace shoved me from behind. The room she was in before was now engulfed in flames.

I coughed the moment I stepped through the window. The smoke was horrendous, yet this room wasn't on fire, and she had closed the door to the room, stuffing whatever she could under the gap of the door.

"I turned on every tap and flooded the hall, but it won't be long. It was only these two rooms it hadn't reached. The moment I opened the bedroom door on the room next door, it became consumed from the open window. I forgot to close the window," my mother said, and I saw her hair was all singed. Her arms were covered in burns, yet she seemed eerily calm, almost like she accepted dying here, or maybe she was in shock.

"On the count of three, we both command her to jump," Tyson said, looking at Ace as he stepped inside behind me.

They tried numerous times, but the smoke was becoming too bad, and all of us were choking, and I knew the fire was about to reach this room. The rest of the house was destroyed, only this room remained, and I could feel the heat growing hotter under my feet.

"Just stop. Get my daughter out of here," my mother wheezed out before slumping on the ground. She started hacking, and the room filled with smoke. My eyes and throat burned, and I struggled to see.

"NO! Try again. It has to work," I rasped out. My breathing was becoming increasingly difficult, and I could hear people outside telling us to get out.

"My brother is the King. Nothing overthrows his commands, Lucy. She can't overthrow him without her wolf," Tyson said.

"I am not leaving her here," I told them when my mother reached for me. I gripped her hands, holding onto her.

"Tell your brothers I love them." I shook my head.

"What, no! I am not leaving you. We will find a way!"

"Yes, you are, sweety. There is no way, and you won't be dying with me," my mother said before kissing my face.

"I love you," she told me, and I shook my head and gripped her arms, my nails digging into her arm as I held on to her.

"No, we leave together!" I told her, and she shook her head, trying to pry my hands from her arms.

We heard a crash somewhere on the other side of the door, and I coughed smoke coming in under the door. Flames had started to creep in the cracks and around the hinges. The door was on fire. Despite having the gap jammed with blankets, the room became unbearable. The smoke turned the walls black. The space heated up like an oven, and the wallpaper peeled away.

"Get my daughter out of here!" my mother choked out.

"No, no, no!" I screamed when I felt arms wrap around my stomach. I kicked and hit when they pried my hands off my mother, calling for Ace to let me go.

"Stop fighting me!" Ace commanded, and I tried to fight off his order when Tyson's aura rushed over me too, forcing me to submit.

Tyson looked at me grimly, and I could feel his heartache. "Get her out," Tyson said while turning away from me.

Ace dragged me toward the window before scooping my legs out from under me, and I screamed, thrashing in his arms and clawing at his back to let me go.

"No!" I screamed when he jumped from the second-story window before landing on the ground below with a soft thud, his arms holding me in a vice-like grip.

"Mom!" I cried out. Tyson walked over to the window, hauling my mother to it as she resisted.

"Jump with him!" I begged her.

"If she does, she will run right back in, Lucy. Right into the middle of it. Just jumping could even kill her." Ace told me what I already knew, but we had to try.

I looked back up at her, and Tyson seemed to think the same thing. Maybe we could take our chances and pray Ryker got here in time when another explosion went off, and half the roof caved in, including the garage roof, before it exploded. The cars inside blew up, and it collapsed, falling to flaming debris and rubble.

Tyson reached for her when my mother suddenly shoved him out the window. Tyson fell backward before twisting at the last second and landing in a crouched position below the window. I screamed, trying to escape Ace's arms to get to her, and Tyson rushed over to help him contain me.

"Get my boys back, and look after Lucy! No one is dying up here with me!" my mother called out when I saw pack members about to try to find another way.

They all stopped and stared up at her when she shut the window.

"No!" I screamed when she walked away, disappearing in the smoke. The warriors around us suddenly howled loudly, the noise tearing at my soul.

"Stop, Lucy! You can't go back in there!" Tyson said, clutching my face in his hands.

"Please, it's my mother!" I begged him, trying to pull free of them.

"And that's why you can't watch," Ace's voice said behind me, turning into a growl before I felt his teeth sink into my neck. I struggled against him, my hands smacking at him when Tyson gripped them. My vision grew darker, and I felt myself slipping away as he buried his teeth deeper into my neck.

Then I saw nothing, just oblivion as I was sucked into the abyss.

Chapter 77

Ryker

"*G*ET OUR BOYS BACK!" Reika said through the link as I raced toward the packhouse. I repeatedly tried to command her through the bond and the mind link, but nothing worked as I felt her grow weaker. My lungs scorched as I tried to get to her. *So close.* Yet the distance felt impossible when she suddenly stopped talking, falling silent in my head.

"Reika!" I called through the link as I ran for the packhouse. Brax pushed us as hard as we could go when he hit the dirt, and a tortured groan left him. My body felt like it was engulfed in flames. Brax writhed in agony as he tried to take her pain when it suddenly stopped.

We were five hundred meters from the packhouse when I was forced to shift back, and I found myself lying in the dirt. Brax suddenly went as silent as Reika, and the bond felt numb.

The mate bond went quiet as I broke through the treeline surrounding the property. My legs almost gave way when I saw the house, and crushing pain shredded throughout my chest, making me clutch it.

I tripped over the wire fence as I forced my legs to move, my claws slashing through the wire to free me.

So much noise filled the air as pack members tossed buckets of water on the house, giving out orders to one another. Yet all I saw was flames, the roof had collapsed, and the front door was no longer accessible.

"Reika!" I screamed and half broke down as I neared the house. I caught a glimpse of Tyson and Ace but couldn't see Lucy as I raced forward when I was hit from the side. Arms wrapped around my waist as I hit the dirt, and his weight crushed me to the ground.

"You can't go in there!" Tyson snarled at me, trying to pin me down.

"She can't be saved. She is gone, brother," he gasped, and I roared. Tossing him off me, Ace suddenly appeared in his place along with some warriors, and my claws slipped out, slashing and attacking anyone that got in my way.

"She is there. Let me through!" I bellowed the command, and they hit the dirt as my rage-filled aura battered them down. Ace fought against it, and so did Tyson as they both charged at me.

I swung blindly at them, and my fist connected with Ace's face, and he went sprawling on the ground when Brax shoved forward, lending me his strength before we tore into Tyrant, Tyson's wolf who tried to block us from getting to her.

I suddenly choked, clawing at my throat as I gasped for air, and my eyes flitted to the house. Brax took over, and I let him have control. Driven on instinct, he searched for the pull to her, letting it lead him to Rayan's bedroom window, yet it was too high for us to jump as the roof had now collapsed in, and Brax whimpered. My eyes moved to a huge hole in the side of the house where the kitchen used to be.

A moment later, I ripped at the hands that tried to hold us back from stepping into my burning home before my foot connected with Tyson's midsection and knocked him down, but I didn't wait to check on him. Instead, covering my mouth and nose with my hand, not that it did much, I stepped inside what used to be the kitchen, the bare frame of the house still standing thanks to the sandstone brick exterior.

Brax tore through the place just as the second floor started collapsing. The roof above crushed half the area and my skin burned and blistered as the flames blew over me.

Brax tried to heal us as quickly as possible when we came to what remained of the foyer; the fireplace running up the center of the house was the only thing holding the roof up where we stood.

However, the roof had collapsed on the stairs, and the scorched brickwork of the structure was barely holding together.

"Reika?" I called out before choking on the hazardous fumes. My eyes darted around, trying to find a way to the next floor. Water running over the landing above and spilling on the floor around me made me look up, and the banister directly above still held firm. Regardless, the walls were covered in flames above.

"She is up there. She isn't dead. She is alive barely," Brax growled. The vibration of the bond barely existed. Still, it was there.

The living room suddenly caved in, sending flames and dust all over me, and I groaned as pain flared across my back, face, and left arm.

"There," I told Brax at the crushed stairs, the tiled roof crushing the ground.

"We will be burned alive," he growled, yet I could feel his determination.

"Now!" I roared at him, not giving a damn. It was the only way up to the banister; we just had to endure it. The collapsed roof made the place a raging inferno as the air fueled the fire. Chunks of concrete fell from the floor above as the house crumbled around us, trapping us in its fiery confines. The only way out now was up.

Gritting my teeth, I ran up what used to be the staircase, the tiles were like hot coals under my feet but adrenaline forced me forward, and we pivoted at the last second and jumped across.

My fingers only just managed to catch the banister above, and a mangled scream left me as my hands locked around it. The metal was glowing red, and I felt the skin of my hands stick and melt to it as I forced myself up. The putrid smell of flesh burning filled my nose.

The inside of my thigh melted to the metal as I swung my leg over, and my skin pulled away as I pulled away from it. The ground was soaking wet but turning to steam and boiling hot as the flames licked at the walls around us.

Dropping to our hands and knees, we tried to remain under the smoke, the toxic fumes making us delirious as we made our way to where the bathroom was, feeling the pull in that direction. The tiles were hot under our hands. The double sinks and the overflowing bath spilled onto the floor.

The ground felt unstable as we tried to make our way to her. The wall shared with Rayan's room was busted through, a hole barely big enough to squeeze through, the broken tiles covered in blood, and the mirror shattered on the floor around the sink basin.

The water poured out, yet the pipes had heated, making the water boil as it streamed out.

"She is in the tub," Brax choked as I clutched the side and pulled myself up.

Gazing into the blood-filled water was Reika, her skin blistered, bright red, and she was not breathing. She boiled herself alive. Diving my hands into the bathtub, I ripped her out of the bubbling water.

It was that hot I groaned and fought the urge to pull my arms out. We pulled Reika out, water sloshing over the sides of the tub, and my back melted against the clawfoot tub as I leaned against it.

Moving her to the floor, I placed my hands on her chest and started compressions. We grew weaker, the smoke becoming too much, and not even Brax could heal us fast enough. I punched the center of her chest with one last breath before collapsing over her body.

My body tingled as life started to leave me when I felt her heave a breath from under me.

Her body convulsed, and she rolled underneath me. "You fool!" she gasped and sputtered before collapsing.

"Get out!" Brax ordered, the words slurred, but the command was our final one as he forced what little strength we had left into forcing our aura over her. I welcomed death with open arms, unable to move as the fumes ravaged my lungs, praying some miracle could get her out. I couldn't live without her, but please let her live without me. My kids could live without a father, but they needed her; she needed to live for them.

"Nothing like a barbeque. However, a cooked wolf isn't a delicacy I want to try. Your ass would be tough like jerky," came a voice.

My mind was unclear about whose voice it was, yet the smell of burned almonds could be tasted on my tongue when I wheezed out my last breath. The smell and taste were somehow oddly familiar to me.

Chapter 78

Tyson

I watched in horror as the house burned around them, my brother and sister-in-law trapped inside. We should have stopped him from entering. Now, two lives would be lost. The fields around full of dead grass made me nervous; the old barns would go up if they caught fire along with the surrounding forest.

Ace placed Lucy in the car, but now we had another issue to contend with; the fire was growing out of control and threatening the neighboring forest surrounding it. A tree was next to the kitchen burning already, embers being picked up in the wind and blown into the treeline. Ace growled while pacing as he stared at our childhood home burning, clutching his hair.

"What is taking him so long?" Ace growled, worried for Ryker, who had not yet come out of the burning house.

"Where is Ryker?" came Aamon's voice behind me, and I jumped. I stared at him in shock, and Aamon clutched my arms, looking me dead in the face.

"Where is your brother?"

"Trying to save Reika," I told him, pointing to the house. Aamon looked at the burning building. He muttered something too low to hear before misting, vanishing into thin air. Sirens sounded in the distance, and all I could do was stare. Reika's screams of agony died out after what felt like hours ago.

"Watch out!" someone screamed before the old oak tree beside the house fell. Warriors rushed to put out the blaze.

"We need to put it out before the forest goes up," Ace yelled, and I saw Melana rush past us, a bucket of water in her hands. I had completely forgotten about her with all the chaos.

Ace growled, also spotting her before he stormed toward her, a terrifying growl escaping him as he grabbed her.

"You did this! You had to have known!" he snarled. Her face changed color, turning purple as he squeezed her throat, crushing her windpipe when yells could be heard.

"Get the pack doctor!" Ace and I looked up, and his hands unwound from around Melana's throat, and she gasped, rubbing her neck.

"Ryker?" I gasped before taking off, running toward Aamon, who was performing CPR on him.

Another warrior was working on Reika, who looked like she was boiled alive. Her skin melted off in parts when she suddenly stopped breathing. Ace pushes the man out of the way, his hands going to her chest.

"She needs blood! Get blood!" I told those crowding around them before biting into my wrist. I kneeled beside Reika, holding my wrist above her mouth while Ace pumped her chest, and I fed her my blood.

"Come on, buddy," Aamon told Ryker before breathing into his mouth and pumping his chest again.

"Where is the pack doctor?" Aamon snarled, and the wolves surrounding him stepped back, his demonic eyes glaring at them.

"On his way, he should be here soon," someone in the crowd yelled out. The sirens were getting closer, and I bit my wrist again, prying the wound open, trying to heal Reika while Aamon tried to save my brother. Ace's hands were working just as fast.

"The forest, the forest!" someone called out.

"Fuck! Avery, be good if you could get here soon," Aamon breathed out.

"How did you know?" I asked, biting into my wrist yet again and placing it over Reika's mouth, my blood flowing down her throat.

"A text message Melana sent to the school mobile. I called her back, and she said Ryker was in trouble,"

I looked at Ace, whose brows furrowed before scanning the place for her but not seeing her anywhere. Focusing back on the task at hand, I went back to trying to help revive Reika.

"What is taking the authorities so long?" I growled. Watching the trees ignite one by one, the forest was going to burn, so much wildlife would be killed when I heard an engine before a loud bang. Jacob's car was plowed out of the way as the bulldozer from the barn crashed through the wire fence and into the side of his car. Thinking of Jacob, I hadn't seen him, which made me glance at the house.

"Quick, move out of the way!" one of the warriors yelled, and I looked at the bulldozer to see Melana bouncing around in it as she steered it toward the house.

"Move out of the way!" she bellowed out the bulldozer's window. I thought for sure she would have taken off after Ace grabbed her, and I was a little shocked to see she remained to help instead of saving her own ass.

The sirens got louder, and I heard a gasp, and Reika took a breath. Aamon was still working on Ryker. Reika's breathing was shallow, but she was alive. Barely, but alive. Her body fell slack, but her chest still rose and fell. The forest was burning out of control, and Melana plowed into the packhouse, the blade of the dozer crashing into the stonework bringing the place down easily and reducing it to rubble. Heat from the flames was blowing over us when Avery suddenly misted here. She appeared just down the driveway, a little bit away from us. Clutching her knees like she was out of breath, her auburn hair falling down around her like a waterfall.

"The forest! Babe, are you alright?" Aamon called, and she nodded, raising a thumb that he didn't see. She coughed before standing upright and staggering, and my eyes went wide when I saw her huge round belly.

"Love, are you good?" Aamon called, and I got to my feet and rushed over to her, gripping her arm and helping her walk.

"I'm fine," she stammered before shaking my hand off and raising her arms. She looked at the sky before muttering to the bright sunny and clear sky. She had on a green maxi dress that did nothing to hide the baby bump I couldn't stop staring at.

"le fiamme si alzano fanno cadere i cieli lo fanno versare, annegano tutto."

Her eyes turned black as coal, her hands shook, and the air rippled. Storm clouds rolled across the sky rapidly, the day turned to night, and thunder and lightning lit up the sky. The thunder was deafening as it cracked and rolled loudly before it poured down.

The sky opened up, and a tidal wave of water crashed down on the flames. Winds so strong I fought to remain upright, and Avery looked strained like she was holding the weight of the world up by her hands. Blood dribbled down from her nose, and steam rose, and the flames died down.

"Avery, enough!" Aamon called out to her over the howl of the wind. Avery dropped her hands and wobbled on her feet before clutching her knees just as the fire brigade tore up the driveway. Ambulances followed behind it, and they looked around in shock as the storm left just as quickly as it had appeared.

"Don't just stand there. Help them!" I growled at the paramedics and pointed to my brother Aamon was still working on. I saw the pack doctor jump out of one of the ambulances unfazed by Avery's magic, and he rushed toward Ryker just as Avery passed out, collapsing, and I rushed to grab her before she hit the dirt.

"Over here," I called to the other paramedic while clutching Avery; her huge swollen belly startled me. When did she fall pregnant?

"Mom?" Lucy's voice trembled, and I looked up to see her standing there, her hands clutching her mouth.

"Mom!" she screamed, rushing over, leaving Ace's car door wide open as she dropped next to her mother. Aamon came over, having the paramedics take over Ryker and retrieve Avery from out of my arms.

"I got you, love. Take what you need," he whispered, brushing her hair from her pale face.

Chapter 79

Lucy

I paced the hall in the hospital ward, waiting for the pack doctor to come and give me news on my parents. Avery was in the room next door with Aamon, and I was shocked to learn she was pregnant.

"Lucy, stop pacing," Ace growled. We had been waiting hours; they managed to revive my stepfather. However, he hadn't woken up, and neither had my mother. Apparently, a few pack members, except those of the original pack belonging to my grandmother, were knocked out along with Ryker.

Only those that served the original Hybrid Queen remained awake and the mutations. Tyson and Ace explained it was some sort of default. Luckily it only affected those he personally brought into the pack and had pledged to him. Despite my stepfather being the King, the rest were bound to my grandmother, Aria and grandfather Reid who were apparently on their way here.

"Lucy, stop!" Ace snarled, his temper bubbling over, and I glared at him. I still haven't forgiven him for knocking me out. Tyson suddenly walked out of Avery's room with Aamon, but my attention was diverted to the pack doctor; when I saw him walking down the corridor toward us, I all but pounced on the man.

"My parents?"

He sighed, looking over my shoulder at my mates, and I growled when Ace stepped closer to listen to the doctor.

"Your mother is in a coma which appears to be induced by the King, same as the rest of his blood-bound members. Until he wakes up, she won't either."

"When will that be? My brothers are out there somewhere. I need them awake to help find them. We don't have the manpower to search the entire city without all of his pack," I snapped, tears brimming in my eyes at my frustration.

Everything was so fucked up. My brothers were god knows where and my mother was knocked out due to her bond. We already had every person out looking for them, and an amber alert had been broadcasted on the radio, yet nothing. It was like they had just vanished. At the same time, I am stuck here, wasting time that could be spent searching for my brothers.

"Ryker has burns to over sixty-five percent of his body. The only thing that keeps him alive right now is the machine he is hooked to. His lungs are burned, we have vacuumed them twice now, and his wolf genes are too weak at the moment to heal him. It is hard to say when or if he will wake up."

Ace suddenly walked off, and I felt his heartache at the news of his brother, yet all I could think of right now was my own brothers. Ryden was completely defenseless since he was a baby and at the mercy of a psycho, and Rayan wasn't much better off. He still hadn't shifted, so he was also defenseless against Josie and god knows who else.

Aamon came over with Tyson, and I listened to the doctor talk to them too. When he left, Aamon turned to me.

"How is Avery?" I asked.

"Fine, for now. She overloaded herself. Her magic isn't at full strength right now."

"But the baby is okay?"

"Yes, our daughter is fine. It's why she was visiting her father, but she felt I needed help. Misting is dangerous while pregnant, and then using her magic drained her."

"You're having a girl?"

"Yeah, hopefully, this one makes it."

"This one?"

"We don't like to get our hopes up, and this isn't her first pregnancy. Avery is a hybrid witch. She is half-succubus and half priestess, her pregnancies have trouble going to term, her power too strong for them, but this baby seems to be holding on."

"I don't understand."

"She is half-succubus. It would be fine if she were just a witch like her mother, but being half-succubus, her body powers up off magic. She feeds on it. We think this baby has made it nearly to term because it is more demon than a witch, so her energy hasn't been feeding off it like it has the others, which killed them. Although now she is growing weaker, the baby is draining her."

"So, she can't use her magic?"

"She can, but it isn't particularly safe."

A few of Tyson's warriors made their way down the corridor, and we all turned to face them when we wandered over to them.

"Anything?" I asked, but they shook their heads.

"They weren't searching. They went to Alpha Jamie's pack," Tyson said, and my shoulders sagged.

"What did you find? Was she telling the truth?" Tyson asked just as three gurneys were rushed down the hallway by paramedics toward the pack doctor's ward.

Chapter 80

Rayan

TWO DAYS LATER.

"Shh... shh..." I hugged Ryden close; he wouldn't stop crying, and he was once again hungry.

"You have to be quiet," I whispered to him, trying to muffle the noises he made by tucking him closer to my chest.

"Does that thing ever shut up?" the woman with evil eyes snapped, glaring over at us.

"Shut it up," she said, pointing a long narrow finger at me. Josie glanced at us nervously before rummaging through the bags she'd brought from some small convenience store. We had run out of formula already. I pushed my thumb in his mouth, and he made hungry sucking noises gnawing on it with his gums.

I missed home. I had been trying to mind-link mom and dad but couldn't reach them. I tried Lucy and my uncle's but nothing. I had no idea where we were as I looked around the dark wine cellar.

"I need to go get more formula," Josie said, and I went to get up and follow her. I liked our chances better with her than I did this crazy witch. Last night, I watched her skin some poor creature as she made something in her cauldron. She didn't even kill it first; its tortured cries would forever haunt me, and I was glad Ryden was too young to remember this.

"No, you wait here," Beryl snapped. Her wild eyes pinned me where I stood, clutching Ryden in my arms. I shielded him away from her glaring eyes when her nasty eyes went to him, squirming in my arms. He was heavy, and I had been holding him for two days, too scared to place him down in case that witch did something to him.

Josie looked over at me and smiled sadly, and nodded for me to sit. A bit too late to feel bad now; she did this. I begged her to let us go. I tried to convince her to let us leave him near the forest edge, knowing my dad and mom would have heard his cries or sensed him, but she refused to leave him.

Josie left but hesitated at the stairs leading outside, looking over at the woman.

"Go, and hurry back. Alpha Jamie will be here soon. if it annoys me too much, I will get rid of it for us." I stiffened, and Josie stopped.

"He is a baby, babies cry," Josie told her, just as horrified.

"I will take him with me."

"Fine, but the boy stays. I will need him in a minute," Beryl snapped at her, and Josie rushed over to the makeshift bed I'd made out of cardboard and hessian bags.

"Let me take him," she whispered, glancing over her shoulder at Beryl.

I hesitated, looking down at my brother, who suddenly cried out, and the woman screamed in frustration before throwing a jar at us. Josie moved quickly, taking the impact, and her back arched as she snatched him from my arms. She made a pained hiss before tucking him close to her chest inside her jacket.

"I'll be back. Just do as she says," Josie whispered, and I looked at my baby brother.

"He's safe," she said, darting out of the cellar and up the stairs.

Beryl muttered under her breath about whining babies, mixing her cauldron that stank like cat shit.

Her hair was wild and gray, her evil eyes gleaming as she stared into the cauldron's contents. One eye was black as coal, the other a whitish-gray; she almost looked blind in that eye because it had no color. She was skin and bone and looked like she was knocking on death's door, her hair falling out in patches leaving bald spots.

She was everything I had ever pictured a wicked witch to be, and she was wicked and crazy.

"Oi, you boy, get here," she said, not even glancing behind her as she called me over.

My stomach growled hungrily. I hadn't eaten in two days, and the motion of standing after spending so much time sitting made me dizzy. She grabbed my arm with calloused fingers, her nails stabbing into my skin, leaving little half-moons imprinted in my skin.

She hauled me toward the cauldron, and I resisted when she slapped me. My ears rang, my cheek burning, and I growled at her.

"Am I tempting your beast, boy? Never mind, you will meet him really soon," she snarled, her teeth black and green in places. The stench made me want to gag.

"Give me your wrist," she said, holding out her hand. "I won't ask again," she snapped, her gray-white eye shaking in her head before it settled on me. She gripped my wrist and yanked me to the cauldron, my other hand gripping the side, and I hissed as it burned me. The boiling bubble inside was black like tar and stank of death.

The cauldron burned through my shirt and burned into my stomach as I clutched it to stop it from falling in. My hand was blistering under the heat as I clutched the side.

Beryl grabbed a knife and sliced it from the inside of my elbow to my wrist. I tried to yank my arm away as my blood spilled out as she held it above the cauldron. My vision flickered and blurred, and I felt faint and queasy as the room tilted around me.

"Jamie wants to hurry up. I need my mutation here," she rambled.

"Suppose Josie will do it if need be," she said thoughtfully before letting me go, and I fell backward on the cold, hard floor. My blood spilled onto the floor as she wandered off to the wall covered in jars. She grabbed a few off the shelf, but I could feel my life essence spilling out of me.

"Not long now, boy, and all will be right in the world. Avery will be dead, your family dead, and Jamie thinks he will be the next Hybrid King. Fool. No one can take that title, but for now, he lives, and you shall play the part and be his daughter's mate. I shall be the next high priestess. Avalon City will be mine, but first, I need to take care of that bitch Avery and get my power back, and you will help me."

She said more, but the blood loss sent me spiraling into the darkness as it swallowed my sight.

Chapter 81

Lucy

"WHAT DO YOU MEAN?" I snapped, taking a step toward her. Melana stepped back, but Tyson dropped a hand on my shoulder, holding it firmly.

"Alpha Jamie always spoke of this place in the woods, his holiday retreat, near some small town, but you said you can't track Beryl?" Melana asked while turning to look at Aamon. He shook his head.

"What about Josie? Could Avery track her using my blood? We are biological sisters. I know witches need an item of the one they are tracking. Would my blood be enough?" Melana asked, and we all looked at Aamon.

"Possibly, but Avery is pretty weak. She can't use magic right now," Aamon said. Tears burned in the back of my eyes, and I couldn't take it anymore. There was always some barrier stopping us from finding them. Instead, turning on my heel, I left.

"Lucy, wait!" Tyson called.

"Let her calm down. She basically lost her entire family in one day. Leave her be," I heard Aamon tell him.

I was sitting out front of the hospital on the bench seats when Melana found me. She sat beside me, and I glared over at her.

"We will get them back," she said softly, staring out at the parking lot.

"They wouldn't be missing if your sister didn't take them," I growled at her. Lucille pressed forward, angry that she would even seek us out after everything she had done, and I pushed her back, trying to subdue her.

"I'm sorry, Lucy. I truly am," she whispered before looking at me. "I don't know when my life got so out of control," she whispered, and I sighed, sitting back.

The sun was hot today, and I found it comforting; instead of the cool crisp air-conditioning inside the hospital that made it feel extra cool inside, I welcomed the warmth and the fresh air, needing to clear my head.

"Yeah, that I can relate to," I admitted. We sat in silence for a bit; she didn't say anything, but it was nice not having lingering attention. Tyson was watching me like he thought I would snap at any moment, and for a second, I thought I would.

Ace was the opposite, feeling like the weight of the world rested solely on his shoulders. He took on the burdens of dealing with both packs while worrying about his brother. His temper became shorter as the last couple of days slipped by.

I felt useless, waiting around for everyone else to make the decisions, but I was tired of waiting, tired of being expected to sit still and wait for everyone else to make up their minds on the next move. Any move was better than not moving at all. So, for once, I didn't hate Melana's presence beside me.

She expected nothing of me and didn't expect me to act perfectly put together when I felt like falling apart or screaming at my lack of being able to help those I loved. Melana was no one to judge, and she made her fair share of mistakes. Any I'd made were nothing in comparison to what she had done, and for once, it felt good not being the target of everyone's anger.

"The place you were talking about that Jamie goes to?"

"They said to wait until Avery is better, so we aren't chasing our own tails. They also said that if I knew about it, the chances are slim they would go there. That's what Tyson said anyway."

"What do you think?" I asked her.

"I think Jamie isn't as smart as they give him credit for. If he went anywhere, I believe that's where he went."

"Do you know how to get there?" I asked her, and she looked over at me.

"I don't think that's a good idea, Lucy. I know you want to help your brothers, but we should listen to your mates."

"My brothers are out there somewhere with some witch. One is a baby, and I am sick of sitting on my hands. You want to make up for all the shit that has happened? You want forgiveness? Then take me there."

Melana looked over her shoulder toward the hospital entrance.

"We can't go alone. That would be foolish. He will have men there, and what about the witch?"

"I just need you to get me in there, and I will send my brothers out."

"You want to make a trade?" she asked.

"Jamie wants a bargaining tool, right? Ryker isn't available to bargain with right now, so the only ones he could possibly cut a deal with are Tyson and Ace."

"No, Lucy, you aren't understanding. Jamie wants your brother to mark his daughter, ensure her future as the next Queen."

"But he has no wolf to mark her with."

"Jamie said the witch could make a blood bond, so when his wolf awakens, he won't accept anyone else but Emily. She is forcing their fates, but I also think she will force him to shift," Melana told me.

"But she can't, not without—" I looked at her, horrified.

"She has to kill him. He is half-mutation. Without him coming of age to shift, the only way to awaken him is to either force the shift with strong emotion or force the hybrid gene to awaken. She will have to kill him."

"She does that though there is also a chance she could actually kill him," I told her. Melana looked away and nodded in agreement. Both of us have endured that horror before. I nearly lost my wolf because of them trying to awaken my vampire side, giving us the ability to shift at will while also giving us the perks of both species, building the army Kade had wanted so desperately. I refuse to let my brothers suffer through that.

"I think that's why Josie took Ryden. I don't believe Jamie will risk Rayan being killed. He will find another way to force the shift."

"You need to get me to that house. I won't sit around and wait for one of my brothers to drop dead before doing anything."

"Lucy, what are you asking of me?"

"What you owe me. I am done being the one sitting on the sidelines. They won't let me help yet are hesitant to do anything. You said you know the way, then show me."

"And what about when we get there?"

"I'll figure that out when we get there," I told her, and she pursed her lips.

"I do this, when everything is over, you let my mate go. Kill me, I don't care, but let him go. Don't punish him for my actions. He has suffered enough."

"You do this for me, and I may just let you live when all this is over," I chuckled. Melana snorted, shaking her head. She looked back at the hospital and back at me.

"When?"

"Whenever you are ready. Now preferably. The sooner, the better."

"They would be onto us instantly. Tonight when they fall asleep." I nodded.

"That will give me a chance to find a car."

"Car I can get, but you are driving," I told her.

"I will meet you at the packhouse," she whispered, getting up hastily, and I saw Ace suddenly walking toward us from the parking lot. Melana rushed back to the hospital, and Ace stopped, watching her leave before coming over to me.

"What was that about?"

"She was apologizing," I told him. He eyed me suspiciously before reaching for me.

Chapter 82

Ace wrapped his arms around my waist, tucking me against him. He buried his face in my neck, inhaling my scent.

"I didn't mean to snap at you," he murmured into my hair. I nodded, wrapping my arms around his neck. Lucille purred, making my chest rumble, and Ace chuckled at her reaction to him, despite the time not being appropriate.

"Sorry," I told him, but he shook his head and kissed my cheek.

"Our wolves make noises. I expect her to purr. I would be worried if she didn't," he said while grabbing my hand and pulling me toward the hospital entrance.

We walked back up to the ward, and Aamon was nowhere to be seen. Tyson was on his phone pacing the corridor, talking to someone angrily. Ace tugged me over to the chairs in the waiting room and pulled me on his lap while we waited for Tyson to finish on the phone. Ace's hand sneaked inside my shirt as he brushed his thumb over my stomach.

"I have sent people to check the airport's security footage to see if Josie flew out of here," Tyson said while hanging up and walking over to us.

"Any change?" Ace asked him, but Tyson shook his head.

"No, but we should go home, shower, eat, and get some sleep. We can't sit around here all the time twiddling our thumbs," Tyson said, and Ace sighed.

Tyson gripped his shoulder and gave it a squeeze. "He will survive, brother. He has too much to live for," Tyson told him. Ace nodded against my back but didn't add anything.

"Come on, we should get home and away from this place, at least for a little while," Tyson said before gripping my chin and forcing me to look up at him.

"You okay? You seem almost calm," he said, and I swallowed.

"Yep, fine, just needed some fresh air," I lied. Tyson turned my face eyeing me suspiciously, or so I thought.

"You smell different, and you feel warmer."

"Yeah, I haven't showered in days. You don't smell so hot either, and it is hot outside," I told him. He chuckled, letting my face go.

"Come on, let's get home and shower." I nodded, and Ace unwrapped his arms from around my waist and let me up. Tyson tugged me toward him before kissing my hair.

"They will all be fine, and we will get them back. We just need to wait a bit longer. Avery or Ryker will wake soon, and then we will know what to do," he said, and I nodded. I already knew what to do. *Fucking search and not sit on our hands.*

We all reluctantly left. Despite being worried about mom, I needed to head home to meet Melana tonight. I needed to bring my brothers home, to make sure they were safe. Right now, that was all I cared about.

The drive home was silent while I tried to figure out what to do next. Leaning between the two front seats, I turned the air-conditioning up. Tyson was right. My scent was so much stronger, the heat really getting to me.

Even Lucille was panting in my head and whining about the heat. Ace glanced at me, his brows furrowed before touching my head, the warmth of his hand making me hotter, and I slapped it away and a growl tore out of me. I felt so uncomfortable in this stuffy car.

"Settle down," Ace growled at me.

"Sorry, it's just boiling."

"It is quite warm today," he murmured, and I saw Tyson's eyes dart to me in the rear-vision mirror.

"I know everyone is irritable, but we just need to be patient. Once Avery wakes up, we will know our next move."

"Anything is better than nothing," I murmured, and his eyes darted to mine and narrowed slightly.

"Are you feeling okay?"

"Yeah, just tired," I mumbled, resting my head back on the headrest and enjoying the cold AC in the car. We pulled up at home, and I instantly started sweating the moment I left the coolness of the vehicle. A shiver ran through me upon being back here, and it felt so long ago, even though it had only been a couple of days and yet a lifetime of drama happened in that time.

The house was quiet as we entered, and Tyson checked the phone's answering machine while I wandered down the hall to the bathroom. Pulling my phone out, I saw a message from an unknown number, and I opened it.

"I will be in the garage at midnight and will wait for you until you escape them. I still think we should tell someone."

I figured the number was Melana. How she got my number was beyond me, but I just thought she either already had it or asked for it from someone.

"See you then. I will get Ace's keys," I replied just as the bathroom door opened.

Ace walked in, and I put my phone down, locking the screen. "Who was that?"

"Just checking my emails," I lied. He nodded while walking over, turning the shower on, and stripping his clothes off. I shook my head. I intended to shower alone, but oh well. I tugged my clothes off.

"Tyson?"

"On the phone," Ace growled. I wondered what had made Ace so grumpy this time but couldn't be bothered to ask.

The water was hot against my skin, and I turned the water down, the steam making me dizzy.

"Freaking cold, Luce!" Ace shrieked when I turned it down.

"It is boiling outside," I snapped at him when he tried to turn the temperature up.

"Doesn't mean we need to freeze in the damn shower," he retorted, turning it up. I rolled my eyes at him and reached for the soap, snatching it from his hands.

"Fuck, what's wrong with you?" he asked.

"Nothing," I mumbled while washing myself. *Only a few more hours*, I reminded myself. A few more hours, and I would be out of here actually doing something other than waiting around and wasting time.

****

The time ticked by slowly. We showered, had dinner, and then stared at the TV, not really watching it. Tyson spent the majority of the night on the phone pacing the veranda. Ace, however, was being annoying as hell and kept touching me. How his mind could even go there with everything going on was beyond me, and I was about to throat-punch him if he didn't stop soon.

All I kept thinking about was my brothers, my mind utterly consumed with their well-being, wondering if they were hungry or warm. If they had eaten. If Ryden had formula. If I was worried this much about my brothers, I would hate to be mom when she woke up. This was pure torture, and I was never having kids if it meant spending all my time worrying about them like this.

The door opened, and Tyson walked in. He shivered, and a growl escaped him.

"It's like an igloo in here," Tyson mumbled, turning the AC down. Ace moved again on the couch, tugging me against him.

"Will you stop?" I hissed at him and his grabby hands. Instead, he ignored me, rolling over and pressing me against the couch and moving between my legs.

"Ace!" I snapped when his lips went to my neck as he nipped at it. His erection pressed against my cotton shorts. Tingles rushed across my skin as he nipped at my neck. He thrust his hips against me, and I fought the moan that tried to escape me. The last thing I needed to do was provoke him more.

"Ace!" I growled while Lucille remained quiet, almost dormant in my head. *I could actually use her strength right now, but no, she runs off somewhere in my head.*

"You smell so good," Ace groaned, nipping at my mark.

"It's called deodorant. You should try it, now get off me."

"She does smell different," I heard Tyson murmur, and I felt Ace's hands grip the side of my shorts as he tried to tug them down. I sank my teeth into his shoulder, and he groaned. I huffed, annoyed as he kept pawing at my clothes, trying to remove them.

"How can you even be thinking of sex right now? Get off me, or I will toss you on your damn ass. last warning, Ace." Yet he chose to ignore me and pinned my hands in his above my head.

"Then let me change your mind." *I will change his in a damn minute*, I thought to myself angrily. He ground himself against me, and I lifted my hips since he had my hands trapped and turned, making him topple off the couch. I landed on top of him, my legs straddling his hips, and he gripped my thighs, his eyes the black of his wolf when I throat-punched him. He choked, clutching his throat, and I got to my feet.

"I fucking warned you," I snapped at him, stalking off down the hall. Tyson whistled and chuckled.

"Well, that's what your stupid ass gets," Tyson told him while Ace gasped behind me. I shook my head, wondering how he could even think of anything other than the situation at hand. I was about to walk into the spare bedroom when Tyson growled behind me.

"No, Ace's room. We are all staying together," Tyson commanded, and I gritted my teeth against the order as it rolled over me, pissed off he would even use it on me.

"Lucy, not tonight. Sleep where you want after all this shit is over, but until Jamie is found, we remain together," Tyson said, walking past me and pushing Ace's bedroom door open. I glared at him before stalking past him and into the room. My blood felt like it was boiling in my veins as I climbed into the bed. Ace came in a few seconds later and mumbled an apology which I ignored.

"He didn't mean to upset you, Lucy. Cut him some slack. Your scent is extra potent tonight," Tyson mumbled, his eyes flickering, and I lay on my back, both of them sticking to the edge of the bed like they were too scared to get too close to me.

I didn't blame them. I was in a terrible mood, and it suited me just fine. Plus, it was sweltering. I sat up, keeping an eye on the clock. Each minute passing felt like an hour, but eventually, they both fell asleep, yet both wouldn't stop squirming in their sleep, and their arousal was ticking me off.

How could they both be so horny while sleeping while I was in a murderous mood and Lucille was anxious and quiet? I could feel how uncomfortable she was, but her anxiousness helped keep me awake.

When it was nearly midnight, I heard movement outside and knew it was Melana. I tried to untangle myself from them and climb over Tyson when he gripped my hips.

He groaned lewdly in his sleep, rubbing me against his erection, and I fought back my own sudden arousal. His hands on my bare legs sent sparks straight up between my thighs. I fought the sudden urge off, struggling to get a grip on myself.

Melana is outside, I reminded myself. *My brothers, my brothers, I need to find my brothers*, I repeatedly chanted in my head, wondering why I was suddenly struggling with control. Tyson murmured in his sleep, and I saw Ace squirm on the other side of the bed. I forced myself to step off the bed, and Tyson's hands fell back to his sides.

I quickly rushed out of the room, tiptoeing down the hall. I had no time to change and scoop my sneakers up from the door. Everything in me was trying to pull me back to my mates, some urge I couldn't explain, and the further I moved through the house, the stronger it got.

I carefully picked up Ace's car keys, making sure not to jiggle them before carefully unlocking the door and slipping into the night. The crunch of the gravel made my feet ache, the breeze caressing my skin like shards stabbing into my skin as I raced up the side of the house to the garage. Melana waited in the shadows and stepped out, and I held the keys out to her.

She took them and pressed the key fob unlocking the doors, and the beep had us both freezing and glancing at the house nervously. When they didn't come rushing out, we opened the doors and climbed in, and Melana tossed a bag onto the backseat. Melana placed the keys in the ignition and turned the dash on before putting the car in neutral. I glanced at her because she still hadn't closed her door completely.

"We start the car, they will hear us before we get out of the driveway," she whispered before stepping out. I opened the door catching on, and we carefully pushed it out of the garage, letting it roll past the house before jumping back in.

Melana steered the car away from the house and down the long gravel road a bit before shutting her door and starting the car. I closed my door, and I glanced back at the packhouse in the distance but saw no lights turn on and figured we were safe.

I let out a breath and turned back to face the front when she put the car in gear and took off. I wound the window down, needing air. Sweat dripped off me, and nausea rolled over me before we were completely off the gravel road.

"You okay?" Melana asked, and I nodded, feeling the blood drain from my face.

I felt terrible. The further we drove, the worse I got; something was trying to pull me back home. We had been driving for over an hour, and our city was miles away from the secluded road that we had pulled onto when Melana suddenly pulled over. She checked her phone.

"Shit, I have no reception," Melana murmured before hopping out of her car. She rummaged in the backseat, pulling a map from the bag and a flashlight. I hopped out when she walked around to the hood of the vehicle, unrolling the map, the flashlight between her teeth. I clutched the side of the car. My stomach was aching, making me double over.

"Lucy?" she asked. I waved her off, and she walked over and gripped my arm before jerking away from me.

"What?"

"Your skin. It's so hot, Lucy," she told me, rushing to the back of the car. She grabbed a water bottle from her bag and handed it to me. I watched as she sniffed the air. My hands shook terribly as I twisted the cap off. I chugged the water down thirstily, and Melana observed me before taking it from me and drinking some.

"How long have you been feeling like that?"

"Since we left," I muttered, leaning against the car's hood.

"You should have said something. You don't look too good," she said nervously, reaching out and touching my face. My skin felt clammy and sticky.

"Have you gone into heat yet?" she asked, and I raised an eyebrow at her.

"More vampire, I don't have a—" My words cut off as it dawned on me. *Lucille*. I had a wolf now.

"Shit, we need to go back now." Melana says.

"What? No, we have already come this far," I told her, staggering toward her. My surroundings spun, and I lurched forward, my stomach contents spilling onto the ground as I heaved violently.

"Nope, we are going back."

"I am fine," I gasped out.

"No, Lucy, you're not fine. You are in heat, and you need your mates. You know it can kill you. You're a mutation, our wolves are weaker than an average werewolf in that state, and we can't transition through heat by ourselves, not without our mates."

Chapter 83

Rayan POV

I tried to open my eyes, and I could hear a voice talking to me, listening to the people in the room as I tried to remember what had happened. Forcing my eyes open, Josie hovered above me. She seemed frantic when it all came back to me. What Beryl had done and my arm burned. I blinked slowly. My entire body felt heavy, and I could hear crying, making my eyes look down when I felt movement on my chest. I tried to move my arm, but Josie held it in the air.

"You bloody bitch! He could have bled to death," Josie snarled.

"Shame he didn't. Would save me having to deal with this mate bond drama," Beryl said somewhere around me. My hand moved, and I tried to feel for my brother. Josie gripped my other hand, placing it on my chest, and I felt Ryden wiggle under my hand and let out a shaky breath.

"He is right there. He is safe," Josie whispered, and I turned my head. My vision blurred when suddenly the door opened.

"Finally, what took you so long?" Beryl snapped. A girl younger than me with her hair in pigtails walked in, holding a man's hand. She looked around the room before looking up at the man.

"Daddy, why are we here? You said I could see mommy," she said.

"Not now, Emily. Soon. We have things to do first. Go sit over there," he said, pointing to a crate off to the side.

He led the girl over to the crate, and as he stepped closer, I got a better look at him and realized it was Alpha Jamie. *The girl must be his daughter, the one Beryl was talking about.*

"No, bring her here, hurry, hurry," Beryl said while waving the girl forward. Alpha Jamie waved the girl to come to him, and she glanced at her father before hesitating.

"Emily, now!" he snapped at her, making her feet move faster. She chewed on her thumb, a rabbit stuffie tucked under her arm. Beryl moved toward her, and she took a step back, only for her father to grip her shoulders.

"Give me your hand, child," Beryl said, reaching for her hand, but she clutched it to her chest. Beryl sneered at the girl before grabbing her toy rabbit and tossing it toward where I lay.

"You won't be needing that," she snapped, reaching for the girl's hand, her dagger clutched in her other hand. She started to struggle, and her father gripped her elbow.

"Daddy, no!" she screamed, and I looked away, unable to watch, but her scream and crying told me all I needed to know. Looking up, Josie was also looking away, her face pale.

"It's just a scratch. Quit your crying!" Alpha Jamie snapped at his daughter, and I bit back a growl that threatened to tear out me. My arm was suddenly healing, and Josie gasped before letting my arm go. I clutched my brother, shocked at my ability to heal. I had no wolf; it shouldn't be possible yet.

MY TWO ALPHAS | 431

Sitting up, Josie helped me, and I clutched my brother to my chest, leaning against the wall. I felt woozy, and my vision still blurred. Turning my head, the girl was watching me, clutching her hand that was dripping blood. Her rabbit was next to my leg. I reached for it, wanting her to stop crying. Meanwhile, Jamie and Beryl spoke above the cauldron, looking into its contents.

"You did good, Josie," Alpha Jamie acknowledged before nodding to her. "Now, bring the boy here." He waved to her. I shook off her reaching hands, and Alpha Jamie growled.

"Willingly, Rayan, or I kill your brother," he said, and his eyes dropped to Ryden in my arms. I clutched him tighter and let Josie pull me up while one of Jamie's men brought a chair into the room.

He placed it in the center, and Alpha Jamie looked at his daughter before nodding to her.

"Emily, come," he said, waving her forward. She hesitantly got up, a sob escaping her. I moved toward them, and Josie held her hands out for Ryden, and I looked at her.

"I won't let them hurt him," she whispered, and I glanced at Alpha Jamie, who was glaring at his daughter. I passed Ryden to Josie before bending down and picking up the girl's stuffie. I glared at Beryl as I walked to the center of the room and stopped by the chair. Jamie dragged his daughter as she thrashed, not wanting to come closer.

He forced her to stand in front of me, and Beryl grabbed a goblet, dipping it in the cauldron before grabbing a ribbon and tugging it from her long unruly hair. She immersed the ribbon in the bubbling brew before handing it to Alpha Jamie. He pinched it between two fingers, holding it away from himself.

"That's it?" he asked her.

"No, you idiot," Beryl snapped at him, and he growled at her, but she ignored him before walking toward us. I held the rabbit out to Emily, who snatched it with wide eyes and clutched it. Tears trekked down her face, and she looked no older than four or five.

Suddenly the goblet was thrust toward her, and she jumped.

"Drink," Beryl said, and Emily shook her head. The smell was vile.

"Drink," Beryl repeated, and the girl sobbed, so I reached over and snatched the goblet from her hand while glaring at Beryl while I gulped some down. I nearly spewed the moment it touched my tongue but held it back, not wanting to scare the girl. It burned as it ran down my throat, the liquid steaming hot.

I choked but forced it to remain down. Beryl went to snatch it from me, but I pulled my hand back before blowing on it, trying to cool the scalding liquid down before giving it to Emily. Beryl tapped her foot impatiently, and when it felt tolerable, I let her take it.

She thrust the cup toward her, and she sniffed it before screwing up her face. Josie watched from the sidelines, and Ryden started fussing in her arms, and I saw her go to the baby bag she had and start rummaging through it.

Emily drank the liquid down and spewed it on the ground. Beryl slapped her up the back of the head, and I growled at her. So did Alpha Jamie.

"The rest of it, now, or it won't work," she scolded Emily. She sobbed, clutching her rabbit tighter before emptying the goblet, and Beryl took it off her before tossing the goblet on the ground. She held her hand out for the ribbon, and Alpha Jamie gave it to her.

"Hands now," Beryl snapped, and I held my hand out, and so did Emily. Beryl placed my hand on top of Emily, and I rubbed my thumb on her hand, trying to stop her from crying. I felt bad for her. I kind of knew what was going on. Emily, however, looked clueless about what her father was doing.

"When can I see mommy? You said I could see her. I can't remember her much."

"After, darling. Soon, really soon," Alpha Jamie said, and she nodded sadly, holding her rabbit still and looking at me. Beryl wrapped the ribbons around our hands in intricate knots while chanting, the ribbon heating up and melting into my skin. I tried to jerk my hand back, and so did Emily as it burned our flesh.

I gritted my teeth, and Emily screamed. The ribbon melted our flesh away the more she chanted in a foreign tongue when I jerked away, falling on my butt on the floor, and so did Emily. Alpha Jamie caught her and set her on the ground gently. I tried to remove the ribbon to find it dissolved onto my skin like some weird tattoo. My skin burned, and Beryl laughed while clapping her hands.

"That's it?" Alpha Jamie asked.

"Yes, for now. Next, we awake his wolf. Bring me that baby," Beryl snarled, and Josie froze, shielding Ryden away.

"No! Don't touch him!" I snarled.

"No? Do you have any idea how to awaken a wolf, boy?" Beryl laughed. I shook my head, and Jamie looked away from her.

"Pain, or strong emotion. I bet your brother would bring your wolf out."

"Pain, I choose pain," I yelled at her, glancing at my brother in panic. Josie looked at Alpha Jamie.

"He is a baby," Josie said, outraged. Jamie looked conflicted.

"You touch him, and my father will leave nothing of you for your daughter to bury. Not even your carcass for the worms to eat, you pig," I snarled at him.

"He won't have a choice. You forget you are tied to my daughter now. Once you mark her, the only way for you to live is if you have your mate by your side. She is underage, and I have control over whether she sees you or not. I have control, and your father will either lose his other son or obey my commands and stand down as the Alpha King," Jamie said.

"You think that will stop him? Avery will break this spell. Avery will put you down like the dog you are, or my uncles will. Leave my brother alone, or you will be planning your own funeral."

"You may regret choosing that, boy. Your brother's death would be quick. Your pain will be slow."

"I don't care, don't fucking touch him!" My mom would have washed my mouth out for using that word. I suddenly wished for Amanda back. She would eat him alive and enjoy his screams for mercy.

"Very well then, let's see how long you last," Beryl said, and Alpha Jamie whistled loudly. Two men came in and gripped my arms before tying me to the chair. Wolfsbane burned my arms, and I barely had time to catch my breath when I suddenly couldn't breathe.

My head felt like it was exploding as immense pressure filled my skull. I screamed, the sound deafening as I thrashed. My head felt on the verge of exploding, and Beryl laughed with her hand outstretched toward me. She twisted her wrist, and the pain got worse. I screamed through the link hoping someone could hear me, praying someone would save me or at least save Ryden and Emily.

Chapter 84

Lucy POV

Melana gripped my arm and tried to pull me back toward the car, but I kicked the door shut as she steered me toward it.

"I'm not leaving. We are so close, please, Melana," I begged her, but she ignored me, reopening the door.

"If I let you die, I will never forgive myself. We can come back with reinforcements. We can convince them to check the place out," Melana said while pulling her phone out.

"Shit, quick! We need to drive where I have reception," she said, leading me around the door so I wouldn't try to kick it shut again when I heard a scream.

I looked around for the scream, recognizing it as Rayan's instantly. The fear in it made my stomach sink, wondering what was happening to him.

"Did you hear that?" I asked Melana, and she looked at me funny.

"Hear what?" she said, looking around into the surrounding forest.

"Dad!" Rayan screamed. A blood-curdling scream filled my head, and I clutched the sides of it, realizing it was the mindlink.

"I can hear him," I spat through gritted teeth, my head pounding from the forced link.

"Hear what?"

"Rayan, we are close. I can hear him," I told her when another scream boomed through the link, this one bringing me to my knees.

Melana tried to pull me up and toward the car, but I shook her off, adrenaline numbing the pain momentarily. I tried to encourage Lucille to shift but got no answer from her.

"Lucille, please," I begged her, hearing his agonized screams on repeat.

"We can't," she panted breathlessly, trying to come forward, but it was like she was stuck behind a veil and unreachable.

"Lucy, we will come back," Melana said while trying to grab my arm, but I slashed her, my claws slipping out.

"Keep talking, keep talking, Rayan," I urged through the link.

"Lucy?" he replied, his voice a hoarse sob.

"Right here, buddy. Where are you?"

"Lucy, please. Get dad, get dad before they hurt Ryden." I didn't answer, trying to figure out direction by how loud his voice was. I looked around at the surrounding forest before pain rippled through me, and I clutched my stomach. Sweat dripped off me, and yet I felt cold, so cold and clammy.

"Lucy?" Rayan cried out, his voice stammering and fading in out as he called to me.

"I'm coming for you, just keep talking," I gritted out through clenched teeth.

Melana tried to grab me again, but I shoved her, forcing myself to run for the trees.

"Shit! Lucy, no!" Melana screamed after me, but I ignored her. I heard the car start up behind me, the tires squealing, but I didn't stop. Instead, I kept running from her before she overpowered me. I was growing too weak, but I refused to leave my brothers behind wherever they were.

"Rayan, I need you to keep talking so I can find you."

"But it hurts," he rasped through the link.

"Focus on my voice. Just keep talking, and I will find you. I promise I will find you," I told him before hitting a tree as I reached the treeline. The air got knocked from my lungs, and I was trying to catch my breath when he screamed through the link again. Adrenaline kept me moving, and I took off, turning every time his voice grew softer, using the boundaries of the mindlink to guide me in his direction.

Chapter 85

Ace

CRIPPLING PAIN WOKE ME and stole the air from my lungs as I lurched upright. My sweat drenched the sheets beneath me and clung to my skin as it covered me also. Atticus whimpered in my head, and I fumbled for the lamp, flicking it on and brightening the room when Tyson gasped, also jolting upright in the bed across from me. Yet, the middle of the bed was empty. Light filled the room, and I glanced around and sniffed the air for my mate. However, Lucy was nowhere in sight.

"Lucy?" Tyson called out, and I jumped from bed to check the bathroom, yet some part of me was being pulled outside, like some tether, and an invisible force was saying to go a certain way. My mate mark burned fiercely, and I covered it with my hand, the mark itself searing hot. I glanced at Tyson behind me, his mark an angry red and almost glowing under his skin; he, too, was drenched in sweat and was a sickly gray color.

Atticus was on edge, and the pull to her had us run into the darkness of the night. Tyson was on our heels when pain rippled through both of us, paralyzing us temporarily as we both hit the dirt, and I slid across the ground, the ground tearing at my arms and hands as I tried to catch myself. The air felt stagnant, and I struggled to breathe as pain radiated through my chest, her pain flooding the bond, and I couldn't stand it.

"Where is she?" Tyson choked out when his phone started ringing.

"Answer it. It could be her?" I spat through gritted teeth, crawling to my hands and knees and trying to regain myself. Yet, her pain was crippling and flooding the bond.

Tyson fumbled in his shorts pocket for his phone before dropping it. He tapped the screen, and Melana's frantic voice came through the phone, and he growled before clutching his chest like he was having a heart attack.

"Lucy is in heat. I tried to stop her, but she wouldn't stop. She has gone after Alpha Jamie. I am... I am on the old road leading to Avalon City."

"Where is she?" I heard Tyson snarl.

"I don't know. I lost her trying to get phone reception to call you," she said, but I took off, Atticus urging me to follow the bond, and we shifted.

Tyson stayed behind while he waited for instructions from him. Opening the mindlink I listened, waiting before speaking.

"Get back up. I will get our mate," I told him before hearing him acknowledge my words and answer.

"On it. Find her, Ace, bring her home. I will get Aamon and hopefully Avery. Fuck, I hope we can wake Ryker," he growled.

"I will find her. Just be ready when I do."

Chapter 86

Lucy

I HAD BEEN RUNNING FOR what felt like ages. My perception of time was off. I thought I was moving quickly. However, I felt Ace growing nearer, the bond trying to pull me toward him, and I hadn't realized I had slowed to a walk. I was delirious as I continued to listen to Rayan's voice leading me to him, but with each step, I grew sicker, weaker, and I struggled to remain upright. Clutching a tree, I tried to catch my breath. Lucille had gone quiet a while ago, and I was starving. Ravenous for blood.

"Lucille…" I gasped for air while trying to pull strength from my wolf, but I felt nothing. I felt hot and then cold, and before I knew it, I had collapsed, the ground rushing toward my face, and the only thing holding me from unconsciousness was Rayan's screams running through my head. Holding me and keeping me from accepting the darkness as it tried to steal my vision.

It started to rain, drops falling from the canopy leaves above and hitting my face. I welcomed the drops, anything to cool the blistering heat that ravaged my body.

Rayan's voice was so loud now that I could hear him so clearly and knew I was close. I had no idea how long I lay in the dirt, but willpower had me forcing myself to my hands and knees as I crawled to the tree to pull myself up. Ace, I could tell, was so close I was worried it would be all for nothing. His voice boomed through the link to come to him but I had to find my brothers first. I was not leaving without them, and I knew he could hear Rayan, or at least I hoped he could by now.

I stumbled through the forest when lights appeared in the distance, flickering among the shrubs and branches ahead of me. My heart rate picked up with excitement as I realized I'd found them, found the place Melana spoke of, and Rayan had managed to lead me to him.

When I reached the end of the forest and burst through the treeline, I found I was at a vineyard. Green and purple grapes lined up in rows filled the vast house's fields. It was a mansion lit up in the night. I had barely taken a few steps when I was tackled from behind. Something warm and hard smashed against my back and collided with me, sending me hurtling toward the ground.

Sparks erupted everywhere, and a growl so terrifying slammed against me; its vibration against my back sent a shiver up my spine.

"I told you to stop," Ace's voice boomed, his aura rushing over me suffocatingly strong, his scent wafting to my nose, and I felt Lucille try to press forward, but she was too weak to push against the veil that separated us.

"I found them! I found them!" I groaned, trying to roll out from under him, but he growled, his teeth grazing down my neck in warning. It was like the energy just zapped right out of me at his thunderous purr, calling on me to submit to him. He pulled his chest off my back, allowing me to roll, and I stared up at Ace, my vision blurry, and he glanced around.

"Rayan?" he whispered, and I felt the mindlink open up.

"Please, god, tell me you're close," Rayan cried.

"She found you, buddy. I am sending Tyson back for you," I heard him tell Rayan, and I growled. I wasn't leaving them here. Ace glared down at me before dipping his face into the crook of my neck. He put pressure on my mark with his teeth against my throat. Atticus tried to force me to submit to Ace's demands and go with him as he pressed beneath Ace's skin.

Ace tried to pick me up, and I thrashed in his arms; his answering growl was menacing as he tried to pin me so he could grab me.

"No, I am not leaving them!" I screamed at him, but his aura rushed out, slamming against me and stunning me for a second.

"You are dying. I can feel it. You need to get back with Tyson and me. We can come back for him now that we know where they are. I need to get you back, we can't take on anyone with you in this state, and I can't reach Tyson for backup. We are too far out," he snarled.

"No, no, I won't leave them!" I struggled against him when Rayan screamed through the mindlink. Ace dropped me, clutching his head, and adrenaline pumped through my veins as I started running toward the mansion. I didn't get far before Ace had tackled me again.

"No, we have to go back. I won't let you die," Ace roared, grabbing and dragging me toward him.

"No, I am not leaving!"

"No, you're not," came a voice that didn't belong to Ace. Ace pivoted, and I saw Alpha Jamie, who stepped out of the trees along with a group of men who quickly surrounded us.

Alpha Jamie held a gun pointed at Ace, and Ace roared his aura, rushing out when the gun went off. Ace fell back against me, and I screamed, clutching him, and my hands became wet with his blood. The bullet hit him in the chest, and his breathing wheezed in a long puff as he choked.

"You're not going anywhere," Jamie said before nodding to his men, who suddenly raced toward us. Ace coughed, blood spraying out his lips, and his spittle hit the side of my face. Lucille wailed in my head.

"Ace!" I shrieked when another bang sounded out into the darkness. Ace moved quickly, blocking me with his body, and this one hit him in the shoulder. He grunted, and I felt the impact as his body jolted against mine. Pain radiated through my shoulder as the bullet passed through him and into me, and the pain was my ending as the darkness finally enveloped me.

Chapter 87

Tyson

I HAD LOST CONTACT WITH Ace, the mindlink not reaching because of his location. Yet I could feel Lucy's pain and anguish. Melana couldn't find the road she was looking for, and the sun was just beginning to rise as I reached the hospital. Aamon was unreachable the entire drive, but I spotted him smoking out the front of the hospital, his clothes all wrinkled, and he looked like shit.

"Any news?" I asked as I parked beside where he stood.

"Avery has grown too weak. She is unconscious and has been for hours. No matter how much energy I give her, she won't wake up."

"The baby?"

"Fine," he said. I felt terrible for him, even more so with what I needed to ask of him. Aamon looked at me before taking a step back.

"What happened to you?" he asked, taking in my sweaty and pale appearance.

"That's why I am here. Lucy took off last night looking for Jamie, and she is in heat," I told him, and he instantly tossed his smoke before gripping my arm. I would never get used to the experience of misting. It was unnatural, and I felt like I was being sucked through a vacuum when we suddenly appeared in Avery's hospital room. Her skin was deathly pale, almost gray.

"She doesn't look so good," I told him, and he nodded before digging for his phone in his bag.

"Shit, I missed your calls. Sorry."

"We need to wake Ryker. I can't reach Ace, and Melana has no idea how to find the road leading to Jamie's holiday house. She said no matter how much she drives down that road, she can't find any others leading off it. She has to keep driving back to get reception to call, and I have a feeling something bad has happened."

"By the look of you, something bad has definitely happened. As for the road, it could be cloaked, which means the only way in would be on foot. You have to walk past the barrier. Makes sense if Beryl is with him."

"What can we do? I am way out of my element here."

"We have no choice but to wait."

"Wait? My mate is out there dying!" I snapped at him.

"Ace will find her, but until Melana finds the road or Avery wakes up, we can't do shit but that's not all. We have no warriors left, in case you haven't noticed," he said. "Your pack is small, and Beryl is strong. She has to be to remain hidden all this time, especially from Avery. No offense, but werewolves stand no chance against witches. You have no idea what they are truly capable of."

I glanced at Avery lying unconscious on the bed.

"I'm not sitting around and waiting for my mate and brother to die," I told him, walking out. I opened up the pack link, ordering all men to start scouring everywhere outside the city. But Aamon knew my pack didn't have the manpower and was hours away.

"Tyson!" Aamon called behind me, but I didn't stop when he suddenly misted in front of me.

"Wait, there may be something we can do."

"If you say wait, I may fucking hit you."

"No, no, I wasn't going to suggest that."

"Then what?"

"I need you to watch my body. I need to travel to the underworld. Asmodeus may be able to wake Avery or give enough energy to her at least. I am not strong enough to wake her."

"You want to bring her father here?"

"Yes, but it's harder for him. He will have to break down the barrier between this world and his."

"How long will that take?"

"I don't know, but if we can bring him up, even if he can't wake Avery, he will be able to find Lucy and Ace," Aamon said, and I glanced toward the doors.

Chapter 88

Lucy

I HAD LOST CONSCIOUSNESS QUICKLY, the bullet in my shoulder taking the last of my strength, and I woke in a delirious state to Alpha Jamie dragging Ace into a small cell. He was bleeding profusely and unconscious still. I groaned, trying to move my hands to find them tied to a chair. It was hot, ridiculously hot, and I could feel each pump of my heart feel the blood pass thickly through each chamber. Hearing a whimper, I saw Melana's battered body on the ground. I blinked, trying to clear my double vision, but it didn't work. Jamie was talking softly to a woman who seemed mad about something.

"They got through my wards. I am not ready yet. Make sure it doesn't happen again," the woman said.

"It won't. Have you awoken his wolf yet?"

"No, the boy passed out, but he is stronger than he looks. Hopefully, his sister might entice his beast out of him." The woman laughed, and she turned. I dropped my head quickly, pretending to remain unconscious when I heard a baby cry. My head instantly snapped up, and I looked around for Ryden, spotting him in a crate crying.

"That thing ever stop whining?" the woman hisses, and I growled at her, turning her attention to me.

"Well, aren't you a clever little thing? Using the mind link to find your brother, perfect timing, really. Your brother has been quite a pain in my ass." She stepped aside, and I spotted Rayan tied to a chair in the center of the room, next to a huge cauldron. Burn ran up his arms and chest, and he had a slash down his face. A pool of blood sat at his feet, congealed.

Lucille was no longer present, and I struggled feebly against my restraints, but it was no use. I could barely keep my head up, let alone do anything. The heat running through me made my blood feel like lava in my veins. The woman walked over to Rayan and slapped his face a few times, trying to rouse him awake.

"Wakey wakey, you have a visitor," she said, and Rayan stirred, drooling blood down his small bare chest.

"Don't touch him!" I yelled, but it came out more of a murmur. The woman laughed.

"Like this?" she asked, picking up a hot poker from the cauldron and running it down his chest. Rayan instantly jolted awake and screamed. I tried to break my restraints, tears running down my face when she pulled it away from him. Rayan breathed heavily, glaring up at her before his lips parted and his eyes fell on me. *I failed him. I failed him terribly.*

"Lucy?" he breathed.

"I'm right here," I gasped.

"Good thing too, or your brother was taking a dip in the cauldron," the woman said, turning toward me with the hot poker. I gritted my teeth when she pressed the poker against my stomach. Rayan thrashed. I felt my skin melt against my shirt, where she prodded before the skin broke. She pierced my skin, the poker plunging into my abdomen, and I choked on my screams and thrashed with all my might. Rayan screamed for her to stop when the door opened. The woman pulled the poker from my stomach, and my head rolled to the side to look at the door. Josie walked in and stopped in her tracks. Her eyes went to me, and a cruel smile split onto her face before it faltered when her eyes darted to her sister. Her mouth opened and closed.

"Melana?" she whispered and rushed to her, dropping on her knees beside her.

"What did you do, you bitch?" she sneered at the witch.

"Your sister was caught driving along the road, so my question is, why is she here?" the woman said to her.

"You said she would be left out of it. You promised not to harm her. We had a deal," Josie snarled at Alpha Jamie. The woman laughed, cackling loudly and holding her tummy. She was a grotesque-looking thing, and Josie stood, pointing an accusing finger at her.

"What did you do to her?"

"Nothing. Jamie's men found her, you twit. She came in like that with these two," she said, pointing to Ace and me. Ryden started crying again and the woman got mad.

"Shut up, brat! So help me, god!"

"We had a deal," Josie said to Jamie. He sighed, and the woman laughed.

"So naïve!"

"What is that supposed to mean?"

"There was no deal, sweety. You think a witch can get your mate out of the underworld?" She laughed maniacally, and Alpha Jamie growled at her. Josie looked to Alpha Jamie.

He shrugged. "You asked for the impossible. You didn't truly think I could bring him back? Why would you even want him back after what he did to your friend?" Jamie asked, pointing to me.

"She spelled him, she seduced him, it's all on her!" The old hag laughed again, finding the drama unfolding comically.

"Sit down! Shut up, or I may kill your sister!"

"So, was it all a lie? You were never going to help?"

"Is she retarded? Did she really… Oh my gosh, the stupidity runs deep in this one." The woman laughed, turning back to me. Josie lunged at her, but with the flick of her wrist, Josie was tossed and smashed against the wall. The woman didn't even look in her direction but instead faced me, and I glanced at Josie to see her get to her feet. The woman waved her hand again, and Josie's head suddenly bounced off the concrete and knocked her out.

"Now, where were we? Oh yes, awakening one's wolf." She laughed, plunging the poker back through my stomach. Rayan growled and screamed for her to stop while I faded out again, the darkness taking my vision.

Chapter 89

Ace

I KEPT SLIPPING IN AND out of consciousness, my lungs burning as one had collapsed when the bullet passed through it. My breathing wheezed with each breath before I lost consciousness, my wolf unable to heal me fast enough.

However, Lucy's scream and agony ripped me out of my pain-induced slumber; my wolf was livid as he rushed to the surface to see the witch plunge the poker straight through her stomach. Her scream was deafening before it suddenly died out. Rayan's screams for them to stop died out the moment Atticus shoved forward and tried to shift, only we couldn't.

My body was strapped down to the chair, and all we could do was watch. I could feel the skin on my legs melting off, and I glanced down to find my legs submerged in a bucket of wolfsbane, yet were unrestrained and heavy as the pain rippled up each leg, my hands, forearms, and chest strapped to the chair, and a collar was around my neck.

The witch laughed. The sound seemed to vibrate around the room, echoing loudly as she laughed before doing it again. I struggled against my restraints. Lucy was dripping in sweat, her skin deathly pale, and I could see Melana lying on the floor not far from her feet. Josie was unconscious on the floor face-down near the door.

"Come on, boy." The witch laughed, and I screamed when she plunged the poker through Lucy's sternum, hearing her flesh tearing and muscles shredding. Her eyes flew open, and her mouth opened with a silent scream when her eyes fell on me. She looked down at the poker protruding out of her. The witch pushed it all the way through to the handle. Blood dribbled from her mouth, and she sputtered, coughing blood everywhere. Lucy looked up at me; her face held shock before she spoke.

"Get them out…" she gasps, blood pouring from her lips and down her chest as she choked on it.

My world stopped. Everything around me stopped as I listened to her heartbeat slow before her head fell forward. Searing pain crushed my heart to oblivion, the bond severing. Rayan called for his sister.

"Lucy?" he whispered. The witch tapped her cheek with her filthy hands, yet all I could do was stare. She was dead. Her heat made her unable to heal from her injuries, and her body succumbed, unable to take anymore.

"Hey, wake up!" the witch snapped at her. Alpha Jamie turned and stared at Lucy.

"I said wake up!" the witch snarled at her, slapping her, and her head just rolled, blood running down her nose and from her eyes, but she didn't move, her heart no longer beating, and I felt the tether to her had snapped completely.

Blinding pain moved through my chest, and Atticus howled and thrashed while Rayan growled. The sound was predatory, yet all I could think about was my dead mate, sitting across from me, unmoving dead. I did nothing and just watched her die; I couldn't save her.

"Whoops," the witch said with a shrug, and I glared at her. She raised her hands before turning back to Rayan and clapping her hands, and her eyes lit up with joy. The sick bitch just killed my mate, and she couldn't care less. Like Lucy's life meant nothing to the old hag.

"Well, will you look at that? Seems your wolf isn't far from the surface, after all, boy."

"I will go get Emily," Alpha Jamie said, turning toward the door.

"Best I do it. I need to prepare her. Don't want the little wolf in pain when she receives her mark, now, do we?" Beryl said, and Jamie nodded, watching her go. When she did, he turned to face me.

"You know all this could have been avoided. Your brother only had to do as I asked, and your mate would still be alive," he taunted, kicking Lucy's foot. Rayan snarled at him, and I peered over at him. His canines had slipped out, and his silver and gold eyes were fluorescent as he bared his teeth.

Alpha Jamie sneered at him. "I own you, boy. Don't you forget it. That marking up your arm ensured it," he said, spitting at Rayan's feet, and I noticed the swirling pattern etched up his arm, the skin raised and an angry red. His hands clenched the armrest, claws digging into the wood.

"I'm gonna kill him," Atticus growled in my head, yet all I could do was watch. I had no point in living without her, my mind numb at what I had witnessed, the way she looked at me. Her heartbeat was forever ingrained in my memory with the way it abruptly stopped.

Chapter 90

Tyson

*A*AMON AND I MOVED Avery into the same room as Reika and my brother so I could watch over all of them while Aamon traveled to the underworld. It confused me, but he explained it was some strange voodoo meditation that would allow him to remain here while his soul traveled between realms.

"Ready?" I asked him. Aamon moved to the spare bed we had dragged in and was just about to lie down when Avery suddenly gasped and sat up abruptly, nearly making me jump out of my skin.

"Avery?" Aamon jumped off the bed, rushing to her side. Her eyes were wide open, and her lips were moving quickly, muttering in some foreign tongue, but her eyes were white. Aamon clutched her face in his hands.

"Babe? What do you see?" he said, shaking her gently when she gripped his hands, her eyes returning to the emerald green I was used to.

"Avery?" he whispered.

"The earth will bleed," she whispered. My brows furrowed at her words.

"The what?"

"The earth will bleed, and so will she, for she touched my hybrids," Avery said. Aamon and I both stared at her, trying to make sense of her words, when pain rippled through my chest, making me clutch it. My knees buckled, and Tyrant howled in my head.

"Lucy!" I choked out before feeling the bond sever. A scream left my lips as unbearable pain ripped at my soul and tore my heart from my chest. Pure agony when Avery was suddenly beside me, her hand over my heart, and Aamon hovered behind her like he was worried she would drop dead like my mate just did.

"Lucy!" I gasped, and Avery nodded sadly. I felt her hand warm against my chest, the pain receding when we heard another gasp turned feral growl, making my eyes dart to the two other beds in the room. Ryker's remained the same, the machine breathing for him, and the soft beeping of the devices attached to him was loud in the quiet room. Looking at Reika, she was staring at me, only it wasn't Reika, her eyes a demonic black, and her canines protruded. A look of pure evil had her nose wrinkle before Amanda growled.

"Reika?" I choked out, holding back tears.

She turned her head, observing me for a second before looking at her hand, and Avery rose to her feet.

"How is she awake when Ryker isn't?" Aamon asked the question I was thinking.

"Hello, Amanda." Avery smiled.

"Where is my daughter?" Amanda said, her voice raspy when she moved with blinding speed. Avery put a hand on her chest as she went to dart from the room.

"Power to the wolf," Avery said.

Amanda laughed. "No power needed, witch. I like to kill with my bare hands. Now, who am I killing first?"

Chapter 91

Ace

Alpha Jamie paced while he waited for Beryl to come back with Emily. Ryden cried out, and I glanced over at him as Jamie wandered over to the crate where he was lying. He rubbed his tummy before pushing his pacifier in his mouth that had fallen out to quiet him. I tracked his movements.

"So, what's next? You get my nephew to mark your daughter, and you think everything will just go to plan? That you will somehow be allowed to live when my brother comes for you?"

Alpha Jamie turned on his heel to look over at me, and Melana groaned on the ground, pushing off the filthy floor with her hands. She shook her head, looking around when Jamie rushed over and kicked her in the head. She put her hands out, blocking it, and the force of his kick shoved her to her feet.

I growled at him when he punched her, knocking her down to her knees again with speed she didn't see coming the second time.

"I suggest you don't test me, girl," he warned her. I growled at him, and his eyes darted to me before they went to Lucy, dead in her chair. Melana cupped her mouth in shock before she looked over at me, and her bottom lip quivered. I shook my head. I already knew how dead my mate was; she didn't need to point it out. Ryden cried again, and Jamie walked over to him.

"Damn babies, never stop crying."

"I'll take him," Melana offered, rushing over, and Jamie glared at her but didn't stop her. Rayan growled at her beside me, and I shook my head at him. Melana might be many things, but a baby killer wasn't one of them.

She cradled him in her arms while sitting on a crate. Melana knew to keep her mouth shut, she had always been able to read a room, and she knew the only way out of this, for now, was playing along and that's what I intended to do when I felt a flutter in my chest.

Hope bubbled within me, and I turned my attention to Jamie, who watched Melana for a second before cursing under his breath. He wandered around the room, looking in the cauldron and at the jars on the shelves in the room.

"You never answered me," I told him.

"Your brother will do as asked. I will have his son's life in my hands," he answered simply.

"And what is it you plan on asking him for?"

"He will stand down as king, forfeit the title over to me." I snorted. Was he delusional? You were born a king, not handed it.

"You think that is funny?"

"I think you're an idiot," I told him, and he walked forward, lifting his hand and backhanding me.

I laughed at his pathetic blow; Rayan hit harder. But I was glad he was closer, close enough and no longer paying attention to Lucy. I felt the bond returning; I had no idea what was going on with her, but I had no doubt the reason the pain stopped had something to do with the strange fluttering of a bond reawakening.

Her fingers twitched behind Jamie, and I knew I was right. Rayan looked over at me, his voice flitting through my head.

"You see that?" he asked, but I kept my eyes on Jamie, who was watching me.

"You don't seem too upset at the loss of your bonded. Not that I blame you; my bonded was weak too. Melana would have been a better choice for you. Instead, you chose that monstrosity," he sneered.

"Alicia was weak, wanting me to stop, wanting to live a normal life," he said, doing air quotes with his fingers. He chuckled, shaking his head.

"Yeah, she was always too good for you. Has a nice set of tits too," I told him, and he growled, stepping forward with his hand raised.

"Tell me, are they fake?" I asked. He snarled, baring his teeth. I knew I had hit a nerve.

"Don't speak of my mate like that!"

"I thought she was pathetic. Since we are comparing mates and all. Thought she was fair game."

"Your mate is pathetic. Mine was weak," he spat when I saw Lucy raise her head behind him. My eyes darted to Melana when Lucy looked around.

"You're seeing this, right? I am not imagining it?" Rayan mindlinked. Jamie looked between Rayan and me, and I heard Tyson's voice flit through the mindlink. I smiled, knowing he was either close or already here.

"What are you smiling about?"

"Nothing. I am just wondering if Alicia is a screamer?"

Jamie scoffs. "You wouldn't even know what to do with her, boy."

"I think I know a thing or two. I bet I could make her scream." It was petty, but I needed him distracted away from Lucy, and one thing I knew that would tick me off was someone talking shit about my mate.

Lucy stretched her neck behind him, and I was trying to keep my eyes off her blood-red ones. I sniffed the air subtly, trying to get a feel for her, but one thing was sure; she wasn't a wolf anymore. I couldn't even sense Lucille at all, and neither could Atticus. Whatever she was, I didn't care. She was mine, and I was just glad she was back. Melana tiptoed in the background with Ryden, and Lucy's head snapped in her direction, making her jump.

Alpha Jamie went to turn when I spoke, distracting him away from what was going on behind him.

"I bet Alicia is a screamer. I will let you know when I drive my cock in her when I get out of this chair. If you're lucky, I may let you watch as I fuck your mate, so you can hear her scream my name instead of yours," I told him. He snarled before his fist connected with my face. I spat out blood and laughed.

Chapter 92

Lucy

I had no idea what was happening. I felt my heart stop and nothing but oblivion when pain ravished me. Lucille's voice whispered to me in the darkness.

"Hang in there, Lucy." I tried to make sense of her words when I felt it. My link to her was just gone, my wolf was dead, and my heart stopped. My breath wheezed out with a bloody gasp. I knew I was dead, yet I felt like I was floating. My nerve endings felt twitchy, and I could feel my blood congealing in my veins, yet I was still here in the darkness. Would I be trapped here? What happened to my mates? What happened to my brothers? Time stopped, and so did I or so I thought.

My sense of smell came back first. I could smell dust, blood, and it made my teeth ache before I could smell Ace. His scent made my mouth water, and my fingers twitched. Yet my heart did not beat. The more I sat there frozen in time, the more I became aware of my surroundings, the dripping sound coming off my side, the bubbling cauldron. The footsteps walking around, the vague crying of Ryden before I heard Ace's voice taunting Jamie.

I had gripped the chair in which I sat to fight back the urge to growl at the monster who tortured my brothers.

Lifting my head slowly, I made eye contact with Ace, whose eyes darted away quickly, and he smiled up at Jamie tauntingly. Rayan was still strapped to the chair, but Melana was no longer at my feet. I glanced around for her to find her behind me, off to the side with Ryden in her arms. Her mouth was wide open, and I mouthed to her to be quiet. My hunger burned, bloodlust consuming my senses, and I felt my fangs slip out and pierce my bottom lip, making me shudder when my own blood repulsed me. Tasted as dead as I felt inside.

I glanced at Melana again and nodded toward Rayan. She nodded in acknowledgment, tiptoeing around the room while I yanked off my wrist, the ropes binding me snapping with ease.

"I bet Alicia is a screamer. I will let you know when I drive my cock in her when I get out of this chair. If you're lucky, I may let you watch as I fuck your mate, so you can hear her scream my name," Ace taunted. Alpha Jamie snarled before his fist connected with his face. Ace spat out blood and laughed, and Ryden screamed loudly behind me.

"Fucking pathetic just like your bitch. Shut that fucking mutt up! Fucking mutations," Alpha Jamie spat over his shoulder, and he was about to turn around when Ace spoke again, pulling his attention away before he did. I rose to my feet before bending over and breaking the restraints on my legs like they were string; the wolfsbane coating them had no effect on me whatsoever and might as well have been water. Ace laughed.

"The mutations are something, alright," Ace laughed, and Jamie chuckled.

"But one thing I have noticed about them?" Ace paused, and Alpha Jamie cocked his head to the side.

"What's that?" he asked.

"They are impossible to kill," Ace growled before kicking his leg out. The bucket of wolfsbane his legs were in flew through the air, drenching Jamie, who screamed just as I pounced on him, sinking my teeth into his neck. My legs wrapped around his waist, and my arms wrapped around his chest. His blood flowed into my mouth, and I heard Ace scream for Melana to get Rayan out. Jamie's claws sank into my leg, and he threw himself back and dropped on his back. My arms let go, my teeth tearing from his neck when he threw his head back, and it connected with my nose.

Ace broke his restraints before attacking him, grabbing him and tossing him off me. I scrambled to my feet when I heard a bang outside, and chaos ensued above us.

Rushing over to Rayan, I broke his restraints. My movements were quicker, and I struggled to control how quickly I moved, and my strength was something I had nothing to compare to. Rayan staggered as he stood, and I gripped his arms when I saw Melana trying to wake Josie, who was on the ground still. Ace and Jamie were trading blow for blow when Josie jerked upright, and I called Melana to help with Rayan.

"Here, I will take Ryden," Josie called. I didn't have time to stop Melana from handing him over when Josie darted out the door with him, and Melana rushed over to grab Rayan when Jamie shifted. His wolf attacked Ace viciously, and I moved to help him, tackling his wolf, and we slammed into the shelves, the jars on top rattling and falling to the ground around us, when an explosion went off outside.

Chapter 93

Tyson

Amanda snarled down at Ryker before moving from the room, Avery quickly chasing her and on her heels before gripping her arm.

"I know where she is," Avery said, gripping her arms and making her stop. Aamon chased after Avery.

"Then what are we waiting for? Take me to them," Amanda snarled, gripping Avery's arms tightly.

"Nothing," Avery said, gripping my arm, and I heard Aamon scream out to Avery when I felt the room fizzle and zap as we misted, the vacuum suction spitting us into the new surroundings. Suddenly, we were in a vineyard. I looked around. Avery clutched her knees, and I grabbed her arm, but Amanda was already stalking off down the rows.

"You alright?" I asked Avery, and she nodded, trying to catch her breath before standing upright. Blood gushed down from her nose, and she wiped it with the back of her hand.

Avery staggered as she took a step, and worry smashed me when I felt a strange sensation rush through me, making my hair stand on end. I glanced out at the vast fields. Amanda walked off with pure determination toward the massive mansion in the distance before she suddenly started running, and a vicious snarl ripped out of her. A growl slipped out of me when I saw men start charging at her, and Tyrant shoved forward, forcing the shift.

"She is alive," Tyrant growled as I felt the bond coming back to life. Tyrant took over and started running down the rows where Amanda was taking down Jamie's men like it was child's play. Her hands tore them apart when she sank her teeth into one's neck, tearing it out and spraying blood everywhere before turning on another. I pounced on the one closest to me, ripping out the back of his neck as Tyrant tore through his spinal cord, paralyzing him instantly.

Avery

Years I have hunted down this woman and now was my chance. Aamon would be furious, but I was the high priestess, and nothing was getting in my way. I knew the moment I woke up to the vision of the ground opening up that if she weren't stopped, she would destroy the world. Her power astounded me, making me wonder how many lives she had taken to gain her power. I gripped the grapevines wrapped around the mesh, trying to find my feet while Tyson and Amanda took down Jamie's small army. Tearing them apart, I could feel myself growing weaker with each step, but this was my job. Beryl was my responsibility, and no more of my people would die because of my mistake.

I felt her power the moment she stepped outside with a small girl, dragging the girl who was resisting when she suddenly turned and slapped the child when her head suddenly snapped in my direction.

She snarled, her evil eyes glinting maliciously, finding me instantly sensing my magic. This ended today one way or another. I created that monster. Now it was time to put it down. Straightening up, she tossed the girl aside before storm clouds moved, rushing above and blocking out the rising sun and turning the sky black as thunder boomed overhead. Her magic rippled, the darkness enticing; something I had fought all my life against, not to give in to it and the madness that came with it.

"One more round, Amy," I whispered, rubbing my bump. Aamon knew this could be my end, but so be it. It had to be done, but I was determined to make sure if it was, I was taking Beryl with me this time. Making up for the mistake of showing this vile woman mercy when I should have only shown her death like the rest of my coven.

Tyson

The earth turned to mud under our feet as rain poured down, a storm coming out of nowhere, and the ground became drenched in blood. Amanda and I took them down one by one. Time seemed to slow when light blasted past me. I only just managed to duck in time. Tyrant followed the light seeing it head straight toward Avery.

Avery put her arms up, crossing them over her face before moving quickly, and green light met the silver as it burst from her. The bang when her magic smashed Beryl's made the loudest noise, pushing Avery back when I heard an angry snarl, making me glance in the other direction to see Beryl stalking into the fields, hands forward, when I got punched.

Another explosion boomed behind me, but I was preoccupied trying to get the bastard off my back as he tore into our side. Tyrant dropped his front leg, tossing him over his shoulder before pouncing on him and ripping his neck out.

Amanda screamed when a black wolf bit into her shoulder, and we tackled it just in time to see Josie run out of the barn in the distance, heading for the forest. The doors bang-opened again, momentarily distracting me when Melana ran out, carrying a bloody Rayan. Amanda suddenly shifted, tearing through everything that got in her way as she ran toward the barn just as Jamie rushed out, and she attacked him.

I slipped in the mud, blood drenching our coat, and Tyrant shook himself before taking down the last of Alpha Jamie's men while Amanda viciously ripped into Jamie. His daughter's voice seemed to echo as she screamed, watching her father get torn apart.

I saw Ace rush out, his entire body covered in burns and drenched in blood. He looked over at the screaming girl before taking off in her direction. Glancing at the barn, my eyes went to my mate, and relief flooded me that she was indeed alive. Lucy looked around before darting off in the direction Melana and Josie had gone.

Turning back to Avery, I saw Beryl getting the better of Avery. Avery tossed her arm out, trying to deflect Beryl's magic when she was launched backward. The blow made her skid across the ground on her feet. When she dropped and punched the ground, a crack split up the aisle, and I jumped out of the way just in time before the earth swallowed me. Beryl laughed manically.

"You're no match for me anymore." Beryl cackled before throwing a fireball at her, which she only just managed to block when a forcefield flitted up around her. She staggered, gripping her knees before lifting her head and glaring at the woman, her emerald green eyes glowing like a beacon in the darkness before they turned black as night. I could hear her breathing from here as she grew weaker. The smell of electricity in the air made my fur stand on end when lightning cracked loudly above before spearing down at Avery and hitting her.

The sky glowed a crimson red as lightning smashed the ground around us and lit up the sky. Turning toward Beryl, the divide in the earth was huge. We backed up, hitting the fence covered in grapes behind us before charging forward and jumping across. Tyrant ran toward Beryl, and Aamon was right. Witches were in a league of their own.

Beryl didn't even look in my direction. Instead, flicking her wrist out and tossing me into the barn. I hit the ground and was forced to shift back when a piece of splintered wood pierced through my side just as I heard Aamon's voice scream out for Avery over the winds. My vision blurred as I got to my hands and knees just as Amanda ripped out Jamie's heart, and Aamon rushed toward Avery when a blast of power exploded out of her.

The blast knocked me back against the barn again and flattened the trees surrounding the place, the grapes exploding with force as everything in its path was obliterated, the barn turning to splinters and bursting, raining down chunks of wood and debris.

The house exploded in fiery rubble when Aamon suddenly dropped where he stood. He collapsed on the ground while I was caught between a magical tornado as Avery and Beryl battled it out. Avery's eyes and nose started bleeding as she tried to conjure up more power to overthrow Beryl, the winds so strong branches were flying off trees. The noise was deafening when I saw a flaming branch coming straight at me. Then all I saw was darkness, and I got knocked out.

Chapter 94

Lucy

Outside was utter chaos. What I wasn't expecting to find was my mother fighting Jamie. She was injured, but it didn't stop her fighting. I looked around, horrified at the carnage, looking for my brothers, when I noticed Ace grab a little girl I assumed had to be Jamie's daughter. She was screaming and thrashing in his arms when my mother called out to me.

"They went into the forest!" she screamed at me as she punched Jamie in the chest, her hand piercing through him. The noise was sickening, but I turned, sniffing the air as the wind picked up. Rayan's scent was weak but noticeable.

I darted off into the trees when I was suddenly thrown forward by a blast behind me. A shriek left me, and pain rippled through me from the bond. I knew Tyson was hurt but still alive. Shaking myself off, I noticed the trees around me broken and flat against the ground like something had just bowled them over when I heard faint voices.

I moved quickly, chasing after Melana and Josie, wanting to get my brothers to safety. Although I had no idea where I would be safe with everything going on; it was madness, and if it weren't for my heightened vision, I wouldn't have been able to see in the darkness. The lightning was crazy, and the winds only got stronger as I pushed forward against them, trying to navigate my way through what was left of the forest. Twigs and branches were snapping off trees and whipping my arms and face as I tried to listen over the howling wind. I felt like I was running on a treadmill, barely making any distance with the winds swirling around me and pushing me in the direction I had come from, when I hit a small clearing and saw Melana with her arms outstretched. Rayan was at her feet when my eyes darted to Josie, who was holding Ryden.

Rayan was screaming at her to give Ryden to him as he got to his feet. My hair whipped around my face as I made my way over to them, Josie's eyes instantly seeking me out, and she snarled, baring her canines at me.

"Please, Josie, just give me the baby," Melana begged her sister, and I growled, baring my fangs at her wondering what was going on.

"They will kill me," Josie said, and Melana took a step toward her, but Josie pulled Ryden closer, her hand on the back of his neck. He was screaming, the wind carrying his voice away.

"Please, Josie, just give me my brother?" I asked, holding my hands out for my brother.

"You took my mate," Josie sneered at me.

"She never took him, Josie. He is sick. Why can't you see that?" Melana tried to reason with her, and she looked down at Ryden in her hands, wrapped in his filthy blanket. She shook her head.

"This is the only way. I give him back, and they will kill me," Josie said.

"No, you can go. Just give me my brother, and you can go, Josie. We won't chase after you," I told her, my eyes on my brother in her hands. Melana nodded to her, holding her hands and stepping closer, but she took a step back again before turning her glare on me.

"This is your fault, all of it. You just had to report him to Avery. You took him from me. Now I will take everything from you," she screamed, and I saw her hand twitch a second before I lunged at her. Ryden went flying from her hands. His squeal pierced my ears and heart as I tackled her, and we hit the ground.

Josie punched me in the head, and Rayan screamed, making me look over at him to see Melana catch Ryden. Just as Josie grabbed my throat, she climbed on top of me, her claws sinking into my throat as she strangled me.

"We were in love! You took him from me! You took my mate," she screamed and gritted her teeth, and panic kicked in when I suddenly couldn't breathe. I clutched at her hands, and she screamed when I felt her wrists breaking but didn't let go. She headbutted me, and I saw black for a second before grabbing her hands, trying to loosen her grip when she suddenly went rigid; her grip loosened on my throat, and a look of shock crossed her features. Josie looked down at her chest. Her hands let my throat go, and I coughed and looked up to see Melana standing behind her, tears rolling down her cheeks. Josie looked up at her sister.

"I won't let you hurt anyone else," Melana choked out before closing her eyes, and I heard a sickening tearing noise before my legs got coated in a substance I knew instantly was blood. Josie's lips parted before she fell to her side. I stared up at Melana, holding Josie's heart in her hands before she collapsed to her knees beside her sister. I scrambled backward, looking at Josie while

Melana sobbed over her sister's body, pulling her little sister into her lap and cradling her head while stroking her face.

Tears sprang into my eyes at what she had done. Josie was my friend once, and it was clear how much doing that broke Melana. Looking around, my eyes fell on Rayan, who was staring blankly at Melana, Ryden clutched in his arms, and a sob broke past my lips as I got to my feet, rushing toward him.

"Rayan!" I cried out, dropping beside him and looking down at Ryden in his arms. He was eating his own hand, sucking happily and unharmed, when I heard someone call my name over the wind.

"Lucy, Rayan!" I heard someone scream, and my head snapped up in the direction of the voice to see my mother burst through the trees.

"Mom?" Rayan called, turning his head to look behind him.

"Mom!" he screamed, getting to his feet, and she started running toward him. I got to my feet, running after him, when my mother opened her arms, and we both crashed against her. Her arms enveloped us both, and she kissed both our faces. I pulled back, relieved to see she was okay, only to notice it wasn't my mother but her wolf Amanda. I wanted to take a step back from her when her hand reached out, cupping my face gently.

"That's my girl," she whispered, brushing my cheek gently before ripping me toward her and hugging me. I hugged her back, and tears slipped down my cheeks. She looked down when Ryden squirmed, crushed between our bodies.

"Hey, precious boy. Come to Momma," she purred at him, taking him from Rayan when the sky lit up and streaked loudly with lightning and thunder.

"We need to get out of here!" my mother called over the wind that picked up rapidly.

"Melana, we need to go!" I screamed out to her, and my mother growled viciously and tried to pass me Ryden, but I stopped her with a hand on her chest.

"I never would have found them if it wasn't for her," I told her.

"She just killed her sister to save Ryden and Lucy, mom. She saved me, too," Rayan told her, and Amanda looked at us before looking down at Ryden. She nodded before her eyes darted to Melana. Melana got to her feet, wiping her eyes but remained where she was, waiting to see what my mother would do.

"Come on, we need to leave," my mother told her when the ground suddenly started shaking violently like an earthquake.

Chapter 95

Ace

EMILY THRASHED IN MY arms but went still the moment she saw her dad drop to the ground. A strangled whimper left her little lips, which were blue from the cold bite of the wind.

"Daddy?" she whispered, and my heart twisted painfully for her when I saw Reika dart off into the forest after her kids. That must have been hard to witness. No matter how much I hated that vile man, he was still the girl's father.

"Shh, shh, it's okay," I told her, hoisting her higher and propping her on my hip when I saw Tyson smashed and knocked out by a flying tree branch. I tried to run over to him when the wind suddenly picked up, and it sounded like we were smack-dab in the middle of a tornado.

The wind pushed me down to the ground, and I tried to shield the girl's body with mine. Glancing around, I saw everything destroyed. Nothing was left standing as the wind ripped the area apart, resembling a war zone. I noticed Aamon on the ground, and I hoped he wasn't dead, but I couldn't be sure. Beryl screamed, frustrated, throwing her magic around blindly, trying to take out Avery. Avery suddenly collapsed on her hands and knees, and plumes of smoke and colored light flew and zapped around everywhere. Beryl walked toward her, laughing maniacally when the ground started vibrating, and she stopped. I screamed out to Tyson, but he remained unconscious.

"All these years, all these years, I have waited for this," Beryl laughed, and she was only around twenty meters from Avery, who was clutching her stomach. Blood covered her face when the ground started vibrating, rumbling and splitting open, lava spewing out of the crack when I heard a furious bellow.

The sound echoed through the sky, and the lightning cracked loudly. Beryl staggered back when I saw a black blur fly up out of the cracked earth into the sky, making me crane my neck to look up.

"Asmodeus," I heard Beryl hiss before turning on her heel and running in my direction. He fell back to the earth, hitting the ground hard and creating a crater where he landed before raising his arms. Lava hounds started spewing out of the molten lava that filled the crack he'd made in the ground. They chased after Beryl, and she screamed, throwing magic blindly, trying to fight them off.

I watched in horror as one pounced on her, landing on her back and tearing into her, her clothes catching fire, and she screamed as it started dragging her toward the crack in the ground. The ground beneath me was hot, too hot, and I rolled, pulling Emily off the hot ground and placing her on my back.

"Hold on!" I screamed over the deafening wind, and she gripped my neck tightly, and I started running toward Tyson. The lava hounds attacked Beryl, who was fighting a losing battle as they continued to drag her toward the crack. Beryl clawed at the ground, screaming. The noises leaving her made my blood run cold when I skidded to a stop coming across another gap where the earth had been divided. I teetered on the edge when a hand grabbed my arm, yanking me back.

Glancing over my shoulder, I saw it was, Aamon. He looked over at Tyson, and I sensed the strong scent of burned almonds flooding my nostrils and the ripple of his power. I was suddenly beside Tyson's limp body, and Aamon disappeared.

"You dare touch my daughter, and my granddaughter?! I have waited decades for you to return to where you belong. A lifetime of pain awaits you there," Asmodeus's voice boomed as the hounds dragged Beryl to his feet. She looked up at him, and the lava hounds escaped back into the lava.

"Asmodeus!" Beryl gasped.

"Your new captor," he said before kicking her, and she tumbled into the lava-filled crevice. The ground swallowed her, and I could hear her screams. Asmodeus suddenly clapped his hands, and the earth started moving again and closing. Then everything fell still, the winds stopped, and the storm cleared like it never existed.

Tyson groaned beside me, and I gripped his shoulder, rolling him on his back. He blinked up at me, and I heard Aamon wail loudly, making my head snap back in his direction to find him clutching a limp Avery in his arms. Asmodeus stopped beside him and gripped his shoulder.

Aamon looked up at him, and the dark-haired figure that seemed like the devil incarnate reached down, picking up his daughter in his arms and taking her from Aamon.

"I'll bring her back to you, son," he said, and Aamon hung his head.

"Whatever it takes, she will return. This life has taken enough from me, from her. I won't allow it to take any more," Asmodeus says before he suddenly vanishes into thin air.

"Ace, Tyson!" someone screamed. I looked around frantically for her voice and felt her getting closer. Tyson sat up just in time for her to tackle him, knocking him backward again, his hands clutching her. He hugged Lucy close, and I moved toward her to see Reika holding Ryden, Rayan, and Melana stepping out of the trees. Tyson clutched Lucy's face looking at her red eyes.

"How are you alive?" I heard him whisper.

"I don't know. I don't know," Lucy sobbed, hugging him tightly, and I brushed her hair behind her ear.

"Lucille?" I asked, and she looked over at me and smiled sadly before shaking her head. So my suspicions had to be correct; Lucy was no longer a hybrid but a vampire, her wolf now gone.

"Is he alright?" Lucy asked, looking over at Aamon behind us. I glanced over my shoulder at him before looking back at Lucy.

"He should be," I told her, hoping that was true.

"You said you had a car?" I heard Reika ask, looking at Melana, who nodded, and I growled.

"It was Lucy's idea, I swear. I only scratched it a little," Melana said.

"There better not be a scratch on it," I growled at her.

"Depends what you consider a scratch."

I growled, and Lucy laughed, the sound making my heart swell, and I reached for her just as Melana removed Emily, who was still clinging to my back.

"I know, sweety, I know but I know where your mother is. I will take you home to her," Melana told her as I pulled Lucy in my lap, inhaling her new scent and enjoying the feel of her safe in my arms.

Chapter 96

Lucy

Aamon transported us back when we discovered Ace's car was a wreck. We all sat in the hospital's waiting room while everyone received treatment. The markings on Rayan's arms told us some bond had been put in place, but only time would tell if it could be undone. Aamon paced and muttered to himself. He was beside himself with grief, and I prayed Asmodeus could bring back Avery and his daughter for him.

"Ryker?" I heard my grandmother's voice, making me look up to see Ace crash into his mother. She wrapped her arms around him and hugged him tightly.

"He will be fine, son. Your brother is strong." My grandmother, Aria, hugged him. My grandfather came jogging through the doors. He looked around, and I watched as my mother approached him. She talked to him, and he followed her into the room where my stepfather was. How our lives had been turned upside down in a matter of days. Tyson came over, sat next to me, and grabbed my hand before kissing it.

"He'll make it. I know he will," he said, and I leaned against him. Now we had to wait. Wait to see if the pack would wake, if Ryker would make it, or if the king would fall.

"Lucy?" came Rayan's voice as he stepped out of the room in a hospital gown. I opened my arms to him, and he sat on my lap. I kissed his little head and hugged him close.

"How do you feel?" I whispered to him.

"What if he doesn't wake up?"

"He will," I told him, and he looked up at me. He was so strong. How he endured what he did without giving in was beyond me. His wolf was close to the surface, but thankfully he never shifted; he might have had his wolf earlier than expected, but at least he didn't complete the transition.

"But what if he doesn't?" Rayan whispered while leaning his head on my shoulder.

"He will. He has too much to live for. He will make it," I tried to reassure him when Luna Alicia walked out. She was deathly pale and could barely stand. Melana was holding her arm, and my mother rushed over to help Melana get her in a seat. She could be another to be lost if Avery didn't return and sever the bond… so many lives sitting on the brink.

"I'm fine, I'm fine," Alicia says, and Emily, who was sucking her thumb, came over and climbed in her mother's lap, glancing around nervously. Rayan stared at her before looking down at his arm; the markings etched by the witch glowed under his skin.

"Thank you for bringing her back to me," Alicia whispered to no one in particular before turning to my mother. "The King?"

"Stable for now, and the bond is getting stronger. I can feel him. He is in there somewhere. He'll come back to us," my mother murmured, looking back at the room where Ryker was with my grandparents.

Gosh, I hope so. We had lost enough to Kade and his minions.

<hr>

One Week Later

I carried the salad bowl out the back of our packhouse; rows and rows of tables lined the fields as all the packs gathered. It was Jacob's funeral today, and a memorial wall was erected in honor of those lost since Kade came about decades ago.

It was funny to think that one misunderstanding by my great-grandfather had brought about nearly a century of terror, ruled by one man even decades after his death. But for once, everyone was hopeful this was the end, the end of one lifetime and the beginning of another.

Avery wasn't able to sever the bond between Emily and Rayan. Asmodeus, too, had returned with Avery after dipping her in the fountain of life. After taking her to the seven sisters of some purgatory who apparently owed him a favor, Asmodeus was able to keep his word, or Amy and Avery would no longer be here. Avalon City would have lost their high priestess, and we would have lost an irreplaceable family friend.

I placed the salad bowl on the table as Ace brought over a meat tray from the spit roast. I looked down at Amy in Avery's arms, her emerald green eyes peering up at her mother. Her jet-black hair matched her father's. A perfect combination of the two of them. Aamon brushed Avery's hair behind her ear before kissing her shoulder.

Glancing down the table, my stepfather sat at the end. He had been quiet today, watching over his family and pack. His somber expression saddened me, and I knew he felt Jacob's loss the most. Jacob was one of his best friends and family to him.

Burns ravaged most of his body, but he still looked like the fearless king he was. The ruler of our kind. I sighed, looking down at the table of three generations of family all in one place—generations of heartache and pain, but we still stood. We held strong. Never have I felt so at home than I did at this moment.

Pack members mingled and talked as all packs came together. Rayan was talking to Emily, her mother thankfully recovered after the bond was severed between her and Jamie, and she took over his pack and seemed to be readjusting to a life outside of the cells. Melana joined Alicia's pack and is now a Beta. She and Nathaniel finally marked each other, and he looked smitten to have his mate.

Looking for her, I found her talking to Mitchell, laughing at something he was showing her on his phone, while Nathaniel and Mitchell's mate looked over her shoulder, watching, too. Melana, feeling my eyes on her, looked up. She smiled and nodded at me. I nodded back, all animosity left behind, the past not forgotten but no longer holding us back. We both got what we wanted, and I moved toward the memorial wall that finished being built yesterday, the plaques all in place. Mom and dad were staying with us until a new packhouse could be built. Each pack now had its own memorial, and the day was placed on the calendar as a day to remember those lost.

Looking up at the wall, Abel sat at the top; it started with him, and it seemed fitting. Looking over the names, I recognized most but not all. Despite Josie causing issues, her name was also etched into one of the plaques; she hadn't always been a monster, and I tried to remember her as my friend.

Mitchell stepped beside me, looking up at the colossal wall of names, our enemies and friends frozen in time but never forgotten.

He grabbed my hand, and I glanced over at him. He nudged me with his shoulder, and I smiled, nudging him back when I felt another hand slide into mine. I gave her hand a squeeze peeking up at Melana, once enemies now friends. Life was too short for grudges, and hate was not something I wanted to hang on to.

Feeling arms wrap around my waist, I looked over my shoulder at Ace; he buried his face in my neck, purring softly.

"I hope I never hear the name Kade again," he muttered, and I hummed in agreement.

"That would be nice," Melana said, and Ace nodded.

"So, what's next for you?" I asked, turning to Mitchell, and he shrugged.

"No idea, you?"

"I have a few ideas," Ace said, bumping his hips against my ass.

"Get a room," Melana muttered, nudging me with her hip.

"Not without me, they ain't. Her parents living with us is the biggest cock blocker," Tyson said, making us turn as he approached us. Ace growled; Tyson was right. Ryker was always at us about doors remaining open despite the fact they were my mates and we were all adults. Apparently, I was still his daughter, and the 1.5-meter rule had been set in place while they lived under OUR roof.

"Gosh, how you will survive them two is beyond me. Ace was annoying enough."

"Annoyingly fantastic," Ace said, and Melana rolled her eyes at him when I was tugged away by Tyson. Ace growled at him, reaching for me.

"Stop being a hog," Tyson snapped at him, kissing my head.

Avery wandered over to us with Aamon.

"So, this is it…" she mused, looking up at the gigantic wall.

"Is that confirmation that the bastard won't be haunting us again from the grave?" Tyson asked, and Avery smiled.

"Something is always haunting us from beyond the grave," she answered, and I shivered.

"But yes, I feel this is the end of Kade," she said, looking back out at everyone gathered here today before she groaned loudly. I followed her gaze, and Aamon chuckled when I finally spotted her father casually leaning against the side of the house, talking to three she-wolves.

"Can't take him anywhere," she muttered, shaking her head. She passed Amy to Aamon and stormed over to him in a blazing fury, her cheeks red with embarrassment as her father was surrounded by she-wolves swooning over him.

"Dad, you old horn dog! Shoo, get away from them!" Avery scolded her father. The she-wolves darted off, and Asmodeus glared at his daughter.

"What? I wasn't doing anything," he said innocently.

"You know exactly what you were doing. They have mates."

Aamon laughed beside us, and Melana fanned herself with her hand. "Is it hot out here?" she laughed, and my face glowed red. There was no denying Avery's father was definitely a panty-dropper. Ace growled as all faces turned toward Avery's father, and I had never seen a man get so many death stares and not by one wolf but every male wolf here as all the ladies, even those mated, couldn't tear their eyes from the dark, handsome, mysterious man. He just commanded attention with otherworldly sex appeal.

"That arousal I can smell better is because I am touching you and not because of the old carcass over there," Tyson growled below my ear.

"He doesn't look old," Melana said, her voice sounding far away. Nathaniel grabbed her hand; she seemed to be in some trance as she stared after Asmodeus.

"The fossil is older than the earth," Aamon said.

"Just something so appealing about him," I mused, and Ace cleared his throat.

"What? We can look?" Melana said.

"I wonder—" Asmodeus smiled tauntingly at his daughter's angry red face.

"You wonder nothing. Dad, stop it, you filthy old man," Avery scolded, shooing him away.

Even a few of the men were watching, drooling over him. My stepfather whistled, and Asmodeus looked over at him, a smile flashing on his face, and half the woman near him swooned. Tyson and Ace growled as he passed us, sending a wink at Melana and me. I chuckled, knowing his demonic ways had us wanting to beg at his feet just to touch him.

He flopped down in a chair beside my stepfather, and even my mother and grandmother were no match against his appeal. My mother was staring at him in a trance. Asmodeus smirked while my stepfather rolled his eyes, only to growl when my mother reached her hand out. I could tell she wasn't with it. Ryker grabbed her hand, tugging her in his lap.

"Stop it, god of the underworld or not, I will drag you to the pits of hell myself," Ryker warned him, and he chuckled, putting his hands up in surrender.

"I'm on my best deviant behavior," he retorted.

"Bloody old fool, we just finished a war. Does he really want to start another by bedding everyone here?" Avery said, reaching for Amy in Aamon's arms.

"You should try living with him. Ten years I had to listen to the noises coming from his room," Aamon huffed.

"Well, you shouldn't have killed my parents, and I wouldn't have locked you there."

"I have been scarred for life. The man is insatiable, a beast in bed."

"I would rather not hear about my father's bedroom adventures," Avery said.

"Hear about them? I had to watch them do the walk of shame each morning. His bedroom was like a revolving door," Aamon muttered.

"I'm gonna see if he needs anything," Melana muttered dreamily.

"Like hell you are, you stay away from him," Nathaniel growled possessively, shooting a glare at Asmodeus, who was clearly enjoying the attention. In fact, I was pretty sure he was reveling in it.

Epilogue

A Year Later

We had just got home from the waterfalls. Today was an absolute scorcher, so we went swimming. Mom and dad had moved out a couple of months ago, and we were glad to have the house back to ourselves. Though I would miss mom's terrible cooking and Rayan's constant "I'm bored."

I rushed into the house, intending to shower, and I screamed, "I call dibs," racing toward the bathroom. Three days in a row, we had run out of hot water, and I was not freezing my ass off again. Yesterday the water was so cold my nipples practically inverted to escape the torrents of icy water. But not today, Satan, not today. That hot water is mine. They could have shriveled balls; my titties weren't freezing because they used all the water again. Stripping off as I ran down the hallway, I rushed in, slamming the door behind me.

I had barely stepped under the spray when the door burst open and smashed into the wall as they shoved and pushed each other, trying to get in the shower with me.

"No, you are both too big to fit," I scolded them.

"That's what they all say," Ace murmured, and I rolled my eyes.

"Oh, I will fit, baby," Tyson purred, trying to shove Ace away. I growled at them, trying to invade my shower. Ace pushed Tyson, making him land in the bathtub. Tyson growled at him as Ace hopped into the cramped stall. I shrieked when my back came into contact with the cold tiles. His hands reached for me the moment he stepped in. Ace was mauling me when the shower screen door opened again.

"Nope, definitely not. I am already squashed," I snapped at Tyson, but he ignored me, squeezing past us when Ace jumped away from him, growling and baring his teeth.

"Gross, bro. Your dick touched my fucking leg," he growled. Tyson growled back at him, yanking me out of Ace's grip.

"Both of you get out! I wanted to shave," I whined.

"I can shave you, though. I am kinda digging the Amazonian look," Ace chuckled.

"Fuck off!" I snapped at him, slapping his hand away that was squeezing my breast, and I groaned when Tyson hit the shower caddy off the wall trying to move in the cramped space, knocking down the soaps and shampoo.

"There are two other showers in the house. Out!" I snarled at them.

"But none have a Lucy in them," Ace purred, tugging me to him while I tried to escape his clutches so I could bend down and grab the soap. I snatched the soap and shampoo bottle off the ground, only to be held down by hands on my shoulders.

"Well, while you're down there…." Ace purred, smacking me in the face with his cock.

"Go on, be a love and get on it," Ace said, thrusting his hips at my face, and I bit the head of his cock when he pushed me back down, smacking me with his hardened cock again.

"Oh, I don't mind a bit of teeth. I will take any attention in the schlong region," Ace purred, gripping my hair and tugging it. I glared up at him.

"No. I got your sloppy seconds last time," Tyson snarled.

"Paper, scissors, rock ya for her," Ace said as if I had no say in this.

I growled as I gripped Tyson's hip, hauling myself up between them. "I will paper scissor rock you to get the fuck out of my shower," I snapped at them.

"I make you a deal. You get a free pass if you get out of the shower," Ace taunted, gripping my hips in his giant hands. Tyson chuckled as I squirmed between them, only for Tyson to press against my back, sandwiching me between them.

"You two are impossible."

"No, I would say I am rather easy," Ace retorted, pressing his cock against my stomach. Tyson hummed in agreement, pressing his lips to my shoulder.

Ace suddenly turns, washing or rather playing with himself. I shook my head at him, turning away from him. Tyson growled at him, wanking himself and hogging all the hot water and I glare at Ace for the assumption.

"What? I am just heating up her dinner," he said. I elbowed him when Tyson's hand slipped between my thighs.

"Well, I'm playing with mine," Tyson purred, his fingers circling my clit. I moaned softly.

"And you think you're not easy?" Tyson growled at my sudden mood change as my arousal perfumed the room. Stupid bond.

"Easily mine," Ace taunted, shoving his finger inside me from behind, and I pressed against him, losing all track of my thoughts.

"Ah fuck, dinner's served then," I growled, gripping Tyson's shoulders and shoving him to his knees. Tyson chuckled, hoisting my leg over his shoulder, and I leaned back against Ace, whose lips went to my neck.

Goddess, Tyson had really gotten good at this in just a year. Ace moved behind me. I leaned my head back until it pressed against the cold tiles. He shifted, making himself more comfortable as his tongue delved right into my slit.

He slurped, lips moving against my clit as he devoured me.

Ace stopped cleaning himself and moved closer, almost pushing me over in the small space. His cock pressed against my back, and he growled softly, nipping at my neck as I was stuck in an endless moan from Tyson's torments.

"Hey, who said you get to have all the fun?" Ace whined.

Tyson didn't answer. He just removed one leg from my thigh long enough to flip Ace off and worked his tongue around my clit, almost sucking it into his mouth.

My legs threatened to buckle, and I grabbed onto his shoulders for support. Ace refused to be left out, and he licked on the skin below my ear, grazing it with his teeth. "Fuck, I love hearing you cry out," Ace growled, grinding his dick into my back.

His spicy scent enveloped me, and I leaned against him, turning my face to his, my nose trailing across his throat. My mouth watered. I parted my lips, sucking on his skin. "Please," I pleaded with a whimper. I wanted to taste him, to have his blood filling my mouth when I was pushed over by the edge by Tyson's newly developed talents.

Ace laughed and gripped the back of my neck. He pushed my face into his neck. "Go ahead, baby," he cooed. "If that's what you want, but in return, you're going to let me fill that pussy of yours."

I would agree to anything at that point, even with being filled with pups. The desire for his blood was too strong. I wanted to be closer to him, to both of them, than I had been in ages.

I required no more prompting. I bit deep into him, letting my fangs sink into his skin. He hissed at the sharp pain but didn't pull away. The spice of his blood hit my tongue, and I moaned aloud.

"Heh, looks like I'm winning," Ace teased with a grin, his fingernails scraping my scalp. "She moans loudest for me." he taunts Tyson.

Tyson made the risky maneuver of lifting both hands off my thighs long enough for him to offer a double bird before he growled deep in his throat and stuck a questing finger up my pussy as he continued to tease and torment my clit with tongue and lips.

While Ace's blood coated my tongue, I went over many similarities in my mind, but Ace was so unique. His blood was refreshing, but also comforting in a way. I chuckled as it hit me after a long gulp.

My mate tasted like a living apple cider.

Tyson's finger hooked deep inside me, and he ran it along my bumpy ridges, searching for that oh-so-right spot. He hit it, and I pulled away from Ace, panting hard. "Fuck," I moaned.

But Tyson was relentless. His tongue swirled around my clit, faster and harder until I didn't know if I was in pain with bits of pleasure or if I was drowning in pleasure with tidbits of pain. I thrashed against Ace's grip before my entire body came undone. My body tensed, and my back arched like a bow as the orgasm hit me.

Tyson continued to devour me throughout it. I was stuck panting, watching as Ace's amazing blood dripped down the open wound I'd left on him. I wiggled closer, licking at the fresh drops while the orgasm continued to wrench its way through me, and Tyson was forced to move as I twisted slightly, his grip on my thigh keeping his face between my thighs.

I was right.

The delicious spice of blood and the orgasm were pure heaven. But I wanted more than this. "Bed," I ordered, touching my elongated fangs to my bottom lip.

Tyson kissed my thigh and grinned. "As you wish, Princess."

Ace rolled his eyes. He didn't waste time. He picked me up, our slippery bodies pressed against each other in the small space, and he cradled me against his body. "Hold on to my neck," he ordered.

I wasted no time and threaded my arms around him. It put my nose directly against his blood again, and I buried my face against it, sucking more of his holiday-themed blood into my mouth.

I was glad the hunger wasn't something I had to deal with anymore or worry about freaking them out. I had an all-you-can-eat mate buffet at my fingertips.

Ace held me close to his chest while Tyson scrambled away. "I'm going to go get our dessert," he called before running out the room, his naked ass moving away.

"Dessert?" I questioned, coming up from my feast to study Ace.

The man chuckled at me. "Don't worry about it. Just some things I mentioned wanting to do, and that Tyson said he wanted to try. It might be fun for you, too." He dropped me on the bed, and I bounced for half a second before catching myself.

Ace didn't give me a chance to rest. He followed me onto the bed, shoving my legs around his neck as he picked me up. My eyes widened, and I squealed as he lifted me, moving me to the center of the bed. I only had a moment to squeal before he licked away at my previous orgasm with big broad strokes of his devil tongue.

I grabbed the pillow, my mouth wide open as he brought me to the brink with his roughness. "Fuck, Ace," I moaned,

He didn't hesitate in the slightest. He kept my body pinned under his grip squeezing my thighs. His tongue twisted and circled my pussy like he was a child, licking away at the last bits of a pudding cup.

I thrashed in his grasp, unable to do anything but moan at his mercy. He brought me almost to the point of coming again when Tyson ran back in.

"I brought a couple. We've got chocolate and strawberry, and I grabbed some whipped cream, too."

I glanced over at him from the corner of my eye. He held a couple of syrup bottles in his hand and my container of whipped cream for my own desserts.

"Hey! That's for my pies!" I growled at him.

Tyson smirked at me. "Yeah, I know, the nice big cream pie," he answered back.

I bit back a groan. Great, just fucking great. I didn't like Ace rubbing off on his brother like that. It was bad enough I had to deal with one sex-crazed idiot.

I didn't worry about the sex-crazed part too much, but the stupid jokes would have to be stopped, and soon. I couldn't put up with double those.

"Nice," Ace encouraged, pulling away from his meal long enough to chuckle. "Here, slap some on there right now. I want to see which one's sweeter."

Tyson trotted over, peeling back the lid for the whipped cream and grabbing a handful of it out. Fucker, now I'd have to get a new one.

But my thoughts weren't with me long as he slathered it between my legs, pushing some of the mushy cream into me.

But Tyson wasn't satisfied with that. Oh no. He grabbed another huge dollop and graced both of my breasts with the stuff. My skin was so hot from the shower that had it melting quickly, so I was treated to the horror of watching the white mixture slowly slide down making me ridiculously sticky and ruining my brand new sheets after they destroyed the last ones with their sordid shenanigans.

"I've got it!" Tyson called with a laugh, getting on the bed and kneeling by my head before dipping his head to lick the slippery cream, his tongue chasing the substance back to my nipple, and he sucked it sharply into his mouth.

Turning my head to the side, I dragged my tongue over his shaft, forcing him to moan and let his current treat go.

However, my victory was short-lived as Ace attacked me with a new frenzy. His shoulders forced my legs open as he forced himself back between them. He shook his head side to side and he lapped away at me.

My squeals turned to moans, and Tyson's hips moved against me, his cock rubbing against my mouth and I opened my mouth so he could glide his cock along my tongue, propping myself up on one elbow

My orgasm shook me hard, and in between my moan and gasp, I bit Tyson. He hissed, and I winced, thinking of the pain he must have been in.

But that's when drops of his blood dribbled onto my lips. I hadn't bitten him as hard as I would to feed, but enough for the sweetness to cling to my tongue.

I'd thought that had been my last orgasm. But just these first bits were enough to make my eyes roll and for my pussy to become soaking wet again. I moaned, lapping at Tyson's blood. He was so fucking sweet. Like honey and something else.

I wanted to bite into him and get a good taste, but I wasn't about to do that to his poor dick. I had much better plans for it. I licked at it, sealing the wound, and gave it a little kiss, running my tongue along the edge.

"Still hot," he groaned at me.

Ace smirked, reaching for the bottles that Tyson had left with his free hand. He grabbed the strawberry and pulled away from me long enough to squirt it all over me.

I shuddered as the still-cold syrup from the fridge liquid dripped all over me and slowly down my body. Not that it had long because Ace sucked away all of it in mere seconds. His tongue was never satisfied until every last sticky part of my pussy was personally cleaned by him.

Not to be outdone, Tyson grabbed the chocolate, coating it over both my nipples and his own cock before moving slightly so his cock was directly above my face his knees on either side of my head. "Careful, you don't bite this time," he encouraged with a grin.

I couldn't resist. I licked at the chocolate, letting it ooze into my mouth and curb the need to taste Tyson's blood more thoroughly.

Ace finally let up with his violent tongue that was relentlessly tasting every inch of me and Tyson moved slightly, getting a better position to continue to suck and nibble on my nipples. His chocolate-covered cock glistened, almost dripping onto what were clean bed sheets.

Bloody hell, I was not letting them get away with that. I grabbed the chocolate before it tipped over, licking it away with my fingers before taking his whole dick into my mouth and letting my tongue scrape off all the chocolate goodness from him.

His tongue danced over one nipple and then the other until he'd cleaned his own treat off. He pushed deep into my throat, and I took it all, letting his tip scrape the back of my throat and hearing him practically purr from it.

Ace pushed my noodley legs to the sides, lining his heavy cock to my sopping wet entrance. I would have to take another shower after this and clean our fucking sheets.

Fuck it, everything felt too good at the moment. Tyson backed off me, leaning close until his lips nuzzled just above my breasts. "You want to bite something? You can bite this, Lucy."

I didn't need any other encouragement. I opened wide once more, sinking my fingers into Tyson as Ace pushed inside me.

That first gush of blood entered my mouth, and I moaned against his flesh. Honey and vanilla. How could I ever mistake this type of flavor for anything else? It was more subdued than Ace's spicy flavor, but I loved it just as much.

I made sure not to take too much, all too ready to be consumed by lust as Ace pounded into me. His hands gripped my hips, ripping my lips from Tyson's cock with a pop, and he pulled me firmly against his body, thrusting deep inside me.

"Come on now," Tyson whined, staring at his brother. "You can't be the only one that gets to enjoy her. I've worked on a lot this year. I wanna see whose cock can make her come first."

Ace laughed. "Fucking ballsy of you to challenge me."

I pulled away, and Ace slapped my ass as I rolled, only for Ace to grip my hips and pull me back against him so I was sitting on his thighs, sated with the blood of both of my mates. I leaned forward, reaching for Tyson "I don't care what you two do as long as you keep making me come," I panted.

Tyson chuckled. "We've still got plenty of lube." He dived for the drawer where we kept all the toys and pulled out the same lube we'd used the first time we'd played Lucy in the middle. He squeezed the bottle tight, letting the mixture ooze onto his fingers before tossing it to Ace, who shoved me forward only for Tyson to grip my hair and bring my head towards his lubed cock. I wrap my lips around him, enjoying the cherry flavor of the lube. Ace's hands smooth over my ass before he leaned down at bit it making me hissing at the same time Tyson thrust into my mouth and making me gag.

My entire body quivered as he brought me to that miraculous space between pain and pleasure.

Ace pushed a finger between my asscheeks, teasing my hole. "Relax," he whispered into my ear.

I nodded, forcing my body to relax as much as I was able. Ace slipped the first finger in, then quickly followed it with another, scissoring the two and working my body up, his arm banded around my waist as he hauled me back against him, and Tyson moved down the bed, slipping his legs between mine before gripping my hips. Ace let me go, his fingers still deep inside me as Tyson seated me on his cock before gripping the back of my neck and yanking me down to capture my lips.

"So tight," Tyson groaned against my lips.

"Fuck yeah, she is," Ace moaned back. "Don't worry, baby," Ace assured me. "I'm going to wait until he's nice and tight inside you. I know how much you love it when you're entirely filled up.

I nodded, biting my lip. Despite coming so many times already, I was greedy. My pussy demanded more. My cunt was a beast of its own, feasting on these men and their cocks, desperate to milk them for every drop. Tyson lifts me slamming me down on his cock, and controlled my movements as he slammed me down on him.

I was older now. Maybe pups wouldn't be so bad, anyway. The thought of myself growing big and expanding our family filled me with an odd sense of pride and lust at the same time. I wanted to give both of them pups.

"There we go," Ace moaned, pushing a third finger in. "Look at how easy that was. You ready?"

I nodded, moaning as he slipped inside me little by little. The lube helped him ease down my tight hole until he was snug inside me. Tyson had the decency to stop his thrusting for a minute to let Ace slide fully inside.

"She likes that," Tyson chuckled, continuing his frenetic pace. "Watch her eyes roll back."

"Kind of hard to do that, Genius," Ace chided. Once I relaxed against him, he thrust hard into me, desperate to match and beat his brother's pace.

I was tossed between their two cocks like a ping-pong ball. First, Tyson was balls deep in me, his cock twitching and tensing as he got close. The next Ace would bury himself deep in my ass, and my body would stretch to accommodate them.

They worked back and forth, picking up their pace and smoothing out into a rhythm. The fullness pushing my insides and hitting just the right spots finally had me clawing at Ace's shoulders as yet another orgasm broke me into a million pieces.

I leaned close to him, biting into Tyson to stop the scream from escaping me. The warm honey-sweet blood splashed over my tongue, and his cock twitched a last time before painting my insides. Ace wasn't that far behind us when he moaned, and his body stilled as his own dick unloaded into my body.

I let the taste of my mates sink into my body, and I smiled to myself at the dual sensations. This was my perfect life. No matter what came next, it didn't matter because I'd found my place in this topsy-turvy world. It was right here, pressed between My Two Alphas, and I never wanted it any other way.

THE END

Printed in Great Britain
by Amazon